Nick Earls is the author of thirteen novels, three collections of short stories for adults and teenagers, and four books for children. He is the winner of a Betty Trask Award (UK) and a Children's Book Council of Australia Book of the Year Award. *48 Shades of Brown* and *Perfect Skin* have been adapted into feature films, and five of his novels, including *The True Story of Butterfish* and *Zigzag Street*, have become stage plays.

NICK EARLS

Analogue Men

VINTAGE BOOKS
Australia

A Vintage book
Published by Random House Australia Pty Ltd
Level 3, 100 Pacific Highway, North Sydney NSW 2060
www.randomhouse.com.au

Penguin
Random House
RANDOM HOUSE BOOKS

First published by Vintage in 2014
This edition published in 2015

Addresses for companies within the Random House Group can be
found at www.randomhouse.com.au/offices

Random House Books is part of the Penguin Random House group of
companies whose addresses can be found at global.penguinrandomhouse.com.

National Library of Australia
Cataloguing-in-Publication entry

Earls, Nick, 1963–
Analogue men/Nick Earls.

ISBN 978 1 86471 153 0 (pbk.)

A823.3

Front cover image courtesy of GS_Photo/iStock
Back cover image courtesy of Big_Ryan/iStock
Cover design by Luke Causby/Blue Cork
Internal design by Midland Typesetters, Australia
Typeset by Midland Typesetters, Australia
Printed in Australia by Griffin Press, an accredited ISO AS/NZS
14001:2004 Environmental Management System printer

Random House Australia uses papers that are natural, renewable and
recyclable products and made from wood grown in sustainable forests.
The logging and manufacturing processes are expected to conform to the
environmental regulations of the country of origin.

1

ROBYN IS THE FIRST to see me when I get to the top of the back steps. She's still a silhouette through the screen door when she speaks.

'Where did you get that cap?' she says, as if our conversation has already started before I got here. 'It's kind of ninety per cent great and ten per cent sexual predator.'

'Exactly the look I was going for.' Drops of sweat are landing around my running shoes and evaporating almost instantly from the warm painted timber. I haven't seen her for nineteen days. 'People think you're cool, and yet they keep their distance, just in case it might all go bad. It's from the factory in Guangzhou.' The cap is odd and boxy. It looked good on the young guys in Guangzhou. Quirky cool. Non-predatory. 'Just wait. All the kids'll be wearing them soon. Remember you saw it here first.'

I got home late last night, on an international flight passing through from Sydney on its way to Hanoi. I called Robyn as soon as it was organised and she said, 'Don't wake me,' when I told her the arrival time. I stumbled through the room like an intruder in the dark, but her breathing didn't change. There was just enough moonlight coming in the window for me to see her hair on the pillow, the shape of it anyway. No detail.

She pushes the screen door open. She's wearing her black-framed glasses, a paisley-pattern top, a work skirt that goes to her knees and flat shoes. She's ready to go to the surgery.

Inside I can see my father and Jack at the kitchen table, with breakfast in front of them. My father is sitting with one of his feet up on a stool, his white hair pushed back like Einstein's but with a little less spark. He has his teeth in. He's still a big man, even with the weight loss. No seat was ever quite his size.

'I'd wear it,' he says, pointing to the cap. 'I suppose that'd be the kiss of death for the youth market.'

'Nah.' It's the first sound Jack's directed my way for more than a week, but he doesn't muster the effort to turn it into a word. 'That'd be Dad wearing it. He's pretty much killed it off in one run round Auchenflower this morning.'

Robyn steps outside and moves to kiss me, but stops when her hand's almost on my shoulder. 'Maybe when you're less sweaty.' She takes her hand away, just as I'm reaching towards her. 'I'll get you some water. And I'll take those inside for you, if you want.'

She means my keys. It's a signal that I'm not to go in yet, trailing sweat across the kitchen floor. She takes the keys as if they're a specimen she needs to drop into a jar.

Then she opens the screen door with her foot and passes me two blue plastic cups full of water before resuming the treatment of my father's leg ulcer. It's a red misshapen oval above his right ankle, surrounded by dusky mottled skin that has seen better years. There's a disposable dressing pack open on the table. A metre away from the raw wound, Jack shovels cereal into his mouth.

My father is in short pyjamas with a pattern featuring mini flags and the top two buttons undone to allow a sizeable flash of white chest hair.

'Nice PJs.' I can't let them go uncommented-upon.

He looks down at them and fumbles to do up one button. 'The hospital administration doesn't like their inmates getting about in the buff.'

Jack mimes gagging and then gets back to the business of shunting cereal into mouth.

'Same goes for the administration here, it turns out,' Robyn says, as she picks at a pile of gauze with a pair of green plastic forceps.

'Four dollars at Kmart.' My father's still inspecting his pyjamas. 'Thanks to you guys and your clever dealings.'

'I don't think Andrew's to blame for that item.' For a second it sounds as if Robyn's sticking up for me. 'If BDK's got that factory making terrible pyjamas, I bet they're making sure they go for at least six dollars.'

'Flags of all nations.' My father holds his shirt front out with his thumb, highlighting a flag with a blazing sun rising from a wavy sea into a red sky. 'Kiribati. I looked it up. Every flag on here except Taiwan.'

He straightens his pyjama top and peers at me over his reading glasses. His other hand is resting on an iPad on which, from the look of the masthead, he's reading the Australian. His long-distance glasses are hanging on a cord around his neck. Bifocals failed him on his only attempt in the eighties.

I've got the door jammed open with my shoe and I can feel my left piriformis muscle threatening to tighten again. The piriformis is in the buttock, deep in the gluteals. I stretched at the bottom of the steps before presenting myself. It was enough to allow me to come into view without a limp.

'Back for good, then,' my father says as Robyn uses the forceps to wipe a square of gauze across his ulcer. He reaches for a piece of toast.

They are evidently used to this, to oozing and wiping and eating, and making small talk at the breakfast table at the same time. This is minute one of my new normal. My father in the granny flat, post-health calamities, Robyn enlisted for the slow and uncertain process of repair, Jack zoned out and fuelling up, Abi somewhere back in the house, running to her own clock. This is my first picture of that great prospect.

I'm home. Home to work, home to stay. Cranking back the frequent-flyer status from platinum to something more like base metal. To the sound of no applause from my family or indeed anyone – none expected – I think we've turned around the apparel company I've been working on. No more jobs will be lost, the Australian business is sound, the factory in Guangzhou is humming, the debt level is nicely tuned. It's not the company it once was, or the brand, but it's no longer corporate wreckage either.

It was planned as a one-year job but took closer to three. Most of it was from a Sydney office or at sites around Australia, but I ended up with a lot more China Southern Sky Pearl air miles than I'd anticipated. We've skyped most times I've been away, but Skype is best at reminding you of what you don't have.

'That's the plan.'

'Good for you,' he says, as if he's unaware that his hand is pushing toast into his mouth at the same time.

In the years my father's spent alone since my mother died, he's lapsed from the habits he once drilled into us as manners. He now eats as soon as his plate lands and he talks at the start of every idea, through food, through conversation, through wound care.

Jack's in his school uniform. For two years, he's been cutting his own hair. It complies with the school hair rules, technically, but he ends up looking like Peter Tork from the Monkees or a Plantagenet king. Except, in Jack's case, it's cut into three blunt unforgiving levels – fringe, ears and mullet. It sits like a thatched roof cut for a human head, though perhaps not his. It would do no good to point out that, to older folk at least, any other choice might seem more attractive. The Buddy Holly-style glasses are new.

I ask him how long he's been wearing them and he looks my way as if he's just noticed me for the first time – as if I'm something unexplained but harmless that's blown onto the screen door – and says, 'A couple of weeks.'

'What made you . . .' I want to ask Robyn why she didn't spend more money on them to get a pair that looked good. 'Were you having trouble seeing the board at school, or . . .'

He sighs and sets his spoon down. 'The board at school . . .' He says it slowly, to make it clear that I've yet again tripped over the fine line between father and idiot. 'Lyrix got them for me.'

'Lyrix? But . . .'

I have never met Lyrix, though I have seen a photo of her. A non-consensual photo taken from side-on, with a third of the shot occupied by the blurry edge of the fruit bowl used to hide Robyn's phone at the time. Jack has a no-photos policy, and we know without asking that that extends with twice the fervour to Lyrix.

Lyrix has a row of piercings down one ear and goes through a lot of black eyeliner. She is fifteen and whatever people are calling emos now. She is neither an ophthalmologist nor an optometrist. In olden times she would have been referred to as his 'girlfriend', but in Jack's world I might as well say they're courting and ask how much he enjoyed squiring her to the latest sock hop or cotillion. She has a status in his life, but I haven't yet been let in on the approved word for it.

Lyrix should be the name of a character from a certain comic-book series set in ancient Gaul, rather than something we have to say straight-faced in life.

'They're nontherapeutic,' Robyn says, offering me a warning glare to go with it.

Jack is wearing two plain transparent pieces of glass or plastic in Buddy Holly frames, his vision remains perfect, and his choice to wear them is clearly not up for discussion.

My piriformis catches again as I change my weight from one foot to the other.

'Butt cramps,' Robyn says, as if my spasm has to be noted. And also diminished in the way that long ago became a habit.

'Do you call it that when your patients have it?'

'Sure.' She sets the forceps down and picks up scissors. 'I have. I've told them that's what we call yours.'

'You're telling your patients about my buttocks? Isn't there some ethical issue there?'

She holds a square of some kind of dressing material next to the ulcer, then starts to trim it to fit. 'I have an ethical duty not to tell *you* about *them*. You're fair game, though.'

I can hear Abi's school shoes in the hall before she walks through the kitchen door. She swings automatically towards the fridge as she comes in, but then stops when she sees me. She's as tall as her brother, but her belt needs to be pulled in to make her school uniform sort of fit. She has the build I did at fifteen. She's lanky in a way that seems timeless and resistant to any awful dietary input. If she's truly like me, she'll have years of that left, and then it'll change when she least expects it to.

Her hair is almost blond at the tips and naturally dark at the roots, with several gradations in between. That's new. It's a style I've seen somewhere – on the stars of K-Pop maybe – while channel surfing. I have a cap for her too, the girl's version of the one I'm wearing. She's always worn caps.

'Oh, it's you,' she says. It's the closest I get to a welcome. 'I thought it was, like, Friday or the weekend when you got home.'

'Well, I got the chance to come earlier, so I did.' There's a longer version, but I always get shouted down when I drift into longer versions.

'Cool,' she says, but as a kind of punctuation rather than suggesting it's actually cool. She's already at the fridge door, pulling the no-fat milk carton out from where it sits between the low-fat milk and the full-fat. Like almost everything else, the household milk selection is the product of much negotiation.

'I was about to make my coffee,' Robyn says, wanting me to make her coffee.

'Let me do it.' I check the deck timber between my feet. 'I've stopped dripping now. If I sweat anywhere, I'll clean it up.'

She smiles. 'It's good you're back. However hard I try, I always seem to overtamp it. Or under. One or the other.'

'I'll show you.' I take a step inside and the screen door slaps shut behind me.

'I don't want you to show me. I just want you to make my coffee.'

She smiles again and points towards the machine.

Black, somewhere between an espresso and a full cup in volume, with one and a quarter sugars. Some people might say the tamping's not the only issue with a coffee quite so highly customised. She has a barista near the surgery who has come to know this as a 'medium black'.

I ask how everybody's day is looking. It's the closest I can risk to an overt conversation prompt. Jack and Abi trample neediness, as Robyn learned years ago with requests for hugs.

Jack says, flatly, 'No bleaker than usual,' and Abi says, 'Ha. Can't top that.'

'I've got a few lesions booked in.' Robyn's wrapping a crepe bandage around my father's leg. 'That'll be nice.'

I can hear the cereal fall into Abi's bowl as I level the

coffee in the filter basket. My father clears his throat, thanks Robyn, and the stool scrapes across the tiles as he moves his leg away. Compact domestic sounds, better than the background talk on CNN in the serviced apartment in the Rocks, better than hotel buffet clamour.

This job has taken me away so much that Robyn started folding the end of the toilet paper in the en suite into a point. When I asked her why she said, 'To make you feel more at home.'

I press the button and the coffee machine surges into action, the needle of its pressure gauge swinging into the perfect caramel-coloured zone and telling me I haven't lost my touch.

'Oh, I've cut back on my sugar,' Robyn tells me as I hand her the cup. 'Just the one now. But I'm sure this'll be great.' She glances down at it. 'It looks great. I don't get that at all when I make it. That crème. That crema.'

'If you can keep making them like that . . .' My father holds out his mug.

He leans forward and there's a crinkling of plastic from within his pyjamas. As I take the mug, a drop of sweat falls from my elbow.

'How's it all going down there?' I find myself nodding in the general direction of his abdomen rather than giving it a name. Maybe it's too early in the day to face the word 'cancer'. Rectal cancer. Carcinoma of the rectum.

'Good.' He pats the front of his pyjamas and the bag crinkles again. 'Good margins around the tumour, nodes all okay and the stoma's putting out what it's supposed to.'

Abi frowns and looks out the window, her spoon stuck halfway to her mouth.

'We've had a couple of leaks,' my father says, 'but you get that. In the early days. A few surprises.'

Abi puts her spoon back in her bowl.

'Should I put a towel down?' Robyn says, pointing to the now two drops of sweat on the floor.

'No, I'm . . .'

'I'll put a towel down.' She's already standing. 'Don't move. Don't shake anything.'

I want to suggest to her that that line would be better directed to a dog just come in from the rain. I want to remind her she's recently had several encounters with rogue liquid faeces, and two drops of my sweat can't be too putrid in comparison.

She fetches a blanket from the floor of the laundry and drops it at my feet. 'Just stand on that.'

'That's a dog blanket.' It's stained, and matted with white dog hair. 'It's a dirty dog blanket. You were about to wash it.' And yet already I'm obediently standing on it, as if it might score me a doggy choc.

2

MY FATHER'S WHY I'M HERE. The kids, and my father. And I've come about as far adrift from Robyn as I want to. Too many lives were going on without me, and his rectal cancer sealed the deal. I was home for three days for his surgery, then gone again. I moved as many boxes as I could to the granny flat. The old house sits there locked up and fully furnished, as if he's on a long holiday.

The ride is over. I'm no longer part of the private-equity pack. As of today, I'm an employee of a company that actually does something, that puts out radio, twenty-four hours of it a day. SPIN99 FM.

The SPINstereo network reached its present shape through the work of a team on the floor above my office. It's still mostly owned by my ex-overlords, BDK – Bamberg Davis Kirchner & Company – but I'm off their books now and on staff at the network.

I met Truman Davis once in New York. His handshake was half-empty and he ducked any eye contact. He's seventy or so and still with the firm, though scaling back. He has a penthouse overlooking Central Park, a small island of his own in the Caribbean and he bankrolls a charity that provides school breakfasts for inner-city kids from disadvantaged backgrounds. The one time I checked, he was ranked the 342nd richest person in the world. He might not be quite that high now though.

Private equity, everyone knows, hasn't had it easy in recent years. A decade ago, it was on a streak that suggested it could get away with anything. We all bought the story and took some losses when it turned. I had already mentally extrapolated my investment returns out to infinity, based on another three or four decades of sunny days. Because that's what we all expected. Even as we paid lip service to the possibility of a downturn, we thought we'd found the smartest, coolest way in history of making money, and that it would be different.

In the en suite I make sure to pile my sweaty running gear in the corner, with as small a footprint as possible.

The bathroom mirror confirms that, rather than TV, it's nudity that adds ten pounds.

I am not fat, but I am pushing a thin man's clothes to the limit. For a while I've been belting up to the last hole, starting to muffin-top. There's only so many months you can tell yourself it's gas and still believe it. I have borderline irritable bowel syndrome, in the part of the spectrum that Robyn classifies as 'being human' and not an actual disease. Some days I'm a gas ball, but on no days now could I call myself lean.

On my better days, I can convince myself that I am the standard forty-nine-year-old sack of shopworn but mostly serviceable parts. I am weeks away from my first colonoscopy and months from one of Robyn's workmates slipping his or her index finger into my rectum for the first time. I have broken teeth on something as lame as breakfast cereal, I have torn my calf muscle running in a manner colloquially known as 'the old man's injury', I have had three conversations already about what glucosamine can offer the weight-bearing joints. I am mostly somewhere on the life spectrum between 'wear' and 'tear', though 'tear' finds me when it wants to, and more often than it once did. Even my earlobes have their first hint of wrinkles, and I can see no reason for earlobes to age at all.

I was born in the Menzies years, in John F Kennedy's final weeks. Warships my age are now dive wrecks. I have been alive for all eleven incarnations of Doctor Who.

I am doing my best.

I can see more scalp through my hair than I once could. Under bright lights, it's almost as if there's an X-ray outline of my skull.

If I turn side-on the picture only gets worse. My lifelong round-shouldered slump looks more like a question mark, and now one with a broader base. The kind of question mark that would rock back into place if you tipped it over.

In my twenties, I went through blood tests and X-rays for ankylosing spondylitis. My back was – is – stiff as well as hunchy. Despite semi-regular attempts at yoga, my muscles are permanently taut, as if stuck in a thankless state of vigilance, like those Japanese soldiers left behind in the jungles of the Pacific decades after the war.

None of this – the piriformis syndrome included, according to Robyn – amounts to an actual disease. I am simply less well constructed than average for vertical life, and on top of that I've given my joints decades of routine rubbing and grinding, and put my spine through too many years of slumping in bad furniture.

Robyn swears by massage. She can pay a stranger plenty to oil her up and dig their thumbs into her. For me it's all wrong – a weird intrusion into personal space, as well as a physical assault that sends the call up in an instant from the musculoskeletal sentries.

Back in my ank spond days, as the investigations dragged on, I was ninety per cent panicked at the thought of having it and my spine setting like fibreglass, but ten per cent wanting it so people would be obliged to stop seeing my posture as a personal failing.

My body, with no known diseases, is more like a pale hairy barrel with the arms of a different model hung on the sides. I have the arms I used to see behind post-office counters when I was young and they hung out of the short shirt sleeves of old men who I assumed had been born behind that same counter and would one day die there.

If I suck in all the wrong bits of myself that are suckable and I tense every muscle, I can convince myself some parts aren't awful, that there's a body in there that could still be salvaged, find some kind of respectable shape if I devoted everything to it. And then I don't devote much to it at all.

I run most days and then I use that as a free pass to treat any buffet as if I'm sailing upon it flying the skull and crossbones. Each time I tell myself it's the last.

Perhaps I'm just entering my wagyu years, face down in the feed trough, muscles silently marbling.

I assume I have about the normal amount of self-loathing for a man my age, but it's not a thing any of us ever compares notes about.

I used to panic about being seen naked. Now I don't even shut the hotel curtains. I'm no more inclined to display myself, but I'm invisible. I've gone from a scrawniness I'd grown accustomed to, to a broader, deeper, run-of-the-mill middle-aged unattractiveness that the world simply doesn't see.

All those billions being spent by the military-industrial complex to develop a suit of invisibility, and all they really need to do is dress every soldier up as a flabby white guy pushing fifty. This is what I am taking into SPIN99 this morning – this seedy bloater cunningly attired, a reasonable grasp of how to operate a business and no idea at all about digital radio. I'm the only person I know who has ever glued broken parts back onto a mobile phone. I can't claim to be an early adopter.

When I mentioned I might be interested in the job, no one at BDK tried to talk me out of it. It was a backward step – away from the power, down the pay scale – but all Carl, the MD, said was, 'Great. Sean's ready to step up.' Sean is now in the office I used to think of as mine. He is thirty-two. He is full of bright ideas.

The glass-half-full take on it is that they knew about my father's cancer, and wanted nothing to stand in the way of my move back to Brisbane. But no one said that.

I've read our pitch on the SPINstereo network. We paid a branding outfit good money to dream up that name. BDK has bought two pieces of failed or flagging networks at fire-sale prices, added two other stations and come up with SPIN. For that notion alone, and its brazen irony, the branding people earned their pay.

The document talked of synergies and, non-specifically, of some shared programming. In my world that means cost-cutting, staff-cutting. It never needs to be explicitly stated. The pitch had all the usual language, with the usual quota of industry jargon, this time from the world of radio, slotted into the right spots to show that some heed had been paid to the specifics.

The aim isn't new. It's to pull it into shape, make it look smart and extract some kind of return on the exit. This time, though, the door's going to shut while I'm still inside.

This will be better than a life spent in Sydney and Guangzhou. I want to catch my children before they're adults. I want to work out who they are, properly, and I want to lodge myself properly in their lives. I don't want to be a shadow on a screen door, a trick of the light that's best ignored for a bowl of cereal because tricks of the light don't last.

★ ★ ★

I'm standing naked in front of the open wardrobe when Robyn comes into the bedroom.

'Second-best suit, collared work shirt, no tie,' she says. My indecision can be read from the door.

'Cufflinks?'

'Jeez, no. Don't be the weird cufflink guy on day one.' She stands in front of the mirror and straightens her top. 'Try not to be the weird anything. Don't let the day-oneness of it all get to you.'

Robyn has never said 'Jeez', but now she does. Cufflinks would be an affectation. It's a radio station. I happen to like cufflinks, but that's not the point.

'Must be different to get to choose from all of them at once.' She means my clothes. 'Try the grey shirt that's maybe third along. The dark grey one.'

I have a pattern to my dressing, usually. I carry a few shirts on each trip and rotate them through the hotel laundry service. Every shirt gets about the same number of turns, and it doesn't ever feel as if there's a choice to be made.

She's right about the dark grey shirt.

She stops halfway through putting on her lipstick. 'I got you the phone we talked about.' She runs the lipstick along her lower lip, draws her lips in and makes a soft popping sound with her mouth as she opens it. She turns back to the mirror to check the result. 'It's the same as mine.' She puts the lid on her lipstick, drops it into her bag and lifts out the phone. 'I'll show you how to get started. Where are your glasses?'

'In my suitcase. I won't need them for this.'

One of the wardrobe doors is a full-length mirror. If I get the shirt right, there's no visible muffin-topping. It looks just like shirt puff over the belt.

'You're not planning to take them into work, are you? You've already decided that.' She's mapped out some sad story of my vanity and she's about to take me through it. 'Too many funky young people in radio for the old man to be fumbling around looking for his readers . . .'

'You haven't been listening to SPIN99 if you think it's overrun with funky young people. I'll be fine without the glasses, that's all.' They're useful for tiny print and not much more. I've told her that. Okay, they're also useful for reading regular print closer than an embarrassingly telescopic distance from my face, but I keep hoping my eyes can relearn their old ways, just enough that I don't have to get arm extensions. 'So, how about the phone? The plain folk's guide . . .'

For a full second she weighs up her response options. She has more to say about the reading glasses, and my attitude to them. She flicks something on the phone and checks the time. 'Okay.' She moves to stand next to me.

The wallpaper seems to be a photo of my father's dog, from a very anal angle. In the entire minute she's prepared to devote to the tute, she doesn't mention this, which leaves me determined not to ask.

She shows me the switch, the ring on screen to flick to unlock the phone, how to hold it to get a landscape-style qwerty keyboard so the letters are bigger for typing a text message.

'Most of it's easiest to work out by using it,' she says. 'You know, the way funky young people do.' She hands it to me, dog's-arse picture still glowing brightly. 'I've got to move to get the kids to school, but there's some left-overs from last night's dinner in the fridge for Winston. Could you take them down to your dad's fridge on the way out, when you take your manky running clothes to the laundry? I'm guessing that's them in the plastic bag. Hoping . . . Just leave them tied up in that. There's not enough sweaty stuff to do a load right now.'

The bag is used shirts from my trip.

'Sure.' I can hear Abi and Jack downstairs, clumping around. There's a blast of music that stops as quickly as it started. Not enough to guess the song. 'So, Jack gets to wear glasses to school as a fashion thing?'

'I pick my battles.' She gives me a look that says I don't have enough data on her campaign to start judging it. 'If I didn't, this would just be one long one. Think of it this way: he's the opposite of you. He has perfect vision but chooses to wear glasses. You have presbyopia that means you can barely read, and yet you refuse to wear them.'

'I'm fine with reading. Anyway, I got the glasses.'

'At a chemist for five dollars after testing different strengths by looking at the creases on your palm. And then you bought a pair in a Dame Edna shade of mauve.'

'They were the ones that worked best.' They were the ones I could pretend were part of a costume.

'Yeah.'

Downstairs, Jack sings something in falsetto and Abi tells him to shut up.

'Let me see how you look.' Robyn reaches for my arm. 'Do a twirl.'

I spin ninety degrees and try to strike a kind of hot office-worker pose. Assuming there is such a thing, outside secretary porn.

'Good.' She smirks, and tugs on my lapels. 'Mature sexy. George Clooney.' She steps back as the dog's-arse picture vanishes from the phone and the screen turns dark. 'How did it feel when they amputated the BlackBerry?'

'Final.'

More than anything else, it was handing back the BlackBerry that made it clear to me I no longer work for BDK. I've stepped outside, and I don't think you get to go back in.

'Well,' she says. 'Have a good first day.' She puts her hands on my shoulders and kisses me.

'Mum,' Abi's voice calls out from downstairs. 'We should have left five minutes ago.'

★ ★ ★

My father's not in when I knock on the door of the granny flat.

He's imposed his own kind of clutter inside in the month he's been there. There are magazines, mostly copies of Rolling Stone, spread across the coffee table and a row of paired hand weights set out on a rubber mat like cutlery at a formal multi-course dinner. He has two large bottles of Cointreau on a shelf in the kitchenette, one almost empty and the other unopened. His vinyl records – hundreds of them at least – are shelved in the bookcases and his professional turntable sits on the dining table with a box of them.

On top of the box there are notes for a set list, written in large unsteady capitals, with arrows and cross-outs. It's a work in progress.

My father is still DJing in RSL clubs and long-forsaken venues from his heyday – DJing in the oldster way, one turntable with a record on it, rambling anecdotal intros about a shared golden past in which he was a god of the local airwaves and today's audience were his listeners. It's his old radio job, narrowcast to a dining area with pressed carpet, seniors' discounts on Tuesdays and the heartless jangle of a nearby roomful of pokies.

I'm not sure if he knows what DJing means this century, though he likes to try to keep up. My father is not deadmau5. He doesn't wear a cartoon bullet-ravaged mouse head, he doesn't do any knob-twiddling when he plays, and he still spells his name entirely with letters. I have never heard the music of deadmau5, though I've seen the name and I know enough to know that 'never heard the music of' is probably an old person's way of putting it. His real name is Zimmerman, which stuck with me for the obvious reason that it's not without precedent for a Zimmerman to change his name and become a big deal in music. At least with Bob Dylan there is no risk that I will one day disgrace my children in front of their friends in a vain stumbling attempt to be hip that ends with me calling the new Zimmerman deadmaufive.

In the early nineties, when my father's radio career had tapered, my parents opened a theatre restaurant. During the day he recorded voiceovers for ads, then he hosted the restaurant shows at night. My mother usually starred in whatever farce they'd cooked up. My father did the intros and his own act that verged on stand-up, but was always marked generously since it was never called stand-up. He worked the tables, shook every hand that was offered and clicked his fingers to produce free drinks for anyone having a birthday. But eventually the hours took their toll, and his audience started dying or stopped going out after dark or stopped spending. My parents sold the business when my mother got sick.

He has the Doors on his set list, and the Animals' version of House of the Rising Sun. I imagined he'd play the same set, time after time, rather than repeatedly reworking it. There's nothing on the list that gives me a clue about the event he's getting ready for, or why some songs have made the cut this time and others haven't.

Beneath the list, the top record is a copy – maybe even my copy – of Ripper '76. It's my first close look at it in years, and you can see goosebumps on the cover model's skin. It was long before photoshop, so the track titles are probably actual writing on an actual buttock, exposed by a savage tear in the short white shorts. In the mid-70s, that album cover bore the promise of some great seamy life waiting in a cooler place beyond the trap of the suburbs. Hip people, shredding clothes, scrawling on butt. Guys lounging in spas with awesome moustaches and proud animal coats of body hair, girls who only ever bought the bottom halves of bikinis and lost them soon enough. All of them high on the kinds of stuff we were lectured about at school, with the record player in the corner pumping out the seductive beats of Ripper '76.

It's only the sleeve we all remember – those of us closing in on fifty – but the record itself managed an impressive ten hits per side, opening with Sherbet's Howzat, closing with 10cc's I'm Not in Love and including Supernaut's I Like it Both Ways, conceptually the raciest hit of the era. I was too young or too unworldly to be confident about what either way entailed, and genuinely afraid that my mother would burst in while I was listening to it with friends. I pictured her interrogating me about my understanding of it, dragging my cluelessness out into the open and then lecturing us on the finer points of both the ways.

No one else I knew had to think about their parents like that. Other people's mothers didn't know what they listened to, or reeled back when they heard some of the words, uselessly fearing corruption of their chaste child. Meanwhile that child had long ago located his own penis and enough porn to get him started along the path to blundering early adulthood and, eventually, the middle years, lard, musculoskeletal compromise and the plateau of self-loathing.

At a time when Queensland parents discovered that one half of ABBA were 'married Swedish-style' and therefore *not married at all* and a threat to our young that needed repelling at the borders, my father was in the business of playing corrupting music to the masses. At our place, it felt to my sister and me as if our parents owned the seventies, defined the era, lived it and shared it out. At our place, you could look like a loser if you didn't know exactly what Supernaut were on about.

Kiss toured in 1980 and played at Lang Park. My father got his regular two backstage passes, and I went with him. I saw Gene Simmons blast fire from his mouth, then come off stage and slump into a cheap director's chair like a collapsed bat while someone else soloed out the front. I don't think I breathed the whole time he was there, in case he noticed me. I could see his black leather-studded chest heaving as he inhaled, and the bloodshot whites of his eyes. He was an arch villain who could take down Gotham City. He was exactly what Gene Simmons was supposed to be.

There's nothing in my father's fridge but a wilted lettuce and half a red capsicum turned in on itself at its cut edges.

At the sink, on the narrow divider between the two tubs, there's a dry teabag sitting in a spoon. It's waiting to be re-used, since there's still tea in there. My father gets enough uses from a teabag to bring the unit cost of a cup under five cents. It's a habit from his mother, from his Dutch childhood.

He's talking to Winston as they get to the door. It's more of a monologue, but Winston's presence legitimises it. Every person should have a dog nearby, if only for the times when they need to rant about the failure of toll-road tunnel traffic projections.

'It never stacks up,' my father says emphatically as he pushes the door open. 'The investment case never stacks up until it's gone under at least once.' He notices me, clears his throat, gives a lift of his bushy eyebrows.

Winston skitters in across the tiles, benign tumours swinging from his abdomen like pompoms on a poncho, a variety of ways of being ugly instantly on display. He pulls up when he sees me, blinks, sniffs. Winston came along soon after my mother died, so I'd put his age at about eight. My father had never before taken a second glance at a bulldog.

'Rob gave me these to put in your fridge.' I'm still holding the two takeaway containers in my hand, despite having already opened the fridge door and then shut it. 'It's leftovers from last night's dinner. For Winston.'

'Oh, great.' My father takes a couple of chews at the gum in his mouth. 'Just leave them on the counter. I'll find a spot for them.'

He pulls a rectangle of foil from his pocket, wraps the gum in it and folds it shut, as if it's given him no pleasure. It's sugar-free and he uses it at the recommendation of a dentist who told him he needed to make more saliva. When I was young, any time I had a packet of Juicy Fruit he was forever on my back about where it'd end up.

'So, did you invest in those toll roads, or . . .'

'No.' He smiles. 'You heard that? No, I . . . That was just wisdom.' He laughs at the word. 'I read the prospectus. That was me doing the "I told you so". But the board couldn't be here, so Winston's the proxy.' Winston pants. A string of drool bungees from his flabby lower lip to the floor. 'He didn't invest either.'

My father is now in sandals, and baggy shorts reined in with a discoloured leather belt. He has a faded Hawaiian shirt on that's not quite hanging right. The fresh white crepe bandage on his ankle is almost gleaming.

'So,' he says. 'First day in radio. Who'd have thought?'

'Not me, I've got to admit. I'll try not to break it.'

'Ha.' He reaches a hand out to the top of the sofa. 'Don't worry. It'll break itself. Or maybe not. Did you read that article on Pandora? What was it? Eighty million subscribers?'

'Yeah.' He sent me the link while I was in Guang-zhou. I can't claim to have understood the concept. Pandora Internet Radio – I'm still stuck in that spot where you think the internet and radio are two separate things. 'Wikipedia says fifty-five million at last count.'

He nods. 'Both big numbers, though, if you know how to make money out of them.'

There's more than the entire population of Australia unaccounted for between the two figures. If everyone's shooting in that kind of dark, at least I'm not alone.

Winston shuffles between my father's feet and starts licking his bandage. Either my father doesn't notice, or his mind's too much on Pandora. 'You've got to admire the model,' he says. 'A radio station that programs its next song based on how much you liked the last one, or based on your suggestions. It's tens of millions of radio stations already, each with one listener. Very smart. But you're not in your new job to reinvent radio.'

'No.' It feels as if I'm supposed to declare exactly what I'm there to do, and to offer some guarantee that it won't be too stupid, that I won't stumble in and realign SPIN99's finances with the subtlety of Vikings sacking Lindisfarne.

Radio, even if I might be catching it on an ebb tide — and who am I to know — is still precious to my father.

Winston shambles across the floor, shoulders a bar stool aside and nuzzles one of my shoes. His back legs scrabble for traction and he belly-flops his soft heavy body onto my foot and starts rutting it.

'Winston . . .' My father says it in a growl, but it does no good. He makes a move forward and starts to reach down.

'No, stop.' I pull my foot back and it drags Winston along with it. 'Don't bend. You can't bend yet, right?'

'Right. Something like that.' He instinctively cradles his stoma through his shirt with his forearm. 'Don't want to bust my arse, I guess.' He smiles wryly. 'I got a million of those. Jack's decent enough to laugh at most of them. Just tip Winston off. It's the easiest way.'

I tilt my foot and Winston flops onto the floor, landing on his side, his legs kicking, his penis jutting from his belly like a hot pink candle.

'It's a side-effect of his medication,' my father says, not for the first time, from the sound of it.

'A shoe fetish?'

'No, not shoes particularly. The need to hump. Usually I get him to take it out on the grass.' He reaches out with his toe, nudges Winston and helps him back to his feet. 'Don't let me make you late for work.' He glances past me at the clock on the wall.

'I only emailed late yesterday to tell them I'd be starting today. I don't think my arrival's time-critical. It was going to be next week.'

He nods and looks me up and down, measuring me against his radio boss expectations, or his memory of the reluctant high-school debater and house captain I once was.

He takes a step forward.

'Don't slouch.' He puts his big dry hands on my shoulders and tries to straighten them, the way he's always done. 'You want to create the right first impression.'

3

BRIAN BRIGHTMAN and Dazz Davis, the Breakfast Bar team, should be in their final hour of today's show when I flick through the stations on the car radio and settle on the one that must be SPIN99. There's music playing – a song I know but don't know, one that's been co-opted for TV ads or promos.

I read the org chart on the plane at the weekend, but I can't recall having consciously listened to the station before, even in its pre-re-branded form as 4BBB. It was 4BB before that, back in its AM days, and plenty of us listened then, though not proudly. It was lowest-common-denominator commercial radio, and the right kind of girl could not be impressed by an admission of being a Double B fan.

Brian Brightman is their most expensive talent. When I'm looking to cut costs, his role in the end of my father's radio career is to remain coincidental.

Brian was only part of that, a rising star of a scrappy new kind. A 1980s gotcha caller and master of the single entendre. It was change that got my father in the end, and he himself was the first to see it. Unlike a lot of the others, he was always watching out for change, listening for its march.

'You should find a job where you feel lucky to be there every day,' he told me when I was at school, and I knew he was talking about himself, and radio. He'd got to it late. He was close to ten years older than the other big stars of his time, and grateful for every week no one noticed that.

He came home from work one day in 1979 with the LP of Bop Till You Drop. It had Ry Cooder on the sleeve looking like a waxworks model of himself, eyelids casting shadows, a mauve suit and mauve background and a sky-blue guitar held high.

It was the world's first album of digitally recorded music.

'You can hear the difference,' my father said. 'I swear. It's not like Moog, but there's a computer involved. It's all ones and zeroes, ones and zeroes. Every sound falls into one slot or another. There's nothing human about that.'

He also had a newspaper clipping headed 'Philips Introduce Compact Disc'. It was barely bigger than his hand but he spread it out flat on the kitchen counter – it had been in his pocket – and made us all gather around to read it, like a dispatch from a battlefront.

'They're changing records too.' He didn't wait for us to finish reading before spelling it out. 'They're going to make them smaller. And not vinyl. No pops, no crackles. They won't even need a needle. It reads it with a laser, or something. And somehow plays it perfectly. I'm not sure I like that at all. Perfect isn't . . . rock. Where's the heart?'

He subconsciously bumped his closed fist against his chest. He was rereading the article, checking he'd got the facts right. He looked like General Custer in those days, and the future was rising out of the grass around Little Big Horn, like Crazy Horse and countless warriors.

It wasn't such momentous news to me, or to Julianne. We were always having futures imposed upon us when we didn't want them, or kept away from us when we did. Mostly the latter. The laser record would happen or it wouldn't, and probably not in a hurry. Change didn't usually make it to Brisbane in those days until it had been trialled thoroughly elsewhere first and had most of the newness and any threat of evil worn out of it. Even mundane change wandered in late. We were the last people left to learn about focaccias, the last left emphasising the middle syllable of Adidas, the last people of the pre-kipfler days, when potatoes were just potatoes.

And now, in the same lifetime as those fears of my fathers, it's the CDs that are going. Their sales have been sliding for years and it's only the non-young who are shuffling through the last terrestrial music retailers to hunt them down.

Along with picking up Ry Cooder and CDs on his radar, my father watched FM coming from a long way off. He smoked more and his habitual sarcasm took on a meanness he had previously kept in check. In my last year at school I learned the word 'misanthrope' and thought of him right away.

He was still clever, though, and funny, and nothing passed him by even when, as he saw it, the end of the world was nigh. He was one of the last kings of the analogue days, the AM radio days, before FM annexed music and AM turned to talk and lazy listening.

He managed another decade in radio, but he wasn't a king any more. He shifted to less ambitious stations, and then to one at Ipswich with a footprint that barely reached Brisbane's outer western suburbs.

'It's an easy gig,' he told me. He was playing the Carpenters all the time, and songs like You've Got a Friend. 'It's a bit of a drive, but it's against the traffic both ways.'

I drove through Ipswich once in the late eighties and saw his face on a billboard, one of a series along that stretch of road promoting the station. But Brian Brightman's face was all over Brisbane on the sides of buses by then, where my father's had once been.

I had always thought radio would just be radio, but he knew it wouldn't. I thought the music might change, and the people, but radio itself would stay as it was. He knew that, once FM went commercial, money would pour in and the sharp new sound would call for fresh talent, and not for him. And now there's digital and Pandora, and more, and it might be the dumbest time ever to put together a radio network, or the smartest.

The song finishes, and a voice I know well enough says, in classic commercial radio cadences, 'Maroon 5 on the Breakfast Bar on SPIN99 with Moves Like Jagger. Must have been written by someone who's seen me dance, hey, Dazz?' It could only be Brian Brightman.

'Last time I saw you dance, someone tried to shove a padded spoon in your gob. I don't see anyone doing that to Mick.'

'Well, you wouldn't, would you? Have you seen that gob? He'd take the spoon off at the elbow.'

Wheezy laughter from both ensues, then an ad for a Toyota dealer.

I'm sure the radio's on every day in Robyn's car on the way to school. I don't know what Abi and Jack listen to. I'd put money on it not being SPIN99. I should have driven them to school today, broken into the family's well-set routine. Robyn, Abi and Jack went about their departure as well-drilled as a gunnery crew, thrown only a little by me stumbling in. I had the time. It didn't occur to me, to any of us.

Brian and Dazz talk costumes, the van, their sausage budget. I've come in late and it takes a while to work out they're doing an outside broadcast. There's clunking and crashing, but it might just be sound effects.

'There we go, mate,' Dazz says, leaning away from the microphone. 'One snag, lightly scorched.' In the background, a teenage voice thanks him. 'Who's next?' There's shouting. He's surrounded. 'This is what happens when you set up the Breakfast Bar outside a boys' school. Go, St Stan's.' A cheer breaks out. 'You lads sure know your way around a sausage. How's it going in there, Bri?'

There's a thump and a scrape and silence, then Brian's back. 'Sorry, mate, dropped the mike for a second. Not a lot of elbow room in the costume department. Hey, do you reckon we'll still get to do this after the new boss arrives? Did I tell you I looked in the fridge and it turns out we've got milk that's been in radio longer than our new manager?'

Dazz laughs. 'Keep it up, Brian. Get it out of your system now while he's not listening. While he's still watching kiddies pick fluff out of looms in China. I hear that's been his gig up until now.'

'You mean he's not sitting there streaming us?'

No, he's listening on radio. In his car, in your city. Crawling through CBD traffic on the way to the station. Checking out drivers in nearby cars to see if anyone's listening, and laughing. None so far.

Is it good radio? Maybe it's not awful. Maybe it shits only me a little. Brian and Dazz can tell me how smart it is, face-to-face, this morning. While I'm not in the habit of turning up to big welcomes, I'm not used to my arrival being broadcast on my way there.

'Got the gear on?' Dazz says. 'I could do with a hand out here.'

'Father Pervy is good to go.'

Dazz commentates as Brian emerges, since it's a sight gag. There's cheering, laughter, clamour, but not so much clamour that it sounds like canned crowd noise. Brian is wearing a priest's cassock and a sign around his neck reading 'free hugs'. And he is running amok outside a Catholic boys' school.

He has a microphone with him. It's mostly picking up chaos, but I'm sure I catch him saying, breathily, 'Okay then, anyone want to play hide the sausage?'

There are adult voices, a man shouting, then sirens in the distance.

Dazz cuts in with, 'Back to the mother ship, Father Pervy. Might be time for a song . . .'

The opening chords of Frankie Goes to Hollywood's Relax punch through and their time at St Stan's is over. And I might be newer than milk to SPIN99, but I think I know something with potential consequences when I hear it. Sure, it's funny, in one of those ways you can't openly admit to. If I had nothing at stake I might be laughing. But in this case, if and when hell rains down on us, I might be the one searching for the umbrella.

I change stations, because I have to. And I try to fight the idea that I have landed back from Sydney and stepped in a turd.

4

THERE'S A SPOT IN THE carpark marked 'General Manager'. There are maybe twelve parking bays at the front of the building and there seems to be more parking beneath. The two spaces to the left of mine – for the content director and the promotions and publicity manager – are both empty. The signage looks new and the carpark is bordered by neat garden beds. So, a tick for first impressions.

My hip starts to click on the way to the car boot. I can hear it more than feel it at first. My piriformis is tight after the drive, but it's not that. Whenever my left foot lands, it seems to trigger it.

Every time I whinge – even to no one but the mirror – about my body's incipient decay, it becomes less incipient.

I've got a box with photos from my Sydney desk – Robyn at a wedding, Abi with a guitar, Jack in a freakishly normal moment. There's a coffee mug in there too, painted and fired by Abi when she was six. It's been carried in and out of every office since. The design started out as a picture of a horse, but ended up abstract. The beginnings of a hunchy lumpy orange horse are there if you look closely and coincidentally happen to be thinking 'horse' to the exclusion of all else.

Even when I pull my shoulders back – imagine the posture of a gorilla mimicking a human gait – my hip still clicks. Or maybe it's lower than my hip. My knee?

When the twins were two and Robyn and I were deep in the bottomless pit of toddler parenting, Jack habitually dropped the beginnings of words. On one shopping trip, my piriformis clenched when I reached for a box of cereal. He saw it on my face. He stood up in the trolley's baby seat, rubbed the back of his shorts vigorously, put a pained look on his face and said, 'Sore muscle.' But, in the absence of the 'm', everyone else in the aisle heard a two-year-old complaining about his sore arsehole. And no one sees any part of that as indicative of good parenting.

'He showed empathy,' Robyn said when I told her. 'That's pretty important developmentally and I bet none of those people gave you credit for it.'

I'm confident she was right about that.

The sliding doors of the building open to a compact polished-granite foyer, with a reception counter, two red sofas, board-mounted headshots of SPIN99 stars and a long glass display case of radio memorabilia.

The woman behind the counter is on the phone, but she holds up her other hand, to say both hello and 'stop where you are, crazy-suited old bloater-ape with box'. She has auburn hair pulled tightly back into a ponytail, ochre skin that's not quite anyone's natural tone, and pearl-coloured gloss nails. Even from a distance her irises look a patented industrial shade of blue, the kind known by a four-digit code and too impeccable for nature, with lashes launching above and below plumped with added volume. She's in her early twenties. Every visible part of her has been recoloured.

I can see myself reporting the epic makeover to Robyn and saying something like, 'And there's every chance that, beneath all that, there's an attractive girl hiding.' There are nanna remarks in me, fighting to get out.

The memorabilia in the display case goes back to SPIN's days as 4BB, with microphones from the fifties, valves of different sizes, bumper stickers, a newspaper front page from 1985 featuring Richie the Rat giving a thumbs up with his Dunlop Volley-clad foot posed awkwardly on the left front wheel of a White Lightning Suzuki four-wheel drive. There's even a row of Goldies, the Brisbane radio awards.

My father won four Goldies in six years in his glory days at 4IP, back when the station was at Queen Street in the city, then Wharf Street, with 'That's Queensland – That's 4IP' emblazoned across the front of the building. After that they changed their call sign to 4IO but called themselves Radio 10, then Stereo 10, then Light and Easy 1008, followed by one final fling as 4IP before being bought by a gambling company and repurposed into 4TAB, the nation's definitive radio broadcaster of horse and greyhound racing.

'I know,' the receptionist says to whoever's on the other end of the line. 'But he signed the text off with an "X". Doesn't that mean something?'

Behind her from this angle, I can see past a pot plant to a large glass-fronted office with its vertical blinds closed. The sign next to the door reads 'Steve Meldrum' and 'Station Manager' on two strips of plastic in aluminium slots.

The woman at reception must be Venice. I've been emailing her. We're about to have that moment where I say her name to her face for the first time, and try to say nothing glib about an Italian city.

She nods, plays with her pen. 'Just one "X". Not, like a bunch of them or anything. And no "Os".' I can hear a female voice replying, but only just. 'I know plenty of people who do "Os". Anyway, look, someone's here with a delivery.' She smiles in my direction and lifts her hand to let me know I'm still in her thoughts. The bangles on her wrist jangle. 'Yeah, righto. I guess I'll put one "X" when I get back to him. Let you know how it goes.' She puts the phone down, gives me a smile that shows bright white teeth. 'Sorry about that. What have you got for me?'

I lean the box up against her counter. 'Pictures of my family mostly. I'm Andrew Van Fleet. I'm guessing you're Venice.'

'Oh, Andrew. Van Fleet.' Her painted eyebrows jump into surprised arches and she pushes her chair back from her desk. 'Hi. Welcome. You're early.' She stands and her hand juts out for me to shake it. 'And it's Vuh-neece, but don't worry. A lot of people make that mistake.'

'Only your parents,' I want to say, but manage not to. Vuh-neece. 'Vuh-neece.' I practise it, deliberately and with eye contact, to lock it at least somewhere in my brain. 'I worked with a Siena once, but that was pronounced . . .' It's a bad idea but she's waiting for me to finish it, or perhaps stop it. 'Siena.'

'Cool,' she says guardedly. She looks puzzled, to the extent that expressions can make their way through the make-up. 'Like Sienna Miller?'

A smart answer might be 'yes'. Cut my losses. Another smart answer might be simply to move on. A dumb answer would be to say, as I do, 'And I had a great aunt on my mother's side called Florence.'

'Good.' She freezes her smile as if it needs to be fixed in place. 'That's nice. That you're close to your family.'

To her, I've just launched into a bunch of random statements. They might be women I've known with the same names as Italian cities, but she hasn't made the link. The urge to help her get there with one more dumbarse example is stupidly strong.

'Andrew can be uncomfortable in social situations,' my grade five school report said, 'but he pushes through doggedly.' Doggedly. Forty years later, I remain dug in down at the 'I' end of the Myers-Briggs introvert/extrovert spectrum. Robyn tests right in the middle, which is as close as I can get to 'E' and still understand what's going on.

'We thought you were coming next week.' Venice is moving us along. 'But this is cool. Obviously. Coming today.'

I mention the email I sent and she reaches across to her mouse.

'Here it is. It's in my spam.' She opens it and reads it. 'Hotmail? I think it goes to spam automatically in our system. I didn't think anybody still . . .'

My BDK address was gone by the time I sorted out the flight. Hotmail was the first thing that came to mind. This conversation will not be improved by me standing up for Hotmail.

'So, the content director . . .' I want to regroup. I want to get out of the spam folder and away from blundering through Italian names and take a step or two closer to credibility. 'Is that who I should talk to about any possible problems with anything we broadcast?'

'Problems?' She's still checking something on screen. 'Yeah, but Gary's in the Maldives this week. He had it booked ages ago. He'll be back Monday.'

'Okay, so who's in charge? Who's looking after things between Steve going and me arriving?'

'Damian. Damian Misso, the station accountant.' She glances past me, towards the glass doors and the carpark. 'But he's not in yet. He's probably dropping his daughter off at childcare. The Breakfast Bar crew should be in in a few minutes too. They've been out on an OB this morning. Outside broadcast.'

This is the point at which, in any US TV crime procedural, it would become clear that Venice was a front, the lone occupant of the shell of a building pretending to be a radio station, with the last of the heroin or rocket launchers or sex slaves driven away in unmarked vans moments before I arrived.

'I've ordered a sign for your door,' she says. 'Is the "V" in Van Fleet capital or small?'

She makes a V with her fingers. I want to tell her I've seen Vs before. Actually, I want to segue into the kind of rambling story my children would punish me for, in this case about the name and its lower-case/upper-case Dutch-Australian history.

I cut it all the way back to, 'It's a capital now,'

and she seems to regard the 'now' as non-endearingly enigmatic.

I want a do-over, but this is real life, so there are none. I want to erase the past ten minutes, disappear until Monday and reappear then to a full complement of staff, far fewer non sequiturs and a V of whatever size on my door.

My hip or knee or some nearby part clicks all the way into Steve Meldrum's office. I can feel something there now. I shut the office door, sit and try a stretch.

There's a video of the recommended piriformis stretch on YouTube. You contort your leg so that the ankle of the affected side rests on the other thigh near the knee, then you lean your torso forward, bending from as low down your back as you can. There's nothing graceful about it, but I can't claim to have ever been much about grace.

I find the exact position I need to, lean forward and put the muscle on the stretch. I give it a minute, though I should probably give it two.

The pain of the stretch peaks and ebbs and, when I stand, there's just the outline of it left, for now. And then I walk. And click.

As documents from Venice ping through into my email inbox, I'm googling 'hip clicking when walking', then 'leg clicking when walking' and taking a crash course in unfamiliar spasming syndromes, free-floating chunks of cartilage and a range of other below-the-waist nightmares.

I take my phone out and toy with the idea of calling Robyn, but I know how it'd go. Robyn is not one to dispense sympathy for unremarkable ailments. One time I showed her an admittedly minor foot swelling and she told me it was unknown to medicine. I thought I had something amazingly rare, and then she clarified. It was unknown to medicine because no one would bother turning up with it.

The screen on the phone is dark, with a couple of new icons on it, and I wonder where Winston's arse has gone. The picture's a test from Robyn — put something embarrassing on my phone to see how quickly I'll solve the puzzle of changing it. But it's vanished already.

I fiddle around, tap the screen a few times. There's a click — exactly the same click that's been pursuing me since I left my car — but this time there's also a flash. And a photo of the leg of my pants appears. With a tiny archive of earlier photos in the bottom left corner. About a hundred black photos of the inside of my pocket. So I can stop googling clicking syndromes now.

An email comes through headed 'Happy News'. It's Venice telling all staff I've arrived early, presumably so that I can be returned to reception, or Steve's office, if found wandering the building taking photos of my pocket.

There's also a ruling from ACMA, the media regulator, on an earlier indiscretion of Brian and Dazz's, a joke competition looking for the best joke beginning 'Jesus, Mohammad and Buddha walk into a bar'. It turns out it's insensitive and inappropriate but not vilification, and the grovelly apology already offered will suffice. Case closed.

By the time the OB van is back, Damian the accountant still hasn't been sighted and I've called the principal of St Stanislaus College and used the words 'insensitive' and 'inappropriate' several times each. In return, he has eased away from using expressions like 'reputational damage' and pointing out how many Old Stanislausians are now judges.

I've almost finished the file note when Venice comes to the door to tell me that Brian Brightman is in the building.

I call him on his landline, but it goes to voicemail.

I try his mobile and he answers and says, 'Chief.' There's an echo. 'Welcome to SPIN. Did you hear the caps? *SPIN.*'

'Both times.' He's in the building, but not at his desk. And there's an echo. 'And thanks for the welcome. Don't take this the wrong way, but are you in the toilet?'

'Well, yeah.' He shuffles around. I can hear his feet scrape across the tiled floor. 'But there's nothing going on down there. I wouldn't have answered if I had one crowning. I've got standards.'

'Okay, well, I'll let you finish.' Obviously not the same standards as a lot of the rest of us. He has spent the first minute of our relationship on the toilet, and during that time introduced me to a new euphemism for shitting. 'When you're done could you let me know? It'd be good to have a talk. You and Dazz.'

'Sure.' I can hear straining. I'm sure I can. 'Be in in a minute.'

I push down harder, focus on giving my piriformis a good long stretch.

And the surge of pain makes me groan in the exact moment that Brian swings the office door open without a pause or a hint of a knock. While my head is buried in my own lap.

'Whoa,' he says as he recoils. 'Nice work, chief. You

know only three blokes in a million can give themselves a blowie? No worries, though. We'd all be doing it if we could.'

'It's an exercise.' I swing my foot down to the floor and push the chair further back from the desk.

'Sure. Most people have to settle for getting that kind of exercise with their hands, though. Or a friend.'

'It's for a tight muscle.' Minute one of my face-to-face relationship with Brian Brightman and the first thing I'm obliged to do is demonstrate that my fly is done up and I don't have my penis in my mouth.

'I'd be feeling a whole lot less tight if I could do that to myself. Probably take my super now and head out of here.' He's grinning, wide enough to stretch the pepper-and-salt stubble on both visible chins. He's standing with his hands on his hips and his feet splayed, wearing the brightly patterned shirt favoured by larger men who want you to know they're all about personality. His abdomen has long ago won its war with his pants and relegated them to low-riders.

'Maybe you could knock next time.'

'What, and miss out on this?'

Brian Brightman has a gold signet ring on the little finger of his right hand, a silver frosting of hair around a tanned bald dome, eyebrow dandruff and a urine stain the precise shape of Sri Lanka on his khaki pants. Which he sees me noticing.

'Yeah,' he shrugs, as if it's something we might as well share. 'Late-emptying penis. What can you do?'

'Late-emptying . . .'

'Mate, if you'd been listening to the show . . .' He waggles his finger at me. 'We do stream, you know. As do I, as you can see.' He frames the stain with his hands, in case I haven't got the point. He only goes double entendre if he's in a position to wave a flag so that no one misses it. 'It rates a mention from time to time. Good fall-back for a slow news day.'

'You're not . . . You are serious.'

'Hey, is this the fam?' He shifts his belt around with one hand, steps over to my desk and picks up the joined photos of Jack and Abi. 'Nice. She's musical, hey?' He sets them down and swivels the picture of Robyn so that he can see it better. 'And this'd be the little lady. Sweet.'

'Let's have a coffee.' Before I feel too violated.

I stand and my jacket falls off the back of my chair. He's too busy staring at the Robyn photo to notice.

'Father Pervy. Coffee.' I pick the jacket up, throw it over the arm of the chair and lift my coffee cup from the box. 'What do you do for coffee round here? Maybe we could get Dazz and your producer . . .'

'Coffee? Sure.' He swivels the photo back around. 'Might just be me, though, if you want to do it now. Dazz is sorting something out down at the OB van and Kylie's cracked a tooth. Went to the dentist as soon as we got off air.'

My phone takes pocket photos all the way to the tearoom. Brian hears the clicking, and of course doesn't keep it to himself. I tell him it's a pedometer. He points out that I could probably mute it.

Somehow, I don't feel any need to prove myself to him, or to get the chat right. He opened with a volley of blow-job lines at my expense and he considers the urine on his pants a talking point. Brian offers no scope for a botched attempt at a polite beginning.

He walks in front of me, since there's not enough room for us to fit beside each other. As his arms swing, they betray the cardinal sign of the fat man walking – the palms of his hands face backwards, since his arms have to rotate to work around his body. Deep inside I am a sizeist arsehole, with my own bigness creeping up on me as payback. I glance down to check my hands. Okay so far.

The corridor is dimly lit, with flat grey carpet. One side has an off-white wall with posters from the 4BB and 4BBB days, the other has a long glass-fronted room with big machines covered with LEDs and cables and dials.

'Don't ask me what any of that shit does,' Brian says, pointing to it with his thumb. 'Everyone asks. It keeps us on air – that's all I know.'

The tearoom is windowless, with more panelled off-white walls and grey tiles on the floor. There are two tables with speckled laminate tops, scattered chairs with their seats and backs in a blue that almost matches the kitchen benchtop, and an old arcade-game console in the far corner. Above the sink there's the inevitable laminated sign telling everyone they're responsible for cleaning up their own mess. I've been in this tearoom in at least four Australian states. The teaspoons are always mismatched, the mugs inevitably strive for quirky and the room can only end up looking like the place morale might come to die.

'We've got a thingo that takes those Nespresso pods.' Brian steps towards the bench and puts his hand on the matt metal top of the machine. 'Those of us who care about non-shit coffee chip in. But you can have your first one on me.' He slips the capsule into place and reaches for my mug. He turns it over in his hand, like a bemused presenter on Antiques Road Show. 'This'd be the work of one of those kids of yours, wouldn't it?'

'Actually, it's from the Miro Museum in Barcelona. The Fundacio Joan Miro.'

'Yeah?' He smiles, takes a closer look and then slips it onto the tray under the milk and coffee spouts. 'The ones I saw there were a bit more . . . distinct. Latte? Cappuccino? Long or short black?'

'Latte. Thanks.'

'Figured.' He pulls the fridge door open and reaches in for the milk container.

He locks it into place and turns the machine on. He's got me with Miro and he knows it. I want to tell him the mug was Dali in his later years, after he developed the tremor, but it says Abi on the bottom and Brian's probably got Dali covered too. The urine mark on his pants has blurred into an oval, less clearly like Sri Lanka.

Behind him there's a noticeboard with a chart detailing last season's footy-tips comp, a note saying someone's selling chocolate to raise funds for a school and a colour postcard of a man wearing 1920s tennis gear and holding a wooden racquet in a rakish pose that looks straight out of an old manual. In one corner, swirly gold writing spells out 'Mister July', above a small calendar for July 1997. Pinned next to it, written in gold and with an attempt to match the font of the card, is a note that reads, 'Before we porked up.'

'That'd be me,' Brian says when he notices me looking at the picture. 'Bit harsh really. I was reasonably porky then. They just put me in a puffy shirt.'

47

He presses a button and the coffee machine starts to hum and then to chug. 'They picked someone for every month. Some promo thing. David McCormack from Custard was January, I think, and it sort of fell away from there. A barista, a handbag-maker to the good ladies of Ascot, me. What the local celebrity pool lacks in depth it makes up for with shallowness.'

He swirls a spoon around in my cup a couple of times, then hands the cup to me without mentioning sugar, which I happen not to take. He sets up an identical coffee for himself.

He turns around while the machine's at work and says, 'Well, here it is. Your new empire. Loving it so far?'

He makes an open-armed gesture to the room and shakes free a shard of eyebrow dandruff, which drops like a lone snowflake to the floor.

'The video-game console's a nice touch.' It's better to say that than to focus on his de-scaling face, the shifting morphology of his urine stain or the shuddering sense of déjà vu that the rest of the room puts through me. 'What have you got on there?'

'A bunch of things. You're talking to the station Galaga champion.'

He picks up his coffee, gives it the same perfunctory swirl with the spoon.

'I used to be pretty good at that.' It's out of me before I can question whether it's a smart thing to say or not, whether there's any risk it might sound like a challenge. 'Or Galaxion. It was before Galaga, right?'

'Yeah. Think so. Sounds like a challenge.'

'About today's OB . . .'

'Want anything to go with your coffee?' He takes a step towards a brightly coloured cardboard box full of lollies on the counter and pulls out a Wagon Wheel. He uses it to poke through the others. The box is a fundraiser and features a picture of a child with a suffocating mid-facial bandage and dark hopeful eyes.

'It's on me,' he says, still making his choice. 'It's for the craniofacial kiddies. Reckon I've fixed two or three myself. This is where diets go wrong.' He waves the Wagon Wheel around, like a remonstrating finger. 'There'd be kids all over the Asia-Pacific with humungous mid-facial tumours if Australians like me didn't sacrifice their own waistlines on a daily basis to chip in for the surgery.'

He settles on a big cookie and drops two dollars into the slot in the cardboard. He takes a bite and cookie crumbs scatter, some catching in his stubble. He glances past me, through the open door, and lifts his non-cookie hand in a wave.

'Brian, hi,' a voice says from the corridor. 'And this must be Andrew.' By the time I turn, there's a hand ready for me to shake. 'Damian Misso. I'm the accountant. I've been filling in until you got here.'

Damian Misso is a worn-down version of late thirties, with facial hair somewhere between the designer stubble of Miami Vice and a proto-beard, and wire-rimmed glasses that have lenses little bigger than ten-cent pieces. He looks as if a fifteen-degree tilt to either side would be enough to send him to sleep.

'I heard you'd arrived. I've got some figures, if you'd like to go through them,' he says, showing me he's got an iPad in his other hand. 'I've been putting monthly reports together for Sydney. Or I can send them to you if you like.' He holds the iPad up, half-offering it to me. There seems to be a spreadsheet on it, but the numbers are tiny. 'Whatever works. I . . . And welcome, by the way.'

'Thanks.'

'Or I could email them,' he says. 'Whatever. I did them for Sydney.'

'Thanks. I used to be Sydney, so I've seen them.' It's a fact but, as soon as it's out of me, it sounds blunt. 'I think we'll work well together. Those reports were . . . really helpful.' I almost said 'good'. 'Really helpful' is at least better than that, maybe.

We're two awkward numbers men, two Myers-Briggs I's, clunky as Lego.

'You need a coffee, young man,' Brian says, taking a step back towards the bench. 'Double espresso, two sugars.'

'Thanks, mate. You're a lifesaver.' Damian watches Brian slip a capsule into the slot, then blinks and looks back my way. 'I've got a two-year-old who doesn't sleep.' He blinks again, hard, as if he's trying to startle himself awake. 'Work issues . . . We don't have a promotions and publicity manager, courtesy of some poaching by Austereo. That all happened in a bit of a hurry.'

'Seriously? Is there anyone working here other than the three of us and Venice?'

'It's a clean slate. Look at it that way.' He takes a step back and leans against the doorway. 'Semi-clean. Brian's still here.'

Brian is holding the coffee cup in place with his right hand as the machine hums, but he gives a thumbs up with his left. 'Semi-clean. I'll take that.'

I ask Damian if he caught any of this morning's OB and he says, 'No, I . . . You've got kids, yeah? Millsie – Millicent, my daughter – she's got a strong personality. That's what we call it. Anyway, It's a Wiggly Wiggly World is pretty much it in our car at the moment. I don't get a lot of turns until she's at childcare.'

'I know that CD. It's the one with all the guest artists?' Common ground. Abi and Jack were two when it came out. 'Slim Dusty, people like that? It spent a few months in our car too.'

'I just forget it's in there. She makes me sing along.' He hums a few notes without appearing to notice. He's almost as pale as the wall. 'I sang along for two-and-a-half songs after the drop-off today. That's most of the way here.'

Brian steps forward with the coffee. It's already stirred.

'Which is why you need this,' he says, handing it over.

Damian takes a sip. 'Perfect. I should let you guys get on with . . .' He stalls, wondering what it is we might be doing. 'Things. And I should . . . I've got to finish putting together this month's Sydney figures.' He turns to me. 'I'm nearly there. How about I bring them in to you when I've got them done and we can talk things through?'

As he leaves with his iPad and his coffee, Brian watches him walk down the corridor. I had to sing along to that CD too. Jack would take the male parts, including Kamahl's, which he'd push right down into his tiny chest, and he'd insist on me doing Dorothy the Dinosaur's in falsetto. You reach a point where going with it is easier than the alternative – resistance, independent thought, suggesting anything else.

As soon as Damian's turned the corner, Brian says, 'She had reflux or colic for ages, his baby. His wife's got postnatal depression. He's a good guy, Damian.' He picks up his jumbo cookie from the bench. 'It's not just the craniofacial kiddies that need a bit of TLC.'

He nods towards the table and points at it with the cookie. It's an invitation to sit.

He pulls a chair around with his foot and lowers himself onto it. Air comes out of the padded seat in a sigh. It sounds more like resignation than protest.

'I was your dad's biggest fan, you know,' he tells me. He taps the cookie on the table and there's another shower of crumbs. 'When he was pretty much the king of 4IP in the seventies. And after that too. I collected the top forties. You know, the cards.'

He tucks the fat cookie between two fingers and outlines the shape of the top-forty cards with his hands. They were close to the size of a DL envelope, in alternating pastel colours – lemon, lime, pink and powder blue.

'Yeah, I collected them too.' Obsessively, week after week. I even graphed the performance of some of the better songs over time.

Each week – I can't remember the day – the new cards would be piled on the counters of record stores in the Valley and we'd grab them between the bus from school and the train home, and work through the rises and falls and new entries as we sat on the platform.

'I wanted to be in a band,' he says before I can. We all wanted to be in a band. 'I wrote song lyrics and I got myself a guitar. I had an old folder for the songs and I painted it gloss black – I had some left over from an Airfix plane model – and I put a 4IP "If it fits, wear it" sticker on the front. You know the one? Like denim unzipping with a record inside?'

I knew the one. I knew them all. 'Colour Radio 4IP', 'Share Queensland with a Friend . . . 4IP', the one where the 'I' was a guitar fretboard lunging out at you, the stickers customised for each local rugby-league team. My father would hand over envelopes stuffed with new stickers, hot off the press and pre-release, as if they were contraband. And I would take them to school and sell them. So, they *were* contraband. Commerce was not encouraged at school.

I sold stickers and salty plums, never on the school grounds, and some of the profits went on arcade games.

'But the band thing was a non-starter.' Brian's story hasn't finished. 'It was Casey's voice I started copying, into my hairbrush. Which just goes to show how long ago it was.' He runs his hand over his bare scalp, feigning surprise that his hair's been whisked away. Then his face turns serious. 'How is he? Your dad? I heard he hadn't been well lately.'

'Yeah.' It's a leap from the Casey Van Fleet of the seventies and the top-forty cards to the less robust present. I wasn't ready for Brian to make it. I didn't know word had got around. 'He's okay. He'll be okay, I think. He's over the surgery and the news was pretty good. So, look, the OB . . .'

'The OB . . .' He sighs, and slides lower in his seat. He takes a mouthful of coffee, then gives me some kind of signal with his hand while he's swallowing. 'Go.'

It's as if Steve Meldrum's just tagged me and I've stepped into a conversation the two of them have had a hundred times and turned into rote. Brian is ready for me to say the usual, summarise the fallout and the remedy, and then extract a statement that sounds like contrition but was prepared years earlier.

'Did you see that Alec Baldwin quote where he said we live in a world where who you are on your worst day becomes who you are in the eyes of the media? I think it was in connection with a blunder that got his show cancelled.'

He glances down at his coffee and then smirks. 'Mate, any day when my pants aren't around my ankles in the company of strangers or farm animals is not my worst day.'

There's a knock on the door, even though it's the tearoom and the door is half-open. Maybe word has spread that I might be found behind any door in the building with my head in my lap. It's Venice, with a laptop.

'Don't know if you've seen this,' she says. She turns the screen to face us and balances the laptop on both hands. 'There's video on the Courier-Mail website. Of the OB. Twenty comments already.' She tilts the screen so that she can see it. 'Twenty-six.'

'How did that happen?' As she turns the laptop back again I can see a freeze-frame of Brian in the cassock, with a 'play' arrow across his 'free hugs' sign. 'I talked to the principal.'

The headline reads, 'Try SPINning this,' and the article opens with, 'SPIN99's Brian Brightman, who always knows how to take a prank one step too far . . .'

Brian lets out a burp and wipes his mouth. 'How did it happen? We've got a publicity department . . . Let's check it out.'

He reaches to click play and Venice steers the laptop down onto the table.

'You mean this was deliberate?'

He gives me a look that suggests I should come back into the conversation when I've gone and got myself a clue. 'Well, unless you've come here to triple our advertising budget, we might keep dreaming up OBs that'll get attention, and we might keep telling the media about them.' He turns to Venice. 'Vee, listener feedback?'

'Four complaints, three of them minor.' She looks down at the table, not wanting to be seen to take sides. 'The other one's from a guy who got touched by a priest and you gave him flashbacks. Quite a bit of positive stuff on Twitter and Facebook. Courier-Mail comments were half and half when I looked, maybe slightly in your favour.'

The video is through an ad and rolling. It looks like it's been shot on a phone. It starts out like a game of tag, with Brian a big old lumbering It draped in a brown curtain tied with a rope belt, as boys duck and weave or try to prod him away with sausages.

'See?' He waves at the screen with one hand and points the other at Venice, as if his case is being made all over the room. 'One guy to sort out and pretty much everyone else gets it. Who are the bad guys here? The Father Pervies. I'm highlighting it. *Highlighting it*. Satirically. It's practically a civic duty.'

He takes another bite of his cookie and somewhere out in the Pacific a kiddie facial tumour gets a mouthful closer to being fixed. Brian's all about civic duty.

On the video he keeps lurching, taking clumsy hugs at the air, a Frankenfather let loose on the village. It freezes with him facing the camera, 'free hugs' sign clearly in view, arms wide open.

'See?' He picks out a blurry face in the crowd and points to it. 'The kids are loving it. Because it's funny. Topical and funny. The bit of you that hasn't been running the station for five minutes could admit that.'

'Okay.' I pick the laptop up and hand it back to Venice. 'I assume there's a system for tracking and responding to complaints?' She nods. 'Let's go with that. And I should talk to a publicist some time to see if we should put out a statement this morning. The most senior person in that area who hasn't been poached or gone to the Maldives. And I've got some notes about what the school wants us to say too.'

She pauses, as though I might want a name straight-away, then says, 'Sure,' and leaves us to our cooling coffees.

Brian's smiling but trying not to, like the naughty boy in class. There's a sheen of sweat across his head, but I'm not taking that to mean anything other than a biological need to lose heat. His fingers are tapping arrhythmically on the table among scattered biscuit crumbs.

The OB is not a calamity. The language is already in place to deal with it – insensitive, inappropriate, all that – and, yes, I would probably have laughed if I didn't have to answer for it.

I want a truce and a better start, so I find myself saying, 'Would you mind not doing anything more like that until I've got my feet under the desk and have some idea of what's what around here?'

'Ha.' Brian sits back and folds his arms. 'Deal. Bloody St Stan's. What's wrong with a hug? Super sensitive. You're okay if I keep having a go at you on air, right?'

'Me?' This was about the OB, Father Pervy.

'The milk gag, the one about us having milk in the fridge that's been in radio longer than you have. That kind of shit. They'll put that in the Courier-Mail too. The punters love it when we bash the boss. It looks independent. Editorially independent. The harder I go you, the better the ratings'll be, trust me.'

He talks like a visitor from a different moral universe, some tentacled creature on a screen with a starscape behind him letting me know how things are calibrated here, now that I've wandered into his bizarre corner of the galaxy.

5

GALAGA WAS 1981, it turns out. So, just after I left school. Galaxion was 1979 in the US, but probably not here. My school memories are probably only Space Invaders and anything newer was at uni.

That's where I go online once I've discovered there are no hits on Google for 'late-emptying penis' that don't involve Brian Brightman.

We played pinball machines before Space Invaders arrived. That makes me look as if I hung out with Richie Cunningham and the Fonz.

Some time in the transition from pinball machines, my year at school grew out of salty plums and stickers and I passed my beat on to my next-door neighbour, Paul Gough, who was two years younger. I moved on to collecting for charities, an endeavour that masqueraded as decent. My mother would give me a lift to Toombul Shoppingtown, where I would stand outside Hades Hot Bread Kitchen, rattling tins and being complimented on doing my bit. No one dropping coins in my tin was aware that my bit amounted to fifteen per cent for travelling expenses and ten per cent for sundry expenses – that is, a quarter of everything they gave me.

Around 1990, in its final incarnation as 4IP, my father's old radio station reverted to its popular denim sticker of the seventies, this time unzipping a CD rather than vinyl, and with the slogan 'A Great Set of Hits'. Brian Brightman was already working his magic on radio by then.

* * *

When I go to the bathroom, Damian is standing at the basin splashing water on his face.

'I think I've maxed out on caffeine already,' he tells me when he notices me. He pulls a paper towel from the dispenser and holds it to his face, blotting up most of the water. 'Venice says you've got twins. I can't imagine twins.'

'It gets easier eventually. The sleep part anyway. You'll get through it. Hard to believe though that is sometimes.'

It was a frenzy after the twins were born. I couldn't understand how anyone could handle it without a full-time staff of six. Then, before we could plan for it, they were on the move. Robyn came to divide two-year-olds into two categories: polyps and bolters. We got two bolters. And, if you have two, they never run in the same direction. That seems to be a simple matter of physics.

Is it wrong to like your kids better when they're sleeping or sick? I had months when I might have.

Thirteen years later, Jack and Abi continue not to run in the same direction. I don't know how I'll do it, but I'm here to catch them both.

'Thanks.' He scrunches up the paper towel, aims it at the bin and misses. He groans and bends over to pick it up. I can almost feel him creaking as he does it.

'You should take the rest of the week off,' I tell him. 'Go home now and get some sleep.'

'But I've got the report to do. And . . .' He can't even recall the other things.

'I know the people in Sydney. They don't actually need it until mid-next week. I'll tell them we'll get it to them on Tuesday.'

'Tuesday. Okay. So I could go home right now and sleep?' He leans back against the basin, working it through. 'We should do a handover.'

'We should. But my official first day's Monday. We can do it then. Along with kickstarting the recruitment process for a new promotions and publicity manager.'

'Recruitment. Right.' He nods. And stops himself saying something. If the big bad BDK man wants to surprise someone, mentioning recruitment on day one is an easy way to do it. Damian pushes himself away from the basin. 'How about I introduce you to a few people and then I'll go?'

★ ★ ★

Venice catches me after I've done the rounds with Damian and met more than enough people to convince myself it's a genuine working radio station.

'Just a couple of things,' she says, and already names are detaching from faces, faces are fading from view and I'm imagining the haphazard round of second inter-actions ahead of me, as people I think I've never met come up and greet me by name. 'The video's up to a hundred and eighty comments on the Courier-Mail website and six thousand views, but I think it's tapering. And, um . . .' She points to my office door.

I point to it too to check what she means, and she nods. She follows me in and shuts the door behind us.

'Yeah, look,' she says, trying to find a thread she can pull to unravel whatever she has to say. There's no eye contact. She stares at the notes in her hand. The cuff of her sleeve has ridden up enough for me to see the tail feathers of a bird tattoo. 'There might be a bit of a problem. I got an email from our systems guy saying someone from this office – and that's you and me at the moment – did a search involving the word "penis".'

'What? There's no . . .' It's me. I can picture the letters two-finger-typing their way into the Google search box. 'That was for late-emptying penis. In quotes.'

Because quotes make it okay. Because 'hot spank porn' would be okay in quotes. Her forehead wrinkles into an ochre frown.

'You haven't got it too?' she says hesitantly. She's surrounded by sad leaky old men.

'No, no. Brian mentioned it earlier. I was just . . .' Failing to mind my own business. Failing to think through the office internet policy before typing 'penis'. 'Doesn't he search for things like that all the time?'

'Yeah, sure, but he's got clearance.' She puts undue emphasis on clearance, as though she needs to slow the word down and say it precisely for me to understand it. 'It's part of his job. He has to look for content. He had to look up "butt chugging" once and the pictures were . . .' She shakes her head. Beneath her make-up mask, it's possible she's gone pale. Or blushed. 'Don't try it. We don't normally have to search for penis info in our area. No big deal. You'll just have to put down a plausible explanation and they wipe it from your record. Do it in a Word document and attach it to the email – if you put "penis" in the email, it'll probably go through to spam.' She's nodding, as if she knows the sound of solid advice when she hears it. 'Or, if you really need to search for penis things, I guess that's cool too. But you probably need to get "penis" taken off the watch list.'

'No, it was just that thing Brian said.' Sounding pathetic now. Sounding like a late-emptier who should have sought a remedy after hours.

'Cool.' Meaning please stop now, before you dig the hole deeper. 'Oh, and there's a thing on at the Gold Coast this weekend.' She smiles, happy to be back on a topic other than my failing genitalia. 'An event down there featuring Brian. Normally the promo manager would go to troubleshoot and manage the Brian stuff, but . . .' She shrugs. I'm already aware that the promo manager has fled. 'With her not here, it's the kind of thing Steve would usually handle . . .'

Steve, who has also fled ahead of the BDK stormtroopers surging in, introducing themselves nonsensically and following up with a self-administered blow job and a porn alert.

'So, I think it's probably you or Damian. You'd get a room and tickets to the dinner. You could take your, ah, partner.' She glances at the desk, runs her eyes over my photos. 'It's at Obsidian. Five star.'

She doesn't know why I'm home, and that I'd turn

down five-star space travel this weekend if it was offered to me. But it can't be Damian.

'I'm not sure I'd back Damian to be awake after dark at the moment, unless there's a baby screaming.'

'Cool,' she says, though positively this time. As far as she's concerned, we have a decision. 'You're going to love Obsidian. Let me send you the link so you can see the details.'

I have arrived home, walked into SPIN earlier than I needed to and signed up to work out of town on the first weekend. In a certain house at Auchenflower, that's how this will be read.

* * *

It's an event called the Mass Debate, so, exactly the right quota of subtlety for Brian. It's part of the Australian Comedy Awards and being shot for TV. Most of the comedians on the bill are solid TV names. Brian could look like a local ring-in if you didn't know about his past TV appearances on Good News Week and Rove. Maybe his spot on one of the debate teams was some smart work of Steve Meldrum's to snag SPIN some attention.

From the size of the logos on the website, it looks as if Tourism Queensland has tipped in some cash to bring the event to the Gold Coast. The celeb deal includes accommodation on both Friday and Saturday nights. They're hoping for a lot of 'having an awesome time at the #GoldCoast' tweets.

Beside the info there's a picture of the beach at Surfers Paradise with mammoth tower blocks behind it jostling for space and light, far more of them than there were on our family holidays there in the seventies. Brisbane, old Brisbane, is really in my face today. I guess there's nothing to prompt it in Guangzhou and not much in Sydney.

But we ducked the high-rises back then and stayed closer to the ground, in brick units where we were low enough to hear and smell the sea. And there's my answer.

Venice is at her desk when I get to my door.

'Change of plan,' I tell her. 'I'll go and I'll give Brian whatever minding he needs, but instead of staying at Obsidian, could you find me a beachfront unit nearby? Three bedrooms. Or two two-bedrooms.' We'll all go. Robyn, Abi, Jack, Dad, me. 'Try to get one of the bigger, older ones. But with airconditioning. If you send me the link, I'll pay.'

'It's five stars, though, Obsidian.' There's hardly any part of today when I've made sense to her. 'Practically six stars. Did you do the tour? There's one on the website. It's got a secret garden and eighteen different pillows on the pillow menu. *Eighteen*. They've got a guy whose entire job is to do origami with the room-service napkins. You even get to pick what he does – storks, a little box, practically anything. Some people put engagement rings in the little box.'

Despite the sales pitch, she relents and doesn't take long to find me Crystal Tydes. It's brick, it's solid, it's low-rise and it's plain that she thinks it's vile. It looks like the best summers of my childhood, even if the recent rush of meth labs on the Gold Coast means there's now an awkward irony to the name.

It's just down the road from Obsidian. Two adjacent two-bedroom apartments with sea views are available. I fill in my credit-card details and, while the form's being processed and a rainbow wheel is spinning on screen, I let Venice know it's perfect.

6

JACK IS POOLSIDE WHEN I get home, after half an hour of listening to SPIN's drive team, Kat and Dave, say nothing offensive at all. He's sitting with wet hair and his towel around his shoulders, working on an iPad on the glass table. He's got earbuds in, with their white flexes leading back to the mothership as he flicks at the screen. I think he's editing video. He stops to watch it and picks at his nails. It's an act I can recognise from the verandah.

The nail-picking was a compulsion when he was younger. It used to make his fingers bleed, so we bought gloves for him to wear. Which he pulled off, so we taped the gloves to his forearms. So then he sat in the stroller picking at the tape. And ended up with shreds of it in his hair. And had almost no chance of being normal.

Jack started to learn to write early. Abi would ask him to do her make-up and he would write things like 'DETH MASHIN' on her face in Robyn's old broken lipsticks. He drew a lot of death machines in those days.

The second step from the bottom creaks on my way down but he doesn't seem to hear it. I wave once I'm in his field of vision.

'I knew you were there,' he says. He pops one bud from an ear. Being offered fifty per cent of his attention is a real concession from Jack.

I ask him how school was and he says, 'Oh, god, we're not going to do that every day, are we?' He doesn't quite scowl because he can't quite bother.

'Well, not now, obviously.'

'Good.' He nods. He picks up the swinging bud and is about to slip it back into his ear.

'Just a question . . .'

The angle of his head changes, letting me know he feels under some obligation to hear me out, though the bud hovers close to his ear.

'Where do you hear about new music? Is it the radio, and what is it if it's not?'

He drops the bud, lowers his arm to the table and gazes across the calm surface of the pool.

'I hear about it.' He shrugs.

'Are you meaning to come across as zen-like or just irritated?'

'Ha.' He gives me the pleasure of approximately a quarter of a cracked smile. 'Irritated. Just enough to put you off. Not rude or anything.' He nods. He's pretty happy with how he's summed it up. 'The radio . . . Look, I know you miss the time when you all came in from ploughing the fields to watch Countback.'

'Countdown.'

Jack is a willing desecrator of other people's memories. It's a sport to him.

'Just fucking with you.'

'Whatever happened to "just kidding"?'

'I hear about stuff. There's this thing called the

internet.' He points to his iPad. 'It operates on machines like these. But I'm not really the one to talk to about music.'

As if on cue, an electric guitar chord jangles in the house. Without shifting anything but his arm, Jack points back over his shoulder and puts on a different kind of scowl – he has a broad repertoire of them, and this is one of the world-weary ones, letting me know he's had months of Abi's experimentation with guitar and it's simply part of the long slow curse that is living with your nearest and dearest in this million-dollar house in a desirable suburb.

He looks down at the screen, flicks something with his finger, taps.

'I'll just be heading inside then.' I say it louder than I need to, and more clearly, backed up by some exaggerated pointing.

'This is an assignment,' he says, without shifting his gaze. 'For school.'

Several more notes spangle from the guitar, then another chord. Jack pokes the swinging bud back into his ear and gives the edit all of his attention.

The garden smells of jasmine and wet soil as I go up the steps. Beneath the surface, there's an intricately planned network of pipes leading from the water tanks to drippers and sprinkler outlets. I know someone comes in at least weekly to keep it all tidy. Jack looks like he's sitting alone in the corner of a resort. If I mentioned that to him, he'd complain that a real resort would have a waiter on hand to bring him drinks and snacks.

I can hear recorded music as I approach the house. It's set at a much lower volume than Abi's amp.

She's in the living room with my father. Abi's still in her school uniform with the fingers of her left hand shaping a chord on the neck of her red electric guitar, and a pick in her right. Her feet are bare and she has her right knee on the arm of the sofa. The sole of her foot is facing back my way, its high arch pale and a vague tattoo of floor grime on the rest of it. She has the perfect footprint you see cartooned in shoe ads before they move on to the aberrant shapes of the special-needs feet. My father's in the same shorts and shirt as this morning and also barefoot, with his hard yellow toenails hooking like talons into the pile of the carpet.

He's holding his reading glasses in his hand, as if he's been using them to point at something. His iPad is propped up on the coffee table, showing a video of Patti Smith's Horses.

What did this family do before iPads invaded the house? Talk to each other?

'We didn't know how important this stuff was here,' he's saying. There's a history lesson in progress. 'We just didn't read it. Most of us didn't. The Saints did. Actually the Saints predated . . . We'll get to them.'

He notices me and nods in my direction.

Abi turns, waves with her pick hand and says, 'Hi.' She looks at me as if she's been focusing hard on the video and is still trying to place me in the room.

'We never gave the Saints their due, did we?' my father says to me. 'On 4IP? Imagine if we'd played some of that stuff.' He reaches down to the iPad and taps it to pause the video. 'Patti Smith's Horses.' He points to it with his reading glasses. One side arm swings down and the glasses almost slip from his hand.

'I know that's Patti Smith's Horses.'

He laughs, but it's a laugh about a fresh thought, not my need to prove that I can recognise Patti Smith at ten paces.

'You've got to tell Abi about the whores,' he says.

'What? There were no . . .' I have no idea what he's talking about. He's grinning, knowingly, as though we're two old sea dogs trading stories. In the lounge-room, with Abi, about sex workers. 'There were no whores. Okay, there was one work function that ended up at a strip club at King's Cross, but . . . it was a work thing. I really didn't know we were going there. I wasn't planning to mention that. And it shouldn't be confused with, you know, prostitution.'

It's the truth. The night was supposed to be a dinner, but the guy we were meeting with wanted to cut loose. He owned a family business making tetra packs for fruit juice so, really, anything not involving folding card into boxes might have constituted cutting loose. But he'd seen work dinners in the movies, so it turned out he expected fat cigars, scotch and a lap dance.

Both my father and Abi are staring at me. I could perhaps have found a smarter word to finish on than 'prostitution'.

'Thanks for that.' My father clears his throat. 'I meant the line from The Boxer, Simon and Garfunkel. We were talking about how easy it is to mishear lines some-times. Remember when you thought it was the horse on 7th Avenue that the guy was seeking comfort from?'

'Seriously?' Abi laughs. 'You thought that was a horse? That's very funny. Now tell us about the strippers.'

'Horses can be really comforting.' I can picture it now. The horse I had in mind was attached to a Central Park carriage. It was tall and white, with an understanding eye and a driver who looked like Santa in a dinner suit.

On the chair next to me a phone beeps. It's in my hand before it occurs to me that it isn't mine.

'You've got a text,' I tell Abi, since that's what it says on the screen. 'Apparently it's from a Fuck Face.'

She groans and lifts her guitar strap over her head.

'I told him to stop.' She leans the guitar against the sofa and comes to get the phone. 'He's such a tool.'

She barely glances at the message, which she then appears to delete. She taps the screen twice and holds the phone to her ear.

'You'll never guess who I just got a text from,' she says as she walks outside onto the verandah.

However hard I listen, I can't tell if the person at the other end guesses it's Fuck Face.

With the house raised, the loungeroom offers long views to the city across the inner suburbs and all their poinciana and jacaranda trees that flare red and purple later in the year, their bean-shaped blue swimming pools I've looked down on from planes, their chunky black four-wheel drives bought for nothing more rugged than childcare drop-offs. Somewhere out there, some poor boy has just sent my girl a text that has already been deleted, and he is now being roundly maligned for sending it, whatever it said.

A breeze sweeps through, lifting the curtains and swinging the French doors so that they almost close, with Abi on the other side.

'Mr and Mrs Face really should have thought the whole name issue through,' my father says, watching Abi and her life — as I am — from this short but impassable distance.

She's leaning against the verandah railing facing the pool, her legs crossed at the ankles. She laughs and says, 'I know. As if . . .'

My father shrugs. 'Maybe he deserves it.' His right hand is resting somewhere near his stoma bag and, for the first time, I notice his own posture isn't what it once was. 'So, day one. How was it? Brian Brightman gave you something to keep you out of mischief, from what I've seen. I can remember hearing him in about 1990 call Hothouse Flowers "Ireland's answer to Van Morrison". I'm sure that was him.'

'He said he was a big fan of yours. Without you he probably wouldn't have got into radio.'

'Sounds like the right sort of line if you don't want the new boss to sack you.' He smiles but at the same time smoothes his shirt front down with his hand and stands a little straighter.

'I'm pretty sure he meant it. Just the way he said it.'

The French doors swing open and Abi surges back in.

'Sorry about that.' She strides straight over to her guitar. 'Just had to report in.' She loops the strap back over her head. 'Now, Patti Smith, Horses . . .'

She's already leaning forward to tap the iPad and start the video rolling again.

7

AS ROBYN'S CAR GLIDES into its spot under the house, I'm surprised how good it feels to know that everyone's home.

'Just don't get straight onto an iPad, okay,' I tell her when she gets to the top of the steps.

'Ha.' She swings her bag from her shoulder. 'Conversation, then? I can give you . . .' She makes a pantomime out of checking her watch. 'Five minutes. And don't tell me that's not the best offer you've had this afternoon.' She stops, as though she needs to take a proper look at me. 'You know, it's nice to have another non-screenhead in the house. You can have ten minutes.'

I ask her if she'd like a coffee, and she tells me that gets me fifteen minutes. And it should be decaf. Any time after three is decaf for Robyn.

She dumps her bag on the kitchen table. It's cinnamon-brown leather, oversized and not quite the shape it was when she bought it in Hong Kong. It was either a designer bargain or an overpriced knock-off. Over the past couple of years more items have been added to its inventory while at the same time I'm sure not one has been subtracted. It's a tardis. There's a field hospital in there, and almost certainly a torch, several tissue packs and three kinds of wipes, that tool for de-stoning horses' hooves, a selection of favoured old paperbacks and a business-class robe and slippers from China Southern, still in their plastic. And, almost certainly in this family, an iPad, perhaps several.

'So, how was your first day?' she says. Something in her bag settles and it changes shape again. 'I saw the "free hugs" story on the Courier-Mail website.'

'Well, that's indicative.' I tap the filter basket to level the coffee. 'Other than that, the breakfast hosts crapped on me on air, every senior staff member who hasn't resigned seems to be on holiday or crushed by life issues, and I got caught googling the word "penis".'

'Why were you . . .' She checks herself, puts the frown away. 'No, I don't need to know everything. Will it get better, do you think?'

'I don't know. Yes. From my point of view, yes, it'll get better. The station anyway, in the short term. The long-term future of radio is anyone's guess.'

'The future of radio?' She laughs. She's standing beside me with her arms folded while I lock the filter basket into position. 'You're not expected to know that, are you? I thought you just had to get the place running smoothly. Who knows the future of anything? There's way too much to keep track of. I had at least a year of thinking Grindr was an app for people looking for quality coffee.'

'Sounds pretty reasonable to me . . .' I've never heard of Grindr.

'It's where gay men post pictures of their bits and hook up to have commitment-free sex.'

'Good to know, since sometimes I find myself in a new place looking for quality coffee.' I put one sugar in the cup this time, not one and a quarter. 'Or, obviously, some of that other thing.'

'Well, you are the one googling "penis".' She leans her shoulder against the fridge. Her eyes are on her coffee cup. 'Most of the Grindr boys post pictures of huge penises. Apparently. Don't know if they're legit or not.'

I'm about to push the start button, which will damn the conversation to thirty seconds of industrial noise.

'Is there such a thing as a late-emptying penis?' I ask her instead.

'A what?' She moves the black frames of her glasses down her nose so that she can give me a school-marmish look over the top.

'It's a friend. An acquaintance.'

'Oh, okay. Isn't it always? I haven't noticed it on your pants, if that's any consolation. But you do tend to wear dark fabric.' She pushes the glasses back into place and stands up, away from the fridge. She tilts her head to make an oblique inspection of my groin. 'I think if you just stand at the toilet another couple of seconds it'll sort itself out. Or, better, sit. That whole standing thing's not such a good idea. It's not a hose. It's not a round tube internally and it's got a diamond-shaped aperture, so you can't expect it to flow straight.'

'It's not me. Seriously.'

She's arranged her thumbs and index fingers into the diamond-shaped aperture, and I'm certain it's not for the first time. This is starting to sound suspiciously like a talk she's given before, to other leaky-penised men who pause at the door of her consulting room on the way out and start their new story with, 'Oh, one more thing,' as though they're about to invite her to golf, or ask her when she thinks decaf time should start.

'Ultimately, the penis is the strongest argument against intelligent design,' she says. 'The penis and that little black bit at the end of a banana. It makes no sense either. But those people's god is always a man, and the first thing a man god would get right would be penis design. It should empty like a . . . like a laser, not like a . . .'

'If we could pull back from this outstanding tangent for a moment . . .' I had no idea that in Robyn's ideal world penises emptied like lasers, cutting through steel plate, pissing without attenuation to Alpha Centauri. 'Is there such a thing? As a late-emptying penis? I know someone who claims to have one and I just want to know if it's real.'

'I remember something . . .' she starts, before stopping to think through the details. 'It's not a disease, but I remember something from a urology outpatients clinic when I was a student. There was an old guy who'd lose a few mils into his pants after going. The urologist gave him some advice on how to squeeze it, but I've never heard anyone say it since.'

'So, there's a way to squeeze it?'

'What? Do you want me to show you?'

She reaches for my belt and cackles as I jump out of the way. We're one move short of her chasing me around the kitchen like a Benny Hill sketch.

'I think you have to squeeze it one time,' she says. 'From the base down to the glans. Like, milk it.'

Subconsciously she demonstrates a milking action that implies that penises are two feet long and banana shaped. 'But just one time or it gets confused and starts contracting chaotically. And you risk ending up with the pants stain.'

From above us there's a burst of recorded voices and a plopping sound effect. It shuts off after a few seconds, as abruptly as it started.

'Jack's editing a video,' I tell her, assuming that's what it is. 'It's for an assignment apparently.'

'Well, who would know?' She looks up at the ceiling, in case evidence might reveal itself. Upstairs, homework is supposed to be underway in both of the twins' bedrooms. 'Whatever he's doing, we've somehow managed to have an entire conversation about penis dysfunction without anyone walking in, and that's got to be a minor miracle.'

The second I push the button and start the coffee machine, I want to tell her about my Gold Coast idea. Which, I realise, I should be thinking of as my Gold Coast *plan*, unilaterally made.

'So, this weird thing came up at work.' It comes out like a line from a stand-up routine. 'There's something on at the Gold Coast this weekend. An event.'

The coffee machine snarls away. The last vestige of Robyn's whimsy about the leaky-penis chase evaporates.

Before I can even get to the family aspect of the plan, a frown line breaks out on her forehead and she says, 'Really? You come back to spend more time with Abi and Jack and then you book in a work trip for the first weekend? Is there no one else who could do it? Are you indispensible already? You told me you'd delegate in this job.'

'It's not like that. The promo manager got poached, the content director's away, the accountant has issues . . . But I have a plan.'

'Seriously?' I want to get to the plan, but my turns don't seem to be lasting long enough. 'Right now you're sounding like the one dumb rat that swam back and got on the sinking ship. And why do the accountant's issues count for more than making up for three years of sporadic visits home?'

'Sick baby, wife with postnatal depression, but here's the plan.' If I talk like a text message I might just get to it before she launches the next salvo. 'The work is only one event, a couple of hours, but I thought we could all go as a family, stay nearby, go for the whole weekend. I've found a place.'

She eases her thumb back from the launch button. 'Okay, I can see why the accountant's off the hook. Fair enough.' The frown stays in place. 'Did you check if anyone had anything planned?'

I rush through a mental calendar of birthdays and anniversaries in case I've fucked up in a bigger way, but nothing's evident. 'What? Like sport? It's not as if Jack ever joined a team. It'll mostly be free time. It'll get them away from their gadgets. It'll be good.'

'They'll bring their gadgets,' she says. 'I hope that doesn't crush any dreams you had of Jack running along the beach with a kite.'

'We had great holidays at the Gold Coast when we were kids. And their age, teenagers. And I was irritatingly cynical as well. It was still good. Let me show you the place. Let me get a computer and . . .'

I make a move towards the door before realising I can't picture the nearest computer. I don't know where I'm heading.

'Here,' she says.

She goes to the table and reaches into her bag, most of the way to her elbow. She pulls out an iPad, which I'm starting to assume we bought by the dozen to get a discount. She taps it a couple of times and hands it to me with Google ready.

She watches as I type in 'Crystal Tydes' and says, 'Seriously? You want us to stay at a place that puts a "Y" in "tides"?'

It doesn't have its own website but I find the link Venice sent me to the accommodation service and click on the Crystal Tydes entry. The picture of the unit block, taken from the beach side of the road, loads and fills the screen.

Robyn adjusts her focal distance, in case that'll improve it. 'It looks like a seventies toilet block, or the kind of place you'd go to refill a gas bottle.'

It's solid and unattractive. I can't deny that. It's functional. It's a sturdy box, but that's how they built them then. Next to the driveway, the name 'Crystal Tydes' is cast in a space-age font in a mass of grey concrete the shape of a curling wave, with speckles that suggest hundreds of shells were pressed into it by hand before it set.

'You and I are obviously going to different toilet blocks. Those look like glass sliding doors to me.' It's not a point that will win Robyn over. 'It's way better than a glam resort.'

'Really?'

She taps the screen and another photo comes up. It's the view from the kitchen across the breakfast bar to the loungeroom and balcony. The breakfast bar is the shape of a comma. A laminate-clad pistachio-coloured comma. The loungeroom has studded green leather furniture and the obligatory massive flat-screen TV. Even old toilets and gas-bottle places have those now. The glass doors open to the balcony and a view of near-perfect breaking surf framed spikily by pandanus trees.

'Okay,' she says. 'It's reasonably awful – I think your parents owned that lounge suite when I met you – but, yeah, the beach is right there. It's not like looking down on it from the fiftieth floor, when it might as well be on TV.' She's thinking about it, mentally scrolling through ancient beach holidays. 'And that's an airconditioning unit, isn't it?' She points to it on the wall. 'If the bathrooms aren't foul . . .' She flicks through the photo options and taps one. 'Reasonably foul.'

There's a compact shower with the generic round twenty-five-dollar shower rose we opted not to buy when we were renovating. The towel rails are a toffee colour and could be either wood or plastic. The white tiles, at least, are still white.

'But clean.' I can get away with that, a couple of words. If I oversell it, I'm gone.

'Clean. Yeah.' She nods and studies another couple of photos before shaking her head and setting the iPad down on the table. 'Shit, we're not *buying* it. It's only for a weekend. Sure. Why not? We can leave straight after school, if you can do that. That'd be consistent with your new priorities, wouldn't it?'

'Yeah . . .'

'I only work mornings on Friday, so . . .'

The deal is done. I'm finishing work early on Friday. Priorities crystal clear.

'You can be the one to crush the kids' weekend plans,' she tells me. 'Whatever they were. My advice is don't show them the web stuff, or play up your nostalgia angle too much but, you know, it's up to you.'

'Thanks. Oh, and there's a dinner on the Saturday.' I'd almost forgotten it. It was supposed to be one of my selling points. 'I've got tickets for the two of us. The kids and Dad can have fish and chips or something. It's the work event, but it's the Australian Comedy Awards. Dinner and a debate. It should be fun. It's going live on TV.'

'Really? As long as it won't turn into one of those work events where you walk off and ignore me . . .' She says it as though she's not really expecting an answer. She picks up the iPad again and flicks back to the picture with the beach view. 'Okay. A family weekend at the coast.' She nods. 'We should do more things like that. And there's no reason not to start now.'

8

IT OCCURS TO ME too late that Robyn's spectacular insights into the workings of the universe – and its penises – are one of the things I miss most whenever I'm away.

In the movie of my life, I'm suave, toned and have a selection of perfectly cut suits – that is, it's a movie in which I look seriously like George Clooney, rather than a lump in a jacket prepared to accept charitable Clooney comparisons in a needy moment – but the real ace up my sleeve is my relationship form. It's several notches higher as well, and thoughts like that would hit me in the right moment, and be verbalised and appreciated.

I'm sure I can hear Patti Smith's Horses playing faintly in the distance as I'm unloading the dishwasher. Abi keeps jumping back and running through the same part of it again. I can't remember if it's about drugs or a guy being raped at the lockers or both, and it's not the kind of question I'll be asking her. She's in her room and my father is back bumping around in his flat downstairs.

There's a plastic takeaway container on the dishwasher's upper rack, which leads me to the takeaway container shelf in the pantry and to chaos. When I last checked, there was a system. I thought we'd all agreed upon it. Double-chamber containers in one pile, single-chamber in another, with the containers stacked in increasing order of depth towards the bottom. Now they're tipped at all angles, taking up at least five times the space, and there's no system at all.

So, here it is – the first piece of direct evidence that I contribute something other than money to the house.

Before I realise it, I have three double-chamber containers stacked in my hand, with lids, and then I have everything out on the kitchen table trying to match it all up. I understand some people get medicated for less but, as one container slips neatly into another and hints of the system return, it really is better.

The kitchen door swings open. Abi's out of school uniform, wearing lacy short shorts and a singlet. When she sees I'm there alone, she starts making stripper music, and bumping and grinding. I beg her to stop, for more reasons than she knows.

'It was all the Tetra Pak guy's doing. I . . .' I'm pointing a lid at her, while cradling a container stack in the crook of my other arm like a mad emperor with a plastic box pug.

She pauses to reassess the situation. It's not what she was expecting. She takes a good look at the work in progress on the table.

'What are you building?' she says slowly, in a way that suggests the answer can't be sane, as though I might turn the whole contraption into a mock volcano held together by tape and spit and revealing the site of a future alien landing.

'It was anarchy in there.' I nod towards the pantry.

'Anarchy? What, the ones with the dividers had a revolution and overthrew the other ones?' Technically not anarchy, but it's not the time to play a pedantry bonus round.

'There was a system. There *is* a system . . . You'll thank me.'

She won't. No one will thank me. No one should thank me. Here's how the domestic workload breaks down: Robyn does pretty much everything for three years, I fly back into town and rearrange the used takeaway containers. It wasn't always that way, before the private-equity beast carried me off and swallowed me whole.

'What's going on with Horses? Is that school, or . . .'

She shrugs, but not in a way that means she's uninterested. 'It's kind of legendary. It's, like, deliberately primitive musically.'

Her hand is playing with the Fimo manga-type character she's wearing on a leather cord around her neck. She used to make things like that. Maybe she still does.

'And what about the content?'

'I was mainly focusing on the chords.' She pauses to think it through, as if it's an oral exam. 'Is it alienation? Is that what it's about? The guy's an outsider and he takes a beating and in his mind he's away with the horses? I get that idea. If that's it.'

'I'm sure Patti Smith would be very happy with that interpretation.'

She tilts her head and her eyes narrow, but then she decides I'm not being sarcastic.

'Mainly it was about the music, though,' she says.

'It was a big deal when it came out. It's part of that punk thing of breaking rules but still making music. Grandad says you've got to know the rules so you can *decide* to break them, otherwise you're just scratching around in the dark.'

'He said that?' All my life, he's never said it to me.

'What? You think I'm paraphrasing?' She bumps her hip against the table and her hand picks up a lid. 'I wrote it down straight after. There's not a lot of wisdom in this family. You don't want to miss it when it happens.'

'I'm going to take that as a challenge.'

She laughs, but as if we're in on the joke together rather than I'm being taken down by it. 'Give it your best shot.' Her hand's back on the pendant.

'Is that Pikachu?' As I point to it, she takes her hand away. All I want is for the conversation to keep going. I want more of her, more of this, more of her smart lines about the scarcity of wisdom. That's what I want to write down straight after.

'Is what?' She glances down her front and then peers at me as if hoping for subtitles. 'Jew what?'

'The pendanty thing . . .' More pointing.

'Oh, Pikachu.' She puts her hand over it. 'God. No. I don't know where to start.' She turns her hand over, slips the pendant onto her palm and inspects it for clues that might help her explain. 'No. It's not Pikachu. But thanks for playing.' She drops the pendant again. 'Anyway, I'm supposed to be getting dinner out of the freezer.'

'I could have done that.' Sorting the containers now only looks more tangential.

'Yeah. I think anyone could. But I was supposed to.'

It seems there's a system for dinner too, one I don't know. She goes over to the freezer, pulls out a wire basket and starts searching through containers.

'So,' she says, still facing away from me, 'are you actually back, or . . .'

'Or what?'

'Or is this just temporary?'

She taps on a lid to make some of the frost fall away, then lifts the container towards the light to take a better look at what's inside.

'I'm back. There's a guy in my office in Sydney. Which is his office now. I'm out of that job. My BDK email address goes somewhere else now. Not to me.'

I need to roll my super over somewhere too, though I manage to pull up short of that fascinating detail. I could make a list for her – the BlackBerry, the last half-box of business cards. I expect they wiped my fingerprints from the drinking glasses before the lift reached ground. But that story, and the blank empty moment on the street with my box in my hands, is not how I'm to prove myself. Not to her.

'What's for dinner?'

'Mystery dinner.' She has a container in each hand and she's comparing them. She holds them out. 'Do they look the same to you or different?'

'Aren't they labelled?'

'They're never labelled. And don't ask me why. I don't cook them.' She wiggles the containers to draw my focus back to them. 'Same or different? And are you thinking they'd go with pasta or rice?'

'I'm thinking it'd be nice to go out to dinner.' I'm now even more certain my container stacking will go unappreciated, if they're dining by chance. 'It's my first night back, so . . .'

'Good thinking.'

Within seconds she suggests Sky, a local Indian restaurant, finds the number on her phone and passes it to my free hand so that I can book. My vague idea takes two minutes to become a locked-in plan with an outside table for five lined up.

★ ★ ★

'Dad's taking us out to dinner,' Abi says brightly when Robyn and Jack simultaneously enter the kitchen through two different doors.

They look first at each other, like players in a French farce who haven't quite hit their marks, then simultaneously turn to me, their choreography snapping back into place. Inevitably they speak over each other, two different perspectives on my wrong move. They both stop half a sentence in.

I take my chance. 'Abi was pulling containers out of the freezer and trying to work out what was in them. Since it's my first night back I thought it'd be nice if we –'

'It's perfectly good food.' Robyn's tone shuts me up. We made an agreement years ago never to interrupt each other in front of the kids. We were setting a good example. 'Just because it's a mystery doesn't mean it's bad. It's just that we occasionally run out of labels. They don't always hit number one on my priority list at the right time.'

'I like mystery dinner,' Jack says. He doesn't like much, so it's a big vote of confidence. 'Remember that

87

chicken one? It was kind of red.' He turns to Robyn. 'But if there's another one of those, I want to try it with couscous, remember? We did a deal.'

I fumble Abi's phone around in my hand until I get the restaurant number up.

'I'm going to cancel the booking.' It's supposed to sound entirely diplomatic when I say it, but I can tell it's come out ten per cent petulant and that's the only tone that'll be noticed.

'No, no, don't cancel,' Robyn says, twenty per cent defensively. 'If you want to go out . . .' She shrugs and then becomes acutely conscious that there are four of us in the room, not two. She draws on her deep well of model parenting and says, 'No, let's do that.'

'Not that mystery dinner wouldn't . . .' I'm digging a hole and tossing most of the dirt into my own hair. 'It'd be great too. I'm looking forward to . . .'

As intended compliments go, this one trips over its own feet on the way out and flashes its underwear to the room before face-planting.

She nods, and then seems to notice for the first time that I'm balancing an almost chin-high tower of takeaway containers. 'As long as you promise not to tell me what plans you have for those.' She frowns, takes a step back towards the door and makes herself say, 'It'd be nice to go out.'

9

ROBYN IS IN OUR ROOM getting changed when I make my move to clear the air.

I'm not sure I can read her the way I once did. If I once had the key, or swipe card, to Robyn's brain, it's no longer the case. Even though she still has the freedom to enter mine through a revolving door.

She's standing in front of the mirror, staring but not really looking at anything. She's in a top and skirt I haven't seen before, regretting a purchase or contemplating accessories or making a list of the several ways I made a dick of myself in the kitchen.

I ask her what she's thinking about and she startles, notices me in the room for the first time and says, 'Oh.' One hand adjusts her collar while she gets her thoughts straight. 'Why we don't use anaesthetic more with anal fissures. We know there's pain on defecation – why don't we give the patient some kind of local to self-administer beforehand?'

'Okay, great.' It's not an answer I'd prepared for. Nor is it one of the first million or so I hadn't prepared for but could have listed in decreasing order of likelihood, given sufficient time. But at least it's nothing to do with what happened in the kitchen. 'That could help a lot of people.' Could it? I have no idea how many people have anal fissures. Even the name makes my buttocks clench, as if that might keep the forces of fissuring at bay. 'Um, downstairs, about dinner tonight, that was just a . . .'

'I know. I should try not to bite your head off too often.' She holds up her hand, signalling that she needs a moment to think but it's still her turn. 'Look, we've had to find things that work for us. You've been running a household of one. I've had a household of four and not one of the other three is exactly a breeze. I cook in batches, and if you want to remember to put labels on the shopping list, or better still to buy them . . .' She stops, to release the beginnings of a build-up of steam. She nods, to the mirror, to her better self. 'And if you were restacking the takeaway containers, Rainman, in some perverse but meticulous kind of order that you call a system, go for your life but don't go explaining its merits to me.' At least she's smiling.

I make an effort to keep my mouth shut and nod.

'Well done,' she says. 'I know it's killing you not to tell me how great your system is.'

'I can do some shopping,' I find myself saying because, if I don't, I won't keep a lid on my need to tell her how much more space there is now in the pantry. 'I know where Coles is. Unless they've moved it. This job is not going to dominate my life. It's not going to take me away like the last one. I want to do drop-offs and pick-ups and whatever.'

'Yeah, that's . . .' She glances back towards the mirror, sees herself from side on and straightens her shoulders. Something's not sitting right. 'I drop the kids off because the surgery's near school, and they catch the bus home in the afternoon – they catch it to school as well any day I don't start work at nine – but, yeah, it'll be good to share things more. You can take maths homework and anything like that for a start.'

'Great.' I'll be no help at all – spreadsheets aren't trigonometry. Assuming schools still do trigonometry. 'I can . . . I'm sure there's lots of stuff.'

'Yeah,' she says, without even trying to sound convinced. She undoes her belt to change her skirt. 'I bet there is. Now, if you're going to have a shower . . .'

★ ★ ★

As soon as I've turned the water on I can hear the TV in the bedroom, the voice of a newsreader. Robyn had the TV fitted to the wall during one of my longer absences. It's turned at an angle that makes me feel it's looking at me whenever I walk into the bedroom – looking at me smugly, as if it's better company than I've been.

Through the steamed-up shower door, I can see Robyn throwing clothes onto the bed, trying on something different.

When I get out she's wearing a top and pants, which are both new to me, and holding my shirt and sniffing it.

'You should wear a fresh shirt,' she says.

'I was planning to.'

She balls it up and drops it on my side of the bed. She steps in front of the mirror again, smoothes down the front of her top and semi-rotates in both directions, giving herself close scrutiny.

'Do I have shelf bosom in this top?' she says, as if I'm such a newbie I might think there's more than one potential answer.

Shelf bosom is a decade-long fear of Robyn's, stalking her like Captain Hook's crocodile through department-store change rooms and past reflective surfaces everywhere. It's a perceived affliction of the ample-bosomed woman of middle years, whose alternative to sag is either the perfect bra and top or a breast-control device that forces her soft tissue into a solid mammary shelf.

'No.'

'I saw the way you said that.' It's a physical impossibility, since her eyes were locked on the mirror, and her nemesis. 'You meant yes. You think I've got shelf bosom.' She's pushing her breasts around with her hands, shocking herself by making them shelfier.

'You think that, and yet what I said was "No". Nothing more nor less.' I know this game. I know the next play. I need to stand my ground. 'Next time email me a photo and I'll email "No" back. You can nominate the font.'

'Ha.' She releases her breasts and stares at the mirror long and hard, attempting to view herself as a sequence of random passers-by. 'Times. Twelve-point Times. It's a totally sincere font.'

'Totally. Now, you look good. There is no shelf bosom.' I'm knotting and reknotting my towel over my belly, since body parts are under serious scrutiny. I want to get dressed. 'Tell me which shirt I'm going to end up choosing.'

'Sky is casual.' She pulls a folded T-shirt, one of my

newer ones, from a shelf in the wardrobe. 'Anything you wore to work today or anything like it would be a mistake.'

I've had Sky takeaway before, but always home delivered. I've seen the restaurant from Milton Road, down a side street. I can picture the curries on the table, along with a basket of naan bread and steel bowls filled with saffron rice, but I think it's from a photo sent from Robyn's phone.

As I'm dressing, Robyn points me in the direction of the right shoes and socks. It's easiest, always, just to go with it. The T-shirt at least hangs loosely below the taut belt-line. Robyn checks me out without any of the inclination to judge that she applies to herself.

'Good,' she says simply. She checks her watch. 'Kids should be downstairs. Your dad will have been there for ten minutes unless there's been a stoma misfire.'

★ ★ ★

Jack clears his throat as we walk past his room. So, Robyn doesn't have every mind in the house perfectly read.

I knock on his door with the knuckle of my middle finger and, just as I'm saying, 'Let's head to the car,' the door swings open to reveal Jack at his desk with a picture of a very buxom swimsuit model on his laptop.

He glances at us each in turn and sniffs. He follows our eyes to the screen.

'Sports Illustrated,' he says and shrugs. 'So, don't go thinking I've cracked the filter.'

He's got the kind of smirk that would only be used by someone who has cracked the filter. Most of his desk is taken up by junk and electronic parts and sheets of paper with schematic diagrams, and his laptop is perched on one edge. He couldn't look more like a filter cracker if he tried.

'Well,' Robyn says, 'that girl really needs to re-think her swimsuit choices. Those boobs need a lot more support or they'll be round her knees before she's thirty.'

Jack gives her a look that lets her know she's spoiled the moment, utterly. She's pushed in with all the sensuality of a matronly David Jones bra fitter, shovelling breast into cup, hoiking the straps and scowling at the change-room mirror. It might reflect a certain preoccupation of Robyn's, but from where I stand it's parenting genius.

10

WE WALK TO THE restaurant by the light of Abi and Jack's phones, with messages and who knows what else pinging in and out.

'Okay, there's a road coming up, people,' Robyn calls out, like a scout locating possible enemy positions.

'Yeah, yeah,' Jack says, stumbling over a tilted slab of footpath concrete.

My father and I are the rearguard, carrying the drinks. He's chewing gum and holding a bottle of Cointreau in one hand and a cocktail shaker loaded with ice in the other. Wine has stopped agreeing with him, he tells me.

I point out that they probably have ice at the restaurant and he says, 'Yeah, they might.' He shifts the gum from one side of his mouth to the other. 'But this way I just need a glass. A water glass. We'll all get one of those. A glass *plus* ice? They might want to charge for that.'

'It's on me.'

He thinks about it, takes another couple of chews. 'Still. Do I want you paying for ice?'

* * *

The gum stays in his mouth all the way to Sky, through the ordering debate and right up to the arrival of the pappadums, when he wraps it carefully in its foil and pockets it. Even though Robyn's insisted it'll be too much food, we've chosen a main each since that allows Jack and Abi to each order something they know the other won't like.

The table is in an area that was tiled fawn and milk-chocolate brown in a checkerboard pattern in about 1980, with tiled steps rising to a row of pot plants and the road. It's open on two-and-a-half sides but the roof extends over us, with a single line of winking fairy lights threaded along its edge.

Like most clichés, the one about business opting for unnecessarily fine dining is a cliché because there's some truth behind it. BDK never did business in a place like this if there was somewhere with fluted white napkins in the vicinity. So the tetra-packers and masters of flagging apparel brands and pesticide takeover targets would find themselves being thoroughly silver-serviced, their minds all the time less on the five-star steak than on their scrappy balance sheets or the prospect of strippers or drinking too much at someone else's expense. Or perhaps just getting the night done, and getting out of there and back to some peace or to their families.

Most nights away, I didn't have dinner in my diary. More often than not I'd find myself working into the evening and realising I'd missed the normal hours for eating. So, dinner devolved into cheese and biscuits and then sometimes just the cheese. It remains a mystery to me that powdered parmesan smells like vomit, yet freshly shaved parmesan is perfect. I bought a tool to shave it. I knew I had to stop when dinner became most of a bottle of red wine with a pile of shaved parmesan.

Robyn catches my eye. She's signalling something but I'm not receiving.

'Well, we're all here,' she says, giving up on the non-verbals. 'This'd be a good time to . . .' She's beckoning in my direction. 'If you've got anything to say.'

My father sets a crescent of pappadum down on his plate. Abi looks up from her phone. Jack keeps tapping away at his with a speed to rival a court stenographer. A deal has been done regarding phone use. As soon as the meals arrive they have to go. Negotiations led to pappadums being declassified as part of the meal. When the first curry, first bowl of rice or first naan bread arrives, phones have to go. Which apparently makes it essential in the meantime to work them till they smoke.

'Yeah.' Robyn's message finally lands in the right part of my brain, away from the miracle that is fresh parmesan and the trials of BDK dinners. It's time to unveil my plan. 'I've had a great idea.' It's not a prospect that, announced by itself, appears to thrill anyone. 'I think we should go away this weekend. All of us. To the coast. It's the perfect time for it.'

'Really?' Abi's phone is still in her hand, fixed there. 'Is this just, like, a random idea? Like dinner tonight? Is this how it's going to be from now on?'

'Yes, yes, maybe it is. Maybe we'll just have ideas about great things to do, and then do them. How about that?'

Abi glances towards Robyn, wanting the conversation to take a turn back towards normal, a place where ideas are kept on a tight leash. Robyn gives me a look that says she threw me a decent pass and I've fumbled it.

'It's not that random, but I think it'll be good. Mum and I have a dinner to go to on the Saturday night with someone from the radio station. So, I thought we could all go, make a weekend of it.'

'I've got a history assignment due.' Abi's gripping her phone in both hands in the way a distraught Jane Austen character might clench a lace hanky. 'Like, *really* due.'

'We'll come back Sunday morning. Sunday afternoon and evening, it's all you have to do. Plus, there's always tonight. And tomorrow night.'

'But April and I were going to get together on the weekend to work on some songs. For the band.'

It's the first I've heard of a band. April Tran is in the twins' year at school. She's the overachieving daughter of parents who work every waking hour running a Vietnamese restaurant. She plays at least four instruments and speaks fluent French as well as English and Vietnamese. And yet I didn't know there was a band. April Tran is tiny, in a way that makes Abi look out of scale.

'Well, there's probably room,' I tell her. 'We've actually got two neighbouring two-bedroom apartments. You and April could have the single beds in one bedroom, Mum and I could be in the other and Jack and Grandad could have the other apartment.'

It seems simple. It seems like an act of low-level problem-solving genius, but Robyn's shaking her head. So subtly that only I can see it, but shaking it nonetheless.

Jack sniffs and glances up from the screen but keeps his body hunched over his phone. 'So, Lyrix can come, then?'

Robyn stops shaking her head, her point made.

'Only if you're in a band together and this is keeping you from songwriting.'

'If she gets to bring a friend, I get to bring a friend.'

Every negotiation with a teenager seems to work like a courtroom drama in which they're playing the brash advocate who's confident they've memorised the statute books. Robyn tops up her wine and glances towards the kitchen in case food might be coming.

'We'll have to talk to her parents,' I tell him. And before Robyn's head has fully swivelled back my way, I amend it to, '*I'll* have to talk to her parents.'

'Good,' my father says. He claps his hands and rubs them together, sending a fleck of broken pappadum flying. 'Great.' He's grinning. Almost all the creases in his face line up to do it. 'We're going to have a lot of fun.' He looks straight at Jack, and then Abi. 'We had a van, you know, an old combi. Your dad and Julianne'd bring a friend each and we'd all pile in, put the boards on top and go where the waves were breaking. Maybe a caravan, maybe a fibro shack or an old unit, one of those two-storey yellow-brick places. They weren't old then.'

'The kind of place that calls itself Crystal Tydes,' Robyn says, 'but with a "Y" in Tydes.'

He laughs and says, 'Exactly.'

It was never quite the blissed-out wave-chasing summer he's implying. There's no crackly home-movie footage of children with tousled blond hair and faded tie-dyed T-shirts running down the dunes. Not once do I recall us being so carefree that we went when and where the waves were breaking. It was all planned and carefully budgeted for well in advance, and my parents both had to make it work around jobs in the city, as well as our school timetable. But all that planning meant it could be anticipated as well as savoured, and my father always maintained that made it even better. We'd count down the days, the same as we did for Christmas.

My father had had the van from his single years, and it never quite lost the smell of unshowered young men on surf trips and their thin musty mattresses. But that smell said we were on our way.

Jack slides his phone across the table towards me. He's online, at a Facebook page featuring the headshot of a man in his late thirties who looks to be a hardened criminal, the kind no one dared fuck with in jail and who had a bunch of lesser hard men breaking the jaws of his enemies in the hope of winning favour. Jack has blown it up enough for me to see a number-two cut, a dented scalp, a buckled ear and an owner who couldn't even manage to take the meanness out of his expression for his Facebook photo.

'Lyrix's dad,' he says. 'Is Facebook okay, or do you want an actual phone number?'

11

ROBYN'S IN THE LAUNDRY when I find her to ask if she wants to share the rest of the wine.

'Five minutes,' she says, pulling clothes from the washing machine. 'Yes, I do, but I'll be five minutes, maybe a bit longer.'

'Why don't you . . .'

'Why don't I?' She cuts me off. She dumps an armful of damp clothes in a basket. 'You're not going to say why don't I take a break, as if the laundry will do itself while you and I finish the wine? You realise this semi-spontaneous trip to the coast means I've got to do laundry now?'

Suddenly, I'm a thoughtless dilettante, and the bottle in one hand and two glasses in the other are the props that prove it. I have brought home laundry and seen it done. I have commented appreciatively in lieu of playing an actual role. I have washed my running clothes in hotel showers, sent my shirts to dry cleaners when I've needed to and grown to appreciate the folding and packaging. Clothes have been dirtying in this house all week and foremost in my mind is the last third of a bottle of sav blanc.

Robyn's sleeves are rolled up, her hair has started to unthread itself and tendrils are dipping in front of her face, and right is utterly on her side. She would not be out of line to mention the laundry fairies that Jack's heard about so many times when his grubby clothes have been strewn across his room.

'That's the beauty of going old school for the weekend and getting an apartment,' I tell her. 'There'll be a laundry. So, there's no pressure.' I tilt the bottle to give her a better look at how much wine is left.

She drops the lid of the washing machine and it makes a loud clang.

'There's really nothing beautiful about taking dirty laundry to the Gold Coast to wash.'

'Okay, look, let me . . .' My piriformis catches on the way down the steps and the wine glasses clink together. 'I'll hang this load out, while you get the next one in the machine.'

I make it to the bench before the cramps set in hard. I set down the bottle and the glasses. And wonder how I might move without hydraulics or a crane.

'Great,' Robyn says happily, unaware of the double fist of pain in my left buttock.

She hands me the pile of damp laundry.

We both look at the clothes. She thinks I'm about to hang them out. I'm wondering if there's any chance, even a small one, that there are actually laundry fairies in the house, and that one or two of them might be close by.

'I can't rotate,' I tell her, feeling as functional as a broken marionette.

'Jesus. Would you just like to fold some hankies or

something?' She takes my arm, says, 'Pivot on your good leg,' and turns me towards the drying rack.

I dump the whole mass of clothes on the top level then draw socks out one by one and hang them, keeping my core absolutely still. It's a pastiche of laundry hanging, as if I'm pretending to be Curiosity on the plains of Mars, tentatively extending my delicate robotic arm to perform a series of small and unremarkable yet miraculous acts.

'I'll go and get the next load,' Robyn says, having to look away.

'Good. I think I can get through most of this.'

'*Most*?' She stops, with one foot on the steps. She turns around to see that I'm up to my fourth sock. 'I might be delayed while I go to the kitchen. I want to get some Alfoil to make you a medal.'

She steps forward, pulls a shirt from the pile and threads it onto a hanger. From where I'm hunkered like a titanium Mars crab, the move looks almost balletic.

'Or maybe just some Nurofen,' she says, relenting, opting to be less directly mean. 'And you should go and do some stretches, if it hasn't gone beyond that.'

'I'll cook dinner tomorrow night.' At least it's an offer that's almost a day away from coming to grief.

'Great,' she says, but bluntly. She thinks I won't do it. She's sure it won't be great. She tidies away hair that's fallen in front of her eyes, and checks her watch. She's always on a schedule, somewhere in the house, somewhere in the world. 'No, that'd be good.' The tilt of her head changes, as if she's actively rebalancing the conversation or the two of us. 'Could you add whatever you need to the shopping list?'

I haven't cooked for ages – a couple of years perhaps – but we don't seem to be going there. I almost suggest a two-kilo block of parmesan and a delectable range of cheese-appropriate biscuits, but there's a real risk she'd think I was serious.

'Actually,' she says, 'could you do the shopping after work? That'd make a difference.'

'Sure.'

'And Jack has to go to a place at Milton to pick up some computer parts.'

'Is that the same . . . That's quite an . . .' Just as I'm about to say 'expedition' I realise how bad a look it could be. I only hang socks. I only buy ingredients when I cook, which is approximately never. I only do drop-offs and pick-ups once the kids have grown out of them. 'What's wrong with his computer?'

It seems to be perfectly good at finding him pictures of large-breasted models, which is surely half the use he gets out of it.

'Why? Would you fix it for him? Ha.' She pulls a large pair of khaki shorts – probably my father's – from the clothes pile, and crouches down to hang them over one of the lower racks. 'This is a different computer,' she says, in the direction of the floor tiles. 'One he's building.'

'Building.'

She stands up and shrugs. 'I don't get it either, but I could make a list of fifty things I'd like him to be doing less.'

'But it'd take money, wouldn't it? To get the parts? Is he doing any of the things he's supposed to do around the house to get money?'

She gives me a don't-go-there look. She turns another pair of shorts the right way out and shakes them to stop them bunching. 'That hasn't really been working for us for a while. As I think was the case in your own adolescence, on the weekends it wasn't all about surfing safaris in the famous van. Your father's pretty sure you only ever swept out under the house three times.' She hangs the shorts on the rack. 'Jack trades smurfberries.' She watches me for a reaction.

'What are . . .'

'If you have to ask, there's no explaining it to you.'

'But how does that convert into computer parts?'

'There are still some socks in there,' she says, jerking one from the middle of the pile and flipping it over my shoulder.

12

JULES AND I REPAINTED the famous van when we were ten and eight. One weekend, apparently on a whim, our father taped newspaper over the windows, set us up with tins of paint and told us to do whatever we wanted. He wore a kaftan in those days, or drawstring unbleached calico pants and sandals.

He became more of a man-about-town when he made it big in radio. His wardrobe changed, but the van stayed in our lives for a few more years. His face started appearing in the ads for 4IP and, if people didn't know his face, they knew his voice, and certainly his name. Casey Van Fleet was a name that sounded custom-made for seventies radio.

My grandparents were always van Vliet, but their boy Cees became Casey Van Fleet in his Sandgate bedroom in the mid-to-late fifties, back-announcing Bill Haley and the Comets over 4BC and static, in the same way that Brian Brightman would end up copying Casey's style years later. I don't even know when my father put through the paperwork to make the name official.

By the mid-seventies, it worked for us all over town. At Baxter's in Deagon a table would always be found, and my father would be asked to join the band for a song. Brisbane was so short on fame then that we had no idea how it was supposed to work. I think we all believed every famous person could sing. My father could, and it seemed natural to us – in the odd place in life into which we'd drifted – that he would. He typically did Rod Stewart's Sailing and Maggie May. Then, at least for the few short years before it became crushingly uncool, he would dance with Julianne to a big band number or two and I would dance with our mother.

My parents made so many shifts in tone and style in the seventies that they often managed to wrong-foot themselves, without it ever seeming to matter. It was often hard to get a bead on what we stood for – beyond general decency – or on what was in or out. On some issues my parents were outrageously socially progressive, on some they hadn't budged from decades before. It wasn't uncommon for them to hold both positions simultaneously.

In the same year as a family friend had a ceremony for her placenta and then ate much of it, my mother referred coyly to her own 'monthly visitor'. I wondered if my parents had an open relationship. I imagined a man who came over the back fence any night my father was away. I was an adult before I heard someone else use the term in a context that revealed it to be a euphemism for menstruation.

My guess is my father moved towards the Maharishi in the wake of George Harrison and started edging away when he became the voice of the top forty. The incense burning became intermittent, the showy meditation became private and then probably stopped. My mother shifted with him, always, but I had the sense that he mostly took the lead. While we were never truly carefree in the seventies, I can't begrudge him any memory that says we were, since he made the decade an adventure. He was ten different men during those ten years, most of them great men, if not always easy. We never knew what he would bring home next – what amazing new object, or idea. It was radio that gave him the chance to be like that.

His parents for the rest of their lives wore the same clothes they had brought from Arnhem, mending them and keeping them regardless of their poor fit for the climate. Anything new was bought with a lot of gnashing of teeth, and only if something had properly disintegrated. Their thick jackets and coats and my grandfather's suits lasted them to the end.

Since Julianne was two years older, or perhaps because she was Julianne, she was the first of us to see Casey Van Fleet and his double-denim 4IP world as uncool. I was still chasing the weekly top-forty charts when she started uni and ran from commercial radio to the arms of Triple Z, where the announcers talked as if a dope cloud hung permanently at head height in the studio, and played punk and songs that openly referred to police – our famously brutal Queensland police – as pigs.

She'd bring singles home on vinyl, most of them wild and anti-musical, though there were occasional bands who paid some heed to melody and to their instruments. If my parents ever tired of hearing any particular three minutes of discordant shrieking, my father would ask if he could borrow the record for work. After that, Julianne would never play it again.

I begged and begged until she took me to a loud thrashy band in a church hall. One of her friends pushed us out a window when the police raided. My heart raced all night.

For a couple of years, Julianne ran wild enough that much of my adolescence slipped by unnoticed. I appear in my father's stories of that time, but I'm not the rebel or the interesting challenge. I'm the one who slunk off to his room, got away with the bare minimum of chores and became a banker.

* * *

I'm lying on our bed with my head on two pillows, flicking through Google hits for smurfberries on Robyn's iPad, when she comes in after hanging out the second load of laundry. The official Smurf village website offers thirteen ways to accumulate berries – option one is to pay for them – but 'trading smurfberries' gets very few hits. Which makes sense if the game is free, and funded by berry sales. But somehow Jack is apparently doing it.

'Have you ever seen anything about smurfberry trading?' I flip the iPad around in case any of the Google hits happens to be familiar. 'I'm not sure it's a legitimate thing. How do we know it's not a scam?'

Robyn unclips her earrings and holds them in one hand.

'I asked if he had to give anyone bank-account details or anything like that,' she tells me. 'He said he didn't. It's probably just a nerd with an entrepreneurial streak.'

'So, if he didn't give bank-account details, how does he get paid? How does he get the money for the parts? He's not paying the computer people in smurfberries. There have to be other steps to it. He could be caught up in trade-based money laundering. There are organised crime groups who . . .'

'What? This is smurfberries.' She frowns, trying to conjure up some picture of this apparently mad notion. 'Little blue smurfs, on your phone, living in a tiny pretend village. Are you seriously saying you think the Russian mafia is trading in smurfberries?'

'Why not? The more ridiculous it sounds, the better cover it is.' I have no idea if that's true.

'This'll be your conversation to have with him, won't it?' She walks across the room and drops the earrings into a crystal bowl on the dresser.

'Sure. We're getting the parts tomorrow. I can do it then.' I prop myself up on one elbow and my piriformis grabs me again. The groan is out of me before I can stop it. 'Would Dencorub work for this, do you think?'

'Sure.' She's checking her face in the mirror, poking at the skin under her eyes.

'You didn't even think about that.'

'I did.' She picks up a pot of cream and unscrews the lid. 'I think it'll be perfect for at least a minute. I'm imagining the silence already. It's a perfect silence. The tube's in the cabinet in the en suite. It's the red and white one.'

She puts a dot of cream under one eye and starts to massage it in.

I swing my legs around and lever myself into a standing position. The en suite is a short hobble away. Even the friction of carpet is an obstacle when my piriformis is bad. The tube seems to be out already. I drop my pants, squirt the contents onto my hand and smear it onto my bare buttock.

'It was on the counter.' I'm expecting a brisk rush of heat, but there's none of that. My hand sticks. 'Is it a free sample from work or a unit dose thing? It's pretty small.'

There's a burst of TV noise. Robyn jumps from channel to channel until she settles on something that sounds like CSI Miami.

'No, that's the super glue,' she calls out. 'The sole of one of my shoes was starting to come off.'

'What are we . . .' I lift my hand and my buttock skin rises with it. 'Who keeps super glue in their bathroom? Who leaves it out on the counter?'

'Um, adults? You haven't . . .' She appears in the doorway, squawks with laughter. 'Oh my god, that's the whole tube of super glue. Pull your hand off quickly, before it sets.'

'It's already set.'

I'm stuck in some arse-slapping dance move, pants around my ankles, piriformis pain still fixing me like a staple to a board.

'It can't have,' she says. 'It's not that super.' She takes a step towards me. 'And you think you don't need reading glasses.'

She has a point. It was red and white and tube-shaped, and that was enough for me.

'I didn't think you'd . . .'

She takes my wrist with both hands, yanks it hard and my buttock feels as if it's been side-swiped by coarse sandpaper as my hand comes away. The noise that comes out of me can only be described as a squeal.

'That's what waxing's like,' she says. 'That's why men don't often do it. Hey, now you have a neat hairless butt.' Neat, hairless and burning as if I've been branded. 'Do you want me to do the other side? Even you up?'

Something catches her eye. She crouches down and turns my pelvis to bring my buttock towards the light. In the mirror I can see a red patch rotating out of view. I check my hand, half-expecting a hunk of buttock on there. It's gunked up with glue, hair, flecks of pale tissue.

'Okay, you've lost skin,' she says matter-of-factly. 'It's not deep enough to bleed, probably, but there's serous ooze already. Probably needs something done to it.'

She opens one of the mirrored cabinet doors. I can feel my pulse pounding in my peeled buttock like a second heart. I almost reach my glued hand out to the counter to lever myself around.

'What about this? What about my hand?' My index, middle and ring fingers are stuck together, bound in a glue mitt. 'I have to type with this. And drive. And eat.'

Robyn swings the cabinet door shut. She's cradling a range of bandage options in her bent left arm.

'We'll use nail-polish remover for that.' With her free hand she opens a different door, clinks around among bottles and brings out two. 'You'll need at least one of those, maybe more.' She looks around the room, in pre-op mode. 'I'm going to need you lying down to do the buttock. Or better still kneeling on the floor and leaning forward over the bed. So, we'll take a bluey and you can get started on the hand while I do my bit.'

A bluey, past experience with medical shorthand tells me, is a sheet with blue plastic on one side and quilted absorbent paper on the other. Robyn has a stash of them in all three bathrooms and possibly the kitchen.

I hobble into the bedroom with my two bottles of nail-polish remover in my right hand, bluey tucked under my right arm, the glue on my left hand setting harder than toffee and my buttock feeling as though it should be releasing steam. I keep dragging my pants along around my ankles, as if stepping out of them will be to admit defeat. As if the evening is a moment's good medicine away from being back on track, if only I can manage not to forsake my pants.

I ease myself into a kneeling position, then spread my body forward across the bed. Robyn starts dabbing something damp and cool on my raw buttock. The nail-polish remover has a wildly chemical smell but seems remarkably effective at stripping the glue from my hand.

'Why didn't we start with this?' I'm trying not to cough or gag. Why do women use nail polish? 'I've got my little finger sorted out already.'

Robyn's on her knees behind me. Her voice reaches me as though she's trying to send it internally, whispering it near my buttock. 'It's acetone. It's carcinogenic.'

'What?' I'm waiting for her to laugh. 'That's a joke, right? Or did you say something other than "carcinogenic"?'

'No.' She leans sideways and puts an elbow on the bed. 'Carcinogenic. As in, causes cancer. But fingernails can't get cancer, and you should be okay with one use on your hand. The skin's pretty thick there. It was just that expanse of delicate buttock flesh . . .'

There's a scream at the door. It's Abi. I am kneeling on the floor, my body splayed across the bed, pants still around my ankles and a blazing raw buttock exposed with Robyn's head next to it. And one of her hands placed firmly on the other buttock for balance.

'You left the door open,' Abi screeches, in a higher register than I knew she could reach. 'That's the code. Everyone knows that.'

'I thought the code was more about knocking,' Robyn says matter-of-factly, levering herself up from my better buttock to a standing position.

'What did you do to him?' Abi's stepping back, peeping through her fingers at my seared butt flesh. 'What did he do to deserve it?'

She reels away, lurches out the door. Her feet thump along the hall as she runs to her room. Her door slams. There's a noise somewhere between a groan and a shriek as the image seared onto her retinas refuses to erase.

13

ROBYN FIXES IT, or at least has the calm, quiet talk that she assures me fixes it. Despite her looking like the perp of whatever lurid crime was in progress, she's the one trusted by Abi to go into Abi's room while I'm left with my buttocks in the breeze, contemplating the day's quiet achievements and litany of pratfalls while painting carcinogen across my hand to reclaim my fingers. Above and behind me, out of view on the TV screen, there's a volley of gunshots, then tyres screeching.

'I told her it was all down to your stubbornness about your glasses,' Robyn says when she comes back in. 'And a few tips we picked up from Fifty Shades of Grey.'

'What?'

'Stay . . .' She reaches out with her toe to keep me in the crouch position. 'I just put it down to the glasses.' She frowns. 'That thing's still oozing.'

She finishes applying the dressing, and I stumble and stagger through the essential parts of my bedtime routine. When I pull off my final awkward three-point landing of the night and lie face down on the bed, she's propped up on two pillows reading a novel on her iPad. She's developed a fiction habit that's zeroed in on free ebook-original medical crime thrillers. It started years ago with Kathy Reichs and then Kathryn Fox, on paper and not for free, but now it seems that anyone who's ever sprained an ankle or taken a tablet thinks they've got forensic fiction in them. Robyn starts plenty but finishes few and treats that as all part of the game.

Somehow I'm across the minutiae of Robyn's fiction purchasing, and yet I can't account for the TV bolted next to the wardrobe or when we signed up for cable.

Despite my cramps and butt scalping, sleep feels like it's a minute away, maybe less.

'Oh,' Robyn says, setting her iPad down on her knees. 'It's probably time for an updated sex talk with Jack.'

'Now?' It sounds even more pathetic said face-down into my pillow. 'Right now?'

'Not right now,' she says. She lifts her glasses and rubs her eyes. 'Not this minute. But he and Lyrix could be getting pretty close, I reckon. You might be giving them the perfect chance with this weekend.'

'Oh, so it'll be my fault?'

'I've met her dad. Big guy, builder, tatts.'

She leans towards her bedside table and I hear her glasses case open with a click. She starts rubbing the lenses with the cloth that she keeps in there.

'Jack gave me a look at him on Facebook tonight. Right up until then I'd been holding out hope that her father was Cacofonix, the bard.'

Somehow his brute physicality and his various ways of showcasing menace all add up to a direct threat to me. My stringbean son with his Buddy Holly specs and self-cut hair gives it to Lyrix on my watch, Lyrix's dad comes over to plant his tattooed fist in my face.

'Everyone's got tatts these days, I suppose,' Robyn says, a blasé bystander to my impending pummelling. 'Everyone younger than us, which I'm guessing he is.'

'My assistant – whose name, by the way, I thought was Venice but is actually Vuh-neece, spelt exactly the same as Venice – she's got tatts.' A bluebird on her ankle, a bird of paradise on her left arm.

Tomorrow I walk back in there with a denuded buttock.

'Ha – Vuh-neece.' Robyn puts her glasses back on and blinks a couple of times. 'With a name like that I bet she's got a tramp stamp.' She tilts her iPad up again. She's about to resume reading, but then she stops. 'With Lyrix's father, they're more like prison tatts.'

'I'm going to talk to her mother, I think.'

'There was a time – I'm sure they said this at uni – there was a time when tatts were some kind of predictor of prison. Almost no one without a tatt goes to prison. That's what it was.' Her mind's off somewhere high in the raked timber seating of a med-school lecture theatre, back when such wisdom was newly minted and long before it wore out. 'I bet Vuh-neece has no pubic hair. Brazilians are trending younger. Did you know that? Girls are getting pubically denuded before their formals. Sometimes I see them if the follicles get infected.'

I can't imagine how parents are supposed to start that conversation with their daughters. The 'it's okay to have pubic hair' conversation. That one can't be mine, surely. Abi and I would both hate every second of it.

'Did you know that eighty per cent of US college students have removed at least some pubic hair?' Robyn's still riffing on her new theme, pretending it's abstract and academic, not looming in our lives. 'I read a journal article. There's a handful of women that age fighting back and going hairy, but pubic lice could become endangered in the US due to loss of habitat.'

'If I was Brian Brightman I'd already have a line for you about Brazilians and deforestation.'

'I saw online that Gwyneth Paltrow actually has pubic hair. Or had it until recently. A woman having pubic hair recently is news now. She talked about her friends being unimpressed with her "rocking a seventies vibe".' She does quote fingers. 'They fixed it, apparently.'

'Just back to the Jack and Lyrix issue . . .' I'm starting to wonder how much material Robyn's got on the topic of pubic hair. 'Didn't you have the sex talk with the kids years ago?'

I can remember the debrief, and finding the etch-a-sketch afterwards with the stuttering outline of a uterus and fallopian tubes on it. I think that was Jack's work, rather than part of the talk.

'Yeah,' she says, 'but there's a top-up talk you need to do when it looks like it's about to happen. I think Jack's due.'

'Okay, well, leave it to me.' I have no idea how it goes, other than being confident I won't be sitting there with an etch-a-sketch. 'I'll do it tomorrow, when we're getting the computer parts.'

Groceries, dinner and a sex talk. It's a far more convincing buy-in to family life than I've managed on day one: spoil mystery dinner, throw weekend into disarray, flash seeping butt flesh at daughter while in an apparently submissive sexual position.

'I also had the masturbation talk with Jack, by the way,' Robyn tells me, so that I'm fully up to date.

'That's a separate talk?'

'It is if you want to keep things tidy. Someone had told him about "blue balls". He thought he could lose them if he didn't empty them at least weekly. I didn't mention that?'

'What did you say to him?'

It feels as if this would all have gone better if we'd kept a chart on the fridge on which these matters had been marked off once completed, the way we did years ago when the kids first took on jobs around the house. I could have come home, seen Jack had a star in his 'masturbation talk' box and no one would have needed to say another word.

'I told him it was fine,' she says. 'Normal. Within limits. I told him blue balls wasn't a thing and please don't develop a porn habit. And dispose of all waste.'

All good solid points. I can't guess if I would have thought of them. If only he could just take it out on the lawn, like Winston, the pair of them rutting away, two happy masturbators.

The TV's still on, though I'm not aware of either of us having any intent to watch it. It's now up to its third ad in twenty minutes about preparing financially for death, so I'm assuming it's not one of the digital channels slanted to the younger viewer.

If I twist my head enough I can see the screen.

Patrick Dempsey holds up a bottle of lotion and says, in his brightest, most rejuvenated voice, 'You wanna be a modern man? Take care of your skin.'

If only it was that easy. If only our own skin was all we had to keep track of.

Robyn nudges me. 'He's talking to you and the rest of the arse-glue crowd.'

From down the hall, I can hear guitar chords being tested and played, the faint sound of Abi still working through Horses.

'Do we tell her it's bedtime or . . .'

'She'll only be a few minutes,' Robyn says. 'Unless she was really traumatised by your red-raw buttock. Could be hours then.'

14

AHEAD OF ME ON the footpath on the final uphill stretch of my run, there's a man standing with his son. The boy, who looks about two, is on the father's shoulders under a shapeless hat – the kind of hat that gets grimy, gets washed, dries in whatever scrunched-up form it chooses and then goes straight back on the head, with the bead on its drawstring tightened just enough to keep it in place. I've been that father, done that laundry, pulled that bead.

They're both peering through a gap in a hedge outside a block of units. Each in his own way is fascinated by whatever's on view.

As I move off the pavement and onto the grass to run past them, the father says, 'That's two grown-ups who love each other. People show they love each other in a lot of different ways.'

I am trying to hold my stride together up the hill. If I stop – if I so much as adjust my jogging rhythm to answer to the instinct to turn and look – there's every chance my piriformis will seize up completely and I'll be stuck here, a leery middle-aged man, grimacing at whatever expression of love is being offered and received beyond the hedge.

Before our third cycle of IVF struck gold and the twins came along, Robyn and I lived in a townhouse. Over the back fence, in another identical salmon-coloured building, lived a guy called Stan who was probably close to seventy. Every so often when I was doing the dishes, I'd look up to see Stan at his own sink, dressed only in a fedora and cravat, one hand gripping each of the taps as the latest in a succession of young muscular shirtless 'gardeners' loomed over him from behind. We were close enough for me to be certain I could see Stan's eyes rolling back in his head as his tanned loose old body shuddered. That's the picture in my brain at the end of today's run. Some weeks Stan ate only home-brand cereal and got his shrubs clipped three times.

The slope of our driveway switches me back to walking pace. The house steeples above it, peaking in two circa-1930 gables that look gothic from the road on a moonlit night, but benign and suburban during the day. We raised it in 2003 and built in underneath. Everyone was doing that at the time, creating tall timber castles with more bathrooms than people.

Ahead of me, everything looks like an obstacle. None of it would on a pain-free day. Robyn's car is parked in front of mine and I have to twist to get around the passenger-side mirror. I take it on with all the caution of one of those svelte movie diamond thieves ducking a laser alarm, and my hair-trigger musculoskeletal system for once plays along.

I'm about to lower myself into position for a stretch on the back steps when I notice my father in the garden. He's chewing gum with the deliberate jaw action of someone counting down bites until he's allowed to stop. His arms are raised into a letter Y and, just as I wonder if he's turned to yoga and is Greeting the Sun, he slowly lowers them to make a T.

It's a remnant of the poster of 'commando exercises' that was on my parents' bedroom wall in the seventies, with stick figures doing burpees and lunges. He has a white dressing square taped to his ankle, but no bandage to hold it in place. Winston is sitting nearby, blinking into the sun.

'Is that okay for your . . .' I find myself miming a pouch on the left side of my abdomen as though, if I never say 'stoma', he won't have one. 'Stoma?'

'Did Robyn send you?' He gradually brings his arms all the way down. 'I'm only doing the top half. Slow-motion. No squatting or straining.'

Just near him there's a Brunswick green bench in an area the landscape architect pitched to us as a nook. It's surrounded by ferns, with a staghorn clamped to the tree behind it. It has a look straight out of Better Homes and Gardens, yet we've all assiduously ignored it almost since the last piece of reticulated irrigation went in and the turf was rolled flat.

Today, though, it can pay its way. I ease myself down onto it and lift my leg into place.

'I hope you wear underpants if you do that in public,' my father says, waggling his finger in the general direction of where underpants would go.

'The shorts are lined.'

'I think some of the lining's . . .'

'That's a bandage.' A bandage that, to those with younger ears, is crinkling audibly.

'Why have you . . .'

He stops and looks along the side of the house and towards the street, as if a passing car or a delivery has caught his attention and taken his focus from the mystery of my wounded buttock. He's squinting into the sun. There's no one around. Whatever he's picturing as the butt-bandage back story, I'm betting it's not a self-inflicted super-glue wound. He steps into the shade and lifts his hand to a nearby tree branch.

'Abi's pretty serious about the music, you know,' he says. 'Or it's a serious conversation we have going at least. I don't mean she's planning to do it as a job necessarily. She's taking it seriously. I'm getting her Rocksmith for her birthday.'

He stops talking to give his gum a few chews. I'm supposed to know what Rocksmith is.

'You're in radio now,' he says, but it doesn't help me.

He shuffles across to a garden bed, crouches with great caution and retrieves his iPad from the low railway-sleeper retaining wall. I should have guessed it wouldn't be far away. He flicks from one page to another.

'Take a look at this.' He sets it down on the seat next to me, a safe distance from the sweat dripping from my elbow. He has a Rolling Stone website on screen, with a review of Rocksmith. 'She can plug in her own guitar. You play along and it shows you chords and notes. There's a lot more to it but that's the gist.'

He makes his way over to the nugget of turd Winston has just dropped on the grass. Winston's sitting next to it, his stumpy tail wagging like a wiggling finger. My father tells him outside is good, which means there's also been inside.

Rocksmith is a videogame for guitarists, or aspiring guitarists. Rolling Stone talks it up and gives it four stars. He's probably right that it's a good choice for Abi. I'm not yet on the lookout for presents, or haven't got my radar set so that it pings when something with gift potential comes into view. I have a grand total of about four people's needs to remember to meet. I know I could have seen the website and not given a thought to buying it for her. It's probably not merely a good choice for her – it's probably perfect.

I flick to another page, reviews of new albums, most of them by bands I've never heard of.

By accident, I touch somewhere different on screen and I'm on Facebook, on the Australian Rolling Stone page. Down the side, where I typically have ads for sugar-daddy dating sites and Volvos, my father has old folks' vitamins and funeral plans. We both entered our dates of birth somewhere before we knew better, and this is the future that marketers expect us each to buy. My father will dose up and die with his expenses met, and I'll turn up to his funeral in my Volvo, its passenger seat occupied by an impoverished student who's sleeping with me for the sake of a less ugly HECS debt.

'You can read more if you want,' my father says, nodding, indicating with his hand that I should pick up the iPad. 'There's good stuff there, every month. In Rolling Stone. Relevant. I still get the Australian print edition delivered. I've got them in my . . .' He points in the direction of the granny flat. 'I've got them in there.'

There might be a tiny part of him that nurtures a hope that I have a love for radio, his kind of record-spinning hit-making radio and the passion for music that goes with it and never leaves. Now that I've sensed it, it's a hard thought to put away.

'Thanks. That'd be good. Maybe at the coast, when I won't fuse your iPad with sweat or wreck the paper version.' On one page of reviews, I can see three genre names I don't recognise, or names that might be genres. I'm not even sure. Metalcore, skronk, indie noir. 'I don't know how Rolling Stone we are at SPIN. We're Hot Adult Contemporary.'

'That sounds like something you got from a website. No, I bet it was from some slick PDF about how you're "repurposing" the network, or something like that.' He's smiling when he says it, but he's challenging me to deny it. Which I can't. It was the PDF. 'Hot Adult Contemporary – which one of those three words applies to Brian Brightman?' He laughs.

He puts his hands on his thighs to brace himself and starts to stoop forward, getting his head into a better position to see the screen.

'Dad.' I'm picturing a range of stoma catastrophes, wounds splitting, bowel slopping out the leg of his shorts. 'You're not supposed to bend over.'

'I'm not bending over. Not any further than this.' It's clearly advice he's heard a million or so times over the past month. 'I'm just taking a closer look.'

He straightens again, ambles towards the nearest garden bed and picks up a branch that's resting against the trunk of a tree. He makes his way back to the turd and, on his third attempt, flicks it into the bushes.

When I pick up the iPad to hand it over, it switches to a page featuring a flashback to an Australian top ten from 1990. It's headed by Jimmy Barnes, with Van

Morrison, George Michael, Faith No More, Mariah Carey and Gloria Estefan below him. No surprises there, no unfamiliar names, most of them soldiering on, each now playing to their own middle-aged army waving smartphones instead of lighters, or overestimating their own suppleness and busting out a few ancient dance moves.

Julianne lives in America now and has thousand-dollar tickets to the Stones fiftieth-anniversary tour. She would never have gone to the Stones when we were young.

My father tosses the stick into the bushes and growls for Winston to stay where he is. He takes a step towards me and I pass him the iPad.

'Van Morrison,' he says. 'Did you know he was charting then?' He scrolls down with his finger. 'I know what you do when you go into these businesses, but try to remember the people at SPIN love radio. They love what they do, whatever their taste in music. Even Gopher Brightman.' It was Brian's first radio name. He'd dropped out of school to become an office junior at Double B and threw around enough wisecracks that he started getting air time. 'It's not generic for them. It's not cans of beans or – what do you people call them – widgets.'

'When did I become "you people"?'

I want to contest more than the timing of it, but I've been 'you people' for a while, even if I haven't been it at home, in my own garden. On this occasion, though, the job is a specific opportunity to let my father down – to step onto his turf and prove there that his worst thoughts about me are well-directed. I carve up companies without a care for the widgets they make or for the widgetmakers, as I prise their spry little monkey fingers from their tools and cast them out into the wild. I bring home a large enough share of the resulting cash pile to leverage a loan that builds our house higher and higher and invests it with more features we don't even want, but that must be put there to prove something to someone. And now I am signing up to be a party to the destruction of the great stately medium of radio.

'You know what I mean,' my father says, the edge gone from his voice. He moves back under the tree and into the shade and, without thinking, rests his hand on the exact same spot as before. 'Whatever happened to the idea of a Brisbane office of BDK? Did someone else get that?'

'It didn't go ahead.' It was a promise for a while, or it had the sound of one. 'It died with Lehman Brothers. We just took a few years to accept that. It'll never happen now.'

The demise of Lehman Brothers can be dated more precisely than the lapsing of the promise: mortal wounds in early 2008, followed only months later, on 15 September, by the largest bankruptcy filing in US history. Hours earlier, Bank of America had swallowed Merrill Lynch – or, according to later testimony to Congress, had had their jaws forced open and Merrill Lynch shoved in. Bear Stearns died on its feet and JP Morgan bought the carcass. Goldman Sachs and Morgan Stanley trembled and shook and haemorrhaged until – with the backing of the regulator – they changed their spots and became bank holding companies.

Not one of these stricken giants was a mirror for BDK but, when they fell, the rubble came through our windows too. Head office in New York got slammed, the Melbourne office closed and BDK Australia still isn't much more than half the size it was in 2007. So, instead of the move up to MD and back to Brisbane to head a new office, my job became about holding on and taking what was on offer.

'It's good you're back,' my father says. The sun is lighting him patchily from behind on his shoulders and head, casting bright spots in his fly-away white hair. 'And the weekend's a great idea. Those kids could do with some fresh air and a bit of time away from devices. I know they'll be bringing the devices, but we'll distract them occasionally, right? We should go for fish and chips on the Friday, at some daggy old place, and eat it on the beach out of the paper. My shout.'

15

YOU PEOPLE.

I've steered six private-equity projects and only two of them had any scope for ugly news, for 'you people' stories. The other four made new jobs, in this country, or at least stopped some from being lost.

On Robyn's orders, I shower with the dressing on and let it peel away when it's ready to. I can swivel just enough to see some kind of gel over the raw area, but I don't know – and don't want to know – if it's medicinal or merely the night's coagulated seepage. Even with the shower lukewarm, the water sears my buttock like a faceful of hot towel straight from the flight attendant's tongs.

You people. You people get off planes complaining that the hot towels are too hot and that your face now has business-class wounds.

Noel Everson was well into his seventies when we took on Everson Initiating Systems. His kids had no interest because, not surprisingly, you can't expect everyone to be fascinated by blasting systems for mining explosives. We paid Noel well enough. He knew the bad habits his business had got into over time. He had three factories in different bits of the country, each using different outdated equipment to make the same things in a slightly different way. Not one site had any scope for expansion. The business was as patched-up as his production lines, ambling towards irrelevance and ruin, despite the strengths it still had.

We shut every factory and opened a new one in Shenzhen, close to five times the size. All Australian production-line workers got their entitlements, and we kept a few on to help with quality control, plus the tech team, some management and the sales staff. Then, when it looked like a venture with a future, Orica bought it as a bolt-on acquisition. I can't guarantee what happened to all the old Everson people after that, but Orica told us it needed them.

Without us, Everson was going nowhere. Noel knew that within five years he'd be spending the last of the petty cash on new padlocks for the gates and walking away. We got the bad press about cutting Australian jobs, but we saved jobs too and that story doesn't get told.

The Haddad family had a good idea with the Patio Shed, but no appetite for risk. They were bunkered down in three sites in outer suburban Melbourne, debt free and shooting their own no-budget quirky migrant-made-good ads. We changed it to Outdoor House, changed the look – up-and-coming businesses were tending to add a lot of optimistic bright orange that year – and put it in every capital city in the right big-box locations. That, and our dividend, meant it was carrying a lot of debt at its IPO, but wasn't everything then? Who knew debt was about to get dirty, and

Outdoor House would soon take its place in the queue to tank?

The only thing – the one specific detail about costs – discussed in the briefing for my new job was that most shows at the station have two hosts and plenty of networks make do with one. The ABC makes do with one. And some hosts cost more than others. And, at SPIN99, Brian Brightman, for all his past glories, costs the most.

★ ★ ★

'It's like I'm running wound-care outpatients,' Robyn says, patting my newly re-dressed buttock to tell me the job's done. 'I think you can probably manage this one yourself from now on.'

'I can barely reach it round there.'

Breakfast has started downstairs. Our two half-households are meeting in the middle, my father up from the granny flat and the kids down from their rooms. There's a TV on, and music, and clattering.

Robyn's in front of the mirror, checking today's work attire. She'll face vomit, blood, the full range of human fluids. I'm not sure I'd be making such an effort. She's ignoring me.

'You keep doing my father's.'

'Seriously?' Instead of turning, she glances at me in the mirror. 'You want me to keep revisiting the fact that you waxed your arse with super glue? He has an actual disease. Several.' She pulls her earrings off and searches around in the bowl for another pair. 'His bandage was missing this morning. He thinks he must have taken it off in his sleep and put it somewhere.'

'Really? Why would he do that?' My father has always been a solid sleeper. 'Do you think he's losing it?' I don't want to picture him down there in the dark, wrapping and unwrapping his leg, bumping into furniture, trying to place himself.

'The bandage, yes. His mind, no.' She says it unequivocally, just as I'd wanted her to. 'I can't explain the bandage. But the ulcer's getting better, so . . .' She shrugs. 'It's probably okay just with that light dressing now.' She checks her watch. 'I'll see you down at breakfast. Unless you need me to put your pants on too.'

She doesn't wait for an answer. She picks a fresh pair of earrings and clips them on as she leaves, making sure to shut the door properly behind her.

Downstairs, Abi's voice shouts out, 'Winston!' And Winston yelps.

With my pants on, my dressing rustles like a chip packet in a cinema as I move around the room, trying to reshape my gait into less of a hobble. I feel like an updated scarecrow or tin man from the Wizard of Oz, stuffed with wadding and plastic and not as well jointed as I should be.

Jack's door is open when I walk past. I can now make some sense of the mess of parts and tools on his desk. The computer-in-progress is itself the size of a small table. It's a timber-look box with a K-tel aesthetic. It looks like he's aiming to build himself the World's Greatest Computer of the 1960s, or a prop for Lost in Space.

The top is off but it's plugged into the mains and the outside is warm when I touch it. The room smells of scorched pheromones. If the house burns down today, I'll at least be able to lead investigators quickly to the source.

What does he want to do with it? There's a ninety per cent chance it'll just make stink and heat, take our climate slightly closer to the tipping point and perhaps run simple games, a nine per cent chance it'll connect to the wider world in a functional way and a one per cent chance our door will be kicked in at dawn one morning because he's hacked into NORAD and is now, albeit temporarily, the dark lord of the planet's largest missile arsenal.

At the back of the desk, behind the tiny screws and plans and microcircuitry, there's a lava lamp. It's my parents', from the seventies. It went to the storeroom under the house not long after that, in an early eighties spring clean. My father must have given it to Jack when he moved in here. I can't imagine what he needed then that took him to that room. Some memory to do with my mother, probably.

When I flick the switch, the lamp still works. The light comes on and the wad of wax at the base takes on an orange glow. No child of today could manage the next part of the process, the forty-five-minute wait for the first bud of hot wax to take flight.

On the way down the stairs, I can hear Winston's claws darting across the kitchen tiles, Jack stirring him up.

Abi's on her feet when I walk in, about to put her cereal bowl into the dishwasher. It's the first time we've seen each other since the bedroom incident. She looks at me and then at Robyn in a way that suggests the three of us have a body in the basement, a secret to be kept from the others at all costs. I want my own chance to explain what she witnessed, but her body language is lining up in capital letters to tell me this isn't the time.

'You can *not* be my friend on Facebook,' she says to me. 'I got your friend request. It's just not happening.'

16

BRIAN AND DAZZ ARE working from the studio today. Médecins Sans Frontières is in the news, and they're making the most of it on my drive to the station.

'You can be anything without borders now,' Dazz says. 'Chemists Without Borders. Librarians Without Borders, showing complete disdain for the Dewey Decimal Classification System. I think they parachute in at night and start crazily filing history in the five hundreds. There's also Geeks Without Borders – sadly, a much smaller outfit than Geeks Without Social Skills.'

'Cheesemakers Without Borders,' Brian chips in. 'Fromagers Sans Frontières.' He's made it up so that he can do the accent, which couldn't be more pantomime French if it rode in on a bike with a beret on its head and a baguette under one arm.

'Embroiderers Without Borders . . . think about it.'

'Gardeners Without Borders.'

It's all safe ground as they go to an ad break and then Katy Perry's Firework, which leads to talk about relationships and their ends.

'I'm so over those My Family stickers,' Brian says. 'The girlfriend walking out this week is bad enough, but what I'm really gutted about is having to pull the chick sticker off the back window of my car. I mean, once it's gone, all I'll have is the words "My" and "Family" and a white outline of a fat bastard.'

'Maybe it's advertising,' Dazz says, offering a crude mock-up of reassurance. 'Maybe it'll work for you. Like hanging your bananas over the edge of the basket in your shopping trolley.'

'Tried that. Reckon it's an urban myth. Everything from a tiny bunch of lady fingers to one whopping Cavendish.'

There's some general boyish guffawing at Brian's laps of the fruit and veg aisles at Woolies with his big yellow metaphor on view, and its abject failure to lure the ladies. Who are surely all dialling the station now, mobbing him for a date. Or alternatively, picturing his lonely drive home from Woolies, car stacked with Coke Zero and frozen pizzas, shop-a-docket in his pocket promising five DVDs for ten bucks at Video Ezy.

Brian switches metaphors, refers to his genitalia as 'sporting goods' and the chat lurches to Maria Sharapova, who is back in the news at a tennis tournament.

'Hey, what about all that moaning and squealing she gets on with?' Dazz says. 'Does that get to you?'

'Only if it wakes the neighbours.' There's a pre-recorded sound effect, like a couple of honks of a rubber-bulbed horn, Three Stooges-style. 'Then I ask her to quieten it down a bit.' More guffawing. 'Hey, what if you were on the nest with Maria Sharapova and she was, like, totally silent? What kind of an indictment would that be?'

'Or if she just politely cleared her throat to let you know she was set to pop?'

Brian clears his throat, in a way that could have no one thinking of Maria Sharapova, and then offers a quavery, 'Now please,' in a cartoon Russian accent.

I'm still wondering what ACMA might make of 'set to pop' when Dazz plays some audio of the match, two young women squealing as if they're being vaccinated with wide-bore needles, or accidentally contemplating a sexual act with Brian Brightman.

From there, Brian and Dazz's dream scenario involves both players at once since, when faded middle-aged losers of a pizza disposition get together, they're obliged to stake their claim to supermodels, movie stars and glam sporting millionaires in ratios more flattering than a mere one-to-one. Because that's what their preferred DVD truths tell them is likely, when their luck finally turns. Denise Richards and Neve Campbell *will* come and wash your sad Hyundai with its solo fat bastard My Family sticker, strip naked in your pool and then douse their breasts with champagne to slake your thirst, because your hands are shaking too much for you to bring glasses from the kitchen.

Brian, on air, classifies this as HLA. Dazz asks him to expand it, and coughs over the middle word as Brian says, 'Hot lesbo action.'

'Did you say "lady"?' Dazz asks him tentatively.

'Something like that.'

'On the subject of trouble, how'd you go with your meeting with the new boss yesterday?' So that's a segue now, from hot lesbo action to me. 'Did he go the whole "no 'I' in team" thing?'

'Oh yeah. But I took a close look at it and I told him I was pretty sure I could see a "me" in there, so everything's okay.' Brian, in this meeting that only ever happened in a Breakfast Bar thought bubble, comes out the sure-footed winner.

'That's right. There *is* a "me" in there.' Dazz makes it sound as if it's a revelation. 'A "me" and . . .' There's a pause, as though he's hovering over a page, pencil in hand, solving an anagram puzzle. 'An "at".'

'I told him he could have the "at". But, look, I'm being unfair. He's probably a breath of fresh air. I bet he's got stacks of great new ideas about radio in the digital age. And he loves music obviously, as well as the tech stuff. When I went in for the meeting he was trying to find iTunes on his Apple Newton.'

Like most of us, I suspect, I have a vague recollection of the Newton from the nineties, the decade Apple didn't fly. The decade when hopes were pinned on a message pad almost the weight of carry-on baggage that showed remarkable creative flair in interpreting stylus-written notes. It had great ideas busting out all over, but they didn't quite land as the package the ideas people had hoped for. I'm not even sure that it was officially called the Newton.

But Brian's line isn't about Apple, or that device. It's about me and my shitty grasp of new music and tech, and he's found my range.

'Speaking of the new boss,' Dazz says, 'I've got something for you.'

There's a burst of trumpets, a pre-recorded fanfare.

'Why, Dazz, how lovely of you,' Brian says warmly. 'That looks like a big fat sandwich with something brown in it. Oh, wait, it's a . . . It's something I have to read at precisely the same time that we let Father Pervy off the chain yesterday. And here it goes.' He clears his throat and draws an audible breath. 'SPIN 99 apologises, and Dazz and I personally apologise to St Stanislaus College for a live sketch that ran at this time on yesterday's show. While it was intended to be humorous and not intended as a comment on St Stanislaus, it was insensitive and prone to harmful misinterpretation, as no present or past staff member or priest associated with St Stanislaus has ever been convicted of offences against children. The College in fact has a proud record going back more than a century of providing a well-rounded Catholic education.'

There's a hint of po-faced newsreader about the way he does it — just enough to imply that the whole thing could be parodied, but not enough to actually parody it.

And then, because we're Hot Adult Not-quite-contemporary, they play the Police's Don't Stand So Close to Me, with the collective memories of listeners, all well versed in the pop culture of thirty years ago, turning to Sting in his academic gown and his tale of Nabokovian misplaced affection.

17

THE FIRST THING I do at the station is check how the morning's feedback is running. I have a sinking feeling this could become a habit, walking in to spot fires to find Brian Brightman holding the matches and Dazz Davis a bottle or two of accelerant.

'No calls, a few tweets, only one of them looking negative,' Venice says.

She turns her screen towards me so that I can see the Twitter feed. The tweet in question reads, 'Why is it that hopeless middle-aged straight men are obsessed with the idea of 2 women having sex? #SPIN99 #brightmanisadick.'

'Pretty fair call,' she says. 'Might deserve a retweet.' Her contact lenses are green today and the nails of her little fingers have diamantes stuck on them, which might or might not have been there yesterday. 'I checked the "Brightman is a dick" hashtag and it's not trending. Yet. He might have to be a bigger dick to get that happening.'

Before I can come up with anything resembling an appropriate response, something on my office door catches my eye. It's a sign – a sheet of A4 paper, held in place by one piece of sticky tape and reading, in a very business-like font, 'Please pause before entering – may be autofellating.'

'I . . .' Venice says, and puts on an apologetic look that gives her little ochre crinkle lines next to her eyes. 'Brian said it was a joke between the two of you. It's not in the dictionary. I looked it up.'

'I thought everything was in the dictionary by now.' I figure it at least entitles me to one free use of the brightmanisadick hashtag.

'Autoinflating is. And autofocus.' She wants these observations to be helpful.

'Well, my advice is don't go searching any wider for autofellating or you might end up having to email the systems guy to get your record cleared.' I pull the sign from the door and the tape curls around my finger and sticks to it. 'I was going to go and see Brian anyway.'

He and I have HLA to talk about, and my untested theory that, in ACMA's world, coughing over something doesn't mean it never happened.

* * *

Brian, Dazz and Kylie are on the other side of the building in a partitioned work station, with a laminated sign hanging above them on fishing line and reading 'Breakfast Bar'. The room is one side of an L, with the other out of view. The Mornings team is behind them and the others are around the corner. I passed through there yesterday on my meet-greet-and-forget tour with Damian.

Since we have their faces on the foyer walls, and since I'm trying to listen to the station, I have a fighting chance of recognising a few of the presenters, though the producers are a comfortably dressed blank to me. The tech team are just as blank, but with tools, and somewhere in the building is a windowless room where promos are cut by as many as three bearded guys who I'm certain are all called Josh.

'Look who's here,' Brian says. 'Our fearless leader.'

He's sitting back from his desk and rocking in his chair, with his feet wide apart riding the castors. It creates the optical illusion that every line in the vicinity is leading back to his crotch and the damp dot on his pale pants. He moves one hand to rearrange the front of his pants and breaks the geometry of it. His other hand is spinning a well-chewed biro.

Through the venetian blinds, I can see the carpark of the art gallery next door and two industrial bins.

'Andrew,' Dazz says, standing and offering me his hand. He looks and dresses as if he's surfed most of the past thirty years. His eyes are bloodshot, his blond-grey hair close to shoulder length and his chin has maybe three days of pale stubble. 'Dazz Davis. Good to meet you. Say hi to your dad for me.' He takes my hand and pumps it strongly. 'I was Darryl then, mostly. As in Braithwaite.'

'As in Hannah.' Brians laughs at his own joke.

'We had a Darren too,' Dazz clarifies. 'Dazz could be either of us. I'm not the Darren.'

'Kylie,' Kylie says, also reaching to shake my hand. She has glasses not unlike Robyn's, a shiny pimply forehead and black hair gathered back into a short ponytail. She's wearing jeans, Converse sneakers and a bowling shirt with 'Vince' over the pocket. She must be close to thirty, making her twenty years younger than her on-air team. 'Sorry I didn't catch up with you yesterday.'

'I hope everything went well at the dentist,' I tell her, before having a crisis of confidence and wondering if that was someone else. 'You did . . .'

'Yeah, that was me. All good now.'

Their work area has a whiteboard on which they're blocking out tomorrow's show in blue and red pen, a mini-basketball hoop stuck to the window with a nerf basketball in it and, on the desks, exactly the amount of clutter I might have guessed.

Dazz has the Smiths Meat is Murder poster taped to the window to the left of his computer screen while, to the right of Brian's and therefore flush up against the poster, there's a picture of Hitler captioned 'Ein Volk, Ein Reich, Ein Vegetarian'. Beneath it is a doctored Courier-Mail clipping of the two of them, with white-out daubed on the slogan on Brian's T-shirt and 'I'm with Tofu Tits' inked in on the bumpy white surface, with an arrow pointing to Dazz.

The divider behind Kylie's computer has a picture of Ozzy Osbourne wearing a space-age jumpsuit and standing in a gleaming tunnel – in the characteristic posture of the senior Steptoe from Steptoe and Son – with a caption reading, 'What's a fuckin' Bieber?' With a bit of effort, I can recall it from a Superbowl ad for a phone, in Justin Bieber's early days, when the rest of us had just worked him out but it was still plausible that Ozzy might not have.

On his desk, in a simple metal frame, Brian has a photo of a baby boy. He's grinning toothlessly and gripping a wooden train tightly with one hand, probably for balance. He has a wisp of weightless blond hair climbing from his head.

Brian notices me looking at it, and swivels around.

'That's Ryan,' he says. 'My boy.' From above and behind and at close quarters, Brian has a head like a knee. 'He's nineteen now. Twenty.'

'Right.' Head like a knee. If I took a photo of it and cropped the context away, people would guess knee just about every time. But the clock's ticking and a semi-competent social response is required. 'What does he do?'

'He's, ah . . .' Brian picks up the photo. 'He lives with his mum, so I'm not sure, right at the moment. Uni didn't really work out for him. It's been a while since we've had a catch-up. His mother's . . . got a few issues with me. So, it's been a couple of years. Or so. But, you know, you move desks, the photo comes with you. Has to come.'

I had plans half-made to deal with the 'lesbo' remark. Brian studies the photo for another moment or two, in case Ryan might reappear at twenty, grown up and in sharp focus and ready to forgive past indiscretions. Then he sets it down again, takes hold of the edge of his desk and spins back around. It's a well-practised move.

The sign from my door is swinging from my hand, still taped to my index finger. The words are facing Brian, rocking in front of him, as if I'm about to make a big deal out of it.

'Thanks for the generous attempt to expand Venice's vocabulary,' I tell him, before he can jump in and say anything. 'I've suggested she shouldn't research it too vigorously online.'

'Hey.' Dazz drops back into his seat and types 'autofellate' into Google. Surprisingly, or not, there are hits. 'There's a bit on YouTube,' he says, as though we aren't all trying to read over his shoulder. 'None of it human in the first few. One video of a bear. Two walruses.' He leans closer to read the text. 'Wow. One of the walruses can go all the way.'

He clicks and the footage loads. It's handheld, probably from a phone. The walrus is a big hunched-over whiskery lump, wedging himself into position with his flippers and fellating himself methodically, his penis sliding like a dusky pink piston.

'What's that walrus doing, Mommy?' a child's voice says, all crisp and innocent.

A couple of seconds pass before a man's voice close to the camera replies, 'He's cleaning himself, Honey. That's all.' The image shudders, but doesn't break from the sight. 'Hey, look,' the voice says, in a brighter, more persuasive tone. 'Over there. Is that a baby one?'

Brian laughs at the parental distraction attempt, and the determination to keep rolling on the creature porn. He swings around again in his seat to face me.

'Coffee,' he says, making it sound more like a statement than a question or suggestion. 'And I think you were going to show me what you're made of at Galaga.'

It sounds like the direct opposite of anything I've ever said on the subject but, the way he's sitting, the old photo of his baby son is immediately behind his shoulder. He's out of that life, out of the picture, stuck carrying this image with him from workplace to work-place, and all the hope and the weight of it.

'I'm pretty rusty,' is all I can say, and that means we're playing Galaga.

* * *

There's not much I know about Brian after all. There was his start, as Gopher, then I think some years out of town in regional radio to learn the trade. By the late eighties he was a star and by 1990 his new contracts were big enough to make news. By the century's turn, younger talent was on the rise, networks were shape-shifting and Brian started to look out of step. Other people were making the news instead. He became someone a lot of us had listened to at one time, but hadn't followed in his moves between stations. I now know he was married once. I don't think this morning's recent ex-girlfriend is real.

'So, Dazz is a vegetarian . . .' That's where I start, because the photo on the desk is there for Brian, not to cue me to ask about his son and any unravelling that went on along the way.

'You can tell, can't you?' Brian says as he swings the tearoom door open. 'Was it his breath? Or just him generally? They sweat differently, vegetarians.'

He automatically steps over to the coffee machine and takes his mug and mine from the shelf, so I drop two dollars into the craniofacial kiddies' slot and tell him this morning's snack is on me. He chooses a Snickers.

My buttock bandage makes an unmistakable rustling sound as I lower myself onto the plastic stool at the game console.

Just as I'm hoping I'm hyper-attuned to it and it's

apparent only to me, Brian says, smirking, 'I'm sorry, but did your buttock just rustle?'

He sits down, the top of his yellow stool vanishing either between or into his buttocks. He sets his coffee and Snickers on the console and shuffles himself in as close as his body will allow. These machines were built with the shapes of scrawny youths in mind. I can't remember where my knees went years ago. I didn't even have to think about it then.

He's expecting an answer.

'It's something in my pocket.'

'And you've still got that limp. That was a butt thing too, wasn't it?' He's putting two and two together and, unfortunately, making precisely four. 'Is it something to do with that?'

'That's the other side.' It's a lie, and not even a good one.

'You've got two arse problems simultaneously? One on each side?' The idea appeals to him far too much.

'Look, maybe. But nothing on air about this, okay? The Newton stuff, yeah, sure, that was funny, but if we could . . .' There's no good way to put it. No way that won't make it a more tempting target.

'Leave your arse out of it?' He laughs. He goes to sip his coffee and slurps it. A drops lands on the glass. He wipes it away with his hand, and then licks his hand and rubs it on his shirt. 'I can try but, mate, look at my file. Every time I do those personality tests the bar for "impulse control" comes up really short. That's why they hired me. If I was all buttoned down I'd have nothing. I'd be a guy in a suit no one noticed, sitting at a desk. Arse cramping quietly away, maybe. No offence.'

'None taken till the arse bit.'

He presses a button and the machine jangles into life, with a shower of thirty-year-old electro arcade music. He tweaks the red plastic knob and taps a button a couple of times to choose Galaga, two-player. He's player one. The game's opening screen loads.

'But you plan the stuff on air, sometimes days in advance. It's not impulsive.'

'It's a bit of both,' he says, firing a couple of test shots into space. 'It's what they want. The audience. They want me to be just a bit ruder than I'm allowed to be. That's why lots of them are listening.'

The enemy craft appear, doing their mechanical alien square dance across the screen. He starts taking them out strategically, with a blast of fire at one end.

'Do they all want that lack of subtlety, though?' It's as good a time as any to talk through his approach.

'Did you hear the MSF suff this morning?' he says without looking up. He's through the first phalanx of alien ships, and his next adversaries are buzzing him like gnats. 'The "Without Borders" stuff? Plenty to play around with there. But the punchline should have been Book Retailing Without Borders. Get it?'

It takes a second to drop. 'The book retailer. Borders. They shut a couple of years ago.'

'Exactly. But it was vetoed as being too esoteric. Dazz said, "Do you think enough of our listeners buy books?" How about that? We asked around the office and drew a lot of blanks. Don't think I'm not trying. We road test this shit and subtle doesn't fly. Ratings murder subtle. You can take your subtle to Radio National, and even there they'll talk you out of it. But for commercial breakfast, crass is the entry level. You know that.'

He's up to level three, with double guns, getting perfect scores on the gnats. He's battling wildly on the screen, going at the red knob so hard the entire console's shifting.

'I'm having horrible flashes that this is like watching the walrus resorting to flippers when his back's too stiff for him to fellate himself.'

He laughs, and instantly loses one ship in a flurry of missiles and the other in a crash. 'Arsehole.' He picks up his Snickers and takes a bite. Nut fragments tumble onto his controls. 'Poor bastard did look a bit like me, didn't he? See, that's where I'd be if I had your flexibility. Nuded up and in a zoo, working all day cleaning the pipes.'

I picture Brian's face on the autofellating walrus and almost lose my fighter in the opening few seconds. I make a scrappy job of the first grid of enemy ships, then sit one click to the right of where I should be for the gnats and miss three of them. No bonus points. Brian takes another slurp at his coffee and sits straighter on his stool, picking plaque from behind his lower front teeth with a fingernail.

'You realise,' he says, gazing past me towards the door, 'that in the movie of this your father gets played by Martin Sheen and you get played by Charlie.'

Somewhere between 'you people' and the shower, the movie Wall Street had crossed my mind too – Martin Sheen as the blue-collar stalwart of the industry and representative of a bygone age, Charlie as the slick-haired corporate rascal.

'Except I'm the age Charlie Sheen is now, not the age he was back then.' I worked that out at home. 'Two years older, actually. And I don't think my dad's put in seven highly acclaimed seasons as the US president, while I'm living with two porn stars, touring a thought bubble called Torpedo of Doom and snagging a million Twitter followers in my first five minutes there.'

'Ha,' Brian says. One of his knees starts jogging. 'Dream on. I think technically only one of them was a porn star and that was all over a while ago. Still . . .'

He watches my fighter, haplessly chugging across the screen firing wildly, miraculously intact. He clears his throat and drinks a mouthful of coffee. Wall Street is still in the air.

'Yes, I get it,' I tell him. Mercifully I reach the end of level one and, for a few seconds, I can look up. 'My father was an industry legend back in the day and I'm the cruel face of capitalism come to make a buck out of the thing he loves. But the Charlie Sheens of this story – the Wall Street Charlie Sheen-type guys – won't ever set foot in this tearoom. They might turn up once or twice to see that there's a building on this site and it is what it's supposed to be, but other than that it's all long range for them. They're in offices in Sydney or Singapore or New York. They're years younger than both of us. Right now there's one in the office that used to be mine. Though he's no Charlie Sheen, not really. Not the Wall Street version or any other kind.'

The baton has passed. It's left my hand. That's the truth of it, and it seems as if I have to tell it to everybody. Sean Campbell may one day walk in here to kick our tyres – someone from BDK will – and I'll just have to deal with that. I'll have to buff this tiny outpost of the empire so that it gleams that morning and our numbers will need to be right. Or good enough. We will need to have value, and I will need to be seen to have added some of that value.

'I bet you went to some rich kids' private school.' Brian picks up his half-eaten Snickers and starts tapping the end of it on the console. His signet ring clicks on the glass.

'I can tell it's a Brisbane job when school comes up.'

'I'll take that as a yes.'

It's a yes, but I have aliens massing, intent on doing me in.

'I bet you were a prefect.' He points the stump of his Snickers at me to add emphasis. 'Or even – what do you call it – head boy?'

'Prefect. And the title was "school captain". And that, happily, went to somebody else.'

The screen is full of enemies and missile showers, and all the jinking and jumping and relentless firing back isn't going to save me. I'm trapped in the corner and obliterated.

'You called me,' a voice says distantly – and from my pocket – as the clamour of intergalactic conflict settles. It's Robyn. 'You don't even know you're calling, do you?'

The phone is tight in my pocket and I have to stand up to pull it out. By then she's hung up.

'You just made your first gut call,' Brian says. 'You were . . .' He mimics my apparently seizure-like firing action. 'And you've got just enough muffin top for it to make the call. Take it from a recidivist gut caller. Once you start making them, there's no going back. Some of my best conversations with my ex-wife have been gut calls.' He glances down at the screen and readies himself for action. 'By best I mean least fucked.'

'But I . . .' I can't call Robyn back and tell her my abdominal bulge made the call. I can't even work out how it happened. 'But it'd have to have flicked the ring to have unlocked it.'

'Mate, if your gut's flicking your ring, you're more far gone than I thought.' He laughs at his own joke, more heartily than he needs to. The alien fleet drops into view and he methodically begins its destruction. 'You should co-host with me any time Dazz gets sick. You're giving me plenty to work with.'

18

WHEN I CALL ROBYN BACK, I put her inability to hear me properly down to the mass of radio equipment I was near at the time and its signal-warping electro-magnetic field. It's a story neither of us will ever have the knowledge to shoot down.

The Courier-Mail covers Brian's Father Pervy apology under the heading 'Mea Culpa, Mea Culpa'.

While I'm online to read the article, I look up Charlie Sheen and Wall Street, all the time making an effort not to type P E N I S accidentally into Google. Charlie Sheen played a character called Bud Fox, son of Carl, union stalwart and life lesson that we should all be creating things of value, not gaining wealth through dirty alchemy with numbers. On the poster, Charlie Sheen looks conspicuously well. He has not been married at all by then, and has yet to become engaged to Kelly Preston and shoot her in the arm. In the movie, Bud Fox leases if not sells his soul to Gordon Gekko, gets nabbed for insider trading and goes some way to atoning once his father's heart attack shakes guilt into place.

I'm not Charlie, or Bud. My father isn't Carl. We are altogether less dramatic and, I think, less Faustian.

But I can still picture scenes featuring Martin Sheen in blue overalls and with tousled hair, ready to battle with a future that stood over him like Godzilla.

Because I can and because I never have before, I google Casey Kasem. It takes a few attempts to get the spelling right. He's eighty now and it turns out that, like my father, he didn't start life as Casey. He was Kemal Amin Kasem first. For many years he hosted the American Top 40. It was the only imported segment on local radio in the seventies, and therefore inherently exotic. It was news from a cooler planet.

My only physical fight at school, ever, was when I'd finally heard one accusation too many that my father had copied Casey Kasem's name. It wasn't much of a fight, but it was the last time the accusation was levelled.

The Dutch name Cees is already pronounced something like 'case', so 'Casey' was no stretch. 'Casey' would be what happened to Cees in any Australian playground.

There's a picture of my father on the day the Cleghorns opened Toombul Music in 1967. He's behind the counter, ready to work, with 'Casey' on his name tag. Toombul Music sold instruments and records. In the early years, some of the records were even seventy-eights.

When he started at the shop, my father soaked up the music and any remark about it from the record-company reps. He talked his way into a radio spot about new releases and he grabbed his chance to do more when it came.

I don't even know Cees van Vliet. He sounds like an ancestor, a mute brown portrait of a long-haired frock-coated Dutchman, an East India company trader, a little-known pupil of Rembrandt. I've almost never heard my father speak Dutch, not even to his parents. My grandmother, my oma, wore thick patterned dresses with petticoats beneath, and beige stockings, and she never smelt Australian. She made speculaas in December, and wouldn't make them any other time. On the rare instances when I smell that combination of spices, it's her I think of. I can hardly picture her face now. I'm sure there are photos, but they're in albums somewhere, not on display.

The day we had an In-Sink-Erator installed, my grandparents came over to watch it in action. I remember it because of how little interest they showed in using the machine or even standing close by, but how much pride they had in their son owning such a thing.

They would never have bought one themselves, though they could have afforded it. Spending money seemed like a last resort, after options such as mending, making and doing without had been exhausted.

My oma mentioned the war only once. She was a teacher at the Arnhem Conservatory and, during the war years, Audrey Hepburn studied there. That was all she said. Roman Holiday or Breakfast at Tiffany's might have been on TV. I read a biography of Audrey Hepburn in the nineties because of that connection. There was a famine in the winter of 1944. Some people died of starvation and were found frozen in the streets. The Hepburns – they were van Somethings then, taking a name from her mother's family as protection – ground tulip bulbs into flour to make cakes and biscuits.

I could picture my oma and opa there, honing their instincts for conserving their resources. I have no idea if they were always like that or if that year marked them indelibly. My father, who was seven at the time, has simply never seemed Dutch enough to ask.

As much as anything, that's what I fought for at school that day – his right to be Casey Van Fleet, and our right to aspire to something. Our right to an optimism that always seemed out of reach for my grandparents. But I couldn't have put it that way then and I can't be certain I'm not implanting those better, broader motives in the memory now. Maybe it's enough to fight someone when they accuse your father of copying, and refuse to take it back.

19

IN THE CAR ON THE way to Umart, Jack picks at his nails while I strike out my first half-dozen draft openings for the up-to-date incarnation of the sex talk. Birds, bees and blue balls have been addressed and all that's left is the Grand Final of sex talks. Version 3.0: actually doing it. To be delivered in the knowledge that the stone-hard fists of Lyrix's dad are in the background, and possibly practising for our post-coital encounter by punching holes in old frying pans.

'So, building a computer . . .'

I'm going to come at it from an angle. I'm dreaming that the perfect way in will simply occur to me in the middle of a conversation, so I need to get us to some kind of middle. My wildest hope is that we'll strike up a rapport, I'll suddenly appear to him as a source of wisdom and he'll come straight out and ask my advice.

My vague computer remark puts us nowhere near the middle of anything. Jack pretends it was never said and keeps picking at his nails. His tongue works its way around his teeth, searching out lost morsels of lunch. He has a cap on and I can't see his eyes.

'Remember when you were four or five and you

were forever playing with magnets? Any time I'd turn around you'd be there with a sheet of paper with iron filings on it.' It's the first memory I have of him that might distantly connect to his project.

He stops picking his nails and sits on his hands.

'Yeah,' he says, since you can only allow so many conversation openers to pass by before it's decent to confirm you're still breathing. 'If I let you do this now, will you promise never to do it in front of people?'

'It's endearing. Who wouldn't want to hear that story? The kid with his magnets and his vial of –'

'All I need is a yes.'

We drive past a restaurant that's opening its doors and putting signs out for dinner, and then a café full of dark suits and straight-haired twenty-eight-year-old women with bony shoulders and the glasses of bigger humans. They're all twenty-eight to me. It's the age that, from my considerable distance, looks closest to perfect. Or looks as if it should have been perfect. You're a decade past high school, you're past whatever was next. You're earning something but maybe not yet responsible for much. Twenty-eight might have been perfect if I'd been anywhere near close to perfect at it. Those people look nearer to it than I was, but it's your job at twenty-eight to look like you're doing it well. I could have been there in one of my dark suits, head exactly as full of uncertainties as it was, Robyn months away from coming into view.

'Is it a career thing, do you think?' It's take two, or three, or twelve of my attempt to spark dialogue, to get us to the middle, where the topic of Lyrix and the prospect of intercourse will spontaneously emerge as a smart thing to discuss. 'The computer thing.'

'Careers are so . . .' He fidgets with his cap and ends up pulling it back into exactly the position it was in before. He's trying to work out how to explain the modern world to an idiot, with the minimum of fuss. 'It's not how things work now.'

'Come on, everyone wants to be something. Didn't you want to be an astronaut when you were six? Once you realised Spider-Man wasn't actually a job.'

He looks out the window, at nothing in particular. 'I think that was you. It was never me.' He smiles. 'I have a very low tolerance for constipation. I hear that's a big deal for astronauts.'

It *was* me, but I thought it was everyone else too. The first time my mother brought home Space Food Sticks, I thought I'd genuinely taken a step closer, as if it was part one of my secret training, line one on the CV I would ultimately send to NASA. I ate them, each and every stick, with my future career in mind. Imagining weightlessness, the distant blue-white earth and swapping stories afterwards with Neil Armstrong about what it was like to kick moon dust and use a wrench in space, and about how our preferred Space Food Stick flavour was caramel.

'I built a raft once. That was fun.'

It seems I'm prepared to put all kinds of shit out there now. I might as well say that, when I was fifteen, I took a girl out on that raft and nailed her. Or didn't. Klutzed it up. Or we talked it through and decided to wait, and stuck to holding hands and going out to appropriately rated movies. I'm not even confident about what I'm to advocate here. My parents, deep into their least consistent decade, offered me no guidance at all on the matter of girls when I was fifteen. Which was fine, since I wasn't on the radar of any girl I knew. The blue balls conversation might have assuaged a few fears, though.

I was ten when we built that raft. Or eleven. There wasn't a girl for miles.

I want to text Robyn, to ask what our consensus position is.

'A raft,' Jack says, just to check that I've truly mentioned something as dumb as a raft. 'You and that Sawyer kid, right? Tom?'

I am trying to win my way back into the life of a teenager in the twenty-first century with a story I appear to have plucked from the nineteenth. This is clearly not a conversation he wants to have. I should tell him sex is coming up next, and watch him smash the cartoon outline of a diving adolescent through the window glass as he flings himself to safety.

The role of the Sawyer kid was played by Paul Gough, my neighbour and constant companion in harmless hare-brained schemes. Maybe Tom Sawyer and Huck Finn were behind it. Or Thor Heyerdahl. I can't remember. We built the raft out of rubbish and old rope and were desperate to sail it on what we took to calling 'the open sea', by which we meant any body of water not within metres of our back doors. We struck a deal with our parents that, if it held together well in the Goughs' pool, we would launch it on Moreton Bay. It listed to one corner, but it bobbed around the pool safely enough for a full hour, with us punting it along with a rake handle.

So we set off for Cribb Island, two fathers and two sons, with the raft in Bob Gough's trailer. As we pushed it out from shore, Bob opened a beer and splashed a little on the bow as a launch gesture. We took it as a sign of genuine respect for our mission. A man and his dog stopped at a safe distance to watch us. I had South America in mind at that moment, a grand voyage. We would catch fish and drink rain water.

We sat down to paddle, our blades drawing more bay silt than water. As we pushed an inch or two deeper, some of our more critical pieces of rubbish started to loosen and the raft began to break up. An entire corner's worth of plastic juice bottles, essential for buoyancy, bobbed away on the tiny waves. Fence palings shifted and gapped and slid one by one into the murky water. As we waded back to shore, our fathers stood holding beers, laughing, watching the debris separate and drift away.

When I last heard, Paul Gough was flying jumbos out of Hong Kong for Cathay. If he flies to Brisbane, he'll pass close to that spot as he comes in to land. It'll be to his right, but invisible, with the old houses cleared years ago for the sake of a bigger, better airport.

★ ★ ★

We get to Umart without having had the sex talk, or having made our way to the middle of anything. It's a single-storey building, with each of its windows entirely covered by an ad skin, blocking out all natural light and prying eyes.

'Have you been here before?' I'm picturing hydroponic marijuana, a meth lab, organ harvesting – the usual parental fears. What's so wrong about a little natural light? Why have I never seen an ad for Umart anywhere?

'Sure,' he says dismissively, but no more dismissively than usual. 'It's where I got everything else.'

The carpark is almost empty, so I park at the foot of the steps that lead to the door. Jack's already undoing his seatbelt before I've got the handbrake on.

'You can wait here,' he says.

'In the car? I thought I'd come in.'

'Really?' He weighs up the worth of more strenuous opposition. 'If you have to. But don't talk. And don't touch anything.'

The door opens and a man steps out in a trucker's cap, jeans and a T-shirt with a slogan reading 'This T-shirt slogan is ironic'. He's carrying a bag that probably contains computer parts, but could as easily carry half a dozen hash cookies or a kidney. As he makes his way past us, as assiduous as Jack about avoiding eye contact, another nerd comes into the carpark in a beaten up old Daewoo and drives into a pole. He doesn't seem to mind. His door creaks like a sound effect when he opens it, and again when he slams it shut.

The first part of the building's interior is like a foyer, but without a foyer's purpose of being a welcoming conduit to other places, or somewhere to be met. There's a poster on one wall, and a long white bench with two piles of brochures. Towards the right end of the wall there's a window with two men sitting behind it, neither of them with body language that hints at a customer-service role.

Beyond them is a wider area filled with rows of plastic chairs, several of them occupied by men of varying ages who all look like they've spent three days solid sleeping on their hair. Their seating choices at first glance appear random, but not one is closer than three empty seats from another. It's as if they've been mathematically modelled to sit as far apart as possible without it being obvious.

There's a red terminal mounted on a post. Jack pulls a note from his pocket, punches in a code and sits down, perfectly positioning himself to maintain the three-seat-space rule.

I'm about to move in next to him when his face takes on a pained expression.

'It's fine,' he says. 'You can . . .' He makes a shooing motion with his hands and flicks a sideways glance to the two nearest nerds to check that he hasn't lost status by speaking or by being accompanied.

One of the nerds is skimming through screens on his phone and the other is gazing slack-jawed straight ahead at the counter that's set into the long beige wall in front of him. No status loss is evident. I'm about to move away when a man appears in the space behind the counter holding a plastic bag. He's in his late twenties. He has the pointed black beard of an Elizabethan privateer, and a check flannel shirt.

He flicks the top of the bag over to check something and calls out, 'Davenport,' as quickly and with as little conviction as he can muster.

Davenport stands and lopes to the counter. There's an awkward exchange and he accepts the bag, rolls the top over with both hands and a loud rustling of plastic, and makes his way to the door, clearing his throat and swallowing, his prominent Adam's apple bobbing up and down.

When I look back at Jack, his face is fixed in a compact glare. He wants the glare to be as clear as possible, but kept between us. His right hand, out of sight of everyone but me, is pointing towards the foyer and the door.

Jack is a man at Umart, an equal stakeholder to the older nerds, and I am shaming him with my continued close presence. Umart is a place where my Jack and other Jacks fit in. He wants it to be his and wants me to give him some space and to end this collision of worlds.

I back away to the foyer and pretend to read a brochure intently. Despite giving it several minutes of close attention, I can't even work out what it's about. I pull my phone out of my pocket, so that I can stare at it and look busy. On the screen is a picture of an elegant carriage clock showing the time in Auckland. Perplexing, but preferable to another gut call to Robyn.

There are bags for Chan and Kovacs, then one for Lambert, which Jack claims in a brief semi-functional interaction that matches all the others. With the bag in hand, he heads straight for the door, his eyes on the flat industrial carpet, knowing I'll follow.

I don't know who Lambert is. I don't know if I'm supposed to. Lambert the smurfberry trader. Jack's already on the steps before I'm halfway to the door, and waiting at the passenger side of the car when I step into the daylight.

I could ask about Lambert, or what's in the bag. I could ask about smurfberry trading and how it converts into computer parts, when no one on the internet seems to acknowledge it. This seems like the natural place to do it, but I've agreed with Robyn that Sex Talk Three takes priority. As I get into the car, Jack's already in his seat with his bag between his feet, bracing to repel any Umart questions I might think of asking.

So instead I say, 'Did I ever tell you about my first girlfriend?'

There's a pause. His expression doesn't change. I wonder if he's heard me and then he says, 'No. I have a bad feeling you might be going to now.'

'It was a different world then.' As I back the car out of its spot, I try to convince myself I've tricked us into the middle of the conversation. 'I used to call her from a phone box down the road so I could talk to her without anyone listening. Not that there was anything weird being said – it was just my business, you know.'

'I know.' His knee starts jogging. He smoothes the leg of his shorts down his thigh and it stops. 'Then sometimes you'd send her a note tied to a pigeon, right?'

'Yeah. Or smoke signals. I'd go to the top of a hill with a blanket and some dried grass and a couple of flints. But too many people can see smoke signals. It's not always easy to keep things your own business. People – people who actually care – are always wanting to give you advice. And some of it might be good advice. But maybe it's better for some of that stuff to be general, rather than specific. Advice about how things might go, rather than advice about a particular situation, or girl. Or whatever.'

Somehow I've managed to merge my parental advice intro with a clause from an investment product disclosure statement.

He picks at his nails and his knee starts jogging again.

She showed me her breast once – just once – and

I wasn't at all sure what I was supposed to do next. I sensed one course of action would be right, but only one, and all the others would be wrong. I froze. I told myself not to freeze. I leaned down and kissed it delicately on the side, like the kiss you'd give a great aunt rather than a breast, and she put it away. Not a word was said the whole time it was out.

If I told him all that, Jack would vomit, here and now in the car and all over his bag of parts.

* * *

The route from Umart to Toowong Village and our grocery shopping is, on the map, a short one. Today it seems to have been vacated by almost every other vehicle in town, so it's even shorter. We're most of the way there in about two minutes, and I'm still coyly tiptoeing around the sex talk.

'When I was twelve,' I tell him, 'my parents gave me Jaws to read. The novel that got made into that film about the shark.'

'Yep,' he says, shaking his head, intelligence insulted by the superfluous footnoting.

'It was the first adult book I ever read. It was a surprise to see the adult point of view. It was like the way they maybe spoke or thought when I wasn't in the room.' This is a wide tangent to Sex Talk Three, a mad attempt to triangulate it, having taken a shot at it already in the context of a phone call to a girl in the seventies. 'It had two descriptions of nipples in it and I'd never seen that in a book before. One of them had a nipple looking like coral, I think. It doesn't prepare you for the real thing. It's hard to feel prepared for any of that stuff, even if you're across the theory and you've given it plenty of thought.'

Jack's knee jogs harder and his calf rustles against the plastic Umart bag at a frequency of about five times per second. He's staring straight ahead. We're at a red light at a T-junction and there's a panelbeater's in front of us. It's packed up for the day, a chain on its corrugated-iron doors.

'What I'm saying is, there's a bit to think about.' The lights change, just as I hit a rich seam of useless platitudes. 'There's a lot to think through.'

We turn right and pass under the rail bridge and into the final ninety seconds of this car journey that I'd hoped might take ten minutes. I'd pictured us at this spot, two men gliding into the Toowong Village carpark with an understanding, closer and – in Jack's case – wiser. The pressure would be off. He'd be secretly relieved. The weekend would pass uneventfully and next week Lyrix's dad would punch someone else, kick a dog, smash a window or skull that I'll never know about.

Jack swallows some mucus and adjusts his cap.

'It's just one body part going into another body part,' he says. It has the sound of a quote, but I can't place it. He's out-manning me, going ultradirect.

The car passes through the dark entrance and dips down the ramp to the B1 carpark. We're seconds away from parking.

'In that case you can just stick your finger up her nose.'

He lets out a cackle. 'After the first few goes that loses its magic.'

I can remember a time, though it now seems like a fairytale world rather than the start of this century, when Jack was a sweet, engaging child, whose enquiring mind led him to ask memorable questions, such as, 'How is it that bathroom water always tastes sweeter than kitchen water?' I wrote them down. They're in an old version of Word, backed up somewhere on an old version of a storage system. 'If something's *re*frigerated, does that mean there was some other time when it was frigerated?'

He maintained a list of carefully thought-out favourites in every conceivable category. His favourite rock type was metamorphic because, to use his words, 'It's a rock twice.' I had to look it up. It's a sedimentary rock, with pressure and heat applied igneous-style until it changes type.

He had so many favourites that he invented the concept of the 'favourite favourite' – the best in show of all the category winners. We were all expected to have one. It surprised him that it was a concept that took explaining to people outside the family. One of his early favourite favourites was nasty unicorns. Maybe that was some hint of the teen to come.

Today, he starts the shopping trip with a clear but undeclared feeling that he's had a victory over me. The wry buckled smile is stuck to his face as we ride the travelator up to ground. He's revisting my idiot remarks about nipples and coral or maybe my final salvo about Lyrix's nose. Or maybe he's just contemplating the two of them going at it like Energiser bunnies between the faded sheets at Crystal Tydes.

As we push our trolley into Coles and park it next to the bananas, I unfold the shopping list. We have fruit and veg in front of us, and the deli, and there's bread in the first of the aisles to our left. I tried to group my dinner ingredients with the items Robyn had already written down, in the hope that the order would make sense to me when we walked in.

'Does your mother . . .' My assessment of the list is complicated by having to peer through my presbyopia at scrabbled doctor's handwriting. 'Does she have a system for the way she sets it out?'

'System?' The concept seems to amuse him. 'When something runs out, you add it to the list.'

'Yes, but in a particular place?' I show him the list, hoping to cue better advice about how to use it.

'Yep. Under the last thing already on there.' He takes the list and studies it. 'Though you seem to have a new way of coming in from the side. She'll want to know all about that.'

There is no system. In a modern supermarket with twenty thousand product lines. It's anarchy, like the pantry at home. And it can never, ever be the subject of a conversation there.

'She usually brings a pen,' Jack adds helpfully. 'She crosses them off.' He mimes it, still helping.

I tear the edges instead, in lieu of both a system and a pen. There's something Hansel and Gretel about it, roaming the aisles, tearing tiny rips into the paper and forever checking our bearings.

Robyn has pasta on the list. I know she prefers long pasta to short, so I pick up a box of pappardelle.

'She means fettucine,' Jack says, moving his hand to block the box on its way to the trolley. 'Pappardelle really shits me.'

'It shits you.'

'It shits me 'cause it's supposed to be long pasta, but it's more about being wide pasta. It's flabby.' He throws his hands in the air, as though his point's self-evident. 'It should just organise itself and be lasagne.'

'What about linguine?'

'I can go narrower than fettucine, just not wider. But Mum doesn't go for narrower.'

'Fettucine, then?'

'That'd probably be best. We usually go for this one.' He takes a packet from the shelf and exchanges it with me for the pappardelle.

Precision madness, and yet there's no system. It would be an exaggeration to call it the longest conversation Jack and I have had in months, but there haven't been many longer. I'd throw in more pasta options to keep it going, if I could.

In the next aisle is one of my additions to the list, and therefore a right-sided tear.

'So there goes all the fun out of mystery dinner,' Jack says when I tell him why we're buying a packet of labels.

As I drop it in the trolley, I hear something in my pocket. A rhythmic metal-on-metal creaking sound. I pull out my phone. The screen features a video of a lanky teen with pale legs, faded denim shorts and faux-fur trim to her raincoat, sitting on a steel swing on a bare patch of ground. The line of text across her knees tells us she is offering to strip. She is older than Abi, but not a lot older. Behind her, in the distance, a tractor makes slow progress across a barren field.

'She's a bit young for you,' Jack says, staring in case she takes anything off right now.

'It's the phone. I don't know how to . . .' I don't even want to tap the screen in case it makes her start stripping.

Jack takes it from me, shrinks the image and hits a key that takes us back a step.

'Okay, so your pocket has gone to Google.' He shows me the screen. 'Then it's put in three Xs and she came up as one of the options. Along with a lot of porn. Your pocket picked her.' He hits the home key. 'And now I'm going to show you how to lock your phone.' He says it slowly, as if any technology more complicated than a fork is beyond me. There's a tiny button on top. He presses it. 'Done.'

'I thought that was for turning it on and off.'

'And also for locking it.'

He taps the screen in several spots to show me nothing will happen. He hands the phone back to me. I press the button. Winston's arse appears, with the ring lock in place.

'Okay, that's good. Very useful. Thank you. We don't have to . . .' Asking him not to tell people will only make him tell people. 'Thanks for that. We should check and see if there's anything else in this aisle. While we're standing here.'

'Did you know her, or . . .'

'I've never seen her before in my life. Of course I didn't know her. It was the phone.' I'm peering at the list, trying to decode Robyn's writing. 'Eggs. We both put eggs. They should be near here.'

Jack points to them, immediately behind me. We take a dozen.

'What do you think's next?' I turn the list around so

that he can see it. Anything to stop him talking about the girl on the swing.

'I don't know.' He takes the list from me and looks around the aisle. 'I come here as little as possible. Of course, that's before I knew there were strippers . . .'

It's three more aisles before everything stops being an opportunity to refer to her. Cereal, mineral water, two different milks – the dullness of shopping eventually wears him down. By then it's definitely the longest conversation we've had in months, which I'd count as a big plus if it wasn't mostly about the stripper on my phone.

Our final purchase, apparently after twice as long as Robyn takes and with several items requiring debate, is frozen puff pastry. I used to think pastry was magical. I saw people on TV cutting and trimming and saying how easy pastry was if you bought it frozen, but I never believed it. I was converted with my first try, though my pies have always looked as if someone's trying to punch their way out of them.

I made one attempt at coming up with pastry from scratch. The twins were about six. It yielded something they ended up calling 'ugly cakes'. I don't even recall what they were supposed to be, but they came out of the oven with the consistency of the hard tack carried on galleons and into long military campaigns. The last of the batch survived about a year-and-a-half in the back of the pantry without a speck of mould. When I threw them into the bin, they landed like slate drink coasters.

Back in the car, I have at most ten minutes to revisit the sex talk, or not.

'Grandad's thinking fish and chips on Friday night.' It's not the sex talk, but I have a phone call to make.

To Lyrix's mother, definitely her mother. 'Does Lyrix eat fish?'

Jack shrugs. 'Yeah, she can't make it. Some family thing. I always figured she probably wouldn't be able to make it.'

'But you made such a big deal of it in the restaurant.' I've had close to twenty-four hours of the prospect of proposing, to a man made entirely of muscle and prison tatts, a potential virginity-losing weekend for his daughter. And now I don't have to.

'The principle,' Jack says. 'I was making a big deal of the principle.' And then, in case I'm not across which principle, he says, slowly and clearly, 'Fairness.'

20

I'M WORKING OUT WHICH kitchen drawer looks the best bet for storing pantry moth traps when I hear Jack say, 'Hey, he's got no pants on. The one in the middle's got no pants on.'

They're watching videos with my father, on TV this time as far as I can tell, and the song playing is the Bee Gees' How Deep Is Your Love.

As I step into the loungeroom, Abi's saying, 'It's Barry Gibb. That's not possible. Barry Gibb would always wear pants. Grandad?'

She's back from her guitar lesson and what's on screen looks like an ancient episode of Rage. My father's in an armchair, fighting to find the right pair of glasses amid a mess of biscuit crumbs, his iPad and today's mail. Winston is asleep on the rug, with his head on my father's foot.

'It's How Deep is Your Love. Of course there are pants.' Abi turns when I say it, surprised I'm in the room, or that I could be so certain. 'Just go back a bit and freeze it. If it's that kind of thing – a DVD or . . .'

I don't know what technology she's using, if any. I nearly said rewind, though the last thing it'll be is a

VHS tape. Whatever it is, she puts it in reverse, finds the spot and stops it.

'Abi's right.' I'm even more confident now that I can see it. 'Barry Gibb would always wear pants, and what you're seeing there is a classic figure-hugging buttcheek-grabbing pair of seventies white jeans, with the mood lighting unfortunately creating the appearance of bare flesh. But the giveaway, and something the veteran observer knows to look for is . . .'

I point to my father, who has pulled his distance glasses out from beneath what I'm guessing is a semifull colostomy bag that's filling out the lower part of his shirt.

'The flares,' he says, leaning forward with forensic intent. He clears his throat, and proceeds in his best version of David Attenborough. 'Always take time to note the calves of the seventies rockstar male, and you'll see confirmation that pants are in fact being worn, as the legs flare outrageously towards the ankles.' He sits back in the armchair. 'I interviewed Barry Gibb three times. Pants on all three.' His hand makes a sweeping motion, dismissing all doubt.

'Why have you got those out?' Abi says.

I'm still holding the moth traps.

'I'm just sorting out the groceries.'

She nods. 'They probably go on the top shelf in the pantry. Poisons go high up.'

'Sure.' The next song is starting. It's Bonnie Tyler's Total Eclipse of the Heart. 'Makes sense.'

She points the remote at the TV, hits pause and turns towards my father.

'This one's a great example of where videos were

heading by the early eighties,' he says. He straightens his glasses. 'Lots of billowing, lots of doves.'

★ ★ ★

The early eighties. I should have been the go-to guy for that era, instead of being stuck on the peripheries, clutching moth traps.

It was a Russell Mulcahy video, with input from Jim Steinman. Those are the important points.

The top shelf of the pantry has Baygon, a lime-scale remover strong enough to have a skull-and-crossbones warning symbol on it and a half-empty pack of Redhead matchboxes. Now I'm there, it looks like the obvious place for the moth traps.

In the seventies I saw the How Deep Is Your Love video – back when it was called a film clip – a thousand times, and the prospect of nude butt cheeks in the closing sequence never occurred to me. This millennium, they look nude. They really do. In the seventies, it would have been inconceivable for Barry Gibb to feature in a video naked from the waist down, so I couldn't have seen it. And in the seventies those were just pants.

Jack and Abi are putting together the best patchy knowledge a person ever can of an era that's not their own. Sometimes those fresh eyes see something in a brilliant new way, often they fill in the gaps with their own wrong stuff, without ever knowing there were gaps there.

For me that's Eva Peron, Marilyn Monroe, the end of World War II – inescapable phenomena, but passed to me second hand, with the story already through multiple

177

revisions and its end stamped all over it, blurring the shape of the rest.

I make a start on dinner, since I'm in the kitchen already and I know it'll take me longer than it should. The classic music videos keep rolling in the loungeroom, though it's not long before I hear Jack's feet on the stairs on the way to his room, since he's a bagful of geeky parts closer to his dream – the mysterious Lambert's dream – of reinventing Pong, or posting selfies of his morose lava-lamp-lit face, or controlling traffic lights in Singapore.

My salmon coulibiac recipe came along just as I'd decided that bought pastry was within range for me and I was looking for excuses to use it. The twins were sleeping through, Robyn and I had some of our sanity back and I had yet to be tempted by the offer from BDK – an offer that meant more travel, certainly, but Robyn could work part-time, as she wanted, and the travel was to be a medium-term thing before setting up the now-forgotten Brisbane office.

I made my first attempts at cooking on the Monday mornings of my last year of school, in the ideally timed lesson before lunch. The subject was actually named Bachelor Cooking, and it was never clear whether it was designed to help us survive in the wild or merely to make us a more appealing catch – someone thoughtful enough that he could snag himself a good lady wife on the strength of one average meal, and then never have to cook again.

We learned chilli con carne without ever pronouncing the final 'E', how best to serve ice cream and tinned fruit – the 'cooking' part of the subject title wasn't rigorously enforced – and how to make a jelly with a reasonable chance of setting. Mostly we sat there eating ingredients, knowing nothing we did was for assessment.

Bachelor Cooking was a highly sought-after haven away from real subjects – the subjects with exams and pressure and a direct bearing on our uni prospects. It had a limit of twenty students from a year of two hundred and forty, and the line-up was top-heavy with prefects, over-achievers and, yes, the school captain. None of us learned a thing, but we never had to buy lunch on Mondays.

I eventually had to learn to cook in exactly the kind of environment Bachelor Cooking had perhaps tried to prepare me for – a student sharehouse towards the end of my degree. I found my old chilli con carne recipe somewhere, picked up the final 'E', doubled the spices and ended up turning it into something palatable enough to repeat.

It was a start, and progress has been patchy since. From a magazine recipe for Rustic Pizza – long discarded, since it was all about the DIY dough – I got into the habit of including 'rustic' in the name of almost anything I make, because it encourages asymmetry, mis-shapenness and imprecise chopping.

The coulibiac, with its seven-minute boiled eggs and its three-quarters-cooked salmon is barely in the oven when Abi appears. She's wearing a short skirt, clunky heels and a top put together in layers that don't quite make sense to me. The outer layer is lace and appears to knot at the front, but beneath it she has two straps of different colours going over each shoulder.

She crouches down to view the pale undulating pastry through the oven door and says, 'Nice. Mum did tell you I was going out, right?'

'Not yet.'

'Okay.' She stands up. 'Sorry about that. I texted her earlier but I don't have your new number. I've got to go babysitting. The Mullers' regular person –' She points in the general direction of the Mullers' house, three doors down '– she cancelled at the last minute, or something.'

I still think of the Mullers as new to the neighbourhood, though Robyn would now count them as friends. I can't imagine Abi changing a nappy in the clothes she's wearing, or even sitting on the floor to play with kids. I can't picture the Mullers' kids. I can't picture Abi babysitting. She looks to me like she's about to head to Professor Humbert's place to audition for Lolita.

'They've got Lean Cuisines,' she says, saving me from the further embarrassment of offering to keep her some of the coulibiac. 'They're okay for me to have one.'

She has lip gloss on, and I think she's wearing eyeliner. My next line, should I prove unable to keep my mouth shut, risks being about the length of her skirt and respecting herself, and it won't go well.

'Sure,' I tell her instead, marking her wardrobe selection down for discussion the next time Robyn and I confer about boundaries and where we're drawing them. 'No problem. What time are we expecting you home?'

21

'BAKE AT 180 DEGREES until golden brown,' the recipe says. It's scrawled on the back of an envelope and taped into the recipe book. I must have seen it on a TV food show.

As I lift the coulibiac out of the oven, my father rolls his gum up in foil and fetches a bottle of Cointreau from the pantry. Robyn's already opened a chardonnay and poured us each a glass.

'Have you got a stash of that stuff everywhere?' I don't remember a time when we ever had Cointreau in the pantry.

He looks up from the ice dispenser. 'No, just down-stairs. This is yours.' He pours Cointreau into his glass until the ice rises almost to the rim. 'Cheers.'

Jack walks in, having smelled food. He has earbuds in, with the white cords leading to a pocket in his shorts. I can hear the treble part of an unidentifiable song crashing away into his skull.

I explain to him, in words and also gestures almost big enough to guide a plane, that we're eating at the table tonight. The oven mitts I'm wearing add to the effect.

He pops an earbud out and looks at me critically. 'Tell me you didn't just say we're eating at the table.'

'We're eating at the table.'

He weighs up his options, takes a careful though not close look at the coulibiac, which is sitting on the bench next to the oven, radiating heat. It's not precisely golden brown on top. More chocolate brown on the high points and yellowish in the valleys. A CWA judge, should they have a coulibiac category, would not mark that well. He inhales again, to be certain of his choice.

'That smells okay.' He sighs, pulls the other bud from his ear and reaches into his pocket to turn the music off.

'Thank you.' I'm still speaking louder than I need to. 'What are you listening to?'

'It's EDM. You wouldn't know it.'

'Electronic dance music,' my father says helpfully, before I can ask who EDM are.

'Sure. And the . . .' I can't say band. Band would be wrong. American Bandstand black-and-white lumbering dinosaur wrong. 'Who was it you were listening to?'

'Big Swedish Homos.' Jack deadpans it and waits for a reaction.

I look around at my father but he gives me nothing. A minimal lift of an eyebrow maybe.

'He just wants you to google that at work tomorrow,' Robyn says, in a tone that makes sure we all know she's over the conversation already. 'Now, can I assume you'll be serving the pie over here and I should put the salad on the table?'

There's a rush of steam as I slice into the coulibiac and, when I pry the brittle pastry apart to check the inside, it looks okay. Not restaurant-quality, but okay. It tastes a little better than it looks, but my best coulibiacs always look a little like an accident's happened under the cover of pastry. It's Russian peasant food, I think, and, rightly or wrongly, no one expects Russian peasant food to look like a Fabergé egg when you crack it open. It's playing to my strength, determinedly rustic.

'This is good,' my father says through his first mouthful, waving his fork to emphasise the point. 'Very home-made, but in a good way.'

Robyn makes an mmm noise to back him up. 'And even nicer because I didn't have to cook it.'

A few bites in, at a lull in the conversation, I ask how everyone's day was. It used to be a rule when the kids were about eight. Dinner at the table, and an interesting summary of your day.

'You didn't tell me we'd be doing that,' Jack says, as if a contract term has just been breached.

'It's not going to kill you.'

Robyn says she'll go first, and tells us she picked a cockroach out of someone's ear. My father follows her and continues the medical theme, starting to talk about stoma care before Jack shuts him down.

'Some of us are eating,' he says, suddenly a master of etiquette. 'Oh crap, that means it's my turn.' He shuffles around on his seat, taking it way too seriously, staring down at his plate as though he's following a speck on the horizon – an enemy plane, an alien craft. He smiles, and jolts to a more upright position. 'Today I hung out with this weird guy who told me about this book with nipples in it . . .' Robyn puts her fork down. 'And it turned out to be my dad.'

'It was in context.'

'Yep,' Jack says, as if he's about to let me off the hook. 'Getting groceries.'

Robyn's watching me and blinking, as though I've slipped for a moment to a problematic focal distance. My father's frowning, wondering if there's a reference he's not getting, some nipple book well known to younger folk.

'And in the grocery context,' Jack continues, 'we took a quick look at a girl on a swing who was interested in stripping for us.'

'What girl?' Robyn's even more lost. 'What swing? There's no swing in Coles.'

'What is it with you and strippers?' my father says to me. 'You were never like this when you were younger.'

Jack laughs.

'I'm not like it now. There's nothing with me and strippers.' It's my father's question, but I'm directing the answer Robyn's way. 'Not since my buck's night. And that was only because of your brothers.'

'Kmart might have a swing,' she says. 'But it'd be flat pack.'

Jack laughs again. 'Classic. There was no swing, Mum. It was on Dad's phone. He didn't know how to lock it. It happened in his pocket. A total fluke. A freak accident of strippage. He wouldn't let her go ahead with it anyway.'

Robyn's still processing it when my father snaps his fingers and says, 'I've got another one. Something else that happened to me today.'

He smiles and eases himself to a standing position using the edge of the table. All his vertical moves have taken on a cautious hydraulic look since his operation. He shuffles across to the counter and picks up his iPad. He flips it open and gets online as he's making his way back. He finds the tab he wants and, with a steady hand on the table edge, lowers himself back down to his seat. Only once he's settled and run his hand quickly over his stoma does he turn the iPad to show us the screen.

It's the Wicked Campers website, featuring an 'iconic five-seater' campervan with the words 'Tame' and 'Impala' painted on the side, graffiti-style.

'Hey, Tame Impala,' Jack says, apparently not thinking to question why a backpacker campervan would be part of his sedentary grandfather's day.

My father peers over the top of the iPad, looking down at the image. 'Yeah. Rolling Stone gave their second album four stars. Maybe four and a half.'

He glances at me and then Robyn, as if we're each entitled to a guess about what's going on. Robyn's been an unwilling participant in the conversation since the nipple-book reference and isn't likely to try.

'I don't know for sure if we're getting that one though,' he says. He taps the campervan picture with his fingernail. 'But it's that model. I've slipped them a bit extra to take the bedding out and fit a temporary seat in the back. All legal. Thought it'd be a nice way for us all to get to the coast tomorrow.'

Robyn reaches under the table and squeezes my knee. Her entire day has now stopped making sense.

22

AT CLOSE TO TEN O'CLOCK, with the coulibiac a modest success and the Coles phone incident fully explained, I'm flat on the bedroom floor with a tennis ball jammed into my problem buttock.

My father even went on to liken our multi-generational roadtrip to Little Miss Sunshine, without appearing to work out that, while it might be cool for him to be played by Alan Arkin in the movie, his death would end up a big feature of act three.

Jack is in his room, fiddling with his time machine or death machine, or whatever it is, and there are no signs of smoke or fire so far. Abi is eighty metres of darkness away from home. Robyn is multitasking, reading on her iPad while paying intermittent attention to the TV, and a couple who aren't quite satisfied with anything in Devon on Escape to the Country.

The tennis ball idea came from a physio. With much of my body weight on it, it's at the ideal point on the spectrum between firm and rock hard, driving pressure deep into the buttock through the gluteals to the troublesome piriformis. On the pain spectrum, it's somewhere between bringing tears to the eyes and unmodified yelping.

I have my phone out to distract myself. It's at arms' length between me and the cream ceiling, and I'm browsing the world of superfluous apps that appear to come as standard. At least I'll know where to look if I ever need to work out my latitude or read a version of Treasure Island the size of my palm.

'Why do they all want an AGA?' Robyn says rhetorically. I'm sure she's said it to the room on other nights when she's been here alone.

The British people are now in the kitchen of the quaint Devon cottage and finding the quaintness closing in around them. He's in a faded blue polo shirt, she's in a shapeless dress and has hair that might have been cut by Jack. They're stooping below ancient black ceiling beams, in a wary way that suggests a beam might take a swing at them if their attention wavers.

Robyn continues her commentary. 'I could never live with ceilings that low.'

Robyn, as a party to modest ideas that became big plans that became our agreed once-only massive Renovation of a Lifetime, will never have to live with a ceiling lower than three metres. It seemed to make sense to lift the house when we first talked about it. It would give us more space, add value. Some people make a lot of money out of property. We've made property out of a lot of money.

The elegant simplicity of the house-lifting plan was gone long before the interior designer joined the team, but I've never been able to pinpoint the day it happened or even the month. She wore suits in taupe and bone and looked and moved like an ageing star from a daytime soap. Which is to say she managed a kind of glide while crossing a room, but her face was an immobile mix of collagen, paralysed muscles, nips and tucks.

For our en suite, she brought out small square metallic tiles in colours called Sparta and Ashanti. For the kitchen's island bench, she produced a shard of polished grey limestone allegedly from the quarries used by the Emperor Darius to build his palaces two and a half thousand years ago.

At the end of it all, we have a house twice as good and five times as expensive as the house we'd been aiming for. If the maths of that outcome isn't perfect, I try to remind myself to appreciate the building we live in and to remember that my BDK time at least put a big dent in the mortgage. We're in a street of mortgage slaves, and are less brutally enslaved than plenty of them.

Robyn is a sixth generation Stieglitz from Ipswich and the valleys to the west, a descendant of one of the lesser-known branches of the several Stieglitz families who turned up here in the nineteenth century escaping a persecution that never had the scale to be more than a footnote to the history of Middle Europe. From their arrival, her Stieglitzes – failed farmers from Bavaria by all accounts – produced a further three generations of terrible farmers before her grandfather set up a hardware and farm supplies store. In that, the Stieglitzes mirror the beginnings of the brothers Lehman in America a century before but, while the Lehman brothers went on to cotton trading and a famous financial empire, Karl Stieglitz made a practice of extending infinite lines of credit to his kin, all the way through one drought-stricken summer after another until the banks showed up to change the locks.

The business was Stieglitz and Son by then, so Robyn's father, Barry, lost his shirt as well. Robyn and her sisters spent two years in a caravan in their grandparents' yard, a time she can recount in six different ways, though she tends to choose the one in which it becomes Old Macdonald's farm, with chickens laying eggs for every breakfast and fresh milk from the house cow. Debts are silent seething things, so there is no verse of that song that begins 'Old Macdonald had a debt'.

As our renovation plans got bigger and bolder and populated by wilder and more dangerous characters – with the interior designer gliding quickly to the front of the pack – I realised that, if Robyn wanted to build herself a castle, I wanted us to do it too.

'Hey,' she says. Escape to the Country is on an ad break. 'I saw an article today that said Amanda Bynes had just tweeted something about wanting a rapper to – and this is a quote –' She backs it up with quote fingers to remove all doubt '–"murder my vagina".'

'Something went badly wrong with Sex Talk Three for her if that came up as one of her choices.'

This is the world we're in. They're probably all saying it, everyone under thirty, or whatever the magic number is. The twins – with Abi at least an Amanda Bynes fan when they were ten – have probably already seen the quote several times each.

'Was it a particular rapper or the next one she bumps into?' Somewhere in America, the Bynes family goes into crisis mode. Meanwhile the rest of us – me included – pretend their daughter is a character in a long-running show that catches our attention, fleetingly, when it takes a wrong turn.

'A particular rapper.' One of Robyn's hands goes back to her iPad, which is resting against her knees. 'Is that better? It's not worse.'

'I saw in the Brisbane Times today that Justin Bieber's worked out he probably shouldn't own a monkey.'

I read the story because it seemed ludicrous that it could be one. I'm about to hit the limit of my tennis-ball-inflicted butt pain. I'm not sure how long banal will hold me.

'Well, sure.' Robyn is up for dissecting banal any day of the week. 'Monkeys need other monkeys, more than anything. They don't need . . . Biebers. Who would give Justin Bieber a monkey?'

'A rapper. I don't know if it's the same one as with the . . . murdering, you know.'

I lift myself from the ball, roll onto my side and then bring myself up onto my hands and knees.

'There's more than one rapper,' she says. 'You're in radio. I thought you'd know that.'

She touches another tab on her iPad screen. Facebook. Specifically Abi's Facebook page, where Robyn appears to have friend privileges. Abi's likes and photo albums are all on view, along with Robyn's customised sidebar ads for discounted designer fashion. No Volvos or sugar babies here. How is it that Robyn's Facebook ads seem totally reasonable, while mine are like an introvert's mid-life crisis?

She peers at me over her glasses and says, 'I check Abi's page occasionally. There's nothing too dramatic on there.'

I set my phone down on the bedside table and put the tennis ball in its spot in the drawer.

'You know you want to look,' she says.

And of course I do. I ease myself into bed, my piriformis now feeling more like a dull bruise. Robyn passes me the iPad once I'm safely horizontal.

Abi likes the TV series Girls, Ellen DeGeneres, The L Word and a bunch of shows that have never screened here and which she can only have seen by illegal download. Which might well be the kind of comment I'd post on her wall if I had friend status, thereby casting her into social purgatory. She also likes 'I shall call him Squishy and he shall be my Squishy', 'I could tell you but I'd rather show you THROUGH INTERPRE-TIVE DANCE!!', 'Am I not turtley enough for your turtle club?' and 'There should be a nap time in high school'.

Her photos are mostly solo selfies, selfies with April and selfies with a bunch of friends I don't know, all striking disinhibited poses that are, ultimately, no threat to society, themselves or their futures. They're just kids in an era when every device is a camera and every waking moment a potential photo op.

'Hey,' Robyn says, flicking between TV channels, 'on the subject of Sex Talk Three, how'd you go with Jack? Or did you choke when you found out Lyrix wasn't coming to the coast?'

'No, I . . .' Choked, gagged, spluttered. I did everything but shock him with competence. 'I did some groundwork.'

'Seriously? That's it? I can't believe you had a stripper on your phone and you couldn't turn that into a sex talk.' Escape to the Country is back from the ad break. She sets the remote down beside her. She's still sitting propped up on pillows. 'How was that not a golden opportunity?'

'Because it was in Coles. Because she was probably a minor and I was thrown for a second. Because any golden opportunity she was offering wasn't one I was up for watching. We made a start. I think he knows that conversation's open now. Remember how my parents gave me Jaws when I was twelve?'

'Oh no.' It's more like a sigh than a comment. 'This isn't the two nipple references thing? That's not what he was talking about at dinner?'

'It was a way in. An opening gambit.'

'Seriously?' She adjusts her position and then her glasses so that she can scrutinise me closely, this odd man in her bed who might be punking her or, worse, telling it straight. 'You talk about that all the time. I'm sorry if it's some —' She contemplates her words carefully '— important coming-of-age moment for you.'

She's picturing me, twelve, not the over-fleshed forty-nine-year-old frozen into a negotiated pain-free pose on the other half of her bed. Me, with my first good watch on my wrist, in my grey school shorts with my socks almost to the knee, making my slow and awestruck progress through the pages of Jaws and into an adult world, shown the way there by my willing parents.

'I'm not even sure there are two nipple references in Jaws,' she says.

She's correct that it was a rite of passage for me. A N I P P L E that looked like C O R A L and one other. I was getting credit for being man enough to read that stuff.

I ditch Facebook for Google and type in 'Jaws' plus 'nipples'. Robyn leans across, looking, like me, to see if Peter Benchley's nipple references meant enough to anyone else that they too kept a tally. It's all nipple clamps.

She laughs. 'You really should stay away from Google entirely at work, shouldn't you?'

The clock in the corner of the screen says it's ten sixteen.

'It was still daylight when Abi left. I hadn't thought through how dark it'd get.'

Robyn reaches for the iPad and turns it so that she can see the time clearly. 'She'll be home soon.'

'Should I go out and meet her, or . . . Maybe just stand behind a tree that'll give me a good view of the street?'

'Because that wouldn't freak her out, would it? You're never going to be her friend on Facebook if you try things like that.' Robyn picks up her phone from her bedside table and checks it. 'There's a plan. There's no way she'd accept an escort, whether it's you or Tim Muller or whoever, but she likes to call the second she's leaving and we talk all the way home. The full minute and a half.'

I can imagine her, my gawky-cool unworldly daughter, making her way along the street, talking Robyn through the dark shapes out there in the night. I can picture threats that almost certainly don't exist, as cars pass, carrying late pizzas to deliver or suburbanites like the Mullers heading home to their beds after a new product launch at an Audi dealership.

'Did you see what she was wearing?' That's part of the picture too. In movies, the kind of movies where something goes wrong, the girl is usually dressed the way Abi is tonight.

'She's wearing what they all wear, girls her age. She doesn't even see that skirt as short, at least not in the way you do.'

'Is it what the Mullers are expecting? Assuming they didn't build their wealth on babysitter porn . . .' I'm sure it's a sub-genre. I read about it once. Naive leggy teen turns up skimpily yet not raunchily dressed, something minimal triggers a comprehensive romp with the man of the house who, surprise, surprise, is packing a bridge pylon in his shorts.

Robyn gives me a stern over-the-glasses look. 'No, but amishbabysitters.com was down all day, so they had to settle.' She moves her glasses back into place. 'Is that what you watch all those late work nights when you want a break from the spreadsheets? Babysitter porn?'

Her phone rings. It's Abi. She's on her way down the Mullers' steps. In a little over a minute, I hear our front door shut.

23

'I PICKED UP A coffee on the way here,' Brian says, in a tone that tells us he's not entirely happy about it. 'Tall. Tall is such an insincere coffee. It's for people who want a big bucket of warm milk, but who want it off-white and in a sippy cup. And, you know, my mouth still doesn't taste any better.'

This morning, Brian has already got my attention on the drive to work by complaining that he slept with his mouth open and woke up with his breath smelling 'like an untidy arse'. I'm imagining him in a silent half-empty flat, hooks on the walls where a previous occupant's pictures might have gone, exhaling into his cupped hand and editing and re-editing his punchline.

'What I wonder,' Dazz says, ladling on a big serve of mock empathy, 'is why there isn't a charity putting on some stunt to fix afflictions like yours. Why is no one thinking of the social impact of malignant halitosis? Or the blow to the self-esteem? I mean, I can't sit on the same side of the desk as you unless you're wearing scuba gear, or at least a snorkel.'

'Exactly,' Brian comes in strongly. 'Exactly. There are critical issues out there not getting support, or their own piece of the calendar. I mean, sure, you've got Movember for prostate cancer, then there's Beardtober for . . . I don't know. I looked it up once but I couldn't work out what it was for.'

'What about Snot-tember, where you're sponsored to collect all your used tissues in September to raise funds for people afflicted by allergic rhinitis?'

'Or April Showers, where everyone puts a dot of water on the front of their pants to encourage research into that scourge, the late-emptying man pipe.'

I need to break this habit. Every morning I'm listening to their show like a censor at a 1950s TV broadcast, finger hovering over the button, ready to bleep anything my oma might have found lewd. No one will complain about 'man pipe'. No one will make an issue of 'arse'. I've heard people on radio who go to less trouble to be less funny than Brian and Dazz. But I'm not paying those people.

They go to a song and Dazz back-announces it as Jason Mraz.

'Hey,' Brian says, a freshly minted thought about to emerge, 'on the subject of things medical, I heard the new boss had a buttock transplant, but it's rejecting him.' There's a pause, which to any other listener is momentary, before he adds, 'That one's for you, Andrew. I know you're out there.' There's an audible intake of breath and he changes gear. 'But it's Friday, folks, and we want to hear from you about what you've got planned for the weekend. Anything you're really looking forward to? Anything you're really not? Anything that could go either way? Give us a call. We've got a couple of Gold Class passes from our friends at Event Cinemas for the best and worst. What about you, Dazz? Rockin' weekend as always?'

'As always. No, actually, Brian, I'm looking forward to going home and putting my feet up on my lady boy.'

Brian leaves a space for us all to think it through. Another choreographed gag is underway.

'Don't you mean La-Z-Boy, Dazz?'

'Speak for yourself. Taksin and I can't abide laziness.' The Three Stooges horn sound effect honks, removing any doubt that we've hit the punchline. 'What's up for you this weekend?'

This weekend, or immediately after it, I'll be going to war on horn sound effects, unless they're delivered by an actual horn, honked from a moving unicycle doing tight madcap laps of the studio.

'Off to the Goldie for the Comedy Awards,' Brian tells him. 'I'm part of the mass debate tomorrow night.'

'Can't think of anyone I'd rather have on my team if I was lining up legendary mass debaters.' Mercifully, a honking opportunity is allowed to slip by. 'Are you staying off the sauce this time? Remember what happened last time?'

'Last time?' Brian sounds as if he thinks Dazz is selling him short. 'Most times. There was that dinner for the Australian Society of Authors.'

'How'd you end up then?'

'Written off. Then there was that panelbeaters' association thing . . .'

'Where you got . . .'

'Smashed.'

'And that sewage engineer's conference where you ended up . . .'

'Wasted. And I don't want to tell you how I was after the Cerebral Palsy League fundraiser.'

Honk honk.

Spastic. Brian Brightman has, on air, delivered a joke for which the implied punchline is the word 'spastic'.

★ ★ ★

Despite that, the main agenda item for this morning's inevitable meeting is a Q&A he's done for a website.

His cerebral palsy line is out in the world, without a single complaint surfacing in the first hour afterwards, and I'm deciding to pick my battles and focus on damage yet to occur. The Q&A makes a fine place to start. In the absence of the promotions and publicity manager, the junior publicist has forwarded it to me.

'Jesus, you've got notes this time,' Brian says in the tearoom when I pull the two pages from my pocket. 'What's that? The head boy's report into my latest batch of shortcomings?'

He hands me my coffee, and I set it down on the table and pull out a chair.

'It's the Urban List Q&A.'

'Oh, yeah.' It's as noncommittal as he can make it. He's got his back to me while he loads a new capsule and presses the button. The machine vibrates and hums loudly. 'Fire away.'

He's still got his back to me. Matadors turn their backs on bulls to tell the bulls they aren't of much consequence, nothing to fear. I heard that on a holiday in Spain.

'Okay.' I wait until the machine stops, so I don't have

to shout. That's another thing I heard once – the first person to shout loses. The coffee machine clunks into silence. 'Celebrity crush: Taylor Swift. Do you really think that's a good idea?'

He swirls the spoon around loosely in his coffee and cackles to himself. He drops the spoon in the sink, pulls at his belt and drags the chair opposite me out from the table.

Once he's sitting on it, he says, 'I don't think it'd be a *bad* idea. A really good idea would be Taylor Swift doing this Q&A and putting "Brian Brightman".' He nods slowly and smiles, giving the fantasy a second or two of flight. 'I wasn't serious picking her. If I'd been serious I would have gone for someone much bigger up top.'

'You're not even supposed to be looking at those parts of Taylor Swift.' Already, he's sucked me into debating the moral fine print. 'How about we go with this: if you're old enough to have fathered them, they're not on your list.'

'She's legal.' It's the kind of argument Jack would raise. Brian has a teenager's eye for detail, and grasp of consequences. 'She's, like, twenty. Way legal.'

'I think you're missing the point here. Points. I have several. To start with, at the level of highest ick factor, you say that – that 'legal' thing – as if she might have sex with you. Repeat this over and over in your head: "To Taylor Swift I am just a creepy old man."'

He raises his eyebrows and contemplates it. He goes to sip his coffee but the sip becomes a slurp. A drop falls from his chin and splashes onto his thigh. He doesn't seem to mind. It's not the only damp drop on there, after all.

'I kind of like the idea that she's thinking about me,' he says, 'even if I'm creeping her out a bit. I reckon I could talk her round, on a good day.' He leans back in his chair. Somehow I've sent another blast of wind beneath the wings of the fantasy. He sniffs and lets his smug smile settle a little. 'What about Hermione from Harry Potter? You've got to admit she's pretty bloody stunning, and she's twenty-two.'

'But she started being Hermione when she was about ten. It's even more wrong if you bring up the fact that she played Hermione. She's twenty-two now?' At least five years older than the stripper on my phone. 'Still way too young for you. Just for a second, please, try to get it. I'm attempting to stop you putting out material that could reasonably depict you as a pervy old man.'

'Oh. Right.' He takes it on board as if it's a new idea, one that might be due some deliberation. 'You realise that, through this job, I do actually have a shot at meeting Taylor Swift? So it's not . . .'

It's bait. It's good bait, but I'm determined not to take it. He trails it around in the water for a while. While an interview is unlikely but not out of the question, no set of circumstances available on this planet in this epoch could see him dating Taylor Swift.

'So, who should I pick?' he says, giving in to my fish-eyed stare. 'Virginia Woolf?'

I can't help but laugh. 'You could do a lot worse than Virginia Woolf. And don't go dropping her if you find out she wasn't stacked.'

'She had a nose on her but, you know, I've got to accept I'm looking for a bit of latitude from her too.' He rocks back in his chair and angles his hands to frame the broad hairy abdomen bursting through his shirt buttons, and the complex stains on his pants. 'What about Tina Fey? She's over forty.'

His chair clunks forward again and his abdomen bumps the table. Coffee sloshes around in his cup.

'You can have Tina Fey. And why wouldn't you? Finally, a living celeb we can agree on.'

He smirks. I'm on some kind of hook after all. 'Your wife looks like Tina Fey.'

'You can no longer have Tina Fey.'

I need to move us along. I'm picturing Brian in our garden in the dark, staring up at the high windows of the castle for a glimpse of Robyn in the en suite or closing the bedroom blinds. We should have battlements up there, with archers for just such a situation. I run my finger down the page, past two relatively innocuous answers.

'Okay, school nickname.' It's the next one asterisked by the publicist. 'Could you maybe think of something other than "Hood, because I was the only one of my friends who wasn't circumcised"? Did you really hang out with people who would . . . of course you did.'

Maybe we all did. Every class in a boys' school has at least someone who ends up with a genitally-based nickname. In my year, Alastair Peel wasn't called Bazz – short for bazooka – because he had a secret stash of military hardware at home.

'Did I get anything right, according to your rules for DULL99 FM?' He reaches across and pulls the sheet of paper out from under my hand.

'A couple of things. You didn't tell a joke where the implied punchline was the word "spastic" and "first album ever bought with your own money" was okay. It's the one time we'd be giving the same answer.' Rumours, Fleetwood Mac.

'Yeah.' It's not a fact he seems inclined to bond over. He looks up from the page. 'Do you see a lot of these Q&As when they publish them? Musos do them all the time, and they always get that question.' He stands the page on its end and taps it on the table. It's a gesture vicars use in English movies when they're about to give a sermon in an ancient cold church. 'I still don't expect it when they go "Jagged Little Pill" or something like that. My first thought, every time, is "Why didn't you buy a record before then?" and then I realise it's because they were a child. They're twenty-eight now, they were eleven then. Jagged Little Pill. It's other people's first records that really date you, not your own. When did you buy it? Rumours?'

'Grade nine. 1977.'

I had no need to buy music, since it came home all the time in my father's car, but Rumours was one I wanted the complete rights to – the right to keep it in my room, the right to play it there whenever I chose, the right not to have it treated as common household property.

'How about that? We're the same age. I'm like your evil twin in some alternaverse where they don't have frontal lobes, or wherever it is the managerial bits of your brain are. And here we are, combined age closing in on the century, keeping the wheels turning at SPIN.' He flicks the sheet of paper back across to me. 'Where do you reckon it's going, all this, when you're not sweating the small stuff?'

'I'm still trying to work that out. I haven't even talked to the content director yet, so . . .'

I've given no sense of direction so far – not to Brian or anyone else at the station. I've played Whac-a-Mole with any emerging problem, but I haven't lined the team all up in a room and talked vision. I need a little more clarity about BDK's plans first. I'm not going to start out lying.

'So, next week, then,' Brian says, shepherding me towards some kind of commitment. 'I think people want to know. We can't guess if there are big plans or, you know, sackings, cost-cutting, poaching from other stations . . . People have taken other jobs because they don't know what's going to happen here.'

'Yeah. I . . .' I owe him something not completely dishonest.

'So, what's the plan? Are you buffing this new network of yours up for a trade sale, or are memories short enough to let you have a crack at an IPO?'

He looks right at me, with no less focus than Robyn might show as her scalpel's about to slice an arc around a lesion. He's watching for my tell. I'm trying to suppress fifty moves that might look like one, and trying not to lurch into a massive facial tick as any muscle at random rebels against the order for supreme stillness. I was never a poker player.

'Ha,' he says, and then smiles. 'I know you're never going to tell me that. Not today anyway.'

'I *can* tell you I'm out of that loop now.' In Sydney, whatever plans there might be are probably already one step or two or three ahead of me. I don't know the exit strategy, other than to be certain that there is one. 'It's no secret that BDK doesn't hold onto anything forever, but their smartest course of action is to make this station and the network the best that it can be – to help it do well and run well.' That's the hypertext link to any job losses, if he wants to take it. 'Whatever the long-term plans, they're contingent on SPIN working out.'

I've taken it to the brink of management speak but not beyond that. And I don't think I've said completely nothing, something my last job encouraged me to hone as a skill.

He drinks a mouthful of coffee and brings his left hand to the side of the mug as he sets it back on the table.

'That's nice,' he says, 'but kind of abstract.' He gives the mug a series of small absent-minded turns, like a safe-breaker getting used to the feel of a lock. 'Fifty this year, hey? It's an interesting move coming back here, leaving the world of high finance for low radio. But I guess you could do a lot of different things if this goes to shit. Management's management. Me? Low radio's my thing and beyond that there's only so long I can get by on my rugged good looks.' This conversation is full of tests. He's forever dipping the pole into the water and tapping for the bottom. 'Anyway . . .' He throws his arms up, in a bigger gesture than he needs. 'Dazz and I bombed our My Kitchen Rules audition and the Blue Man Group turned me down on the basis of my nude shot. Too hairy.'

'You had to send a nude shot to the Blue Man Group?' I have a feeling I'm again playing straight man to a line he's spinning. Hands and heads – that's as far as the blue goes any time I picture the Blue Man Group.

'I didn't *have* to. I just thought . . .' He shrugs. 'I figured they'd want to see what they'd be making blue if they ever decided to ramp it up a bit. Now, I need some sustenance.'

With one hand on the back of the chair and the other on the table, he pushes himself to his feet. He rummages around in his pocket and feeds a handful of loose change into the slot at the side of the craniofacial kiddies' box, which I badly need to start thinking of as the 'charity box' or any other semi-respectable name. He peels open a Twix and bites the ends of both fingers.

'Oh, sorry,' he says, spitting crumbs. 'I should've . . .' He points to the two Twix fingers and then to me. 'Except that's not how you're handling fifty, is it?' He holds one hand near his mouth, since that makes it okay to talk through biscuit and chocolate. He makes himself swallow. There's something he wants to say. 'Mate, you want to be scared how quickly things go off the boil. Go to Wikipedia and put in the name of any one-hit wonder you can think of from the eighties. Not one of them just lay down and died. Or cashed in, invested brilliantly and laughed ever since. They pretty much all settled for twenty-five years of grim petering out, still chasing the dream. Each one of them has just put out their twenty-third album, now independently, and is managed by their second or third wife or husband, who started out as a borderline crazy fan who mailed them panties.' He pushes the ends of the Twix fingers further out of the packet. 'They've still got ambition, you know. However quixotic some of us might think that is. And some of them might even be doing their best work, despite the fact that next to nobody's bothering to listen.'

'It can't be all bad news.' I don't want him to be right. It's a picture of failure I could have laughed at once. 'What about Santana coming out with Supernatural?' It's the best I've got. 'And Brian Austin Green played a nerd on 90210, then he vanished for a decade and reappeared with a new show and Megan Fox.'

'Here's what I reckon,' he says, Twix now gripped in his hand like a fuse. 'You think our ratings – which I accept are a bit shit – are the problem, and I'm part of the problem. I don't know what you're planning but, whatever it is, it's some fancy finance thing. It's not radio. At some point, you fuckers need to pause before buying more radio stations and look at what they actually are. And what prospects they have. You need to work out what they might be next. Someone needs to take their eyes off the IPO and do that. We are on a train heading full speed for a brick wall labelled "the future" and we need a way through it or a way over it. Digital might be that, but it won't end up as commercial radio as we know it. By the time Gangnam Style clocked up its billionth YouTube view on the day the Mayan calendar ended, those views alone added up to fifty million hours of lost radio listening. I did the maths. Music is everywhere, on every device smarter than your toaster.'

The heat from his hand has melted the chocolate from the Twix, and it's now smeared along his index finger. He lifts his hand to lick it, then computes the cost to conversational momentum, sets the Twix down and holds the hand out to the side, as if he's hoping that chocolate on skin might air dry to nothing.

'So how do we bundle it up in a way that makes people want it from *us*?' he says, not for a second pausing to wait for the answer we both know I don't have. 'What is it, from the kerbillions of options they have, that makes them ask *us* to make their music choices? 'Cause we're not winning it with our wit and our interviews any more. If they want comedy, they can podcast Gervais and Merchant for nothing, exactly when they want to. If they want interviews, why wait for me to talk to some semi-famous semi-random schmuck when you're three clicks away from Alec Baldwin interviewing Chris Rock? Alec Fucking Baldwin, Ricky Fucking Gervais and all the music ever recorded on tap on Pandora or Xbox Music or Last.fm – that's what we're up against. Not Mix and Triple M and all that shit. You come up with the marketing spend and we can beat *them*. We can compete. But I haven't worked out yet how we compete with the future. Which, by the way, has already arrived.' He licks his lower lip and the skin beneath, picking up some lost chocolate that had landed there like a jazz dot. 'Just a thought.'

24

SO, BRIAN'S PUT HIS cards on the table. Or quietly backed in a truck and tipped out a high rollers' room worth of cards, aces and queens and red sevens piling up in front of me to around eye level as I've clutched my hand to my chest.

Obsolescence isn't owned by one-hit wonders and the crass heroes of yesterday's radio, or the medium itself. It's more suburban, less dramatic, entirely more common than the way he tells it.

Before I leave the station I check some of the figures again.

On the strength of low-level TV infamy and sporadic weekend shows in comedy clubs, Brian's hanging on to several thousand interstate fans who are streaming the Breakfast Bar. We can't even tell our advertisers because the advertisers are all local and they'll come away convinced we're charging them for listeners they can sell nothing to.

I take a look at the websites of SPIN's stations in Sydney and Melbourne. When we start to network some shows, whether it's breakfast or drive or anything else, Brian's the one Brisbane presenter who counts nationally and who could be pitched to the network as part of any team. But that thought lasts about a minute before I picture him the way they will, as a grisly grey radio rogue who peaked in the days of guessing the secret sound.

This part of the process isn't new for me. Between the numbers that came in at the start and the numbers I put out at the end, BDK jobs always had a time when I needed to pull the lid off the black box and square up to the people. I had to look them in the eye and tally a rough sum of their parts – their shortcomings, their great ideas that had never found the ear of management, their will to keep turning up, their transgressions and fears and at least some of their less deep secrets, the buried bodies of their past mistakes, their high hopes and hubris and the windmills still awaiting their charge. I had to estimate them, and their value to the business, and then, almost always, I had to let some go.

Our afternoons host, Trevor Hempstead, does nothing wrong all the way home. He plays it safer than Brian and Dazz, but he's a pro in his own way. He's steady.

Parked outside our house, with its sliding door open and Robyn dragging a suitcase towards it, is a multicoloured campervan with Jimi Hendrix's head airbrushed in black, white and grey on its side, plate-sized eyes closed in mid-riff ecstasy. An entire Jimi Hendrix on the same scale would tower over the street, his grey flares beating at the canopies of the poinciana trees as he strode by. To remove all doubt about his identity, his name is airbrushed curling out from his ear, in a font with a groovy late-sixties feel, along with the words, 'Are you experienced,' followed by three black question marks.

I pull up in the driveway and call out to Robyn to let her know I'll finish the loading.

She tilts the suitcase upright and pushes hair out of her eyes.

'It's okay,' she says. 'This is the last one. Then there's just April's when we get to school.' She puts her hands on her hips and turns towards the van, giving it the look she'd give a band moving in next door. 'Your dad's pretty proud of himself. He's already calling it Jimi.'

★ ★ ★

My father, who I thought would jump at the chance to ride shotgun, insists on sitting behind me on the drive to the school, with a battered Gladstone bag at his feet and a broad grin full of the best moments of ancient and modern times and the alchemy he's pulled off to make them happen simultaneously. He rests his mottled forearm, chipped and flaked with sun damage from too much driving like this, along the base of the open window, his fingernails tapping without any rhythm. The wind whips in as we go, tossing around his platinum lion's mane and the collar of his Hawaiian shirt. He's as happy as a kelpie in the back of a ute.

The van has airconditioning, but airconditioning is not what this drive to the coast is about. Robyn, her window wound to the top, is over the romance of seventies non–climate-controlled travel already.

My father has a second bag on the seat next to him and from it he draws a long tangled flex, which turns out to be connected to his iPad. With one hand guarding his stoma, he leans forward and pushes the free end of the flex across the console between the front seats.

'There's a port for that on the dashboard,' he says to one or both of us.

'Oh, right.' Robyn picks the connector up and scans the dashboard.

Jimi Hendrix is fitted out more like a space shuttle than a van from the seventies. It has ports for more devices than even we own, plus a Navman, a toll token, windows tinted dark enough for the CIA, a concealed bar fridge and about forty-two more cupholders than I remember us having in the old days, when the only cupholder was the human hand.

'Next to the MP3 one,' my father tells her, but I know it won't do any good.

'When we're not moving,' Robyn says, putting on a motion-sick face.

At the next set of traffic lights, he directs us to the right port, almost resorting to calling out, 'Warmer, warmer, colder, colder,' to get us there.

'Random,' he says and, just as I'm thinking it's a summary of our efforts, Racey starts playing loudly from the van's speakers. 'I've got some good stuff on there. Let's see what it picks.'

Racey is still booming out as I ease Jimi Hendrix into a parking spot among the black four-wheel drives ganged up outside the school. Parents, mostly mothers of children younger than ours, are in their cars or standing around in capri pants and designer school pick-up shoes, chatting with each other or checking their phones. Or, more and more, staring in our direction and sizing up the dubious Jimi Hendrix. One of them tilts her phone and, nowhere near as surreptitiously as she means to, takes a photo of our number plate.

'People who know us are looking at us like we have weed,' Robyn says.

'Ha.' My father cackles from the back. 'Makes you want to roll one just to see what they'd do then.'

Perhaps the very same thing happened in the seventies, when he pulled up outside my school in our old van. The other parents and their responses are a complete blank to me. The students, though, saw that garishly painted combi with boards on top and bedding in the back, and they pictured surf movies and famous music festivals that none of us had been to, and a better kind of freedom than their weekends could hope to hold. It was a cooler exit than I ever let my parents know.

'I'm not getting out,' Robyn says, retreating to the 'I' part of her introvert-extrovert spectrum, no doubt coming across my footprints there by the hundred. 'I don't want to get into this. Just don't play any drug songs, Casey, okay?'

As students surge through the gates, a wave of hats and bags and limbs at all angles, I'm the one who gets out to pull the sliding door open. A mother I've met a few times, but have no chance of naming, recognises me and laughs as if the van's okay now and not occupied by roaming child stealers. She waves, then points at Jimi Hendrix, tilts her head and screws her eyes up quizzically, turning most of her body into a middle-class-shaped question she seems not to want to put into words.

'My dad's a fan,' I tell her.

My father leans across the interior of the van and gives a half-wave half-salute.

The tide of children hits the cars, conversations break out, doors start slamming. The mother has a teenage son who towers over her and a daughter years younger. We're ignored as soon as they arrive.

'This?' Abi says when she turns up with April. She stops a few steps away from the van, taking it all in. She laughs. 'This is how we're getting to the coast? Cool. It's got wi-fi, right?'

She and April drop their bags and snap a few quick selfies, arms around each other, with their free hands doing peace signs. They race each other to post them on Facebook.

Jack wanders up, a crumpled smile on his face at the sight of Jimi Hendrix, his wide-brimmed school hat pushed way back on his head so that it appears to be hovering there like a marauding flying saucer. He flips the hat through the back door onto the bags, slips off his blazer, pulls off his tie and climbs inside, claiming the added seat next to the luggage as if we do this every weekend.

Abi gets in next to my father, with the boost of the middle seat making her tower even more comically over April. They sit almost primly with their hats in their laps and their ties still on as we pull out from the kerb and U-turn, heading for the coast.

Soon they're swivelling cup holders in and out, opening the bar fridge and clicking any button they can find. They flick through the playlist or range of playlists on my father's iPad and decide on a music-related quiz where they appear to make up the rules as they go along. The essence of it seems to be selecting a song that allows you to one-up the rest of us with your knowledge of a dazzling but obscure related fact.

Abi plays the Beach Boys's Good Vibrations and gives me half a point for naming the theremin as the instrument making the sci-fi soundtrack noise. Apparently it was an electro-theremin or, as she corrects herself, *the* electro-theremin. Only one was ever made.

Robyn chooses Soft Cell's Tainted Love and then can't think of a question. 'Oh, okay,' she says, 'this is all I've got. Who was the lead singer?'

Jack groans and says, 'Seriously? Marc Almond. Marc with a "C".'

April takes her turn at the iPad, says, 'Right,' and starts skimming through the choices. 'Okay, okay, I think I've got one. There's a connection to the last one. Slight connection. I think.' T-Rex's Children of the Revolution starts to play. 'It's to do with the lead singers.'

'Both dead?' Abi tries. 'Except Marc Almond's not dead, I don't think.'

If Brian was here, he could fill in his version of the details – the massive hit, the descent that followed, the years of fighting not to peter out, the reunion tour playing to thousands of forty-year-olds, the wife-husband-partner who mailed panties and now runs the show. Marc Almond may well have managed three decades of songs every bit as good as Tainted Love, but they didn't break through in the same way, and now teenage girls in vans are speculating about his death.

'Ha,' Jack calls out from the back. 'They both spelt Marc with a "C".'

'That's it,' April says, sounding happy about it. Happy perhaps that her turn is over and that her fact of choice took at least some work to unearth.

In the rearview mirror, I can see her holding the iPad up, waiting for the next player to take it. The afternoon sunlight hits her black ponytail, making it gleam.

My children, coasting through this game on facts gleaned mostly from their grandfather's vast mental archive of western music, don't stop for a moment to consider April's feat with her two Marcs. One of her grandfathers never left Saigon. The other speaks English in the way I speak German, half pointing, half basic nouns. I met him the one time I dropped her off at her house. He walked with a stick because of an old fracture and he had no front teeth.

Jack declares it's his turn, but the iPad cord doesn't reach.

'It's okay,' he says. 'I know what's on there. I've got a double play. Could somebody find them for me?' April hands the iPad to Abi. Jack assumes someone has it and keeps going. 'So, the question is, what's the connection between the songs? You can buzz in as soon as the second song starts. Grandad's not allowed.'

The first song is Bruce Springsteen's Fire and, as it's fading, he asks Abi to find Patti Smith's Because the Night.

'Ooh, ooh,' she says as she's flicking around looking for it. 'Bzzz. Bzzz.' The song begins. 'Springsteen wrote or co-wrote them both.'

'Correct,' Jack announces. 'And something extra for a bonus point?'

I don't have it. Robyn doesn't have it.

'I didn't know Springsteen wrote them both,' Robyn says. 'I've got no chance.'

'Grandad?' Jack's voice calls out from the back.

'Springsteen wrote them both . . .' my father says, building up to his shot at the bonus point. In the mirror I can tell he's got it. '*On the same day.*'

This is what I'm home for. The three generations of us, making sport of something, inventing a game and rolling with it. This is my reward for bailing from BDK. I hadn't pictured it would first come here, on the southeast freeway, while I was piloting the land shuttle Jimi Hendrix, beating the peak-hour traffic to the coast.

'You're loving the van, aren't you?' Robyn says to me, in a way that suggests she's not loving the van. Because the Night hits the chorus one more time. 'Loving the whole seventies flashback. People in other cars are looking at us, you know.'

She wants me to understand that, at a certain level, she feels the need to frown upon the whole caper – the van, the ugly Crystal Tydes, no doubt the minding of Brian Brightman that triggered the plan in the first place. In the seventies I never drove the van, the seats were cracked vinyl that needed a towel to make them bearable and the AM radio signal gave out less than halfway to the coast. What I happen to be loving is not the van but a brand new experience, a moment that couldn't be designed or faked but has just been given to me, without anyone else appearing wise to it.

★ ★ ★

It's perfect for a full five minutes before a dog yaps. My father clears his throat in a lame attempt to cover it. He warily opens the Gladstone bag and Winston forces his head out, slurping my father's hand.

'I thought you were sorting something out with the neighbours.' I'm sounding parental with my own father.

Abi bends down to pat Winston's head and says, 'Hey, Winnie,' sounding not at all surprised that he's there.

'You were going to make plans for one of the neighbours to look after him.' Parental did nothing, so now I'm going for whiny. The website made it clear that pets aren't allowed at Crystal Tydes.

'Yes, well,' my father says steadily. 'He's off his food a bit and he's constipated. Plus, I need to clean his rope daily.'

'Don't you have more than one rope?'

'His rope's the bit that goes over the nose. It's part of him.' He points it out on himself, looking at me in the mirror. It's as if he's applying invisible zinc cream to his face. 'Moisture accumulates and it can get infected. Also his tail, which is unusually curly. I have to put some ointment there.'

Winston's head appears in the mirror between my father's knees. He's pushed himself further out of the bag.

'What? We have to bring him with us because there's some medical need for you to apply ointment to his unusually curly tail? How do we even have bulldogs in the world? How did natural selection not knock them on the head a million years ago, before they had staff?'

'I didn't even mention the hip dysplasia. Everything else is . . .' He waves his hand around dismissively. 'But he takes treats straight from your mouth. How could you not love him? No one'll notice him.'

'Really? Because every time he barks you're going to cough like that?'

'We can take turns,' Jack calls out from the back. 'I'm cool with that. And we can mix it up a bit too.'

He howls, like a wolf at the moon.

'But we'll be going out to eat.' In the mirror, Winston is fixing me with a boggle-eyed stare. 'He'll be locked up in the unit, and you think he's not going to bark? Also, someone's going to come and service the room.'

'Service the room?' My father reaches a hand out to scratch Winston's head. 'It's a grotty Gold Coast unit that spells tides with a "Y". When did they start servicing rooms? Anyway, we'll get him in and out in the bag. It already worked to get him past you. And I'll tell the café people he's a registered assistance dog. He picks things up for me.' He pats his shirt front. 'And I'll say I'll lose my bowels into my bag if they make me do it myself.'

This time it's April I notice in the mirror, glancing at the Gladstone bag nervously as though my father might have some way of spurting his bowels down there to make his point.

★ ★ ★

'Hey, this is like the Amazing Race,' Abi says as Robyn and I debate the wisdom or otherwise of the Navman's recommendation about our turn-off from the highway.

I'm backing 'otherwise'. Robyn can never say no to advice from a gadget, especially one with a superhero name and access to satellites.

'Robyn and Andrew, Long-distance Couple,' Jack calls through from the back in a clipped high-energy narrator summary. It's a badge we'll wear all series, the text on the screen any time we're stuck doing aimless laps of a Paris roundabout or gagging on dried grasshoppers in a Bangkok market.

In the mirror, I can see the back of his head, with the road receding behind him. It looks as if a lifesize puppet of a teenage boy is part of our luggage.

'What footage are we watching the first time we see them?' Abi says. 'Skype call. Mum in the kitchen, Dad a mess of pixels with a voice like a criminal doing a TV interview.' She puts on a warped electronic voice. 'Well, hello everyone.'

April laughs and nudges her.

The Amazing Race is a show we've tried to share while I've been away. It was part of the deal we struck. We all tried to watch it, wherever we were. It gave us something to deconstruct on our Skype calls, in a normal way, as normal as Skype allows. Each week, they'd have to do nothing more than turn on the TV. If I was in Sydney I could do the same. If I was away it took more imagination. In China, I couldn't even download it or go to most of the online forums.

Not even I made the mistake of persisting with that one. It's one thing to be busted at a Brisbane radio station googling an alleged penile disorder – finding a way around the mighty Chinese firewall to download forbidden TV would take a lot more fixing. I can just imagine the Foreign Minister having to weigh in on my behalf, pleading that the pair of ex-Harlem Globetrotters had finished last the week before on a non-elimination leg, so how could I *not* watch as they tried to fight their way back from the rear of the field with no cash on the unfriendly streets of La Paz?

So I fudged it all too often, like the semi-detached member of a book club who's in it for the mid-week drinking and pizza and two hours away from the kids, but who wings the book chat on a close reading of the blurb and a scan through the relevant Wikipedia entry to see if Mister Darcy lives or dies or gets brutally wasted on laudanum or ends up as anyone notable's one true love.

Jack continues his narration. 'He's a fly-in/fly-out number cruncher . . .'

Abi paints the picture. 'Footage of Dad in a big factory, holding a spreadsheet and frowning, working out who he's got to sack . . .'

'It's always the sackings.' The way it comes out of me, it sounds like the sort of protest that should be preceded or followed by me saying 'oy, vey'. 'You people have no idea . . .'

'She's healing the sick,' Jack says, in the reverential tones used for a person waist-deep in good works.

'Mum in a white coat, taking a little old lady's blood pressure.'

They're ignoring me. Robyn's noble, I'm an evil capitalist and they live unappreciatively in a castle that must have been built by luck or the kindness of strangers. I could sit them down and take them through it company by company and show them – no, prove to them – that it's not about the sackings. And then, in the weeks ahead, restructure SPIN and have to let some people go.

Sometimes when I was away, I'd find myself somewhere changing planes, running out of chances to get up to date with the Amazing Race. I'd be with a couple of the others from BDK and we'd get to the lounge, flip open our laptops to suck up some free wi-fi and they'd be typing at speed, batting back emails, while I'd be sitting there wondering how Gay Father and Son had got it so wrong and been eliminated, when the previous week they'd been the only team able to spell Chekhov.

We all liked Gay Father and Son. They were people like us, with the exception of being a gay father and son, and the son happening to have written the Jack Black movie School of Rock. Maybe our CVs and theirs didn't exactly overlap, but we could imagine them having dinner at our place. That was a designated topic: team who would most fit in at dinner at our place.

Favourite team was a different matter. Our favourite teams are Hillbillies and Stunt Dwarves. Hillbillies appear semi-regularly on the Amazing Race, though not usually for long each series. Hillbillies have grown up in a life characterised by third-hand hats and no dental care, and not one life skill that works outside the Ozarks, while stunt dwarves muscle their way into everything without fear. They're usually wiped within two episodes of the Hillbillies.

Our least favourite is any team with a roid rager, since we're not fans of partner abuse.

Least regarded? Number one candidate: Grandma and Granddaughter. Wisdom can be baggage on that show. Grandmas take their eye off the prize, take in the view and give far too many pats on the back for shit. Grandmas take familial pride in multiple generations' worth of being a bit crap, and they take personal pride in simply not being dead yet. Please try harder.

Number two candidate: Soccer Moms. Grandmas in the making, but a pair of them. Way too many high-fives for mediocrity. Far too much inclination to award participation medals and no idea it's actually about winning. No idea what winning is.

'Teams have to navigate their way to a condemned strip mall,' Jack goes on in his narrator voice. 'No, make that, retro apartment block to find their next clue.'

'Cue footage of Long-distance Couple arguing about the sat nav,' Abi says, 'then finding themselves down a dead-end backroad in the dark.'

I can visualise it. I know I could make that happen.

I cave and go with the Navman, since that puts us all back on the same side and, more importantly, means that I won't be carrying the can for any errors. The audience groans. They'd been hoping for drama.

Winston, who has been sleeping on the floor, wakes from a twitchy dream and immediately starts humping April's shoe.

'Ah, Abs,' she says, squirming and inadvertently dragging him across the floor. 'I see something pink. I think he's having sex with my foot.'

'Always pushing the lipstick where the lipstick don't go,' Jack shouts from the back.

My father stirs. It's possible he was dozing. He instinctively leans forward, Robyn shouts for him to stop, April shrieks, Abi shouts at Winston. For about ten seconds, I'm the only mammal in the car not shouting or rooting something.

Then it's over. Winston's been flipped from April's foot and has his legs in the air, his tongue lolling out and his penis back in. Soon he's asleep again, as is my father. And then snoring, both of them, in a chorus of snuffles and whistles.

'I think that's a D minor chord,' April says, intending it for Abi's ears alone. She leans across her, closer to my father. 'It's coming from your grandfather's nose.'

Abi puts one hand over her mouth to stop herself laughing, and shoves April with the other. 'Don't.'

25

WHEN WE PULL UP OUTSIDE, Crystal Tydes looks no more nor less appealing than the pictures on the website.

I open the back door to free Jack, and he steps out wearing Converse sneakers, skinny black jeans, a white T-shirt and a red silk smoking jacket. Somehow, without me noticing a thing, he has managed a complete wardrobe change during the drive.

As he slides out with a loose-limbed al dente ease I can only envy, the side door jerks open and Abi tackles Winston in mid-escape. His tongue, rope and bulging eyes make it into daylight before she yanks him back inside and joins my father in a loud and clumsy attempt to stuff him back into the Gladstone bag, with Winston barking exuberantly the whole time. As he's clipping the bag shut, my father remembers to cough. At the rear of the van, Jack tilts his head back and howls at the sky.

The side door slides fully open and Abi leans out looking so innocent she might whistle.

'I've got an idea,' I tell them. 'Why don't you all just wait here until I can get a house-sized helium balloon with the word "dog" on it and tie it to his collar. Then we can smuggle him in.'

'I think the worst of it's behind us,' my father's voice says from inside.

Fortunately the mock-orange hedge has grown enough to hide the pantomime from any ground-level eyes in Crystal Tydes, and that includes the manager's unit.

The office door opens onto a balcony one step up from the grass and covered with olive and dusky yellow tiles. Rust has bubbled under the bronze paint on the wrought-iron railings. There's a white plastic table with faded red-wine rings on it and a plastic chair with a plump cushion.

'Hello,' a male voice calls out from inside, in an accent that sounds South African.

I hear chair castors roll over vinyl and a man appears in the doorway. He's sixty or so and over-tanned, wearing frayed grey shorts and a faded blue VB singlet.

'Dave,' he says, reaching his hand out to shake. 'Welcome. Is it Andrew? Two units for Andrew?'

The office has racks of brochures for theme parks and scenic flights and glow-worm tours, and two rows of key hooks on the wall. He has the keys for our units ready on a desk blotter. His office chair is at the edge of a hard clear-plastic mat, two of its castors nudging the grey carpet. The room smells of old sweat and the incense he's been burning in front of a small Buddha on the bookshelf.

He pushes the keys to one side of the blotter and checks details on a sheet of paper.

'Oh, yeah,' he says. 'Have you got a contact number?'

I pull my phone out to check it, since it must be on there somewhere.

'It's a new phone,' I tell him, fiddling around in the hope that I'll stumble upon the number. I could offer him a contact latitude, but that's not much use until I can find a longitude app as well.

'No problem.' He laughs. 'You can check with your wife and get back to me. I bet she knows it.' He leans to one side to look out the window. There's nothing out there but carpet grass and hedge. 'Two units, hey?'

'It's a family trip. We've got my father with us.' And his stupid high-maintenance dog. 'They're at the . . . car. Cars. I've got a work thing on, and . . .'

'Oh, yeah.' He seems interested in the work thing, in the imprecise way holiday unit managers can be. They're people people, or supposed to be.

We are about to begin a pointless five-minute chat, no doubt his stock-in-trade, and I have led us there. Robyn wouldn't have done that. She wouldn't have tripped into a feeble don't-mention-the-dog over-share about work. Meanwhile, back at the van, her awesome arsenal of conversational skills goes untested.

Dave asks, as the five-minute conversation requires, what line of work I'm in and, for the first time ever, I say, 'Radio,' which instantly feels like misrepresentation. 'I'm behind the scenes. I'm here for the Australian Comedy Awards. One of our presenters is part of the event. Brian Brightman.'

'Brian Brightman, hey?' It would be wrong to look for anything positive in the tone. He glances at my face, with plenty ready to say about Brian. His eyes are blue, but a flat faded blue, as if the sun's taken the life out of them as well as his clothes. 'And you're the minder, are you?'

'Something like that.'

'That's got to have its moments.' He scoops up the keys from the blotter. 'Two sets for each unit. Hope that's enough 'cause it's all we've got.'

He takes me on a tour of the keys, three to each ring, and runs through his usual routine. Somewhere after the part about washing sand off feet before entering the pool area, my attention wanders and doesn't make it back until he's well into a lament about the civil war in Rhodesia and how badly the British betrayed Ian Smith.

It turns out my gaze has come to rest on a framed black-and-white photo of the farm that once belonged to Dave's family but was seized by the Mugabe government in the eighties. I have at the most a scratchy grasp of Zimbabwean politics, and decide it's best to nod until we exit the rabbit hole.

Out at the van, Robyn will be checking her watch, Winston will be gagging on the manky air inside the Gladstone bag, and everyone else will be wandering into the traffic looking for wi-fi.

The photo is in a living room just beyond a waist-high wall that creates a separation between Dave's office and the flat. Next to it is one of a series of tapestries garish enough to frighten a child, but with frames suggesting complete sincerity. They turn out to be the work of his late wife.

He points to the nearest and says, 'That one's the Mona Lisa,' only semi-redundantly, as he could also have said it was a pale chimp with Bell's palsy in a blue dress.

'Better get the family in, hey,' he says, pressing a Crystal Tydes fridge magnet into my hands on top of the pile of keys. 'And I won't blow your cover, but if you wouldn't mind telling Mr Brightman that family's the word around here – if you get what I mean . . .'

I find myself nodding and saying, 'Sure,' because that's what his body language and his tone both call for, and because I need the conversation to end. Enough Zimbabwe, enough of the stitch-by-numbers assault on the old masters.

I'm halfway back to the van before I work out that he thinks Brian's staying here, and I'm trying to keep it a secret.

26

THE FIRST THING ROBYN does when I unlock the unit is stand in the doorway scanning the living area and kitchen, putting together an inventory of their shortcomings.

The cook top, even from this distance, looks like it might have an early bloom of rust, and there are three whimsical ceramic fish rising up the kitchen wall in decreasing sizes. Above them is a clock with its hands stuck on quarter past eleven. The living area has a glass-topped dining table poked impractically into one corner and all the furniture is beach-typical cane with bright swirly fabric. The coffee table and TV cabinet are big and heavy and in the Balinese style, with one cabinet door adrift from its upper hinges. On top of a small cane hutch next to the cabinet sits a lamp with a base the shape of a nautilus, spray-painted gold.

The room is the result of three distinct shopping sprees to discount furniture retailers over the past twenty years. It doesn't add up in a way that could be called tasteful or even consistent, but it's true enough to the website photos and there's nothing here that could give anyone a disease.

'You can't complain about the view,' Robyn says, determined that the first note hit should be positive.

The van won't fit in a parking bay, so it stays out on the street, with a complicated relay running luggage into Crystal Tydes. Among that organised chaos, a bulldog in a Gladstone bag goes unnoticed.

Soon enough, Robyn is struggling to work out the coffee machine, Abi and April are shrieking at a huntsman spider they've found in their room, and I'm trying to sneak in a piriformis stretch on a saggy foam cushion while checking there are no work emails needing urgent action. That is, it's already almost exactly the weekend I pictured whenever my view wasn't clouded by wild optimism.

'Did we bring the right coffee?' Robyn says behind me, clunking plastic parts together noisily. The coffee machine's a dripolator, and I know she's not a fan. 'You're meeting Brian at a coffee shop, right?'

'Yeah, at his hotel.' I can see where it's going, one of my worlds swinging towards another's orbit. 'It's just a quick catch-up to make sure everything's on track. I'll be back –'

She cuts me off. 'It wouldn't kill us to have coffee somewhere actually nice. I mean, don't think I'm not loving the nostalgia but . . . do you think they ever clean this?'

When I turn around, she has the stained plastic filter holder in one hand and a glass coffee pot opaque with limescale in the other. Exhibits A and B. I can't deny that the inside of the filter holder is a lot browner than the outside. Plus I forgot to bring coffee. Plus filter coffee seems to make her angry. All I've got to offer her is four sachets of sugar and an insanitary machine designed to make a beverage she doesn't want.

As she stands there making her point, she looks even more like Tina Fey than usual.

* * *

Jack's in the loungeroom when I arrive next door, smoking jacket swishing around him like a pimp or a dancer, or a dancing pimp. From the bookcase beside the TV cabinet, he's pulled a pile of fat paperbacks so old and breeze-worn that the edges of their pages are coloured somewhere between caramel and rust.

'Dad, check it out,' he says excitedly, picking one up and jiggling it around in front of me. The cover features a familiar massive shark launching itself vertically at a tiny human swimming freestyle. 'Nipples . . .'

'Twice, yeah.' I take the book from him, as much as anything to stop it shedding pages. 'Apparently to most people it's a story about a big fish. But you and I know better.'

My father's standing in the hall that leads to the bedrooms, staring down at his toes and unwrapping a fresh stick of Extra gum. He offers me the packet when he sees me. It's Cool Breeze flavour.

'Look at that,' he says, reaching out with his toe. There seems to be a gap of about a centimetre between the wall and the floor. 'It must be sand below here. When your mother and I built, they went all the way down till they hit rock. Twenty-three feet in one corner.'

This is the crew I'm rounding up for coffee with Brian, or at least coffee near Brian.

I try telling Jack he'll be too hot with the smoking jacket on, but he insists on keeping it, assuring me that natural fibres breathe.

Next I try telling Abi and April that they'll be too cold in the implausibly short skirts they've changed into, and Abi says they can borrow Jack's jacket if they have to.

* * *

Obsidian stands a block inland, a black chisel forty storeys high. Already its shadow is falling past Crystal Tydes and onto the beach.

Its forecourt is a sweep of dark grey cobbles with a portico marked by gold columns and dark glass doors through which only the glow of chandelier bulbs can be seen in clusters, like planes in a hazy night sky lining up to land.

The foyer is dominated by a huge shard of tortured black glass on a central plinth, with a brass plaque reading 'Obsidian', and nothing more, as if the attention span of the guests is unlikely to extend to a second word. The forest of gold columns outside extends into the foyer, but I can't see Brian or any other comedian I recognise among them. The coffee shop, Lava, is over to our left, with staff dressed in black – or perhaps obsidian – taking orders at the counter, between the coffee machine and a glass cabinet full of cakes and slices.

I shepherd our group over before too much random dispersal occurs and ask what everyone's having.

When it's Jack's turn he says, 'Just a Red Bull and the password for the free wi-fi, thanks.'

I send him off to get Abi's and April's orders while I take my place in the queue. Meanwhile, Robyn pulls two tables together in a far corner and my father wanders about like the Duke of Edinburgh, hands clasped behind his back, head off in a sky-high idea.

No one in Lava looks anything like our party of six. The men are in polo shirts and deck shoes, the women are wearing their everyday pearls. Several older pairs of eyes follow Jack across the room, trying to place him in pictures they've seen of boy bands or other showy teens. The watchers are safely decades into the invisible age, though, so he won't notice them.

He picks a different way back through the tables, fiddling with his iPad as he walks. When he arrives, he clicks from the Smurf village to the Lava website, and slides the cursor across to the log-in box.

'So the smurfberry hunt continues . . .'

He glances around. 'Who told you about that?'

'I've got my sources.'

'I don't actually use them. The smurfberries.' He frowns and hugs the iPad so that the screen presses into the front of his smoking jacket.

'I know you don't use them.' I don't even know what using them means – I could take a guess that Smurfs make pies from them – but that doesn't stop me attempting to deliver the line like Jethro Gibbs in NCIS or Horatio Caine in CSI Miami, as if I've seen it all a thousand times and am wise to the whole caper.

'Look, it's legit.' He swallows. I actually see his adam's apple bob up and down. 'At least, semi-legit.'

He rattles off an explanation that could really do with a whiteboard. Robyn might be imagining smurfberries as the new century's version of stickers or salty plums, but Jack has found an app that allows them to be traded for a coupon that he then exchanges for a mainstream gift voucher, which he takes to a credit-swap website to convert into Umart credit.

'I guess the people who buy the berries from me are selling them somewhere and undercutting the market,' he says, 'but I don't have anything to do with that.'

We shuffle a step forward in the queue.

Who's he dealing with out there? Whatever I said to Robyn, I'd still been hoping for a safe simple answer, and what Jack's told me isn't that. I can't picture who would run a smurfberry racket. Well, I can – some app-happy kid out to make a buck, but he's quickly pushed out of the frame by the Russian mafia, Chechen arms dealers and anyone else who might be extremely violent and have an interest in laundering money.

There *is* a blackmarket in smurfberries, and Jack's a player. When I signed up to be a parent, this scenario was definitely not in the manual.

'It might be working for now, but I think even you've got doubts about it,' I suggest to him. 'You appear to be operating under an alias.'

He turns around to check the tables and make sure no one else is nearby. 'Okay, I just put "Lambert" the first time and then I had to keep using it,' he says quietly, keeping it barely above a whisper. 'I use a lot of different names on the internet.' He stares at my shirt. 'Everyone does. There was a guy called Lambert who imperson-ated a prince once. I read about it somewhere.'

'Mate.' A hand takes my arm. A hand with big hairy knuckles and a chunky signet ring. It's Brian. 'I'm the first one here, aren't I? You've got to make out like we've been doing business or something. I can't be the first one here.'

He's looking at Jack as if he's a new species – the kooky hair, the Buddy Holly glasses, the op-shop couture. When I introduce them, Jack says the bare minimum, then glances down. It's an instinctive move, but his eyes instantly bug out and he swings his gaze away from Brian's pants with such physical force that his jacket swishes.

I want to tell him the damp spot is practically a trademark. That's what I'm dealing with in this new job.

Once our order's in, I suggest a vacant booth to Brian for the two of us and he says, 'Well, sure, but I should meet the rest of the fam first.' He's spotted them, in a Father Pervy kind of way, and he's leering in their general direction and hitching up his pants. 'You don't have a picture of the little Chinese one on your desk yet, do you? Is she new?'

Jack gives me the kind of look I'd expect if I introduced him to a minotaur. The pants, the general inappropriateness, the left-field assumptions – Brian is several sizes larger than life, and nothing like the regular dull workmates I've brought home in the past. Jack will need to be debriefed later.

Abi and April stay around the other side of the table for the introductions. Brian shakes Robyn's hand and then my father's. My father addresses him as Gopher and he seems to like it.

By the time I've fetched water and glasses, the two of them are deep in a discussion about radio, with Brian nodding deferentially.

'The ABC'll be okay,' my father says confidently, loving the chance to broadcast his views, 'and not just because it's already got the older audience who aren't so distractable.' He nods towards the far end of the table, where Abi and April are texting and Jack is no doubt finessing barrow loads of smurfberries to sell to Somali pirates or al-Qaeda or tiny blue undercover cops from the Smurf village. 'The ABC's got a role to play – they get information out. And they're breaking more state political news than anyone. But commercial?' He shrugs. 'I guess it's converging into something. Or diverging. Who can tell? I can tell you what it won't be. It won't ever be a big walnut box the family gathers around to listen to kings or prime ministers or the latest Benny Goodman record.'

He looks distracted for a moment. Brian's nodding, taking it all in as wisdom from a tribal elder. My father watches his latte as it's set down in front of him. I know the Benny Goodman record. It was my opa's favourite – the Carnegie Hall concert from 1938. Benny Goodman wasn't a name plucked from the air.

I sit in the chair to Brian's left, to put a desleazified zone between him and the kids.

My father glances my way, sips his coffee and leaves a thin line of foam on his upper lip.

'Forty years ago, 9am to midday was the women's session,' he says, 'and now it's politics and breaking news if you're a station with content.' He sets the cup back on the table, but keeps both hands on it. 'And the afternoon presenter would call himself Uncle Whatever, since the kids were listening after school. That'd sound wrong now, wouldn't it? Change is going to kick both your arses about another fifty thousand times, and that's just how it is. People went nuts when Ry Cooder put out Bop Till You Drop.'

Brian looks as though the thread has slipped from his grasp.

It's my turn to chip in. 'First digital album.'

'Good.' My father points to me, as if I've passed a test. 'But there was no use in going nuts. Music was changing anyway, because it always does. Like everything else. Grandmaster Flash was already at work, people were scratching and starting to sample, the word "rap" was about to take on a whole new meaning and we white guys on this side of the Pacific had no idea. No idea.'

He takes another mouthful of coffee, checks his watch, then drinks again.

'Yeah, I guess it's changing all over the shop,' Brian says. 'That's the thing. When I got into radio, it looked like we could just front up and keep playing the Eagles forever.'

'Nothing wrong with the Eagles,' my father says. 'Or Benny Goodman. But I've got to get some . . .' He drinks the last of his coffee, sets his cup down, pulls a scrap of paper from his pocket and checks it. 'Apple cider vinegar. My bulldog's constipated. You can't get it everywhere, but I found a place online that's just near here. Shuts at five though.'

It's quite a feat to go from complete sense, even wisdom, to the blocked bowel of your bulldog without missing a beat. Brian's still searching for a link as my father eases himself to a standing position and steps past the corner of the table, giving Brian a reassuring pat on the shoulder as he goes.

He waves towards the kids, calls out, 'Winston's bowels,' and holds up his scrap of paper. It seems to be no surprise to them.

'Right,' Brian says. 'Apple cider vinegar . . .'

Abi and April go back to a conversation about a song, though I can't tell if it's one I should know or one they're writing.

'So what kind of music do you play?' Brian leans in front of me to say it, nudging my coffee cup with his forearm. 'You play guitar, don't you, Abi?'

'Yeah.' She shifts back in her seat. She glances down at her phone, which is on the table. 'Alt-country.'

'That's my favourite alt.' He gives her a wink. Even when he's not setting out to be sleazy, his instincts drag him there. Either that or he's using her as target practice for his mythical encounter with Taylor Swift.

He's still leaning, looming. He doesn't realise how finely he's balanced it. An inch closer to me and I'd be intoxicated by the stale smell of his neglected armpit, an inch closer to Abi and Robyn might take his right eyeball out with her teaspoon. She's holding it as if impromptu surgery isn't out of the question.

'Of course it is,' Abi says dismissively, cutting him dead with no need for parental assistance.

He's more of a misfit than I am in a conversation with teenagers. Without a cassock, a sausage and a microphone, he's the dodgy old uncle you steer clear of at parties. Twenty years ago, he owned that slice of the radio market. Robyn's still watching him, ready to take him out if she needs to. She hasn't picked up that Abi's already done the job.

I pull my coffee out from under his forearm. 'We'd better get a booth while there's still one to get.'

Until I pull my seat out from the table, Brian stays stuck in his failed lean as though he's crash landed there.

The last thing we hear as we leave is April saying, 'Alt-country. Hilarious. That is so 2003.'

Brian's shoulders sag but he maintains a gaze on the entrance, as though there's some purpose to it. He's the one-hit wonder on the twenty-fourth album after success, ditched by the panty-mailer, slugging his way around RSLs, with pokies for a backing track. He is all about radio, but radio is no longer all about him.

We claim a booth and he slides into his side and checks the time on his phone.

'Fuckers,' he says, to stop me trying to say the right thing. 'All wanting to be so important that they walk in last. "Sorry I'm late, but I've just been taping something for The Project."' He tosses imaginary hair and rolls his eyes. 'Fucking Meg Riddoch. It's not like my number's not in her phone. She could call.'

He up-ends the cup of sugar sachets onto the table and starts playing pick-up sticks, as though an idiosyncratic gesture might compensate for timely arrival.

Behind me, a child with a Transformers mask and separate big plastic ears looms up and makes repeated attempts to get Brian's attention, sticking his tongue through the mouth of the mask and doing Klingon salutes.

'Back this way, Riley, please,' the boy's father says, in a tone that's had a lot of practice at sounding both clear and patient. 'Let's give that man some peace.'

Brian checks his phone again, glares at the door, glares at Riley, who's ignoring instructions.

'Riley, please.' The father's tone is even clearer. He turns around and his head appears next to his son's and close to mine.

Just as he's about to speak, Brian says, 'Excuse me, but does your kid have some disorder or is he just eccentric?' He does quote fingers to go with 'eccentric'. 'Because eccentric really shits me.'

The father's face, set to sheepish apology, hardens and colour appears in his cheeks. His hand is on his son's shoulder but now, instead of guiding him down, it's holding him right where he is.

'Didn't you used to be on radio?'

Brian's almost on his feet before he stops himself. His forearm skids forward on the table and scatters his sugar sachets. He grabs the tabletop to steady it, as if it isn't bolted to the floor and wall.

He laughs. 'Nice one. That's probably us about even.'

'Oh, I don't know,' the father says, the edge in his voice as sharp as before. 'I didn't just take down a kid with Asperger's.'

'Righto.' Brian's glance flicks my way and then down to the table. His hands move to start collecting up the sugar sachets, sweeping them into a pile again. He looks up at Riley, an enforced kindness on his face, and says, 'Sorry, Riley.'

He sticks out his tongue, jams his thumbs in his ears and wiggles his fingers. Riley jumps in his seat, laughs and turns to tell his mother.

Brian flicks his phone on again to see the time. 'Forty minutes late. This is bullshit. I've got props to line up.'

'Really? Is that part of it?' I'm imagining Brian browsing somewhere like Naughty But Nice. Props mean trouble, trouble means complaints, complaints mean more for me to unravel on Monday.

'I'm going for a leak.'

★ ★ ★

He's been gone about a minute when a comedian I recognise as Meg Riddoch arrives with a minder. Without a glance around the café, she sits at a table for two, pushes her nest of auburn hair aside, puts on black-framed glasses and peers at a Kindle.

'Honestly,' she says loudly, 'this novel is shit. I want my ninety-nine cents back.' It's a performance, however small the room.

The minder's thin mouth makes a smile, but I can't hear her reply. Her bony fingers are gripping a phone that looks too big for her, and her shoulder blades are pushing at the fabric of her top like a pair of axe heads. Meg Riddoch must be in her forties now, and the minder's fifteen years younger.

Brian comes back in, in no hurry. I look everywhere but at his pants.

'Meg Riddoch,' he says loudly, pretending he's just arrived.

As his arms lift in the first inkling of a move towards a friend kiss, she stays in her seat, puts out her hand to shake and says, 'Yes. I think we might've met before . . . Brian?'

He nods, shakes her hand with both of his and chokes back his list of previous encounters.

Then he smiles. 'If I'd known you were about to turn up, I would have washed my hands . . .' He tilts his head to indicate where he's come from. 'Kidding. I wouldn't have washed my hands.'

'Ha,' she says. 'Glad to know I won't be lowering the tone, then.'

There's a ripple of conversation around the café, eyes turning towards the entrance. If the team has a big star, it's Toby Field and he's walking in with two minders, dark sunglasses and his fine blond hair gelled like a big lick of soft-serve ice-cream. He looks like he's wearing the suit his father wears to funerals, and he has an iPad mini in one hand, in an ironic faux-crocodile-skin case.

Brian's team is here and my job, technically, is done for now.

As Toby's minders each simultaneously introduce him to his fellow debaters, one to Brian and one to Meg, he gives them a shared, nasal, 'Hi, team,' without really looking at either of them. 'It's hot in here.' He puts on a puzzled face. 'Is everybody hot?'

He slips the jacket from his coat-hanger shoulders and one of the minders takes it from his hand without him appearing to notice. Toby Field's schnauzer has ten thousand followers on Twitter, so presumably he regularly hangs jackets on air and people are there to catch them.

I pull my phone out of my pocket and attempt to clench it with a publicist's urgency. When I arrive at his side, Brian's hand is still falling back from a failed attempt to shake Toby's.

I touch his sleeve and say, 'Brian, I'll leave you and the team to it, but remember you've got that live cross to The Project at seven fifteen, and they'll get a bit antsy if they don't see you by seven.' Toby glances towards us. 'And I've got a couple of other things to add to the itinerary, but I can talk to you about them then.'

Brian's look is blank for another second. Then he nods.

'Yeah,' he says, a study in nonchalance. 'Yeah, righto, mate. Good. Seven o'clock, then.'

As I step away, I hear Toby's voice say, 'The Project, hey? Do you find it's much easier to do when you're in-studio and everyone's right there, or is that just me?'

I don't have to keep listening to know that Brian can safely bullshit his way through that one.

Back at the family tables, there's now a woman in Brian's former seat talking animatedly to Robyn. She's forty-something and dressed in a salmon-coloured singlet with a Lorna Jane logo on the back. Among the legs of the chair, I can see she's wearing running shoes.

Robyn waves as I get closer, and the woman turns, swinging her greying blond ponytail.

'Andrew,' Robyn says, 'this is Lydia van der Graaf. We went to school together. She's here for the awards too.'

'Andrew Van Fleet.' It's her surname that makes me go for my whole name, though the second I've done it, it sounds too formal.

'Another Dutchie, hey?' She smiles and shakes my hand. She has rings on several of her fingers and teeth so good they must be capped. 'Did you have to go through the crap at school about your weird lunches and all that?'

'Not so much. About the name, sometimes . . .'

'Andrew's mother wasn't Dutch,' Robyn says, 'and I don't think his dad made a lot of lunches.'

'Robyn tells me you're working with Brian Brightman,' Lydia says, in a tone that suggests it's a positive thing. 'I'm here with the team doing the TV broadcast of the debate. Should be good to see him in action.'

'Yeah.'

Brian in action tomorrow night is a whole squirming sackful of risks I haven't fully faced yet. It's lost in the distance somewhere, behind all the other mis-steps he might take before then.

Lydia checks the time on her phone before slipping it into a pouch on her arm and fixing it in place with Velcro.

'Better get going and fit this run in,' she says as she pushes her chair back and moves to stand.

As I step away to let her through, the rotation twinges my piriformis again and instantly I'm as fixed in my pose as a human statue busking in a mall.

'Don't worry,' Robyn says as Lydia pretends to look somewhere else. 'That's something that happens to Andrew. We call it butt cramps.'

★ ★ ★

As I come out of the en suite, my buttock muscles seared by the hot shower but no more responsive, Robyn is again sniffing the shirt I've been wearing.

'Do we have to keep doing that?'

'You sweat more when your piriformis is off,' she says matter-of-factly. 'It's perfectly normal. I'd recommend a fresh shirt.'

'I need a fresh buttock.'

'Did you bring your ball?'

It makes me sound like a three-year-old or a puppy or someone with very special needs. And, no, I didn't bring my ball.

A physio once used to sink his fist in there, deep, deep into the muscles until the piriformis relented. Robyn's the only other person who can find the spot.

'Okay,' she says, knowing precisely what I'm thinking. 'On the bed, face down. Hug a pillow if you need to.'

I drape my towel across my side of the bed and manoeuvre myself onto it. Robyn hitches up her skirt and straddles my thighs. Even the rocking motion of her getting into place cranks the spasm up a notch.

'Left side?' she says, setting her hand on my buttock. 'At least the oozing's stopped.'

'Yeah. Thanks.' I'd be happier if we never had to talk about that particular oozing again. 'Go hard. Really break its spirit.'

'Okay,' she says, in a you-asked-for-it kind of way.

She drives the bunched knuckles of one fist down, using both arms to push. A whimper comes out of me before I can stop it.

'I need you to be a man now,' she says.

I try to reply, but the sear of pain makes it come out like a yelp. She's hit the spot. I just need her not to be put off if I happen to cry.

She's working my buttock rhythmically. There's a whining sound, like an airlock in a pipe, and I realise I'm probably making it. I've broken out in an entirely new sweat and might need another shower.

'Keep the noise down,' she whispers. 'You realise Abi and –'

At that moment, the door is flung open with enough force that the breeze from it reaches me on the bed. Abi's there, with April beside her. I can see them both in the mirror.

'Aargh,' Abi screams, swinging her hand up so quickly to cover April's eyes that she hits her in the face. 'Aargh,' she screams again.

She grips April around the head, like a struggling swimmer gripping a lifebelt, and the two of them reel back into the corridor.

'No . . .' Robyn says, in a fake super-calm voice, as she dismounts, removing any doubt that I'm entirely nude and splayed across the bed with her fisting me hard. Without thinking, she wipes her sweated-on hand on my towel.

'I thought it was Winston making that noise,' Abi shrieks in a mixture of fear and anger, backed up against the opposite wall of the corridor and clutching onto April. 'I thought he was stuck in something.'

Robyn grabs the door and closes it enough to put me out of view.

'It's just deep-tissue massage, darling,' she says, pulling her skirt back down to her knees with her other hand. 'Everything's all right.'

27

THERE'S A CERTAIN FROSTINESS at fish and chips on the beach, despite the balmy sea breeze. Robyn has insisted she's fixed things with the girls, with the aid of some reassuringly weighty Latin terms and an anatomical diagram of a piriformis muscle hurriedly located on the nearest iPad. Robyn will always resort to science, because science is in her corner and can always be made to sound implacable, and the antithesis of the possible bacchanalian rampage the girls think they have just witnessed.

They're treating her story as plausible, but by no means a sure thing.

And they can't unsee what they've seen – me naked, face-down and gripping the doona, Robyn bent over me, pile driving in my anal region. People put videos of that kind of thing on the internet, and not one of them does it with science in mind.

'Remember when fish and chips was cheap?' my father says wistfully, off in a better world.

He has a mug from Crystal Tydes leaning against his bottle of Cointreau. Robyn and I have a beer each. The Cointreau is weighing down the upwind corner of the sheets of greasy butchers' paper, which are carrying a mighty pile of chips and assorted deep-fried marine creatures. We're relying mostly on the light spilling from the esplanade and a close-to-full moon, but it's not enough to give anything any colour. The chips and the paper are the same grey as the sand and the mound of crumbed items is a shade darker.

There's a separate glow on my father though, casting his craggy features into relief like a campfire shaman. He's brought his iPad, with the express purpose of providing music. It's sitting in his lap, sending its light directly upward and nowhere useful.

Abi leans over and says something to April, but it's too quiet for the rest of us to hear. That's probably for the best.

Jack looks at them, knowing he's missing something.

'It would've been good if Lyrix could've made it,' he says. He reaches forward and takes a handful of chips.

'This one's for Robyn,' my father says, arranging his facial crags into a grin as he taps the screen.

It's Tainted Love, the twelve inch.

Robyn goes, 'Woo,' throws the chip she's holding into her mouth and breaks out some daggy and shameless upper-body dance moves.

'Oh, god, brace yourselves for eighties dancing,' Abi's voice says from the other side of the food. She's silhouetted, with the esplanade behind her and the lights of Obsidian over her right shoulder. Her face is completely dark. 'Or worse . . .'

'Maybe Dad doing his Vladimir Putin,' Jack says.

There's a video online of Vladimir Putin dancing at a wedding. Somehow, most times I brought a work laptop home, the video would end up loaded on there and set to play as soon as I flipped open the screen. Allegations have been made that it's how I dance.

Jack stuffs his mouth with chips, jumps to his feet, cascading sand, and knocks out some moves that look like eighties dancing done by a Soviet-era apartment block.

Abi laughs. 'Better than your jerkin'.' She turns to April. 'Jack's into jerkin'.'

'Well, okay.' It sounds like a really unfair place to have taken it, so I can't help but step in. 'It's perfectly healthy for fifteen-year-old guys to . . .'

'It's a kind of dancing,' Robyn explains, loudly and quickly, as Abi squeals 'Eeew,' and buries her head in her hands, and April sits entirely still waiting for the moment to pass.

'A West Coast hip-hop thing,' my father adds, pretending we're back at the safe topic of music and its spin-offs. He leans cautiously forward for another piece of fish. 'There's plenty of it on YouTube.'

'I'm not even into it,' Jack says, as if it's the crucial point to clarify. 'That was just one time.'

28

IT FEELS LIKE THERE'S a lot for me to sort out with Abi and April, and a lot that I don't want reported to April's parents. Or anyone. I imagine them asking her about her weekend the moment she arrives home, and her saying something like, 'Well, I got to watch Abi's parents having weird brutal sex, then we all went to the beach, ate prawn cutlets and talked about her brother masturbating.'

When we pitched the trip to the Trans as a 'family weekend', we weren't planning to look like that kind of family. It sounds like a European arthouse movie with the potential to seriously divide critics.

The ceiling of the master bedroom in unit four at Crystal Tydes is exactly as I would have pictured it. It's covered with spray-on grit all painted white, like a relief map with the tiny grit mountains casting shadows to break up the white and mask any grime. I'm lying on the floor on my own fist, beside the bed, fully dressed and out of view of the door, should it fling open.

'I'm going to have to wing it,' I tell Robyn, who is out of sight on the bed, deep in one of the more readable Kathy Reichs wannabes.

If I plan my explanation to Abi and April, chances are that it'll come out wrong.

'You can't let it go, can you?' Robyn says, in her consulting-room voice – the one used to reflect a nonjudgemental reality to the dysfunctional. It's all about the subtext and the subtext is that I *should* let it go, because she's covered it and because I will only make things worse.

I can't let it go.

When I open the door, the hall is dark. The door to Abi and April's room is ajar and it's dark in there too. They've been in the loungeroom working on a song, but all went quiet a few minutes ago. The lamp next to the TV cabinet throws yellow light across the loungeroom and into the kitchen.

As I get further down the hall, I can see Abi's guitar leaning against one arm of the sofa. There's an iPad on the coffee table with its screen taken up entirely by the black and white rectangles of a keyboard.

On the balcony, caught in the streetlights and with the black shapes of the pandanus trees and the roaring sea beyond them, Abi and April are standing, holding hands, still as statues. They're looking out at the grey foam of the breakers, with the breeze picking up their hair and tossing it around. I can't tell if they're talking. April leans her head into Abi's arm.

I can't guess how long I'm standing there before I work out that my only course of action is to retreat without a sound. It might be no more than a second or two. I duck back into the hall and stick close to the wall, my head full of the noise of the sea, imagining their voices in it somewhere, but out of reach.

I step into our room and ease the door shut.

'That was quick,' Robyn says, glancing up from the screen. 'Did you change your mind?'

'Not really. Yes . . . I didn't talk to them.'

'So, what's the "not really" . . .'

'Tell me what you know about Abi and April.' It's a movie line, a line from a movie we aren't in, one where the special agent reveals someone's other life.

She smiles at this new outbreak of oddness and meets it head-on. 'Well, obviously they're spying for North Korea. I thought I told you that.'

'That's not what I . . . You know how we were thinking about Jack and Lyrix? I'm wondering if we might have picked the wrong twin.'

She nods, but she's not there yet. She's still busy being pleased with herself for her North Korea line.

'Abi and April are out on the balcony holding hands. I'm kind of wondering if . . .'

'Holding hands?' she says and sets the iPad down beside her. 'People hold hands. Everyone holds hands except grown men, and in the Muslim world . . .'

'Thanks. Great sociological footnote but, you know, there's holding hands and there's holding hands. And this was . . .'

'Holding hands?' she says slowly.

'Exactly. Have we thought through that they might be a couple?'

'A couple.' The notion is now getting serious consideration.

'She hasn't said anything about boys to me. She got a text from one the other day, but he was down in her phone as Fuck Face and he got pretty short shrift.'

'Well, if you knew Fuck Face . . .' Her look makes it plain that he's not highly rated.

'Not that it's any issue for me what they do in there . . .' Their room is next to ours, with two single beds and teenage-girl mess, squared. It looks exactly the way I'd expected it would.

'Would you say that if she had a boy in there?'

'She wouldn't have a boy in there.' Okay, screaming double standard noted. I'm just glad I'm on the winning side of it. 'Look, April's cool.'

'Cool? April's cool?' Robyn takes her glasses off and rubs one of the lenses on the doona cover. She holds it up to the light to check it. 'April's a miniature nerd, and what does that have to do with it anyway? Cool? Just don't tell Brian. I heard him this morning. HLA . . .'

'You've got the iPad. Maybe there's some hint online.' It sounds wrong as soon as I've said it.

'Oh, really, so we should spy on her now? She might like girls, so we should spy on her?'

'We should see if we can get any background information, that's all. The more we know before it comes up in conversation, the better prepared we'll be.'

'Why would we need to be . . . Facebook's the obvious place to start.'

Robyn taps her way there as I join her on the bed, propping myself on a pillow next to her. Suddenly, the liking of Ellen DeGeneres and The L Word stand out from the rest. Then I notice her relationship status has been updated.

'Look.' I point it out to Robyn on the screen. 'It says "it's complicated". I'm sure that wasn't there before.'

'I didn't know people still put that. How very 2010. Complicated. Hmm.' She scrolls down. 'You're aware that's not an invitation for you to step in and try to make it less complicated for her, right?'

'But we have to . . . Okay, not an invitation.'

In my mind I had already ridden up on my white charger, slayed the marauding beasts of complication, freed my princess from the tower and delivered her to the arms of her compact elbow-high lady love.

'Oh dear,' Robyn says. 'That's not good.'

She's pointing further down the screen. Abi's signed up for a new Facebook group called 'I think my parents still do it – LIKE PORN STARS!!! Eew!'.

'We have –' Robyn checks on a different part of the page '– forty-two friends in common. I guess they're not . . . It doesn't mean they know what she's seen. People just sign up for stuff, right?'

Abi has also signed up to groups about lint and naps, so parents-as-pornstars might not be the main game here, despite the excessive capitalising, exclamation marks and spelt-out squeal of horror. Based on this evening's experience, the squeal could do with a lot more vowels.

'It was a truly tender moment,' I tell her, because it feels like it needs to be said. It was a small gesture that could not have looked more affectionate. 'Do you think we should say anything?'

'Why?'

'To let them know everything's okay by us.'

'Why would they not think that already?' She frowns and puts the iPad down. 'How many more gay friends do I have to bring over? How many more gay men do you have to hug in front of her?'

It's true. Our friend circle is batting comfortably above the national average for gayness, with regular HLA. I come from a family of total non-huggers and now I'm so practised I can make a hug work regardless of gender. I've kissed plenty of men on the cheek and come away with stubble exfoliation. Well, several men, but I've kissed them plenty of times. But this isn't about my prowess at kissing men.

'If Jack's going to get a talk because of Lyrix, then Abi's entitled when she's . . . in similar circumstances.'

Robyn frowns. She looks at me and then at her knees. Idiocy has broken out all around the room and she doesn't know where to swat first.

'Similar and yet not,' she says, turning to face me again. 'You do realise the risk of pregnancy's significantly reduced without a sperm in the room?'

I can't deny that. I might have been aiming for a twenty-first century edit of it, but I was falling back on a standard when lining up for my talk with Jack. It was to be about readiness, consequences, safe practices and, yes, those famous troublemakers, sperm, with the comforting knowledge that we were talking about a place I'd gone myself. Not at fifteen, admittedly, but we didn't all get those opportunities.

'I'd heard that,' I tell her. 'But there's more. It's about, you know, where you are in life. I'm ready to handle that one. The one about what you're up for. Thinking it through. How to deal with it in the wider world.'

It'd be my second chance within a couple of days to botch a sex talk with one of our offspring, but Robyn nods and says, 'Okay. You're right. She needs to know we're on her side. And she might need a chance to talk it through. And you want it to be you, don't you?'

'I do.'

'Just don't open with Jaws, okay?'

The balcony door shudders shut on its salt-seized runners. The sea noise drops. Robyn raises her eyebrows and points in the direction of the loungeroom, in case I'm about to shout something that shoves Abi out of any closet she might for the moment be in.

There's a fuzzy feedback noise and then guitar chords start chugging away with the volume down. Abi's playing Patti Smith again, maybe putting horses into her mind rather than parental fisting. Or maybe the idea of being an outsider. I don't ever want her to be outside anything, unless she wants to be.

29

THE NOTION OF THE beach run is often roman-
ticised, almost certainly by people who don't run on
beaches. Unless you're immediately above the edge of
the waves, the softer sand sucks the energy from every
step and turns it into a drowsy stagger.

At least the image of it holds true this morning, with
the dazzling blue sky and sea, and waves crashing like
glass. At the end of the run, I stick close to the water
until I'm lined up with Crystal Tydes and then I let
myself cross the dry sand at a cool-down pace.

While I've been out, a volleyball net has been set
up on the inshore part of the beach, next to the rock
wall and the pandanus trees. There are maybe twelve
people on either side of it, aged sixty or so on average
and, just as I'm expecting them to start an overcrowded
game of volleyball, one lobs the ball gently over the net
and another catches it. She throws it back and the cycle
repeats itself. It's a kind of nerf volleyball for people who
don't want to move. Or compete. Or play volleyball.

Robyn would tell me they're 'doing something',
as though a choice to embark on any physical activity
beyond resting metabolism should make them immune

from critiquing. I am — I want to be — a million miles from that surrender still. I pick up the pace and run over the soft sand, pushing myself to look able, spurred on by the fear that any sign of decrepitude might see me invited to join them.

The others have gone out for breakfast by the time I get back to the unit. Robyn's left a note that tells me I've missed them by five minutes. She says she'll text the name of the place they decide on, so that I can meet them there. There's nothing on my phone yet.

I take my running clothes with me into the shower and wash them in the time-honoured work-trip fashion, by dumping them on the shower floor, sluicing them with shampoo run-off and trampling them. It's no match for a machine, but it works well enough and means the weekend can continue to be laundry-free. Not that I couldn't have put them in a machine myself but, for Robyn, even the idea of bringing powder took us halfway to spoiling things. If you bring powder, grubby clothes mass and ambush you, apparently.

The genius of the work-trip wash lies not in the washing itself, but the wringing.

With only the living area big enough for the drying rack, I set up for business out there. It's a two-minute job so, with everyone guaranteed to be out, I stick with the exact routine I've perfected in hotels. I drop the towel, dial up some music on the iPod I've travelled with — one long ago discarded by Abi or Jack, in favour of newer tech — and I get to work.

I spread the towel out, arrange the clothes on it, avoiding overlaps, and then roll the towel tightly. It's not a job that demands to be done naked, but that's how it's worked out. If you do it dressed straight after the run, the exertion of the next phase puts new sweat in good clothes. And if you don't do it straight after the run, you have a ball of sodden clothes to contend with later, and perhaps pack and carry.

The next phase is the wringing. With the Strokes' New York City Cops blasting in my ears, I put a foot on one end of the rolled towel, then pick the other end up and start twisting.

As the bundle corkscrews and develops a kink, I give it one final twist, while singing along off-key with the big sneery line about New York City cops not being too smart. My foot pivots on the towel, and I swing towards the front door. And a woman in her twenties holding a bucket full of cleaning gear and wearing a hijab.

She drops her keys and her hand starts flapping, as if I'm on a whiteboard and she's trying to erase me. She says something before I've got the earbuds out.

The iPod slides across the table and onto the floor. I pull the towel out from under my foot and shake it hard to get the clothes out. I want to explain myself. I look like some weird tuneless hairy threat who's been lying in wait for her.

She backs away, scraping her keys after her with her foot.

I cover my groin with a handful of towel and shout, 'Washing, washing. It's the best way to do it.' I grab the singlet and hold it in front of me too, rubbing to show how much moisture I've removed. 'Come and touch it.'

She screeches something wordless and then, 'Bad. No touch.'

With one more flick of her foot, the keys skid outside, she lurches backwards and the door slams.

There's another screech and the sound of soft-soled shoes running on concrete.

★ ★ ★

The others are almost finished breakfast when I get to the café. Winston is lapping water from a steel bowl, Gladstone bag by his side. Robyn has a bowl of over-priced toasted muesli waiting for me.

'I tried to call you,' she says. 'I took a shot at what you'd want.'

It's almost certainly what I would have ordered anyway. When I pat my pockets down, it's clear I've left my phone back at Crystal Tydes.

'But you texted me after you'd got mine about where we'd come . . .' she says.

It makes no sense to Robyn that I might have forgotten the phone between then and leaving, but Robyn knows nothing about the extenuating circumstances. The nudity, the lewd suggestion, the set-back for multi-culturalism. The seconds spent grabbing dry clothes with thoughts of pursuit. The realisation that the cleaner and I had enough common language to make the situation worse, but not enough to make it better.

'I got distracted,' I tell her. 'A work thing. But this looks like great muesli.'

A work thing. Brian Brightman, with the exception of his ill-advised remarks about the kid with the mask, has been issue-free so far. Obsidian is still intact, still looming over this stretch of the coast with all the charm of a death star, and no one's called me to report any comedian cat fights, late-night parties or rampaging priests with bad touch on their minds. Props. He said he needed props.

Meanwhile, in this café, away from work at the idyllic family weekend, my father is frowning at websites about bulldog constipation, Jack is trading somewhere in the darker recesses of the internet, and Abi and April are sharing tastes of each other's omelettes, while I shovel in muesli and contemplate how to rewrite my already imperfect version of Sex Talk Three so that sperm no longer figure.

* * *

When we get back to Crystal Tydes, Dave the manager is waiting on the carpet grass. He has a paint-splattered cap pulled down over his eyes and he's finishing a cigarette.

'Andrew,' he says, raising his hand and scattering ash. He glances past me, at the others. 'I wonder if I could have a word.'

'Sure.' It comes out of me too quickly, and pitched higher than I'd like it to be.

I tell the others I'll see them up in the unit and I follow him towards his office. It feels like fronting the principal at school, except this principal's barefoot, bare-shouldered and smoking. And at school I never came close to flashing a Muslim cleaner and backing it up with what appeared to be a sexual overture.

I want to get a towel. I want to demonstrate what happened. If the floor tiles in his units weren't so slippery, I wouldn't have spun around and she could have retreated after nothing more than an accidental flash of bare wounded arse.

261

He steps onto his balcony, picks up a bent metal ashtray from the table and grinds the cigarette out.

'There's been an incident,' he says, gravely. 'Someone in one of your units, and I'm assuming it's Mr Brightman, has approached a member of staff while nude and asked her to touch his penis.' He pauses for the allegation to sink in. I fight the urge to air-punch, and the inclination to instantly slander Mr Brightman. 'Now, I know he's into all kinds of rubbish, but I didn't know he was into that.'

'Right.' I work on a face that says I'm taking this very seriously.

'I've been trying to call you. The lady in question is a Muslim person, so she would have found the penis extra shocking. This isn't how we work here at the Tydes. We're a family outfit. Lots of repeat business.'

'Of course.' I need to offer something, and not a comment that repeat business at the Tydes is a miracle for which Dave should be forever grateful. 'I'm sure it's a misunderstanding. It's not, um, Mr Brightman's style. You're right about that. Maybe he was just out of the shower? But clearly something's gone wrong and we need to fix it. It's probably safe to say that a face-to-face apology might traumatise her further . . .'

He nods. 'Hadn't thought of that. You're probably right.'

We're on the same side. We're all about the solution now.

'I'll move him out and get him to stay somewhere else. Even if it was just a misunderstanding. And maybe he could send her something as an apology? Like a bottle of . . .' Wine. I'm about to say wine. 'Halal something . . . Some really nice olive oil?'

'Olive oil?' I've lost him. The olive-oil apology is, to say the least, non-standard. 'Look, if I can pass on that he's sorry and that he'd just got out of the shower, I think we'll be okay, particularly if you put him up somewhere else. And, really, she doesn't pick up what people say all that well. Him leaving sounds a bit harsh if it's an innocent . . .'

'I know.' I hold up my hand to stop him. He's one step short of suggesting a truth-and-reconciliation meeting where his traumatised staff member encounters a fully dressed man she's never met, with a stain on his pants. 'I know it does, but it's about perception. And about letting your staff member know that her concerns have been taken seriously. She's got to feel safe here. You won't see him again. I insist.'

* * *

On my way back to the unit, I'm expecting the cleaner to come out of any door. My plan looked brilliant until I realised I'd have to spend the rest of her work day thinking like a fugitive.

As soon as our door's shut behind me, there's a shriek from one of the bedrooms. It's April. Abi laughs. Robyn's on a sofa with a pile of pillows behind her and her knees bent. She's reading a novel. For a few seconds we both listen. I can hear voices, but not any of the words.

'Probably another spider,' she says. She swings her legs around and brings her feet to the floor. 'Was there any problem with the manager?'

'No.' The drying rack is just behind her, my running clothes flung on in such haste that I can see the singlet's already slipped onto the floor. 'He wanted to give one of our unused car spots to someone else.'

I'm going to need a spreadsheet to keep track of all these lies.

When I pick up my phone, I have three voicemail messages. They're all from Dave, sent while I was at breakfast. I'm about to delete the third one when the phone buzzes and shakes.

'Incoming,' Robyn calls out, in case I don't recognise what's going on. 'Go to the top, pull the bar down and you can answer it.'

It's Brian.

'Mate, I just got the weirdest call,' he says. 'From Calliope. You won't have met her yet. She's on reception on weekends. At the station. Apparently there's some South African guy down here on the coast who reckons I got my tackle out. Something to do with a Muslim chick. He tried to get onto you, but . . .'

'Yeah, look . . .' I signal to Robyn that I'm going outside, onto the balcony. I mouth the word 'work' and roll my eyes. 'It's sorted out. I've spoken to him.'

'Sorted out?' His voice drops in and out. He's probably in his hotel room. 'No one's talked to me . . .'

I slide the door shut behind me. The pounding surf should mean Robyn hears nothing.

'It's okay,' I tell him. 'It was a misunderstanding.'

'Pretty bloody big one, I'd say.' He laughs. 'Just as long as I don't have to marry anyone. What would make him get that kind of idea? It sounded pretty specific.'

Through the sliding doors I can see Robyn in the kitchen, pouring a glass of water.

'Well, here's the thing . . .'

Down on the street, a lycra-clad dog owner turns her back and checks her phone while her dog lifts its leg and pisses on the rear wheel of Jimi Hendrix. The phone is pink, the dog is a cavoodle or some other breed concocted for fluffy cuteness and its lead is encrusted with diamantes.

'I had a shower after my run this morning.' He doesn't need to know everything. 'The cleaner came to the door when I happened to have nothing on. She didn't speak much English.'

'It was *you*? Ha.' He laughs. His phone scrapes against his stubble. 'They're calling the station to complain about me flashing a Muslim chick, and it was *you*. And what's the bit about you offering her the penis? Did she walk in on you going down on yourself?' There's another guffaw of laughter as the gift keeps on giving. 'How did she get to the door of your bedroom without you hearing her?'

'Yeah. Not the bedroom actually. I was in the living room. Doing laundry.'

'Nude laundry.' He can barely get the words out.

'Nude laundry, yes. Just running clothes.' Because that makes it a whole lot better. 'With an iPod, so I didn't hear her come in.'

'Get to the bit where you offer her the penis. Please.'

Down at Jimi Hendrix, the cavoodle is ready to move on, leaving a glossy black parabola of urine on the dusty rear tyre. Inside the unit, Abi and April are in the kitchen with beach towels around their shoulders.

'Okay. So, it was a surprise for both of us.' I let him know how it went, casting myself as almost a second innocent victim in my story.

'Oh crap,' he wheezes when I get to the part about picking up the singlet and suggesting she touch it. He laughs until he coughs and the phone rattles down onto a hard surface. Eventually the coughing settles. The phone clunks as he picks it up again. 'Sorry.' His voice still sounds strained. 'Just had to make a few notes for Monday's show.' He takes a long breath out. 'Okay, maybe not. There's one thing I'm not clear on yet, though. How did this get to be about me? I'm not even staying there. I don't even know where you're staying.'

'The manager thought you were staying here. And then he thought it was your sort of thing.'

'And you've explained . . .'

'Well . . .'

There's a sharp intake of breath. '*You haven't.*' There's another squawk of laughter. 'You've totally dumped me in the shit, haven't you? You dirty dog. Maybe you're on my team after all.' He sighs. 'You so owe me. Ha. You'll never be the head of the IMF now. I don't know why he didn't handle it your way. That Strauss–Kahn guy. Why didn't he just put it down to nude room laundry?'

30

IT MIGHT HAVE BEEN that no one would have believed that the head of the IMF did room laundry. It might have been the semen DNA. For whatever reason, the art of towel wringing never seemed to come up in the fallout from the encounter Dominique Strauss-Kahn came to describe as a 'moral fault'. They cycled through that line a few times on BBC World during one of my stays in Guangzhou.

At the back of Crystal Tydes, separated from the cleaning of vacated units by a fence and a bed of straggly palms, is a pool, with a waterslide set into a mound of brown-painted textured concrete boulders.

Robyn attempts a few breaststroke laps with her hair gathered up on her head, in the hope of keeping it dry, but there are far too many screaming rampaging children for that. She gives up and settles for reading in the shade.

Abi and April topple down the slide like jacks, arms and legs everywhere. Jack goes down headfirst, because there's a sign saying it's not allowed. I settle for the approved luge style, aiming for speed and a clean entry. Too many dads are hitting the water like dropped whales.

The new UV caution and return to near-Edwardian pool fashion has been perfectly timed for me. It's too much to claim my black rashie is in any way slimming, but at least it's normal enough to wear it now, even if it's turned out to be a minority choice at the Tydes. So, I get to keep my expanding pale hairy self to myself. And Robyn. And the cleaner. And Abi and April.

'Bogan of the day,' Robyn says when I join her on the banana lounges. She nods towards the pool. It's a challenge.

'Not easy.' I scan the queue at the slide, the pool itself with its teeming multigenerational crowd, the sunburnt tattooed families clumped under market umbrellas with the first or second beers of the morning, or spread out on towels upgrading their UV beating. 'The Tydes is much loved by bogans.'

I settle for a guy who's poking around at the barbecues. It might be recent discussions about Lyrix that have me thinking it, but he looks like Obelix from the Asterix books in later life, with a grey rat's tail, plump grey moustache and a selection of fading tatts, including a dragon and a Polynesian dancer.

'He's good,' Robyn says, 'but take a look near the pool steps. Slightly more obese than yours, forehead past the vertex, ringlet mullet – which might just trump grey rat's tail – but the clincher is the ink.'

I angle my head away from him, pretending to read her iPad and sneaking a glance back in his direction. 'I count three skulls with snakes coming out the eyes.'

'And the front. Check the belly job.'

It's a Hooters scene, with the venue name in orange and the owl part of the logo ghosted in behind. It features a bar, well-norked wait staff and four flanno-clad men with pool cues. This is a bogan with a tattoo of bogans. No, it's better. The second bogan from the right in the tattoo is a less bulky younger version of the owner of the abdo-canvas. It's his buck's night, or some other evening so memorable it demanded to be captured in a broad tableau across his own body. It's bogan tattoo genius.

'I've got a picture of it,' Robyn says, as though I might need or want one. She flicks back through images on her iPad. Some are of the family, others are studies in boganry.

'Stop.' I flick forward, to one of Abi plaiting April's wet hair. 'Please don't take any more photos of bogans. They might have to hit me.'

'It's an iPad. No one knows. They think you're reading.' She flicks the screen to show me more. The next image is of me coming down the waterslide.

'Okay, you've got to delete that.'

'Why? It's good.' She pushes my hand away. 'You look fine. I know the rashie's riding a bit high . . .'

'The rashie's not the issue. It's the . . .' I can't even say it. 'Head.'

'It's not thinning, it's just . . . gleaming. It's the angle of the sun.'

'Gleaming like a monk.'

I tap 'delete' before she can stop me.

'No,' she says, just as I hit 'confirm'. 'Why did you . . .' She knows why. 'Now *there*'s a sight worth taking a photo of.' She nods towards the unit block.

It's my father, with a XXXL black-and-white Rip Curl rashie draping itself well below his stoma bag and halfway down the legs of his hibiscus-print board shorts. He has his sandals on, his iPad in one hand, a bright new ulcer dressing that I think Robyn has okayed for the pool and big ancient tortoise-shell-framed sunglasses with a detachable nose guard that hangs over his mid-face like the pink bill of a plastic pelican.

Bogan stares follow him as he claims the banana lounge beside me. It turns out that their pool game is Watch the Freak.

'Dad, what's with the . . .' I tap my nose. I'd call it a nose guard, but I'm not even certain that's what it is.

It looks like someone else's discarded prosthesis, or part of the phantom costume for an impoverished amateur theatre company's Phantom of the Opera.

'It's better than newspaper.' His hand reaches up to check that it's perfectly placed. 'With newspaper the print comes off on your nose.'

'When did you ever use newspaper? On your nose? When did anyone?' A long-repressed memory of it breaks the surface, my father folding the inky beak and wedging it in place with sunglasses.

'Before this came along.' He leans past me, to make sure Robyn's included. 'Office secret Santa, 1978. Maybe '79. But it still works.' He taps it with his finger-nail.

'Sure it does. They really meant it when they made flesh-coloured plastic in the seventies.'

He looks right at me, his eyes lost behind large discs of black glass. He's like a gigantic elderly fly with a plastic nose. 'It's French. Europe made things back then.'

His iPad pings. He lifts his glasses, squints at the screen and then touches and drags something.

'It's a shame they didn't surgically attach your iPad to you when they did the colostomy.'

'I know.' He tucks it back under his arm and sits up straighter. 'Don't think I didn't ask. Apparently there's no Medicare item number for it.'

Behind him, about twenty metres away at the end of the pool area nearest the unit blocks, Jack is standing on a boulder and forcing himself head-first through the palm fronds and over the railing.

Robyn notices him too. 'What is Jack doing?' She adjusts her glasses, in case that might set his feet back on the ground and pull his head out of the plants.

My father turns to see, and appears completely unsurprised. 'If he's smart, and we all know he is, knight to king's bishop three.' He shows us his iPad. They're playing chess. 'I pay for wi-fi. He has to pick up the free signal. I've got to have something to give me an edge.'

I can now see that Jack has his iPad too. 'You know the chess people also make those pieces in wood and a range of other materials to get around the wi-fi problems.'

He smiles. 'I'd heard that.'

Jack's next move pings through. My father pushes his glasses up onto his head, with the nose guard jutting forward. From the side it looks as if his forehead has grown a thumb. He checks the state of the board. His index finger hovers and then he draws it back.

'Clock's ticking,' he says, and makes a move. 'Was it your opa who taught you chess, or me?'

'A bit of both. Mainly Opa.' With a chess set reputedly carved by his grandfather from elm one cold nineteenth-century winter. I don't have much from the van Vliets, but I do have it. 'The radio in the walnut

271

box . . .' It came up in the conversation with Brian yesterday, that and Benny Goodman, which I know to be from life. 'Did you have one of those in Arnhem?

His eyes don't shift from the screen, waiting for Jack's next move. 'Yeah, we did. Everyone did. Everyone who could afford one.'

'What were the big announcements you listened to?' Kings and prime ministers, he said, and I can fake a picture of a boy with short hair and one of his neighbour's handed-down shirts, called in from outside by his parents to listen.

'It was a long time ago.'

He lifts the back of his rashie up, slides his hand around until he finds a pocket in his shorts and pulls out a piece of folded foil. His gum is between his front teeth and he takes it out with his thumb and finger, places it carefully in the foil and turns the edges onto it. Jack still hasn't made his move.

'Liberation,' he says. 'In 1944. That'd be the first one. Queen Wilhelmina. I was, what, seven? My father cried, just that one time.'

'Do you remember how you felt?'

'What is this? A test?' He glances past me, towards Robyn. 'Hungry. It's a safe bet that's how I felt.'

The iPad pings and he lifts it from his lap, warding us off with it, warding me off, studying every piece on the board, every square.

He shakes his head. 'He's got me. I think he's got me this time.'

Behind him, Jack jumps from the boulder, grinning, arms raised in victory.

My father turns around and shouts out, 'You've got me.'

31

'WHEN I WAS ABOUT twelve,' I tell Abi, 'my parents gave me Jaws. The book Jaws.'

I can't say I have my act completely together when my chance comes. April's in the shower after the swim and Robyn's out walking. Abi freezes, with the remote pointed at the TV and home shopping on the screen. She's in shorts and a singlet, with her wet hair in a ponytail, about to settle in for some pre-lunch trash TV. She gives me a warning look. Her radar has detected impending weirdness. And correctly, as nipple references are approaching.

'It was an adult thing, when I really wasn't expecting it. Wasn't ready for it. It's an adult book.'

She makes an Mmmm noise, draws her knees towards her chest and backs further into the pile of cushions behind her. It's not done to make space for me on the sofa, but I take the chance anyway and sit.

And decide against the nipples. 'Sometimes things come along before you're ready for them, before you've thought them through. It's easy if it's a book, but sometimes it's life.' So far, so enigmatic. No disasters, but I have to stop circling and land this sucker somehow.

'The first time your Auntie Jules saw a penis she was horrified.'

It's a true story. Julianne sat in her room crying after the confrontation, and the penis hadn't even touched her. But it was so unusual-looking – a one-eyed blind limbless creature periscoping out of its nest – that she didn't think she'd ever want to have anything to do with them. She got over that pretty quickly.

Abi wraps her arms around her knees and bunches herself up smaller than a magician's assistant in a saw box. 'If this turns out to be about Auntie Jules and how in the end she was cool about . . .' She makes one hand into a fist and jerks it back and forward, miming what she thinks she saw her mother doing to my anal region. 'If you're going to tell me that's just a standard part of adult life . . .'

'No, that was deep-tissue massage. Strictly medical. But it's good to get the chance to clarify.' It's a tangent, but for now I'll take it. It's also on my list of topics. 'The first person who did that to me was a physio. A man. He'd been a physio in the army.'

She dips her head down so that only her eyes are visible over her knees. The reference to the army was supposed to make it less sexual, but now she's picturing a private military tattoo on my buttocks.

'I also use a tennis ball sometimes.'

'Oh god,' she groans and pushes her face into her knees.

'It's the muscle. Nothing to do with the . . . anus.'

'Dad . . .' She starts rocking, as much as the squishy sofa will allow.

Bring in medical names for body parts, Robyn has

assured me. It takes all the heat out of it. Fallopian tube maybe. Piriformis maybe. Anus apparently not.

'Some people never get around to liking penises . . . And that's okay.'

'This is starting to creep me out.' The words are muffled, since they're spoken into her knees. Her forehead is red and the veins are standing out. 'Creep me out *more*. Is it okay if you never say the word "penis" again when I'm around? If there's some really important penis-related message you need to get to me, maybe do it through Mum. Or text me.' She lifts her head. Her entire face is flushed. She's red all the way down to her shoulders. 'Mum said you were googling penises at work on your first day. Is there some . . . No, don't tell me. Whatever it is, don't tell me.'

'That was an accident.' And clearly there are no secrets in this family.

'Sure. At least you didn't say it was "research".' She does quote fingers. The redness in her cheeks retreats to pink.

'So, you and April.' I'm going back in, from a different angle. No more anatomy. 'What's up with that?'

She looks at me as if I've just spoken Aramaic or produced a live flapping fish from my shirt.

'"What's up with that?" Don't you mean, "What's up with that, homey?" I can't believe I defended you all those times.'

She makes room for a pause, in which I'm at liberty to contemplate frequent derision at the hands of unnamed people, with Abi gamely warding it off.

'You're really trying, aren't you?' she says, awarding me approximately a quarter of a brownie point for effort. 'Trying something.'

She reaches up to her shoulder and straightens a slipped singlet strap. Down the hall, the shower stops running.

'Okay, I'm going to stop trying whatever it was. Let me just say, I'm proud of who you are and who you are becoming.'

She nods. She's almost back to her usual pale self. She says, earnestly, 'Thank you.'

'I'm in awe sometimes of how able you are. There are some things I've never found easy and you don't seem to have a problem with them. You can really express yourself.' I want to tell her about the hand-holding and how it rates as a moment, how she needs to keep it in her head. I want to tell her I almost envy her for it. I do envy her for it. 'You're your own person, and in a great way, and I wish I'd been around for more of the past couple of years. But I'm around now if I can ever be . . . useful.'

I can't in this moment conceive of a situation in which I could be. I'm an oaf come back to lumber around in her life, and if I don't break too much furniture she'll think herself lucky.

'I know most of the time you'd like me to focus on not being embarrassing.'

She smiles. 'Mum calls that insight, in the medical sense.' She stretches her legs out and puts her feet in my lap. 'Good for you.'

'Abs,' April calls out from the bathroom. 'I forgot my towel.'

32

WHO COULD HAVE guessed that Sex Talk Three (girl-on-girl version) might end up being as much about me as about the girl in question? Okay, so the big issue never made it to the surface, but the two of us have something. We got somewhere. It's a first step. I'll take that, even if there's nothing to report to Robyn.

After lunch I take my first look at the old novels shelved next to the TV. In daylight and at something short of arm's length, I can still read them without my glasses. Tucked between two Readers' Digest condensed books — four novels in each — are a folded chessboard and a box of wooden pieces.

Jack's on the balcony with the girls, laughing at something further down the esplanade. My father is apparently sleeping next door.

I lift Jack's keys from the coffee table, slip out of our unit and let myself into theirs. My father is sitting on the sofa, iPad next to him, snoring loudly. Winston is on a towel in a corner behind the dining table, eyes closed, snuffling, looking bloated. The news on the constipation is still not good.

The chess rematch my father demanded is on his

iPad, paused for lunch, so I open the board out on the coffee table and set the pieces up to recreate it, square by square. I even place the captured pieces in rows beside the board to mirror the way the software does it. White looks backed into a corner, but still has a queen and both bishops so it's not over yet.

When I go to make my final check of their game, I accidentally touch the corner of the iPad screen and bring up the internet. My father has it set to the Brisbane Times. The third headline down reads, 'Come and Touch It.'

There's a file photo of Brian sitting in the studio and, below it, the Crystal Tydes picture from the booking website. The article opens with, 'Some of us might dress for laundry. Not SPIN99's Brian Brightman. At least that's his version of the story, after his controversial exit from a Gold Coast unit block this morning.'

Brian's quoted as saying, 'I was just doing room laundry. I might have had the music up a bit loud. And, when it's your own room, who doesn't like to hang out with their kit off?'

The next paragraph talks about the shock of the staff member – name withheld at her request – first at discovering the nude Brightman and then at his move towards her and urging to 'come and touch it'. I don't remember moving towards her, but it's probably not the time to seek a correction.

Brian then says, 'No one goes harder at the wringing than I do. I just thought she'd appreciate my handiwork.'

The piece closes with Dave putting it all down to a misunderstanding, with Brian's apology duly accepted, and assuring readers that the Tydes remains 'the perfect venue for a classic family holiday'.

'So it was you who took my keys,' Jack says behind me, quietly so that he doesn't wake his grandfather. 'At least you left the door open.'

'I just thought I'd . . .' I point to the board. 'Do this.'

He tilts his head, as if some effort's required to find the angle that will allow the sight to make complete sense.

'Cool,' he says. 'That's just like chess.' There's irony in there, I'm sure there is. He takes a step to the left, and then another. 'Except with a really nice . . .' He shapes his hands in the air as though he's marking out a globe or a box. '3-D perspective.'

33

'IT'S LIKE A DATE NIGHT.' I'm not sure if I'm saying it to convince myself or Robyn.

We left Abi and Jack arguing over a Thai takeaway menu, Abi pushing for less meat, Jack for more. I'm back in a suit, this time with a tie, and Robyn's wearing a dress I haven't seen before. It's royal blue, with thin straps, a fitted bodice and a skirt that finishes around knee high. I'm sure that's not the right way to describe it. I've stuck to telling her she looks great, and I've done that three times. She's told me she has room in there for about two canapés.

The lights of Obsidian are ahead of us, in a tall stack over the low-rise unit blocks. I can smell a barbecue. A Dominoes car pulls up and the driver takes his red pizza satchel through the brick archway outside a two-storey block called Pa-Sea-Fique.

'A date night, but with a slight element of work function,' Robyn says. She takes her eyes off the dark footpath to glance my way. 'But mostly a date night, once you've got Brian safely to the stage, right? And it's a nationally televised comedy event. That doesn't come along every week. Just don't say, "What could possibly go wrong?", because it all goes bad when they say that in the movies.' The path dips down for a driveway and she steps carefully, reaching for my arm when her heel wobbles on the uneven surface. 'It'll be good.'

The approach to the entrance is less busy than I'd expected. I'd imagined limousines, cameras flashing. I'd pictured an event in a big city where most of the attendees aren't already staying in the building, and therefore go through a process of arrival. The TV OB van is parked to one side of the entrance, out of the light.

There's a sign in the foyer, gold letters on black felt saying, 'Obsidian Welcomes the Australian Comedy Awards – Grand Ballroom.'

'I'd say follow the well-dressed people,' Robyn suggests, and it looks like sound advice in a foyer dominated by sneakers, bum bags and a Korean tour group marshalling around a woman with a plastic pineapple on a stick.

★ ★ ★

The ballroom is set up with rows of round tables in front of the stage, each with eight chairs. There are chandeliers suspended from the ceiling on steel rods. Drinks and canapés are circulating on trays and, around the edges of the room, there are long tables covered in white tablecloths awaiting the arrival of food for the buffet dinner.

A few guests are seated already, gazing up at the screen that dominates the stage. Below the bottom of it, there's a hint of the set built behind it for the debate and the awards to follow. At a table in a far corner, a sand artist is silently at work, and it's her hands and her sand we can see flitting across the screen. At first the image she's creating reminds me too much of the etch-a-sketch uterus, but when she dots the windows in I realise it's Obsidian, with the fallopian tubes becoming the horizon and the hinterland hills.

The bright light she's working with leaches the colour out of her face and arms, except for the red lipstick marking the thin flat line of her closed mouth.

Already the image on screen has changed. It's an owl in flight.

'Ludmila Kirilenko,' the voice of Robyn's friend Lydia says next to us. 'Ranked sixth-best sand artist in the world, apparently, though who decides those things I don't know. Best known for a half-hour show called "A Short History of the Ukraine in Sand".'

'I think I read a novel with that title once,' Robyn says.

Lydia's holding a glass of mineral water in one hand and her phone in the other. She's wearing a dress that's either silver or grey or shades of both. It's made of irregular panels of different fabric, some matt and some shimmering in the light from the chandeliers.

'I thought you'd be flat out,' Robyn says.

'Some of the crew are, don't worry.' Lydia points with her phone hand to the back of the room where four men wearing headsets appear to have built their own temporary version of the control deck of the Starship Enterprise, with panels and monitors and taped wads of cable. 'We did a tech run earlier. It should all be okay.'

Her eyes follow one of the cables out from the desk and along the floor among the tables, safely gaffer-taped all the way.

'I love the dress,' Robyn tells her.

Lydia touches her stomach self-consciously with her phone hand and says, 'Thanks.' She takes a good look at Robyn. 'Yours is . . . wow. I'm getting a Michelle Obama vibe. Don't tell me that's Jason Wu.'

'It is.' Robyn does half a twirl before she can stop herself.

'Should have picked it the moment you walked in.' Lydia takes a step back to give the dress the appraisal it apparently deserves. 'I get to read a lot of magazines in this line of work, so I see my share of what celebs are wearing. Well done, you. Doctoring must be going nicely. Or running radio stations. It looks great.'

'There was a sale,' Robyn says, working hard not to catch my eye.

'I never seem to get my timing right,' Lydia says. 'Some people have that knack with sales.'

'Robyn's amazing at it.' I don't know Jason Wu, but I do know that. 'Always has been. It's like everything she buys is a label, but it's always on sale.'

'Everything?' Lydia laughs. 'That old trick?'

'No, I've seen the tags sometimes. They're massively marked down.'

'Really?' She gives me a pitying look that should be reserved for someone who's quit their job on the strength of an email promising twenty-five per cent of a vast unclaimed Nigerian inheritance. 'They've retagged them? There's a new price tag? An official one?'

'No, it's done with a pen.' My right hand makes pen moves, in case familiarity with pen motion might make my argument more convincing.

Lydia laughs again. Robyn fights back a smile.

'But sometimes it's a red pen and sometimes it's black.' Case closed, surely.

'I don't want to shock you,' Robyn says, 'but these days the wife is allowed two colours of pen. They changed that law.' She touches Lydia's arm with her hand. 'Not that Andrew's tight or anything. Well, not with money. With wine maybe . . .'

'No. Not "red dot" wine. Do I really deserve this?' I'm being ganged-up on on date night, but at least Robyn's having fun. I want to google Jason Wu to check his prices, and then I definitely don't want to.

Robyn turns towards me, placing one hand on my side and the other on my shirt front, like a parent about to shepherd a child through a vaccination.

'Red dot wine,' she explains to Lydia, 'is technically about marking special-occasion wines so they don't fall victim to that whole midnight why-don't-we-open-one-more-bottle thing.'

'It's mutual.' We devised the system together.

'It's not mutual,' she corrects. 'Because only *you* have the thing about special-occasion wines, and only *I* am ever still awake to open a bottle after midnight.' She pats my stomach. 'We had a few pouty mornings when someone woke up to discover what he'd missed. It all got a lot easier when the serious work travel kicked in. Turns out those dots don't stick all that well. Grange it up, baby.'

There was no Grange. Wait, there was one bottle, a gift from senior management after closing a deal in my early BDK days, pre-GFC.

Robyn steps back and laughs. 'Don't worry, I only had a glass of it.'

That's what Munck's The Scream was about, I'm sure of it – a man who woke up to discover his gift bottle of a good-to-very-good vintage of Grange had been opened by a pissed person with shoe leather for a pallet, who quaffed one glass and then left the bottle on the bookcase.

'I was saving it so the two of us could . . .' I'm going straight for guilt. I'll get nowhere moaning about it being an eight-hundred-dollar bottle of wine.

'You've got nothing, have you?' Lydia says. And she's right. 'You were saving it so you could save it. Such a romantic.'

'Ha.' Robyn's with her, ready to go bad-cop, bad-cop on me. 'The most romantic thing he does is go along with things.'

It's true. It's that horrible bright window of truth that's occasionally flung open when you're in a room of seething mockery. I go along with things. And I prize it as some kind of virtue. I drag myself home from wherever work has tossed me, I half wake up and I go along with something. And then leave. That's my track record.

'What about this weekend?' I've at least got that. I'm back, I'm organising. A no-star forty-year-old brick unit that can't even spell 'tides', maybe, but I'm organising.

'Sure,' Robyn says, nodding, maintaining a half-smile that tells me there's trouble coming. 'If I'd helped your dad change his colostomy bag a couple less times it could look a little more romantic, but . . .'

Brian Brightman is to Robyn's left, maybe ten metres away. He's standing next to a group of people but not with them, holding a glass of wine in one hand as he gazes vaguely across the room and picks behind his lower front teeth with a fingernail. I can't hear it, but I know he's working on his plaque again.

Lydia notices me looking at him and, perhaps thinking I'm due some mercy on the romance front, says, 'Brian Brightman. I'm looking forward to seeing him in action. He's so bold.'

'That's one word for it.'

'Don't worry,' Robyn says. 'You're bold too, Andy. One time you rubbed out that grocer's apostrophe on that sign, remember? At the Rosalie shops. You just went up there and did it. Didn't care who saw you.'

It draws another easy laugh from Lydia. Me, striking a blow for pedantry, orange chalk smudge on my hand.

'Wow, yeah, bold,' Lydia says. 'Not quite "Free hugs" or "Come and touch it" but . . .' The way she says it makes it sound as though my laundry incident now comes with a label attached, like something that's out there being widely discussed. Albeit now starring Brian Brightman. 'Have you seen how that story's going?'

'I was hoping it was gone.'

She frowns. 'I was assuming your people put it out there. I don't think it's over yet. He comes out of it all right. Well, in the usual Brian way at least. Fascinatingly crap, no malice intended.'

'Yeah.' She's summed up my interlude with the cleaner pretty well. 'I'd better round him up and get him backstage. See if I can maximise the "fascinating" part of that and maybe tone down the crap.'

I can still see the look on the cleaner's face, her eyes like two lasers zeroed in on my dangerously liberated penis. I take a step in Brian's direction and then stop myself.

'This isn't me walking off and ignoring you, by the way,' I tell Robyn, only making it look more as if I'm walking off and ignoring her. 'I'll be back as soon as . . .' My hand starts signalling something. I have no idea what.

'As soon as you've got Brian safely to the stage,' she says, patiently. 'After that it's a hundred per cent date night. Before then it's make your own fun, and I've been doing okay at that so far.'

A waiter stops, and she lifts a glass of white wine from his tray and makes a toasting motion. Lydia swaps her own empty glass for another mineral water.

Brian gives me a low wave when I catch his eye. He raises his eyebrows, as if the scope of the room and the event, and the place of his own shabby self in it, has just dawned on him. He's wearing a black jacket and a black collared shirt. It's the first time I've seen him without colour bursting out all over.

'Is it that time?' he says. 'Just don't make me the first one there again.'

★ ★ ★

He's the first one there. The green room is two doors down the corridor, and there's not a debater in sight.

'Shit.' He stands just inside the door with his hands on his hips. 'You're making me look bad, mate. Making me look like a try-hard.'

The green room is a section of a high-ceilinged function room, with trestle tables, an assortment of chairs, a hot-and-cold buffet and ice bowls with bottles of wine, beer, water and juice. The eight wait staff are all standing watching the two of us. There's a palpable absence of guests. Unlike the ballroom, where the lighting seems just right, the green room is lit to be noticed from space.

Brian downs his wine in one untidy gulp as staff converge on him with more. His eyes are bloodshot and he's blinking. The glass shudders in his hand as a waiter refills it.

I tell him we should take a seat and he points to a long dark bag on one of the tables and says, 'That's mine. Props. Dropped it in earlier.' He takes a step towards it, bumping a table corner as he passes. 'Went out with a mate to get it. Had a couple of beers.'

Someone should have sent me the page in the minder manual headed 'Ten Ways to Stop the Talent Getting Drunk'.

The bag is much larger than I anticipated. It looks as if a small person might be dead in there. Brian sits and rests one hand on it.

'What . . . Should I ask what's in there?'

He gives me a weary look. 'Still the head boy. Maybe it's just my limbless inflatable girlfriend slash resusc doll.' He waits for the fear to show itself on my face. 'Don't worry. It's entirely PG. Anyway, she dumped me.'

I tell him I'll get some water, and it's only when I arrive at the ice bowl that I realise they've buried all the water bottles on the bottom. The only thing I can reach without going elbow-deep is apple juice.

Brian's sitting with his right hand still on his bag and his left gripping the stem of his wine glass when I get back to the table.

'Got to take a leak soon,' he says to the vacant space in front of him.

He opens his glassy eyes wide and blinks hard, as if there's something he's fighting to bring into focus.

I open the apple juice and slide it up against his wine. 'Maybe try some of this.'

Already I know apple juice is not the answer, and that I've stepped in too late. I have framed Brian for the cleaner incident, allowed him to roam free all day and right now – forty minutes away from national TV – I wouldn't be shocked if his eyeballs started spinning and came up cherries or Aztec gold.

'Bloody Gen Y.' He burps, and there's a smell of wine, hops and stomach acid. 'Green-room toilets are out of commission, so one of the staff went off to find me another one. Haven't seen him since. Slapdash generation. Gen Ys were born without a concentration span and we never made them grow one. Even Gen Yers who think they're anal can probably find their arsehole only about fifty per cent of the time. Actually, I might just . . .' He brings the keyboard up on his phone and has a stab at typing what he's just said. 'I'm the guy who invented the catchcry "I'm naked under these clothes" and they don't even know that. Does Tom Chastain know that? Does Josh Thomas know that? You know that, right?'

'Sure.'

Tom Chastain is the opposing team's biggest star. Josh Thomas is nowhere in the building, but rates a mention as the Ys' flag bearer – and Tom's occasional team captain – on Talkin' 'Bout Your Generation. The catchcry claim is something else to google, when I'm not at work and it's safe to google 'naked'. It doesn't sound like a line anyone had to invent in our lifetime.

There's an argument over at the door. Ludmila Kirilenko is on a break and has turned up smoking. She's a shade less pale away from her machine.

'You don't understand,' she says loudly. 'The stress of this . . .' She waves her bony arms, mimicking sand art and painting an air picture of stress. 'And if I leave this room to smoke, they send me outside. And if I am outside, there are signs saying I must be many metres from building. And soon I am standing in the street looking like a prostitute.'

Brian makes his lips into an 'O' and exhales noisily. 'Better,' he says. He rummages around under the table and pulls his phone out of his pocket. 'She's one to rearrange a bloke's intimate anatomy. That'll keep the floodgates shut on the bladder for a minute or two.'

'We should find you a toilet.' It's been at least five years since I've said that to either of my children. I can picture him taking to the stage with a damp patch on his pants, and offering three minutes of rambling non sequiturs about his genitals. 'And on the subject of bladders . . . the late-emptying issue. Design's not really on your side there, it turns out. Robyn's passed on a few ideas . . .'

'Oh, really? You're going round talking to people about this now?' He looks down at his drinks, blinking when he notices the apple juice for the first time. He turns it around to check the label. 'But go on. I'm all ears.'

I stare straight ahead, he stares at Ludmila Kirilenko and I give it my best shot. I explain the penis to a forty-nine-year-old who never got the instruction book, or had the chance to get the news about his shoddy man pipe straight from Robyn. I take it from the diamond-shaped aperture all the way to the laser it might have been, had there been a god on duty that day.

'Cool,' he says. 'Laser, hey? Anyone who can give you that kind of material, you can talk about my penis with them. I can work with that. Now, I've got to pay a chick a compliment, and see how that plays out for me.'

Ludmila Kirilenko is smoking sullenly, ashing onto a side plate, while a manager is sought. Brian stands, stumbles over the legs of his chair, rearranges the front of his pants and heads towards her.

'The toilet's probably more of a priority,' I tell him, but he doesn't seem to hear.

I'd be a better minder if the job came with a tazer, or at least a net. Instead I look like his needy friend, unable to stop shadowing him.

'Loved your work in there,' he says to her. He holds out his hand for her to shake. 'Brian.'

She eyes him warily, then decides to smile. 'Ludmila.' She transfers her cigarette to her left hand and extends her right, keeping it as limp as a stunned bird. 'Thank you.'

'Yeah, great, very . . .' He searches for the word, any word that might genuinely sound as if he came over to compliment her, anything that might keep him in the game. 'Evocative.'

'Good.' She takes a step to the left, to place Brian between her cigarette and the functions manager, who has just arrived in the room.

'I've got to say – since I won't get many shots at this – you're right in my sights, lady.'

Brian points a finger pistol at her, double-clicks with his tongue to cock it and fires. I can feel myself going red, and no one's even looking at me.

'I've always been into that look,' he says, powering on as she focuses on his index and middle fingers, in case they're still pointing at her for a reason. 'The one where the chick's nose is, like, a size too big for her face. You, Virginia Woolf – you've both got that going on. That rocks my jocks, that kind of thing.'

She lifts her right hand to cover her nose. 'Rocks what?'

Robyn's friend Lydia walks in, still clutching her phone, scanning the room as if she's searching for something or someone.

'Jocks. My jocks.' Brian enunciates it carefully, assuming good diction will do the job, land the lady. Instead it merely shares the word with most of the room. 'It might be short for jockey shorts. Underpants. It makes me muscle up in the underpants.'

From behind, the accompanying mime looks like a gorilla with an itchy groin rash. Ludmila draws back on her cigarette, blows the air briskly sideways. And I make my move.

'I'm sorry to interrupt,' I tell her as I grab his arm, 'but I really need to take Brian somewhere.' And have him shot.

I steer him towards Lydia, since I figure he's got plenty of moves left to run and she might as well experience some of his messy boldness first hand. It's time for her to learn to appreciate the less bold, who have pushed no further over the barricades than the grocer's apostrophe.

'We've met,' she says, when I start to introduce him. 'I'm really looking forward to the debate, Brian. I just came back here to wish you luck, you and the others I haven't caught up with yet. There's still Tom . . .'

On cue, Tom Chastain appears in the doorway in an

old greatcoat and battered trilby, buffered by a phalanx of minders. He's looking theatrically crestfallen, in case we need reminding of 'There's Something Not Right About Tom', TV's fictionalised account of his mopey life, hunt for the perfect cheese sandwich and ironic collecting of snow domes.

Lydia pivots on her heel as though pulled by a string. 'Tom . . .'

The light spangles on the silver sequins on the back of her dress as she leaves us.

'Some people can't do anything without minders and sycophants,' Brian says, glaring as a woman with a publicist look about her steps in to check that Lydia and Tom are already acquainted.

'Sorry we're short on sycophants,' I tell him, but he's not listening.

Tom utters something in his famously soft voice and Lydia throws her head back, laughing in response.

'He's the dickhead who trashed the toilet,' Brian says. 'Throws up before every gig. Probably has four of them holding his hair back. Drank a bit much this time and his aim was off.'

He's jiggling on the spot now, and that was never a good sign from Jack when he was five.

Lydia leads Tom Chastain and his party our way. The others fall in behind him, forming a V.

'Brian,' Lydia says, 'I'm sure you know Tom.'

'No we haven't actually . . .' Tom says in the same moment that Brian mentions their time together on Talkin' 'Bout Your Generation.

Brian's smile, already fake, sets into something identical but grimmer.

A noise somewhere between a squeak and a whistle comes out of Tom and he puts on a lost look and says, 'Awkward,' in a tremulous falsetto.

Brian nods, then points to Tom's face. 'I think there's a crumb of snot caught in your nostril hair on the right. You might want to . . .'

'Oh,' Tom squawks. 'Oh Christ.' His hands rush to his face, forming a tent over his allegedly snot-laden nose. His cheeks flare red. 'They're broadcasting this tonight. And I always get loads of close-ups. Nightmare. Thanks.'

He reels away, minders and Lydia moving into protective formation and shepherding him somewhere that can offer him a private moment with a mirror and tissues.

Brian watches him all the way to the door. 'Ha. Works every time.'

He jiggles, overbalances and reaches out for a table to steady himself.

'I'm going to find you a toilet,' I tell him. 'Now. Try to stay out of trouble.'

Ludmila has been talked down from her indignation, or some compromise has been reached. She appears to have smoked one cigarette hard and fast and agreed not to light another. Her ash plate is carried away as though it's bearing radioactive waste.

'No more helping visiting Ukranians out with the etymology of "jocks".' I can see that Brian's eyes are back on her. 'Maybe eat something or take some time to go through your notes.'

'Yeah, right,' he says. 'Notes.'

34

THERE'S STILL A YELLOW SIGN blocking the door of the green-room toilets. The first staff member I find tells me the ballroom toilets are around the other side, sweeping his arm in an arc that suggests it's a long way.

'Your best bet might be the ones next to Lava,' he says, 'if they're still open.'

As I make my way through the lines of people at the nearby ballroom doors, my phone beeps with an incoming text. My first thought is that it might be Brian, telling me I'm too late and he's back in the green room, an essentially continent adult, sitting in a cata-strophic lake of his own urine because he couldn't be bothered to find a toilet himself before now.

It's from Robyn. 'Serving buffet now. Looks good. Didn't want you to miss out if they haven't fed you in there.'

The corridor is curved, and I can see the lights of the foyer ahead.

'Eat and I'll join you for dessert,' I text back. 'Am currently looking for toilet for Brian . . .'

A flight has just arrived, perhaps from Japan, and there's a clump of pink and blue and Hello Kitty suitcases in the foyer, handles all raised like antlers. Their owners have their phones out, taking photos of themselves or each other or the mysterious central shard of black rock.

'Obsidian,' one of the group says, pointing to it. And then he says something in Japanese and they nod.

Once I'm past the rock and its new fans, I can see that the Lava toilets are still open. That's all I need to know. Now I simply have to line up a party of bearers, outnumbering Tom Chastain's minders by one, and have Brian carried to his moment of relief.

He's sitting with his bag when I get back to the room. He has a plate full of biriyani and a stack of pappadums. He nods in my direction and brings another forkful of food to his mouth.

'I've found one,' I tell him. 'Other side of the foyer, next to Lava.'

He chews, shifts his food around in his mouth and moves his hand to cover it. 'Yeah, don't worry about it, mate. It's kind of passed.'

'What do you mean? How did it . . .'

'Let's just say, thanks for getting me the apple juice.' He pats the top of the bottle. The lid rattles and he hurries to tighten it. 'And thanks for making it the big bottle.'

His seat's at an angle to the table. The ideal angle for me to see the tell-tale damp dot spreading on his pants. Brian, in the middle of the green room, has urinated into an apple-juice bottle.

'What were you thinking? Are you high?'

'Shit, I hope so after what I paid for those tabs. But don't worry, I'm just taking the edge off.' He laughs. 'I'm kidding. I just picked up a couple of fluid tablets.

I wouldn't mind dropping back to two chins before the show. You know, TV and all . . .'

He pats the flabby flesh under his chin with the back of his hand.

'Are you serious? Now you get vain on me? And you mess around with drugs and you . . .' I force myself to crank the volume down. 'Piss in a bottle because *one* toilet was out of action? This is a five-star hotel. They have more than one toilet.'

'Yeah, but I kind of needed it right then.' He shrugs. 'No biggie. I took a leak in a bush outside earlier.'

'What?'

'Hey, I got out of the pool.' His tone is unreasonably close to indignation.

'What are you? A dog? Suddenly laying claim to this whole hotel? Or did your parents never introduce you to the concept of a toilet? They've been around since the Romans. Excellent for pissing into.'

'Sure.' He snaps a pappadum in two and puts the smaller piece in his mouth. 'And so would pools be, if there wasn't always the slight threat that they've got that chemical in there that goes purple with wee.'

'That's a myth. I'm sure that's a myth.'

'Good to know.' He says it as if we're a pair of sly pool pissers now, in on the secret together.

'You are never swimming at my house.'

Tom Chastain reappears in the doorway next to Savannah Burke, another member of his team in the debate. Their separate clumps of minders are temporarily dammed by the narrowness of the space before spilling in behind their respective stars two at a time. Tom looks Brian's way, points at his nose and puts on a kind of scowly shrug. His own nostril inspection has come up negative.

'Must have dropped out of its own accord,' Brian calls out to him. 'Some of the dry ones do and it looked kind of crusty, so . . .' He shrugs. 'Probably on the carpet somewhere.'

Tom keeps the scowl and glances at the floor. A minder takes his elbow and turns him towards the buffet.

'Little shit,' Brian says quietly, keeping his lips completely still. 'Pair of little shits.'

Savannah Burke is in her school uniform as always, with plaits wired out to the side and a heart drawn on one arm in pen, with an arrow through it. She's the youngest debater, I think, and here on the strength of a Raw Comedy win, a few TV guest spots and her one touring show, Seriously Take Me Seriously.

'Look at her.' When he says 'look', Brian in this instance appears to mean 'stare'. 'Too young to even know how derivative she is, but so's her audience . . .'

'I can tell you're conflicted. You hate her for her youth and success and yet that poor old late-emptying penis of yours can't help but notice how she fills out that school uniform.'

He twitches and turns to look at me, feigning a startle. 'Read me like a book, chief. Alarming.'

'Don't be conflicted. It's just another game your penis isn't in.'

'Yep. Ain't that the truth.' He slides lower in his seat and pokes his fork into his biriyani. 'Free to be a big fat old hater, then.' He sets the fork down. 'I've been on Talkin' 'Bout My Generation with both of those two.

Once each. We were two generations apart. *Two*. They keep putting me in Boomer, fuck them. Don't they know we're on the cusp?' He points to me and then to himself.

'I keep saying that. Every time someone calls me a boomer.' Every time Robyn calls me a boomer. 'Bill Clinton's a boomer.'

'Whereas Barack's one of us.'

'I'm sure he feels just the same.' The three amigos – Barack, Brian and me. 'I bet he's standing in a green room right now, getting ready to deliver some planet-changing talk, trying to work out what to do with a sneaky bottle of piss.'

'Man, that'd be the job,' Brian says, sighing and ludicrously contemplating a turn as Leader of the Free World, probably one concurrently dating Taylor Swift. 'I bet he has a whole relay of people handling the piss bottle.'

No, Brian, he finds a *toilet*.

'Speaking of which, we'd better . . .' My phone starts ringing. 'We'd better do something with this bottle before it causes any trouble.'

I'm expecting the caller to be Robyn or someone related to the event – maybe the head of security, who's just reviewed certain footage featuring Brian and a bottle. It's Jack.

'It's my son,' I tell Brian. 'I should . . .'

'Sure.' He scoops up some biriyani. 'Better get some of this in me anyway. I'm starting to feel a bit, I don't know, hazy.'

'I'm with Grandad,' Jack says, sounding tense. 'We have an anal situation.'

'But Grandad doesn't even have an anus. Does he?'

Brian coughs, and splutters biriyani across his plate.

'It's bad.' Jack's voice starts to wobble. 'It's Winston.'

He sounds far away, like an astronaut on a mission that's gone to crap, gazing forlornly at a distant blue earth and wondering how he'll save the day with no more than a pair of tweezers, a wad of chewing gum and some Space Food Stick wrappers. I have to be Houston, calm, dependable. I need to steady him and bring him home.

'I need you to be a man now.'

Robyn would have twelve better lines than that – Robyn who is killing time grazing the buffet until date night starts, Robyn who has the skills to master any anal situation. But he chose to call me.

'It's the bandage,' Jack moans. 'You have to come now. Just come.'

I have wanted to be so wanted, even if not for a crisis involving an unexplained bandage and an anus a block away in the Gold Coast night.

'I've got to go,' I tell Brian. 'I'll be back as soon as I can. Just stay right where you are. Unless they call you to go on stage.'

Brian is holding a serviette to his nose. He nods and blows loudly, then opens the serviette to check the contents.

'I knew it was more than just rice . . .' he says, but I'm already on my way to the door.

I tell myself to keep it to a brisk stride as I push through the foyer, but my legs break into a jog whenever there's space. A liveried staff member waves at the doors to open them before I get there and, once I hit the night air, I'm free to run. I leap over the concrete tracks of driveways, a dropped bottle and a panicking black cat. Less than two minutes from the call, I'm on the steps to the unit, with a long low doggy yowl guiding me to the door.

Abi opens it as soon as I knock.

'Oh, Dad, god,' she says. 'It's Winston.'

April is in the far corner of the room behind a chair. My father is on the sofa, leaning forward, with Winston's head in his hands. Jack is jumping around near Winston's hind quarters, trying to keep him still. And Winston is straining and stretching, splayed across the rug, with several metres of grubby crepe bandage extending from his anus to a couple of twists around the wrought-iron leg of the glass-topped coffee table, to two dining chairs which are now sitting askew, with brown marks on their legs where friction has occurred.

'The mystery of the missing ankle bandage,' my father says when he looks up. 'And the constipation. The bandage seems to have got stuck. I would have tried the extraction myself, but . . .'

'No, no, that's okay. Leave it to me.' All of a sudden I'm a superhero whose special power is extracting bandages from the anuses of bulldogs. 'This kind of thing used to come up all the time at BDK. Dad, you keep talking to Winston, but sit up. Abi, you get down there and take the head. Jack, I need you to mix a sachet of laundry detergent with some hot water in a bucket. April, could you get all the spare towels?'

I run into the kitchen for the dishwashing gloves as Abi and my father attempt to pacify Winston.

I had vainly hoped that the trip to the coast would do it, but it turns out that my chance to reconnect with my family has come through drawing the last of a bandage from the anus of a yowling dog.

I'm on my knees, snapping the gloves on as Jack dumps the bucket beside me and swings a lamp towards the action. Winston's bright pink anus is puckered around a knot in the bandage. The smell coming from him is glandular and panicky. I dip my hands in the bucket, rubbing soapy water across the gloves, before remembering that surgical handwashing actually comes before the gloves are on.

'Lubrication,' I tell them, in the hope that it reassures us all.

I put one hand on Winston's pelvis and give the bandage a tug with the other. Nothing. Nothing but a growl and, in the lamplight, a flash of white bulldog teeth. The anal skin strains but the bandage doesn't budge. The smell turns acrid. He's let some urine go.

I'm fighting the urge to gag, trying to convince myself I'm watching one of those TV birth shows, at the brink of the delivery of a little baby knot.

Someone's breathing rapidly in and out as though their baby's crowning. It's me.

I take one more breath in, let it slowly out and pass my index finger into Winston's anus and around the knot. His legs scrabble wildly, kicking at the air. I press his pelvis down, hook the knot and yank it out. He yelps and falls forward and the last of the bandage slips free.

My father applauds. Winston stands up, panting, damp with urine and rank with the smell of an awful death narrowly dodged.

'Awesome,' Jack says. 'And the crowd goes wild. Dad, how did you . . .'

'Some people are born heroes,' I tell him, rolling the right glove from my hand and fighting another impulse to gag. 'Some people have heroism thrust upon them. Now, I just have to scrub my hands until the first few layers of skin are gone and then I'll get back to the event.'

I run into the kitchen, shove the gloves into the bin and go to work on my hands with the scouring pad until they're bright red. Then the pad follows the gloves into the bin and I'm on my way, disappearing back into the night with my good deed done.

But not exactly flying square-jawed back to my bat cave. I don't know how it works for Batman, but I'm running, dry-retching and screeching, all at the same time, while shaking my right hand hard in the hope of shaking it all the way off my arm. This is Robyn's job – her *job* – interfering with anuses for the greater good. The imaginary stink of panicky dog's arse chases me all the way back to Obsidian.

The first thing I do in the foyer light is check my hand, expecting brown, but it's pink and pristine. I might even have scraped off a couple of age spots.

Back in the green room, the debate moderator, Lyle Hartley – host of a range of second-tier reality TV shows I've never seen and that have names like Who Wants to Renovate My Goat – picks at a plate of salad with his fork and gossips with Di Clark, the token oldster on Tom and Savannah's team, whose shtick is the seventies and later-years cleavage, and who claims to have once almost porked Bon Scott in the early days of AC/DC.

Brian is doing a TV interview, standing with a bare piece of wall behind him, demonstrating something that I hope is not the screwing or unscrewing of the lid of a urine bottle.

When I get closer I can hear him saying, 'You wrap it in the towel and twist it hard as buggery. You'd be amazed how much it sucks the water out.'

I had wanted Lydia to be wrong. I had wanted 'Come and touch it' to have gone away.

When the interview wraps up, he drops the smile and heads over to me. He looks pointedly in the direction of Ludmila Kirilenko. Tom Chastain is holding one of her hands and inspecting it closely, as if it has magical powers. She's laughing, feigning coyness. He's stroking her fingers, as though they're little bony pets.

'I struck out with the Russkie,' Brian says, sounding surly. Then he raises his voice. 'With Pencil Tits.' I get another rush of stale wine breath.

'You can't call someone that.' I almost clamp my hand on his mouth, but it's only marginally less toxic than Winston's hindquarters. 'You just can't.'

'But take a look at her. Two pencils in a dress. All nipples on sticks, no fun bags. She could put an eye out . . .' He starts to rock on his feet and grabs the back of a chair with one hand. 'Might sit down again.' He points towards his bag.

'At least you got rid of the bottle.'

'Yeah.' He peers in the direction of the table. The bag is exactly where it's always been, with a half-finished plate of food and scrunched-up serviette to one side. 'Well, no, actually. Though it does appear to have gone.' He looks over to the buffet. 'Hey, they all have. Look at the bowl. No apple juice left.'

He blinks vigorously and his face goes blotchy. He

pulls the chair over and slumps onto it. He groans, and swats one cheek with his hand.

'Mate, I think it's the fluid tablet,' he says. 'I think I'm having some kind of reaction.'

I put one hand on his shoulder to steady him, pull my phone from my pocket and call Robyn. She answers in one ring.

I can hear music in the background as she says, 'Hey, how's it going? I'm with Lydia. She knows how to rock a date night.'

Lydia shouts something, but she's too far from the phone for it to come through clearly. It's at least possible that it included a reference to HLA. I can hear Robyn laughing.

'I've got a bit of a medical issue here,' I tell her. 'Brian's taken a fluid tablet . . .' Brian holds up two fingers. 'Two fluid tablets, to look a bit less jowly and –'

'Dickhead,' she says.

Brian's looking up at me, gazing divergently. It's a look I've seen on bug-eyed goldfish before they go belly-up.

I give him a thumbs up. 'Robyn's happy to help.'

'Next you'll be telling me he has no idea of the name,' she says, maintaining her previous tough tone, 'but they were white.'

I ask him the name and he stares at me blankly.

I ask him what colour they were and he says, 'White,' giving me a look of defocused optimism.

'Yep. White. No name.'

'Figures,' Robyn says. 'Okay, if he's got any cardiac or kidney conditions, you need to pull him from the debate and get help. Otherwise get some fluids into him and, if he's still dizzy, lie him on the floor with his legs elevated. You're missing a pretty nice dinner, by the way. Did you realise date night wouldn't start until after the main? I'm not sure I knew that.'

I pass the details on to Brian, who gives me another thumbs up before leaning forward and resting his head on the table.

As I get close to the buffet, a staff member asks if he can help.

'I just need a couple of bottles of water for Brian,' I tell him. 'He's a bit dehydrated.' I pull one out of the bowl with each hand. 'We had some apple juice, actually. Did you see where that went?'

'Apple juice? That shouldn't have been touched if he was drinking it. It might have gone if it was a full bottle though.' He looks apologetic. 'There's punch as part of the dessert buffet and they were short of apple juice . . .'

'Have they made it yet?'

He checks his watch. 'Oh, yeah. Probably finishing it now. It'll be out there in a minute or two. They want everything in there before the debate. So . . . We might be able to get some apple juice from the restaurant.'

He wants to help. He wants this to be about a simple diva demand concerning juice. He has no idea of the margin by which he has missed the point. I have a swooning star, my date night is happening in the next room without me and somewhere in the sparkling stainless steel kitchens of this five-star hotel, punch is being made from Brian Brightman's urine.

'I need your food and beverage manager to call me,' I tell him. I reach over to pull a pen from his pocket.

'Okay, I don't know my number. But I need to talk to him, or her. As a matter of urgency. There's been an incident.'

'You're in the debate, aren't you?' he says, smirking. 'You're, like, punking me.'

I lean forward and put it as steadily and calmly as I can. 'Some of Brian Brightman's urine has accidentally gone into the punch.'

'Ha,' he says. 'That's good. That's a good one. Didn't they do that on . . .' He clicks his fingers, trying to remember the show.

They did it here, tonight.

'I'll give you my wife's number.' It's easy enough to find it on my phone. I write it down on a serviette.

'So you want the F and B manager to call your wife about some urine.' He glances at the number and folds the serviette. He's still smirking. 'Sure.'

The debaters are being rounded up to get miked. I'm going to have to find another way. Brian has pulled himself sluggishly to his feet and has two of the wait staff hefting his bag.

On my way across to him, I crack open the first bottle of water. 'Drink this.' I push it into his hand. 'All of it. Don't drink the punch. Don't ask why.'

His head wobbles, strafed by the rapid-fire orders, but he obediently takes the bottle and drinks. There's a smell of fish. It seems to be coming from somewhere near him. He's dehydrated, probably also drunk and smelling of fish, and his urine is about to be distributed around the ballroom unless I can stop it. I'm the babysitter you never ask back.

As I swap the empty water bottle for the full one, an

event organiser takes me by the elbow and says, in an unnecessarily calming tone that's obviously designed for a painless de-mindering of the talent, 'Let's get you to the ballroom. I'm sure you won't want to miss this.'

'I need to talk to the food and beverage mànager,' I tell her. 'There's a problem.'

'There's plenty more food in the ballroom.' She's smiling even as she steers me away from Brian, his sherpas and his props bag.

Her name tag says 'Monet'. With this being the Gold Coast, it's entirely possible the 'T' isn't silent. Her fiercely blond hair is gathered in a black clip that complements her stiff black Obsidian jacket. Her skin is the same shade of orange as Venice's.

'It's a food safety issue.' We're already in the corridor. 'I really do need to talk to them.'

'Is it gluten?' She's no longer actually holding my elbow, though her hand is hovering nearby in case I need more steering. 'I think we marked anything with gluten in it. But Rochelle's in there already so, if you show me where you're going to sit, I can get her to come over.'

The doors to the ballroom are about to close. Monet picks up the pace.

35

LIGHTS ARE SWIRLING as we duck inside and the sound system is pumping out Coldplay's Viva la Vida. Robyn catches my eye from one of the tables and points to the empty seat to her left. I make it clear to Monet that that's where I'm headed.

As I sit down, Robyn says, 'So, that Moroccan thing was pretty good. Did you get it, back there with the beautiful people? The one with couscous?' She's halfway through a glass of red wine. 'My other date had to go and check something.' To her right, Lydia's plate sits half-finished, her chair pushed back from the table. 'How would you rate date night so far?'

'Yeah, look, it's been kind of crazy for me . . .' Winston, the bandage. She has no idea where my hand has been. 'I did think we'd be having dinner together, but . . . Those Indian gurus – they sometimes drink urine, don't they?'

'What?' She leans closer and scrunches up her eyes, trying to find different words in what I've just said. 'Did you just . . .'

'Work with me. Is there anything wrong with drinking urine? Can you catch anything?'

'No.' She moves to sit straighter. 'Well, you shouldn't. Not usually. What have you been doing out the back? It should be sterile. Faeces though . . .' Instantly, there's a horrible picture in my head of Brian taking a dump in a punch bowl. I can't say it'd never happen. 'Why . . .'

'Oh, nothing. Just a question someone had. Don't drink the punch.'

'Don't drink the punch?'

'It's got . . . You know how you hate fennel? It tastes just like fennel.'

'Right,' she says, pushing to see the full picture when I've handed her only a few small pieces of it. 'Don't take this the wrong way, but I don't think you're suited to this minding thing. And I don't think it's really compatible with the idea of a date night. I think that might have been evident if we'd talked it through. It's not going to be a regular part of your job, is it?'

'I don't expect so.' Not after tonight.

Around the room, I can count four large bowls of punch and plenty of people who appear to be drinking it. I try to convince myself it's diluted, with the urine no more concentrated than in the water of a public swimming pool. People drink that all the time.

As I'm wondering if I should shout 'fire' and then run around tipping the bowls over in the rush, a staff member appears beside me. In the low light, I can just make out the name Rochelle on her tag. She's holding a tray with a bottle of apple juice on it, and a glass.

'You're Andrew Van Fleet, yeah?' She's already lowering the tray towards me. 'This is from Mr Brightman.' She puts on a serious look. 'And if you're having any more issues with your insulin, we can get medical help. Just give any one of the staff a wave. They'll all be watching out for you.'

I look past her, towards the door. Two of the wait staff are standing monitoring our interaction. One of them gives me a discreet thumbs up.

'What?' Robyn says. 'Insulin?'

'Thank you.' I lift the bottle and the glass from the tray. 'I appreciate it.' As the victim of this comprehensive punking, I want to move beyond it as quickly as possible.

The bottle is still warmer than room temperature. There's a post-it note stuck to it on which Brian has written, 'Barack says hi,' and a smiley face.

Rochelle nods, tucks the tray under her arm and steps away.

'Insulin?' Robyn's not letting it go. 'Since when were you . . .'

'Since never.' I check that the lid is tight and place the bottle carefully under my chair. 'It was a misunderstanding.'

She looks at me as if I'm a newly arrived middle-aged alien who only vaguely resembles the man she married. 'You are having a very strange night.'

The music stops, abruptly. There's a fanfare, and a voice comes over the PA system telling us the broadcast is about to begin. I've been robbed of any chance to explain, and that can only be a good thing. A very strange night? Unless Brian's found a way to warm chilled apple juice, I appear to be minding urine.

The screen at the front of the stage slips silently up into darkness, revealing a lifesavers' watchtower in the centre and, on each side, three deckchairs under a beach umbrella, with an esky. There's a smaller screen overhead, with text on it reading: 'The Future of Comedy: should we get our laughs between the flags, or is there a place for blood in the water?'

Brian is on the pro-blood team.

Lyle Hartley steps out from backstage with his finger to one ear as instructions come through from the control desk. He's dressed like a lifesaver, with the red-and-yellow cap, a daub of zinc cream on his nose, and a yellow surf-rescue shirt that's just long enough to maintain the threat that there's nothing beneath it but standard-issue lifesaver budgie smugglers.

There are sporadic claps and some woo-wooing, which he ignores.

Someone shouts, 'Thirty seconds.'

Lyle walks forward, his eyes down on the stage, like someone who has dropped his keys in the sand. He finds his mark. In front of the tables, a camera slides into place. He waits. Someone somewhere is counting down.

I check my phone. No more calls from Crystal Tydes. I can only hope that's a good sign. Robyn's watching Lyle Hartley, ready to be won over. I want to tell her all about the Winston incident, but we're seconds from show time.

Lyle looks up, finding the cameras, assessing the audience.

A man near the stage in a black T-shirt calls out, 'In five,' counting down with his fingers. He waves his other arm to summon applause.

Lyle's first few lines might be great for TV, but they hardly come through in the room at all. There's a pop, and his voice is suddenly booming, then it drops to a normal volume.

He introduces the teams, and they come on with a shambolic high-stepping sand march, paying out invisible line over their heads and generally apeing surf-lifesaver moves. As they take to their deckchairs and Lyle talks through the topic and the rules, the text vanishes from the overhead screen and Ludmila Kirilenko is back in action, this time freestyling, opening with a shark's fin breaking through waves.

Lyle turns to climb the tower ladder, giving a flash of blue buttock, and Brian shouts out, 'Hang on a second. That's not a lifesaver.'

He and Toby Field rush over, each grabbing a handful of fabric and giving Lyle a wedgie so vigorous it lifts him two rungs up the ladder. There's a gasp from the crowd, and then a cheer. Brian gives one of Lyle's bare buttocks a slap, and he and Toby scurry back to their seats.

Lyle pivots onto the top of the tower, eyes wide, looking flushed. He wriggles around. Ludmila manages a quick sand cartoon of a panicky man clenching his knees, his hands a blur as he tries to cover himself.

'Much better grip,' Lyle tells us once he's settled in the seat. 'Just like in the surf boats.'

That earns him a laugh and some applause while he reaches around and rearranges the fabric.

Di Clark is the first speaker, making the case for comedy swimming between the flags. As examples of blood in the water, she makes scathing remarks about each of her opponents, and then chastises herself for doing it, saying it's not funny at all. Meg Riddoch heckles. Brian unzips his props bag to check the contents.

Di is in a bright floral dress that goes to the knee and Ludmila gets a laugh by drawing her as Carmen Miranda, with fruit piled on her head.

Di glances up at the screen, which is almost directly above her, and says, 'That's right. Draw me like a bloody drag queen. Everybody else does.'

Ludmila wipes the fruit and draws in some feathers.

'Does a drag queen have these?' Di shoves her breasts up and almost out of her dress. 'They try. You know they try, but it's all pecs and padding.'

Lyle rings his bell. Di seems surprised her three minutes is up, but recovers to take a bow.

Robyn leans my way and whispers, 'What's in Brian's bag?'

'I don't know.' I should know. 'He's an adult . . .'

'Really? You're relying on that?' Further recognition of my minder failings. 'He's a thirteen-year-old implanted in a sixty-year-old body.'

'Next up,' Lyle announces, 'we have our first speaker for the negative team. They're outside the flags, where anything goes, as he proves time and again on Brisbane radio, on regular TV panel show appearances and sometimes in Gold Coast motels. It's SPINstereo's Brian Brightman.'

Brian stands, dragging his bag out from under his chair. He waves to acknowledge the applause, which is more generous than I'd expected.

And then the colour drains from his lips and face, his knees sag and he mumbles, 'Rebuttal . . . rebuttal . . .' on his way to the floor.

The crowd cheers. Brian's flat on his back, arms and

legs moving as if he's trying to climb a ladder. He lifts his head, but it clunks down again.

The audience is still laughing when Lyle, with an aerial view that must make Brian's slow-motion flailing look like landlocked backstroke, works out it's not part of the act.

'Um, we might just take a quick break . . .' he says, peering through the lights in the hope of catching the right person's eye.

Brian points straight at him, dropping his other three limbs and focusing on getting that one arm lined up the way he wants it. 'No. No break. This is my . . .' He rolls his head to look at his team-mates. 'Just get my legs up. Get my legs up.'

All five comedians jump from their seats and scramble into haphazard action.

Brian's microphone is still live, so we can hear him saying, 'It's a fluid thing. I'm dangerously dehydrated. But it's cool. It's cool.'

Somehow it ends up with a comedian holding up each of his four limbs and Savannah Burke on her knees pushing both his thighs towards the vertical.

'Well hello, Savvie,' Brian says, finding some of his old syrupy sleaze as blood runs back into his head. 'Never thought I'd see you down there.' The audience cheers. 'Where were you when I was doing room laundry this morning?'

Someone at a table down the back shouts out, 'Come and touch it.'

'Exactly,' Brian says, freeing one hand to punch the air. 'I'm okay. I'm okay. Think you've got me where I need to be, folks.'

He rolls and lifts himself to his knees. Meg Riddoch fetches him a chair.

'I'm okay,' he says again as they help him into it. 'Just wanted to sharpen the look up a bit for TV.' He pats his jowls, and his microphone picks up a jubbly slapping sound. 'Ooh, nice,' he says, and does it again. 'Reminds me of when I last had a girlfriend. But thanks, team. Teams.' He turns to his opponents and nods, and then to his own team. 'So, yeah, wanted to sharpen the look up a bit. Scored a couple of fluid tablets from my mum when I was filling her dosette for the weekend. Hey, how hardcore is Mum? This shit hardly touches her.'

That draws a cheer. Brian swivels around to face the other team again.

'Hey, Di,' he calls out. 'I just wanted to clarify something. Just from when you had my arm up and I thought the last thing I'd ever see might be your front, looming over me. Do you call that cleavage or is there a larger lady doing a naked duck dive into your dress?'

This time he pulls a mix of cheers and boos. Di's cleavage has its own Facebook page.

'Hey, that's rebuttal. I'm entitled. Outside the flags. Blood in the water. Get it? I could have said "fat chick" but my mum brought me up right. Anyway, without a whole lot of architecture in place below, it's only temporary, all that . . .'

He heaves his own ample breasts into the cleavage zone with his hands.

'I'm not saying set the puppies loose, Di. I'm not going that far outside the flags. Not in minute one. What I'm saying is, don't think you're the only game in town when it comes to breasts, ladies. We fat bastards have our own share of magic moments in the shower. Contact lenses out, bit of steam . . . sometimes the reflection's a welcome surprise for a second or two. Anyway, breasts, they're not easy are they? Bloody gravity. Anything above a D cup you can eventually tie in a bow.'

His props bag is sitting on the stage at an angle to his chair. I'm wondering where his line of thought might take him, and if there really is a resusc dummy in there, which he's about to use in a manner that could set CPR back fifty years.

Ludmila is hurriedly sand-sketching a shirtless Brian in a Soviet-era double-D bra.

Robyn's sitting with a grin fixed to her face, as if she smiled once a long time before date night and then got stuck transitioning to a wince.

'But don't get me wrong,' Brian says, shuffling around to sit more squarely on the deckchair. 'I'm fat friendly. Any time I'm at a modelling agency party, I head straight for the plus-size chicks. The regular models are always scrawny and up themselves and not taking in enough nutrients to make sense, but the plus-size girls, whatever they say, those chicks always have shithouse self-esteem. And you fellas know the chick with shithouse self-esteem's always your better option, don't you?'

I can almost hear Robyn's teeth gnashing.

'Anyway, I know my way around fat.' His thighs are almost at right angles, forming a V that points straight at his groin. For now, any damp patch is lost in folds of fabric. 'Look at me. I went to the beach today. Had to put sunscreen on three chins first. It's like lubing up Jabba the Hutt. I have to rock to get off a couch. Still, at least I don't look like some of those old bastards down on the beach. I saw one guy who was so tanned and wrinkly he looked like a scrotum with eyes.'

He reaches his right hand up to his cheek and bends the stalk of the microphone to put the tip closer to his mouth. I'm not certain he's on topic, and I'm not certain it's as PG as he promised, but it's after 8.30pm, just, and the audience is hooting and laughing.

'But I'm only fat because I care. We've got one of those lolly boxes at the station. For craniofacial kiddies. First time you go there it's for chocolate. Second time it's because you've seen the pic on the box of the kiddie with the alien mid-facial tumour the size of his baby brother. Suddenly it's a moral obligation. Chocolate. It's like, if I don't turn up today and chip in my two bucks, little Ezekiel will still be on that island with his head taking second place on his shoulders. I tell you, I reckon there's a lot of that sacrifice going on here at the Gold Coast. A lot of lolly boxes on a lot of counters. A lot of ladies at the beach today with elboobs. You know, the breakout of boobage on the back of the arm just above the elbow?'

He wobbles his own arm flesh and shakes his head in sympathy.

'And it doesn't end there. I don't just have a body for radio, I've got a pelt for it. I grow more hair out of my ears than I grow on my scalp. And I moult. And it all comes off looking like pubic hair. So if you ever get a parcel from me, you can be pretty sure there'll be one or two of them trapped under the sticky tape. But don't worry — they could've come from any bit of me, and at my place a good seventy per cent of parcels aren't wrapped nude.'

He holds his hand up to settle the laughter. Ludmila reworks the Brian on screen. He's a bear, with large pendulous breasts and a parcel taped to his pubic region.

'It's not easy being a larger, pelted person. You can see the chick down there . . .' He shapes his hands to indicate his groin. 'With a handful of happy sack, and she's thinking, "Do I need to slap some kind of marker on this so I can find it again?" So pretty soon you're back to flying solo. You can tell when a fat bastard's been single a while, because he's waxed his chest to remind himself what tits look like.'

He undoes a button, pulls his shirt open and exposes a diamond of pale hairless breast.

Robyn leans over my way and says, 'You're thinking Jaws, right? Or that first girlfriend who popped it out? That was you, wasn't it?'

Yes, a special if perplexing moment, now destroyed forever, with Brian Brightman's breast photoshopped into my memory.

'And waxing's everywhere, isn't it?' Brian says unhappily. 'What is it with porn now? Where has pubic hair gone? I've seen dummies in the windows of Myer with more pubic hair than porn stars these days. There must be some big bloody mat of it quietly rotating in the mid-Pacific with all those plastic bottles. But it's not just porn stars. It's apparently standard school formal prep now. Is there a new talk that parents have to have with their daughters that says, "It's okay to have pubic hair?"'

Robyn groans and turns my way. 'Did you? You didn't . . .'

'No. As if I'd tell Brian . . .' As if I'd ever talk to Brian about schoolgirls and Brazilians. 'You and he have just read the same articles, that's all.'

Brian waits for the laughter to peak. The audience is his now. He's crass and shabby, slumped in his chair like a partially cracked Humpty Dumpty, and they're hanging on every word as he rips the Bandaid from his lonely hairy life.

'And the pressure doesn't end there,' he moans. 'Have you noticed how much porn's gone round to the trades-man's entrance? And you know what that calls for? Anal bleaching. Anal bloody bleaching.' He looks down below the lights, at the tables, and points to someone. 'How are you going with the sticky date pudding there, mate? Nice, isn't it? I mean, I'm not a prude. I'd be totally prepared to brighten up the old arsehole if it meant some perky young thing might be prepared to slip a digit up there at the moment of climax. As if I'd get that lucky. Last time I got a blow job it was like trying to give a cat a tablet.'

The man next to me laughs so hard he almost loses a mouthful of dessert. He sets his fork down and wipes his eyes.

'And just tonight I've learned that the penis has a design flaw,' Brian says.

Somehow he starts quoting almost verbatim every-thing I told him in the green room in his diuretic-addled state, all the way from the diamond-shaped aperture to the laser the poor maligned organ should have been. The audience, with the apparent exception of my date, is baying for more.

'In case you're wondering,' Robyn says, and not

warmly, 'this was not an ambition of mine, becoming a scriptwriter for a bozo like that.'

'It's great material. They're loving it.' The neighbour to my left is now slapping his thigh. I didn't think people actually did that. 'I paid attention. I know you think I don't. Your spectacular insights into the workings of the universe are one of the things I miss most whenever I'm away.' It's true. I remember plenty of them almost word for word, days later. 'And I never said a thing about the schoolgirls. Just the penis. Because Brian's got that problem.'

'Okay,' she says. 'That's half-saved, I suppose.'

On top of the lifesavers' tower, Lyle Hartley rings his bell.

'Mate,' Brian's head whips around. 'That can't be three minutes. That was just my intro.'

Lyle points to his watch. Brian strokes his stubble.

'Okay, okay, summing up.' He pushes himself out of the deckchair and turns towards his bag. 'Here's my point. If *we* don't cut through the crap all the way to the truth, who will? If we go soft, if we play safe, if we take prisoners . . .' He goes down on his knees and unzips the bag. 'How bland do you want it to be? I'm here to say . . .'

He slips both arms into the bag. He's got his back to the audience, so we can't see what he's doing. He lifts one knee from the stage and pushes himself upright. The empty bag flops to the stage. Brian is hugging a dead bull shark more than a metre long. An actual shark.

He changes his grip, hoists it above his head and bellows, 'Let the friggin' sharks back in the water.'

He stands like a weightlifter waiting for three white lights. The audience cheers madly. Phones flash, taking photos. He lowers the shark, swivels it around in his arms and plants a kiss between its gills and its mouth.

There are shouts of, 'More, more, more,' so he kisses it again. Then sporadic shouts of 'tongue', building to a chant. 'Tongue, tongue, tongue.'

Brian's laughing, soaking up his moment of triumph. He hugs the shark's face to his cheek and waves his free arm, winding the chant up, as though he might reward it if they take it far enough. He's the daredevil who needs the crowd to send him through the fire, over the jump, into the water tank in chains.

Di Clark pulls herself up the ladder, snatches the bell from Lyle Hartley and waves it around, but the ringing can barely be heard above the chanting for tongue.

Brian raises the shark above his head again, tail pointing straight up in the air.

He looks into its eyes, sighs and says, 'We were made for each other.'

He levers its jaw open with a thumb, wiggles his purple shiraz-soaked tongue around in a way that might scare children, and then thrusts it into the shark's mouth.

His eyes roll and he staggers as a new bout of dizziness swipes him. His thumb slides out, the jaw clamps shut. He yelps and slumps into the chair, holding the shark in his lap, his head bent forward, his tongue punctured by dozens of teeth. His fellow debaters are rolling their eyes, making a show of checking their watches.

Down at the front of the audience someone screams, killing the last of the nervous laughter from the back.

The bell clangs until Di Clark realises something has gone horribly wrong.

I'm already on my feet by then, pushing past tables and running to the stage, charging forward with my useless repertoire of business skills, the first minder in history to allow the talent's tongue to become snagged in the mouth of a shark.

As I take the stairs three at a time, new sand artistry appears on the overhead screen. There's an outline of a head like a knee, with a dick and balls drawn on the forehead. Beyond the far side of the stage, in a room now otherwise consumed by panic, Ludmila Kirilenko sits placidly on her stool, next to her glowing glass sand plate, drinking a cup of punch.

Brian's eyes are blinking hard and there's a panting moan coming out of him. He's pushing the shark's face into his to stop its bloodstained teeth drawing back harder on his tongue.

'It's okay,' I tell him when I reach him, because that's what you're supposed to say in a crisis, whether you have a clue or not. 'Just hold on. We'll get this fixed.' Because I brought my miraculous freeing-tongues-from-sharks'-mouths tool?

I kneel down and take the weight of the shark. I have no idea how to start the fixing. I'd get Robyn up here, but it's a simple grim matter of mechanics, not a GP problem. Brian holds its face and keeps panting. His hand bumps his microphone and the sound thumps through the room.

I lean in closer. 'Someone tell me we've called an ambulance.'

Down in the dark, I can make out dozens of people reaching for their phones.

Lyle Hartley appears on the far side of Brian, with a finger pressing his earpiece as a message comes through. 'It's done.' He puts his other arm under the shark. 'Five minutes.'

36

BRIAN GRIPS MY HAND as they lift him onto the ambulance trolley. There's sweat on his forehead. I keep my free arm around the shark and one ambo takes it from the other side.

I'm so focused on the shark and on Brian's tongue that I get a sense of a crowd as we pass through the foyer, but I don't notice a single face. I keep my spot all the way to the ambulance and crouch to step inside as they swing the trolley's wheels up and lock it into place. The siren whoops into action and we're gliding down the driveway and onto the road before I realise I'm part of the trip, going all the way, still holding Brian's hand.

The ambo in the back with me settles Brian on his side, so that the trolley takes most of the weight of the shark. He sets a mask over Brian's nose and pulls the elastic over his head. The mask sits half on Brian's face and half on the snout of the shark.

'Just some nitrous oxide,' he says. 'Take a bit of the stress away.' He puts his hand on my shoulder. 'Are you right with the shark while I get down a few details? You're next of kin, yeah?'

Brian makes a wheezy sound that's almost a laugh. He's lying in the fetal position looking like someone we found in the street. His stubble is the start of a grizzly beard, there's a gob of brown wax lodged in the hair of his ear canal, his nose is running onto the white pillow case, he's drooling spit and blood and, from the smell, it's distinctly possible he's urinated. And I'm sitting with one buttock on his trolley, one arm cradling his shark and the other hand tightly gripping his, looking as life-partnerish as anyone could.

The ambo has a pen poised over a clipboard.

'Only if you mean is he my evil twin.' I'm losing feeling in my fingertips, but Brian isn't letting go.

We race up the highway, past tower blocks and rows of dark palm trees. Through the back windows, I can see the dishevelled traffic in our wake – cars that have pulled onto median strips to let us by, or squeezed to fit two to a lane. The siren switches up to a more urgent tone to take us through red lights, then drops back to its usual rhythm on the other side.

We glide onto a bridge and the Surfers Paradise skyline takes shape behind us as more and more tall buildings shrink to window size. We swing off the main road and pass through roadworks, leaving men in hi-vis gear stepping into ditches. We turn a sharp left up a ramp and there's a flash of a sign that reads 'Ambulance Entrance' – red letters on a white background – and then the angle becomes too steep to see it.

The moment we stop, the back doors are pulled open.

There are three or four sets of sliding double doors leading into Emergency. Brian releases my hand and

I slide off his trolley to let the ambulance and hospital staff manage his exit. I'm shepherded in after him.

The lights are bright inside, highlighting every trolley scrape and stain on the walls and every defect in the lino floor. The new Gold Coast hospital is months away from opening – somewhere else – and it shows.

There's a nurses' station behind a blue laminate counter and Brian is shunted into the bay next to it, beside shelves loaded with fluid bags and IV lines. It's a busy night but the staff are waiting for him.

My hand is numb, several parts of me have cramped in the bizarre semi-rotated posture I've maintained throughout the drive, and both piriformis muscles are weighing up whether or not to go out in sympathy. I step away from the action and back towards the sliding doors with all the agility of Woody from Toy Story.

Meanwhile, Brian is in the hands of experts with moving parts and Robyn is back at Obsidian doing who knows what. The show might or might not be going on. Date night will be remembered, and in all probability held against me, for the rest of my days.

My phone rings.

I catch the call just before it goes to voicemail. It's Jack.

'Oh my god,' he moans. 'Oh my god, Dad. Grandad's thing's come out. He went to pick up Winston and it popped out. It's all pink.' There's a murmur in the background, my father briefing him. 'The stoma's prolapsed. Bowel's come out. It's . . .' There's a sharp intake of breath. 'It's in the bag.'

I sit down on the floor with my back to the wall. I can feel sweat break out all over my scalp. There's a loud buzzing in my head, but it passes.

'It's okay,' I tell him, since I'm in the habit of saying that tonight when disaster strikes. 'We'll get it sorted.' There's a picture I'm trying to push out of my mind of my father squirting bowel through his surgical site, metre after metre of it. 'Don't let him strain and don't let it out of the bag. That's got to be the first thing, right?'

'Right,' he says, his voice steadier now that he's handballed his panic to me.

'Get him to sit down, if he's not already. Sit or lie down. This sounds like a hospital issue. I'm actually at the hospital already, with something else.'

A nurse places a paper cup of water on the floor beside me and touches my shoulder lightly to let me know it's there.

'I'll call your mother,' I tell Jack. I came home to be the parent with the answers. 'She's a couple of minutes away from you. I think we need medical expertise this time. She'll know how quickly things need to move.' It's the truth. Robyn's the choice. He called me, but Robyn's the choice. 'One of you make your grandfather a cup of tea.' As soon as I drag it from my repertoire of out-of-date treatments for shock, it occurs to me he might need surgery. 'But don't let him drink it. I'll call your mother.'

Robyn's phone rings until it goes through to voice-mail. I'm about to call again when she calls me.

'Sorry,' she whispers. 'I've got it on vibrate. They're trying to keep the show going. They figure it's what Brian would have wanted. How is he?'

'Not as dead as that makes him sound. There are surgical people taking a look at him now. But I'm not actually calling about Brian.'

I explain the stoma situation to her and she says, 'Okay. This kind of thing can often look disastrous when it isn't. Not that it's good, but no one should panic. He probably needs to get to hospital, but nothing terrible's likely to happen in the meantime. This'll get sorted out. Leave it with me. Just call Jack back, tell him it'll be okay and tell him I'll be there in a few minutes.'

I do what she says, and I keep Jack and then my father on the phone until Robyn turns up at the door of the unit.

When I stand, the sliding doors open and a breeze runs through. It's cool when it hits my face. I take a mouthful of water. I want my father to be okay.

'Mate, could you . . . You're with . . .' A guy in his twenties who might be a doctor says to me, pointing in Brian's direction. He's wearing surgical scrubs and has a nametag that's turned itself around the wrong way.

Brian's propped up on a trolley, with two nurses holding the shark. He has an IV line in. I nod. I'm with him. Not in that way maybe, but with him to an extent no one else is tonight.

'We're just going to take the shark off,' the maybe-doctor tells me, matter-of-factly, as though this is a syndrome he deals with three times a shift. 'We'll give Brian a drug called midazolam, which won't knock him out but should totally stop him caring. He'll need to go to theatre afterwards for us to sort out the lacerations, but in the meantime we'll need someone to hold the dressing on his tongue, just to keep some pressure on there. And we're a bit short-staffed.'

Me. He means me. I'm being recruited as a back-up nurse, for the purposes of tongue-holding.

He sees me nodding as I work through what he's asking, and he takes that as all the agreement he needs. I'm part of the team.

He goes back to Brian, talking loudly and clearly, as if deafness is a side effect of a shark bite to the tongue. He pushes the drug into Brian's IV line and calmly gives a succession of orders to everyone around him. One of them calls him Jared.

A nurse tears open a packet and Jared removes an instrument that looks like a strong pair of secateurs. Another wave of sweat and buzzing washes over me, and I have to back up against the wall to stay confidently vertical. My first thought is that there's a tongue-ectomy about to happen, with retrieval and an attempt to sew it back on to follow, but Jared hooks the secateurs into the corner of the shark's mouth and carefully crunches them through the jaw bone.

That's enough for me. I turn sideways and gaze out through the sliding doors at the quiet Gold Coast night as there's another crunch. Jared's done the other side.

I pull my phone from my pocket and call Robyn.

'It's, uh, yeah . . .' she says, before a clunk and a rustling sound. 'We're getting him to Jimi Hendrix now. It looks dramatic, so be ready for that, but it's the kind of thing that can happen. He's not in any danger. They had him sitting next to a cup of tea . . .' She half-covers the phone and shouts instructions to someone before coming back to me. 'Lydia's driving us since she's stuck to mineral water.'

'Excuse me,' a voice says behind me.

It's a nurse, and he's pointing back towards Brian. The shark is lying on the floor between the trolley and the wall, and Jared has his hand in Brian's mouth. He's holding his tongue, which is wrapped in a wad of gauze. Brian's staring ahead like a doll.

I leave Robyn to her patient and return to mine.

'Okay, it's pretty straightforward,' Jared says as the nurse offers me a box of latex gloves. 'You just need to maintain moderate pressure over all the puncture wounds. Brian'll be off with the fairies for a while, so don't expect him to get it. He might try to fight you, or he might not even notice.'

He slides off the stool and guides my gloved hand into place. He hooks the stool out from the trolley as a sign that I'm to sit on it.

'Good,' he says once I've wedged myself in. 'Keep it just like that. If he gets feisty or there's any issues with bleeding or his breathing, let us know. The nurses' station's right there.' He points to the wall on the other side of the trolley, then he steps past the curtain and says, to someone I can't see, 'It'll be the appendix first and then this one.'

Brian's gaze doesn't shift as Jared and the nurse leave. He's a long way from feistiness. For the first time, I'm conscious of the Emergency Department noises around us – the low conversations, the beeping machines, a drunk and cantankerous man with the fight not all out of him several bays down. My field of view is framed by the nurses' station on the far side of Brian's trolley and the curtain behind me, and it's barely wider than a widescreen TV. Most of the action's happening out of shot, but nurses stride past from time to time, full of business, and a shoeless man with dirt-matted hair and a drip stand to lean on shuffles back and forth, talking softly to himself and counting on the fingers of his free hand.

He's wearing a faded AirAsia X T-shirt from the airline's launch of flights to the Gold Coast a few years ago. BDK was looking into plane leasing then, before the world had surplus passenger jets in their thousands parked in rows in desert boneyards, waiting for a change of luck.

I pull out my phone and take a look at the China Southern website. Just when I've found what I need, I hear more feet approaching, and Robyn's voice rattling through my father's recent medical history.

37

JACK PUSHES MY FATHER into view in a wheelchair.

'Fancy meeting you here,' he says, lifting one hand to wave. 'They made me sit in this thing.'

His other hand is guarding his colostomy bag in which a length of bowel sits like a pink boneless beagle that's scoring some lap time as a reward for fetching slippers. Between his thigh and the arm of the wheelchair, he's managed to wedge his iPad, which appears to be open, yet again, to Rolling Stone.

'So, this is for real?' Jack says, pointing to Brian's tongue. 'We thought it was, like, a stunt shark when we saw it on TV.'

'Every bit of it. Real shark, real teeth, stuck in his real tongue.'

'Cool.'

My father pulls his iPad out. 'Did you know they've just released the entire Beatles catalogue on vinyl? Thirteen kilos, it weighs. Imagine if I tried lifting that. Imagine a world without the Beatles. I'd push my liver out for the world to have the Beatles.'

'I don't think that'll be necessary,' I tell him. 'The world has the Beatles.'

'And I think we need to be more about pushing your organs back in now, Casey,' Robyn says, stepping clear of the nurses' station.

She's been talking the talk, but her Michelle Obama dress is so wrong for the scuffed lino and fluoro lighting of the Emergency Department that she looks like she could only have arrived in my view in post-production. She's nowhere near shabby enough, or shuffly enough or confused enough.

'We've got adjacent bays,' she says, 'so . . .'

She steps across and pulls the curtain back. Jack wheels my father and his pink bowel pet into position next to me, puts the brakes on and goes around to check out the shark.

Robyn looks at my father in the wheelchair and me sitting gripping Brian's tongue. She shakes her head and smiles. 'Date night. People in sitcoms have more sensible date nights than this.'

'I remember reading an article a few years ago,' my father says. 'Brian'll like this. Can he . . . ?' He doesn't wait for an answer. 'It was about a record factory. CDs were in trouble but vinyl was coming back. The Arctic Monkeys, people like that. They were all doing things on vinyl. It just sounds better. It's not just me saying that. So some guys bought the factory that made Sgt Pepper's and Dark Side of the Moon and Tubular Bells and it's still going. The original pressing machine, all of it. The turntable that did the first play of every new album. I think it was a Garrard.' He pokes me in the side. 'Don't slouch.'

He has everything in there, in that multigigabyte brain. Every musical fact that ever drifted close enough to be hoovered up. It's all still there and easily accessed, even when he's wearing some of his organs on the outside.

On the other side of Brian's trolley, Jack is on his knees on the floor, posing the shark for a photo.

My father shifts around in the wheelchair, trying to get comfortable.

'I think I need to go to the little boys' room,' he says, to no one in particular.

'Is something wrong?' Robyn moves towards him, turning instantly medical.

'No, no,' he says, holding up a hand. 'All normal. I might have had a couple of Cointreaus after the bandage incident and that tends to . . . I have a fair bit of ice with it. I just need someone to wheel me to the right spot.'

Robyn glances at me, stuck holding a tongue, and Jack, who's still on the floor.

'Okay,' she says, trying to sound happy about being dragged into my father's toileting once again. 'I saw a wheelie toilet back around the corner.'

She takes the handles of the wheelchair and flicks the brake off. I talked the night up, we failed to have dinner together, I ran off with Brian Brightman and a shark, and now she and her designer wardrobe are wheeling my father and his rogue bowel and full bladder to a toilet. She's Cinderella back from the ball to her chores, and I'm the entire cohort of ugly sisters and a slapdash ageing prince who needs to get the details right next time.

'Thanks,' I call out to her before she's pushed him out of sight. 'Is there any chance of a date night re-do?' She stops, and I keep talking before she can get a word in. 'This one didn't exactly go as planned. And you really do need to get more mileage out of that dress. I'm sure that Wu guy would feel the same if he saw you in it.'

'It *is* a great dress.' She draws her shoulders back.

'Running out of time . . .' my father says, trying not to sound impolite.

Brian lifts a hand to wave as they go, and his gaze seems to drift after them.

Jack stands up and shows me a shark photo on his phone. 'I bet you're totally thinking nipples now.'

Brian goes, 'Huh,' at the mention of nipples and attempts to turn his head.

'It's a Jaws reference,' I tell him. 'No nipples here. My son's just . . . He doesn't mind throwing in a literary reference or two. You need to keep your head still. The shark is gone and they'll be fixing your tongue soon. Don't try to talk.'

His eyes slide over my way and he blinks and says, 'Uh huh.'

Jack's flicking through shark photos on his phone, deleting the ones that look less dramatic.

'You did well tonight,' I tell him. 'You did a good job looking after your grandfather till help arrived. That must have been pretty stressful. And thanks for calling me first, even if it wasn't really the kind of thing I could fix.'

He doesn't look up. 'Hey, you were like some kind of anal emergency superhero earlier.'

'We might find a different term for that, but thanks. Thanks for calling me first then.'

'Yeah. Mum didn't pick up. Probably had her phone on vibrate. She practically never feels it unless it's right in her hand. You were great though. And I called you first when Grandad dropped his ass out the front. You and those gloves. That was something. The video's already got 142 likes on YouTube.' He taps the screen several times and turns the phone around for me to see. 'Two sixty-eight. And look at the view numbers. See how clear it made the picture when I turned the light around?'

There I am, with the harsh white lamplight glowing on the bandage, the anal margin and the bright yellow gloves, and driving through my hair to my scalp. In the background, shapes that must be Abi and April hover spectrally. The autofocus settles on the gloves and the anus, occasionally resetting when my panicked face leans into shot. I'm talking in a high-pitched voice, half-random reassurances, half squeaked-out orders. I come across as a lot more likely to soil myself than your classic superhero. I'm not entirely proud to be sharing this side of me with the wider world.

'That's why you turned the light around? To improve the quality of the footage?'

'Sure. People are starting to really care about production values.' He says it as if I should already know that. 'You can't just put anything up there. But I need you to go online and say it's not faked, say it's legit. There's a few haters coming out and doubting it, but you get that. And, hey, you totally fixed it. The constipation. Winston's back there shitting like a bandit now.'

'Oh god, how does a bandit shit? Tell me it's not all over the floor.'

Brian raises his hand, as though a question's been asked in class, presumably a class called Bandit Shitting 101.

'Ah thim . . .' he says, which I take to mean 'I think'. 'Ah thim a bambih thipth whereber he wampth.' I think a bandit shits wherever he wants.

'You should talk as little as possible,' I tell him, mainly because him talking involves lips, teeth and heavy breathing all over my hand, all of which can be felt too easily through the thin glove.

Some drool trickles from the corner of his mouth and down my thumb. He doesn't appear to notice.

'I worked something out while I've been sitting here.' I wave my free hand in Jack's direction, to get his attention. He's busy refreshing YouTube to update his 'like' and view counts. 'I have a proposal for you. I've got a whole lot of China Southern air miles that I don't see myself using any time soon. It turns out they can be converted into gift vouchers at a lot of big retailers, which you could then convert into Umart credit in exchange for jobs around the house.'

'Like gardening?' he says, with an expression on his face that suggests gardening is a sentence equivalent to regular bulldog anus bandage extraction.

'No, I think your mother's got someone doing that. I've got something different in mind. Think of all the time you'll save not having to earn smurfberries.'

'I've got a few cheats that work pretty well.'

'Think of how much less time you'll spend dealing with whatever crime syndicate is taking those berries from you. And I didn't tell you the jobs yet.'

Brian lifts his hand again. His eyes flick between Jack and me. 'Bib you thay thmurfbeweethe?'

'I did,' I tell him. 'Smurfberries. It's not the drugs doing that to you. And if it's important, we can talk about it later, sometime when I don't have your tongue in my hand.'

Jack refreshes the YouTube page and looks up at me. 'The jobs . . .'

'Number one is a half-hour lesson teaching me how to use my phone. No Smurf villages, just the regular stuff. Number two is a half-hour briefing, including discussion, about Pandora, XBoxMusic and all that, and how people under thirty-five use them. It's going to be that sort of thing.'

Jack sets his phone down on the blanket and nods. 'Deal. Smurfs shit me.' He sticks out his right hand, ready to shake mine. 'Obviously we can save a few minutes with the phone one, since you know how to find a stripper already.'

Brian's eyes flick my way and he raises his drip hand in a thumbs up.

38

IT'S A START WITH JACK, a toehold, even if he doesn't know it yet. And even if it has an element of commercial transaction to it. We'll talk, beginning with a topic that's not about him and girls and life, but one where he has plenty to say.

A nurse wheels my father back into view, now with a blanket over his protruding bowel, and parks him at the end of the bed.

'Back with us, Gopher,' he says, as Brian makes an effort to pull him into focus and gives a wobbly left-handed salute. 'Robyn's with Lydia and the girls. They were parking Jimi Hendrix.'

'Hembwipth?' Brian frowns and makes what looks like a manual attempt to refocus. His head rocks back and forward, and I have to let my tongue hand be carried along by it. 'He beem bom for yearth, Haythee. Am I wipe?' He's been gone for years, Casey. Am I right?

My father looks at me, cups his hand to his ear. 'Sorry?'

'Hendrix is dead.'

Before I can explain the van, Brian mumbles again to my father, all vowels and glottal stops and an upper lip flapping away on my index finger. I tuck the drape in next to my hand, figuring I might as well get used to the spit rush that's coming my way. My father shakes his head slowly, struggling to make sense of the sounds. Again, he looks to me for a translation.

'He said, "Is Robyn around? I want to thank her for her help with that penis stuff."'

'Sure,' my father says, examining me closely in case I'm inclined to throw out a subtle signal that Brian's brain is still paddling in the shallows of a calm sea of midazolam. I give him a nod – it beats an explanation and it's at least partly true – and he smiles and pats the blanket where it's tented over Brian's foot. 'She's a gem, isn't she? She'd push my arse back in if she could.'

Heels click-clack across the lino. My father glances past the nurses' station. Every sequin on Lydia's dress seems to sparkle in the Emergency Department fluoros as she walks into view.

'You've done it, Brian,' she says, waving to create a bigger target for his drifting vision. '"Free hugs" and "come and touch it" were good, but the fish brought it home. The hashtag's "brianbiteman". You've cracked the global top ten trending on Twitter.' She pauses to let it sink in. '*Global* top ten.'

Brian gives her a thumbs up. The corners of his mouth draw out in a misshapen smile.

'We put the clip up right away and the views are past twenty thousand. We put the whole piece on. Funny stuff.' She checks her phone and flicks something on the screen. 'They're loving it. How about this? "The guy's a dickhead, but he's exactly the kind of dickhead I want to watch." Did you get that?' In case he didn't, she runs it by him again, with emphasis. '*Exactly the kind of dickhead*. All of which adds up to a big fat green light for the show.'

Brian manages a slow-motion air punch. Green light. Show. I seem to have slipped into a nearby but parallel universe to this conversation, one in which Brian's well-being is inconsequential and his particular dickhead status really counts.

Lydia looks down at her phone again. 'We should have a crew here in a few minutes. We'll cross back and break into the awards. Don't worry if you can't talk. I just wish we'd planned that stunt. I would have had a chopper in the air, following you all the way here. It would've rated its arse off.'

I ask what's been green-lit and Brian mumbles, 'Thowee, I . . .' and waves in Lydia's direction.

'Ha,' she says, smiling at me, before I get any time to wonder what he's sorry about. 'You don't know, do you? Hmm.' She takes a breath and glances at Brian, who nods. 'Okay. It's called A Bride For Brian Bright-man. It'll be like The Bachelor, but old, fat and ugly, and with hair in all the wrong places. That's Brian's line, so I'm okay to use it. We'll promo to the max over summer to get the ladies to sign up, then Brian picks his top fifteen, moves into the mansion with Dazz as host and wingman, and we take it from there. Ratings gold. Sorry, Andrew. Poaching's never pretty . . .'

Brian is leaving SPIN. Brian is taking the fall. In one move, he is pulling his fat salary off my books, and Dazz with him, and countless future letters from the regula-tor. My job is instantly a whole lot easier.

And maybe a Bride for Brian Brightman is crass

comic genius, night after night of middle-aged dating train wreck, big hairy scenes in the hot tub, boozy awful lines slurred across cocktails and candlelight.

I can't guess how many of the audience will be laughing with him and how many laughing at him, but Brian has not once tried to balance that equation.

'The things you'll do to get a date, Gopher,' my father says, and laughs. 'Good on you.' His iPad clunks against the arm of his wheelchair, and he grabs it before it slips out.

Brian's looking up at me, waiting for a reaction.

'Maybe Lydia should glove up and come and take a turn holding your tongue,' I tell him. 'Congratulations. In its own frightening way, I bet it'll be compulsive viewing.' He lets out a sound that's almost certainly a laugh. 'I'll be getting you back for the apple juice before you leave, by the way. When you least expect it. And it may or may not involve urine.'

There's another laugh, most of it passing through his nose.

Lydia's eyes are back on her phone. 'You're up two spots in the global Twitter top ten, behind "just sayin". And something's obviously going on with Rihanna . . . I don't think we were expecting you to be quite this big with the Twitter crowd.'

We. I'm picturing the meeting at the network where they talked through the pitch for A Bride for Brian Brightman. There are glossy poster-sized photos of their young stars on the walls and a characteristically dishevelled Brian on screen, in need of a shave and a fresh shirt. Maybe there's even a close-up of his pants, with focus group results showing a mix of empathy and morbid fascination. When I think of the network promos, every one of them centres on bright, shiny stain-free people doing playful things to the logo. I want to see Brian there, stumbling into the party, tidy as last weekend's pizza box, a contender despite himself.

'I thought you were the youth network.'

'Youth don't do TV,' Lydia says, apparently failing to notice that there's a youth right next to her, tapping madly at his phone, presumably sharing news of the show with the world. 'We're changing. If you're eighteen to thirty-five and you want to watch TV at all, you download it illegally from America. Thirty-five to fifty-five – we've got to get a piece of that. Middle-aged late adopters. That's the new battleground. They'll be the last people alive who'll watch when we tell them to and sit through our ads without knowing there's a better way.'

She's described me and she knows it.

An ad starts up on my father's iPad. It's extolling the virtues of wheat grass. The purveyors of life extension are on his case again. He scowls and taps the screen to stop it.

'What crap,' he says, staring at the frozen image. 'As if anyone with any choice . . .' He stops himself and gets rid of the picture.

'Oh,' Lydia says, pointing to Brian's tongue as though the injury's brand new and I've only now shoved my hand into his mouth. 'How are you, by the way? That must have hurt.'

He answers her, but it comes out as, 'Wipe fipping a mimba fpar.'

'Oh, I got this one,' Jack says. '"Like shitting a ninja star."'

Brian goes 'Mmmm' and points to him. He's got it.

'Gold,' Lydia says, and starts tapping at her phone. 'It's cool if I tweet that, yeah?'

As Abi and April arrive, stepping past Lydia with their phones in camera mode, I remember something about my father and grass, eating grass. Something I heard long ago.

'Is that the actual shark?' Abi says, and Jack says, 'No, that's its body double. The actual shark is back in its trailer, learning lines for its next scene.'

She tells him to move his head and lines up a photo. 'Great weekend, Dad,' she says without taking her eyes off her target. 'We'll have to do this again.'

A nurse appears at the back of the growing crowd and calls out, 'Mr Brightman, we'll be getting you ready for theatre soon. I'll just come and check that tongue.'

Lydia steps aside to let her through, and the nurse reaches into a box on a shelf above Jack's head and pulls out some gloves. From the shelf below she picks up two packets of gauze and a fresh drape.

With the shark and its entourage of amateur photographers blocking her way on that side, she comes around the end of the bed and past my father's wheel-chair towards me.

'Let's take a look, then,' she says, and it seems to be the signal for me to let go.

I step back, fearing comic-strip spurts of blood from each of the puncture holes, but the gauze stays in place. As she moves onto my stool, I bump into my father's left wheel. He grabs his iPad with both hands to stop it falling.

'Let's give them a bit of space,' I tell him, though no one else seems inclined to move.

I take the handles of his wheelchair and pull him back from the bed.

'Had enough of the blood?' he says.

'No, I just remembered something.' I'm not sure how to begin it. 'Something Oma said once when I was about six or seven, but I think you changed the subject.' He stopped her, but that's not the most diplomatic way of putting it. 'Late in the war, before the relief trucks got to Arnhem, you ran out of food and you had to eat grass. It was one of the things you ate, at least.'

I don't know how long it was for, but she told me that. It was so odd, such a perverse idea to a six-year-old in a time of plenty who knew from books that cows ate grass and sheep ate grass. My grandmother, my grand-father, my father eating grass – I had nowhere to put an idea like that. The relief trucks brought flour and sugar and condensed milk. My father stopped her saying more by telling me they got condensed milk soon enough. They were in Arnhem for a few more years, with food still rationed. My father listened to the BBC, worked on his English.

There were two things Julianne and I were never allowed to say when we were young: 'I'm freezing' and 'I'm starving'. Our father took the line, always, that we were barely even cold or we were merely between meals. Put on a jumper, eat a banana. Get over it. You don't know what it's like to be freezing. You don't know what it's like to be starving.

He looks away from me, back to the nurse working on Brian's tongue. He licks his lips. His mouth sounds dry.

'Is that where your encyclopedic knowledge of music

has gone? Over all that?' About once a decade I rattle family protocol and put something to him directly. Maybe this is my turn for the two thousand teens.

On the side of his face that I can see, his crows' feet deepen and his mouth lifts into some kind of smile. 'Was it commerce law you did, or some kind of pop psychology? You think I'm blocking it out? The end of the war? Maybe I just appreciate music.' He taps on the arm of the wheelchair with his hard fingernails. 'I don't know. I know I don't appreciate grass. It wasn't a symbol, not then. It was just . . . shit we had to do. The grass was there. It had nutrients in it. It's not as dramatic as it sounds.'

Brian is now holding his own tongue, having passed whatever nursing test of competence he had to. It's wrapped in fresh gauze. The nurse folds her gloves in the disposable drape along with the old gauze, shoves them into a bin and goes to wash her hands.

Abi and April move in and, apparently with Brian's consent, sit either side of him on the trolley with the shark draped across all three of them. Their phones flash wildly in a volley of selfies.

Abi checks hers and says, 'My hair is shit. We can't post any of these.' She pulls at her fringe to fix it up.

April reaches across and says, 'Here, just . . .' She takes the hair and shapes it gently into place. 'Yeah.'

If Brian's eyes bugged out any more, they would leave his head for an independent life. He's still perched on a fading midazolam cloud, his show's green lit, national stardom is officially in his diary for next year, his tongue is in his hand, a shark is in his lap and some moves hinting seriously at teen HLA are happening right in front of him. Somewhere in his still-addled brain, he's wondering if he pashed a shark and woke up a rock star.

More selfies are taken, and this time they're approved. The girls slide from the trolley and instantly forget they've left Brian pinned down by the shark carcass. As they fiddle with their phones to post the images on Facebook or wherever such things go, he looks around twitchily as if a fly's buzzing him. He turns to the left, locating the noise that's intruded on his evaporating fantasy. Jack is next to the end of the trolley, between Brian's head and the wall, messing around with a spare IV unit, trying to turn its various beeps into a tune.

'You know what you do with Abi and music?' I say to my father. 'I think it's time to do that with some other stuff. They've got to know more than they do now. We've built them such a safe little world.' So safe a hospital is toys and photo ops. 'If change is going to kick my arse fifty thousand times, they're up for at least twice that. It won't all be good – it won't all be some cool new app – and we need to make them . . .' It takes a second or two to find the word I want. 'Resilient.'

'I don't think we need to pitch them into a war either,' he says, 'but I know what you mean. They're good kids, but . . .'

'They need to hear about a few other things. We need to give them something to think about, and not just gadgets. You've been doing that with the music talk, but . . . I'm going to tell them everything I can, but I haven't seen a war. They need to hear a bit about that. And, frankly, so do I.'

'We'll see,' he says. His thumb and index finger pinch the folded edge of his hospital blanket and rub the two starched layers of fabric against each other. 'There's some of it . . . I can come up with something. Sure.' He twists his head and looks up at me. 'How about Brian? He's done you a favour, hasn't he?'

'He has.'

I will not understand digital radio. And I will not make that my mission. I will set out to do my job reasonably and sensibly, run the place well, give the people there some kind of prospects and get home every possible day in good time. I will not conduct real life by the sloppy pixilations of Skype, or by text message or email or two-minute phone calls that serve no more purpose than to confirm both parties are still alive. Not every foray into the digital world has helped us. Sometimes, it's allowed an imperfect plan to last far longer than it might have.

'Someone should lift that shark off him,' my father says. 'He'll be getting no blood to his feet.'

Brian is by himself now, the kids' attention steered away by something else the Emergency Department offers that beeps or buzzes or flashes, or maybe just their phones and the world that's looking in, sharing their photos and links to their videos.

I push the wheelchair closer to the end of his trolley and lock the brake. I wrap my arms around the body of the shark and lift it, with as much care as I can manage, free of Brian's lap and the trolley and set it back on the floor.

'Famp,' Brian says. Thanks.

'No problem.'

When I climb back onto the stool, my body automatically assumes its slouchy tongue-holding position and my hand almost reaches for the gauze.

Brian has a big year ahead of him. I don't know yet if there's any sincerity in him about the bride part of it. It makes for great alliteration in the show title. Lydia will mine it – will mine his next life – for all the laughs it might yield and so, willingly, will Brian. But the silences in his empty house must be closing in. He's a talker, even with a lacerated tongue. He's a sad clown, like so many clowns, even when he's a coarse hilarious debating beast.

'You should call your son,' I tell him. There's a space in that part of his life too, another silence.

Brian frowns and points to his tongue. 'Aboup thith?'

'No. I mean, sure, tell him about that if you want to. I think he's going to find out anyway though. Your video looks like it's the new Gangnam Style. But you should just call him. Get an up-to-date photo for your new desk, or maybe the wall of the mansion.'

Brian stares at the sliding doors, which are shuddering open and shut as a cleaner sweeps outside with a broom.

'I wath kwap ah mimepeem,' he manages to say – I was crap at nineteen – almost gagging on the word 'crap'. 'Heeb pwobwee thap am ubwee mow.' He's probably fat and ugly now.

'That's highly likely, but he's your son.'

The cleaner moves along and the doors finally slide all the way shut.

'Yeah.'

Our phones beep simultaneously. It's a picture from Abi, featuring Brian semi-stoned, the flaccid shark and its poor bent mouth, April flashing peace signs and Abi herself close to camera, her hair looking just right.

I can hear heels again, hard high heels and the softer clump of rubber-soled shoes.

'Casey's my father-in-law,' Robyn's voice says before she and a tired woman in her twenties appear. 'He's the one in the chair.'

The woman introduces herself to my father as the resident who will be admitting him, and she reaches behind me to pull the curtain along the rail.

Robyn puts her hands on her hips. 'Nearly there. They'll be coming to get you soon, Brian.' She watches him to see that he's understood, then turns to me. 'The kids are outside with Lydia, waiting for the TV crew. Apparently the phone signal's better out there.' She shakes her head.

Behind the curtain, my father is recounting the incident with Winston and the bandage. Somewhere nearby, a door opens. Five people talk at once. Jack, Abi and April bounce back into my narrow viewing window, followed by Lydia, two nurses, the TV crew and then the wandering shoeless guy with the drip stand, still counting on his fingers.

'This is so cool,' Jack says, his eyes locked on his phone screen as he shoots more video. 'Who gets to keep the shark?'

'Winston was quite traumatised,' my father tells the resident quietly on the other side of the curtain. 'But only emotionally. My son did a very good job of the extraction, considering it's not his thing. He's in private equity, or he was until recently. He put deals together all over Asia. He's home now.'

Robyn laughs and ignores them all, keeping her eyes on me. 'Welcome back to your life, I guess.'

'Is it always like this?'

I vacate the stool again as Lydia steps in with clear ideas about the shot she wants. One of the crew comes over to lift the shark back onto the trolley, arranging its head in Brian's armpit and fussing over the aesthetics of its busted snout.

'Mostly it is,' Robyn says. 'There are rare moments when they're all asleep at once and you get to breathe. But mostly this is it. Welcome home.'

My star is leaving the radio station, and for the moment he looks like a doped Oliver Hardy with a grey, stiffening Frank Laurel cradled by his side. My children are gambolling like fawns in a wi-fi paddock, never still, shooting video of video being shot, uploading, shrieking at the comments coming in from Sydney, Melbourne, London, Gdańsk.

Someone in Gdańsk has commented already. One day, maybe even tonight, I'll hold them still for a moment and tell them about Lech Walesa and the fall of communism in Poland, find some video of all that and tell them it felt like it really meant something in my life, in all our lives, back in that other century. The last century of analogue.

My father is quietly recounting the disgorging of his own bowel into the bag in his lap. Robyn is standing with her hands on the hips of her Michelle Obama dress, calm in the midst of all this, as distinct and as disconnected as a picture. But maybe that's just from where I'm leaning, trying not to be inconvenient, trying not to bomb my way into the TV shot or my father's consultation.

Through the crush of people and cameras and all the

noise around Brian's trolley, it's Robyn's eye I manage to catch.

'What'll it take?'

She looks my way and almost answers, but she stops herself because she knows it's about everything. The kids, my father, the two of us, the glancing conversations she and I have had and the bigger conversations we haven't. The perfect fit we can fake but need to learn how to make again.

'Deeds, buddy,' she says, meaning not words. Meaning my credits for the deed of returning will carry me only so far.

'Okay,' I tell her. 'I've got a whole lot of deeds lined up.'

On this frantic Gold Coast night, it's precisely as glib and untruthful as it sounds. But I am here, and there is time and room to make it true instead, and that's what I will do.

ACKNOWLEDGEMENTS

No middle-aged business executives, radio present-ers, comedians or their associates were harmed in the making of this novel. SPIN99FM, BDK, Obsidian and the woefully spelt Crystal Tydes are all fictional. Brisbane's legendary radio station 4IP and Umart were or are real, but any people in this novel purporting to have any association with them are invented. I'm sure you're getting the picture. You might be in radio, you might be a comedian, you might even have piriformis syndrome and body-image issues, but you're not in this book. (Oh, wait, that was me with the piriformis syndrome and . . . enough said. I have an appointment with a tennis ball.)

While novels typically start in one brain and with one pile of notes (in this case including an unusually high number of crass remarks as I got to know Brian), it takes fresh eyes and the right questions to find the shape of the finished product. Moral support doesn't go astray either. For all of that, I'd like to thank Pippa Masson and Tara Wynne at Curtis Brown Australia, Meredith Curnow and Sophie Ambrose at Random House Australia and Will Entrekin at Exciting Press.

I'd particularly like to thank Sarah and Patrick for the continuing welcome adventure that we share any time I step away from the keyboard.

Also by the Author

THE FIX

Josh Lang went to London with investigative journalism on his mind, but he carved out a reputation as a fixer instead and mastered the art of spinning any client out of a crisis.

Now he's home in Brisbane, and this time the job is supposed to be good news. The client is a law firm, the talent is Ben Harkin, and the story is the Star of Courage Ben is about to be awarded for his bravery in a siege.

But it was Josh's messy past with Ben that was a big part of his move to London in the first place, and the closer he gets to Ben's story the more the cracks start to show.

Throw in a law student who's an exotic dancer by night, and a mini-golf tour of the Gold Coast, and Josh's pursuit of the truth becomes way more complicated than he'd ever expected.

Written with warmth, humour and a touch of the detective, *The Fix* will keep you guessing until the very last page.

ALSO AVAILABLE AS AN EBOOK

THE TRUE STORY OF BUTTERFISH

Curtis Holland wanted to make music. Derek Frick wanted to be a rockstar. Derek won that one. Luck and sales in the millions came Butterfish's way, and Derek lived the rock dream to the max, with Curtis on keyboards, just holding on.

It was a relief, really, when the third album tanked and Butterfish imploded, letting Curtis escape back to Brisbane, to a home studio where he could produce other people's music away from the glare of the spotlight.

When Annaliese Winter walks down his driveway, Curtis is ill-prepared for a sixteen-year-old schoolgirl who's a confounding mixture of adult and child. He isn't at all ready, either, to find himself drawn to the remarkably unremarkable family next door. To Kate, Annaliese's mother, who's curvy in a way that's sometimes unfashionable and sometimes as good as it gets. Even to fourteen-year-old Mark, at war with his own surging adolescence.

But Curtis has to work himself out before he can bring anything positive to the lives of the Winter family, and Annaliese makes it all the more complicated when she begins to show too much interest in him.

Then Derek flies back into town . . .

ALSO AVAILABLE AS AN EBOOK

ZIGZAG STREET

Here I am, on a work day of some importance, riding out of town in a cab with a babe I've just concussed with footwear.

Richard Derrington is twenty-eight and single. More single than he'd like to be. More single than he'd expected to be, and not coping well. Since Anna trashed him six months ago he's been trying to find his way again. He's doing his job badly, he's playing tennis badly, his renovating attempts haven't got past the verandah, and he's wondering when things are going to change.

Zigzag Street covers six weeks of Richard's life in Brisbane's Red Hill. Six weeks of rumination, chaos, poor judgement, interpersonal clumsiness . . . and, eventually, hope.

'A comic masterpiece' – *Who Weekly*

ALSO AVAILABLE AS AN EBOOK

WELCOME TO NORMAL

An Australian wine-maker tries to crack the Taiwanese wine market. Two holiday-makers in Spain decide to tell a lie about each other at every meal. A man drives home from work trying not to dwell on what he has just done.

From Arizona to Taipei to suburban Brisbane, Nick Earls's characters lead ordinary lives that, in these stories, become far from ordinary. Ranging widely in style, setting and narrator, *Welcome to Normal* vividly captures the uniqueness of the everyday through its author's eye for detail and his capacity for bringing the people in his stories to life.

By turns playful and thought-provoking, these stories showcase the calibre and versatility of Nick Earls at his perceptive best.

ALSO AVAILABLE AS AN EBOOK